P9-CEB-222

Sins *of* the Father

Also by Angela Benson

UP POPS THE DEVIL
THE AMEN SISTERS
ABIDING HOPE
AWAKENING MERCY

Don't miss the next book by your favorite author.
Sign up now for AuthorTracker by visiting
www.AuthorTracker.com.

Sins *of* the Father

Angela Benson

AVON

An Imprint of HarperCollins*Publishers*

This book is a work of fiction. The characters, incidents, and dialogue are drawn from the author's imagination and are not to be construed as real. Any resemblance to actual events or persons, living or dead, is entirely coincidental.

SINS OF THE FATHER. Copyright © 2009 by Angela Benson. All rights reserved. Printed in the United States of America. No part of this book may be used or reproduced in any manner whatsoever without written permission except in the case of brief quotations embodied in critical articles and reviews. For information address HarperCollins Publishers, 10 East 53rd Street, New York, NY 10022.

HarperCollins books may be purchased for educational, business, or sales promotional use. For information please write: Special Markets Department, HarperCollins Publishers, 10 East 53rd Street, New York, NY 10022.

FIRST AVON PAPERBACK EDITION PUBLISHED 2009.

Designed by Diahann Sturge

Library of Congress Cataloging-in-Publication Data
    Benson, Angela.
        Sins of the father / Angela Benson.—1st ed.
            p. cm.
        ISBN 978-0-06-146852-0
        1. Adultery—Fiction. 2. Father and child—Fiction. 3. Family—Fiction.
    I. Title.
    PS3552.E5476585S56 2009
    813'.54—dc22   2009001279

09 10 11 12 13   OV/RRD   10 9 8 7 6 5 4 3 2 1

This book is dedicated to absentee fathers and the children, young and old, who need them. Fathers, it's never too late to make amends. Children, forgiveness is not always easy but it's always worth it.

You shall not make for yourself an idol in the form of anything in heaven above or on the earth beneath or in the waters below. You shall not bow down or worship them; for I, the LORD your God, am a jealous God, punishing the children for the sin of the fathers to the third and fourth generation of those who hate me, but showing love to a thousand [generations] of those who love me and keep my commandments.

—Exodus 20:4-6, New International Version (NIV)

Prologue

Sonny,

I know you hate it when I call you Sonny, but if you're read-ing this letter, I guess it's okay since I've gone on to glory. I picked up the pen to write on Tuesday, November 15, 2006, right after you left my apartment, the one you bought for me. I had to write because I couldn't tell you all the things I wanted to say. I don't know when it happened, but some-where along the line I stopped being your mother and became your dependent, one of the people in your life who received money from you but very little else.

You've done a lot for me, Sonny, and I appreciate it more than you will ever know, but I don't think I've been a good mother to you. It was much easier when you were a boy and we had very little when it came to material things. My job then was to keep you off the streets and out of trouble, to make sure that you went to school every day and that you got your homework done each night. I cheered you on when your football or basketball team won and encouraged you when they lost. I went without so that you might have the little extras that most kids took for granted—a new pair of off-brand sneakers or a new CD. I celebrated your every accomplishment and always told you that the world was yours if you worked hard and believed in yourself.

You made me so proud. When I sat in the coliseum at that fancy Ivy League school and watched you walk across the stage, I knew I had done my job and done it well. A single, uneducated mother with only her faith in God for support had raised a son who had not become a statistic— dead or in jail before twenty. I thanked God because I had done my job so well. I even took a bit of pride in what I had achieved. My pride increased with each of your accomplishments. That's my boy, I would tell folks, and watch their eyes widen in surprise, as though they couldn't believe it. You went beyond what I'd prayed when you started keeping the promises you'd made to me.

One of these days, Ma, you're going to have a big house in one of those fancy neighborhoods.

Ma, you're gonna have one of those foreign cars. I'll make sure you get a new one every year.

Once I make it big, Ma, you'll never have to worry about money or work again because I'm gonna take care of you.

You're gonna visit the places in those travel books, Ma, just you wait and see.

Every promise you made to me you more than fulfilled.

So why am I writing this letter? Because today I realized that I had failed you. Somewhere along the line I forgot to warn you to take care of your heart. Sonny, I fear you've lost it in your quest to make money, to fulfill the promises you made to yourself and me. I worry that money and power have become your gods.

I tried to tell you some of this today, but you didn't hear me. It's been a long time since you've heard me. I've become another check you write each month. Oh, how I wanted more for us than that! But it's too late for us. I realized that today.

But it's not too late for you. While in many ways, you've been a wonderful son, you've also been a disappointment. I blame myself for not providing you with a male role model who could show you what it meant to be a man. I tried to show you, but I failed. All you learned from me was that a man provided for his family. You didn't learn that a man also cherished his family. Maybe you mistook providing for cherishing. But they're not the same. Not by a long shot. You've got some housekeeping to do, Sonny.

You met your match in Saralyn. She's put up with more from you than many wives would have. Unfortunately, in order for you to straighten up the mess you've made of your life, you're going to have to cause her and Isaac more pain. You've got to deal with Leah and those kids. Yes, I know about Michael and Deborah, have known for years, but I never said anything. I kept waiting for you to say something and you never did. I have two grandchildren that I never got to know because I was too intimidated by you to challenge you on your decisions. A good mother would have challenged you and made you do the right thing. A good mother would have welcomed her grandchildren even if her wayward son didn't. God help me, but I haven't been a good mother in a long time.

I love you, Sonny. No mother could love a son more. But I want more for you and expect more from you than you've shown. I want you to know love, that sacrificing kind of love that a poor single mother shows her only son. With all your money and all you've achieved, I don't think you know that kind of love. How can you? Everything and everybody in your life have been second to your work and your goals.

I hope to be a better mother now than I was when we were together. Know that I'm watching from heaven and looking for you to become a better man than you are. You know where to start. Take that first step. God will lead you the rest of the way.

Your always loving mother.

Chapter One

Four months later

Y ou can't buy me," Deborah Thomas told the distinguished
man with salt and pepper hair seated across the table from
her in Justin's, Diddy's trendy Atlanta restaurant. The pre-
viously tasty salmon she'd been eating unsettled her stomach.
She met Abraham Martin's dark brown eyes. "Or my love," she
finished as she put down her fork. She picked up her white linen
napkin and blotted her lips, fighting back the bile that rose in her
throat. "Neither is for sale."

She put down her napkin and was about to push back her
chair when he reached out and grasped her hand. She looked at
his well-manicured nails, the expensive gold Rolex watch on his
wrist, and then back up at his face, making sure her displeasure
was evident in her glare. The mirth she saw in the eyes that met
hers only added to her rising ire.

"I'm glad you find this humorous," she said. She attempted to pull her hand away but he only held it tighter.

The mirth still in his eyes, he said, "You remind me so much of my mother. You have no idea what it does to me to see my mother's face in your face, to know that her spirit lives on in you. She would have loved you so."

Deborah snatched her hand away, remembering the contradicting emotions of joy and pain she felt the day he'd shown her pictures of her now deceased grandmother, Iris. Those pictures had answered questions she'd held for a long time. They told her why she was short and big breasted while her mother and brother were tall and lean, why her complexion was light while her mother's and brother's were dark. Those pictures had also made her ache for what she'd missed. "And whose fault is it that she never had the chance?" she asked him. "Whose fault is it that I never knew my own grandmother?"

He sobered, releasing a deep sigh. "I'll go to my grave regretting the mistakes of the past."

Good, she thought, but she didn't voice the word. The sincerity and pain in his voice stopped her from taking any pleasure in his regrets. A part of her was glad he felt remorse, because it meant that he cared a little, maybe. For so long, she'd never dared to hope that he would care, couldn't even dream that he loved her. His absence from her life year after year after year had been too much evidence for a young girl's wishes to overcome. He didn't love her. He never had.

"I'm not trying to buy you or your love," he said, his gaze holding hers. "But there was a time when that would have been my strategy."

Deborah didn't respond.

"Look," he said, leaning toward her. "I made you the offer because I think you're right for the job. If nothing else, I'm a businessman. I don't take the future of my company lightly. Even though Running Brook Productions was a steal and brings needed diversity to my existing holdings, I admit that I had you in mind when I bought it."

Lord help her, her heart beat faster at his words. She felt like the little girl she'd once been, the one who longed for a daddy to make her hurts go away. "I have a job that I love," she said, overstating the truth. "Why should I even consider your offer?"

That sparkle returned to his eyes. "You might love your job, but I'm offering you your own production company. Will Pearson Entertainment do that for you? Though you've been in and around the broadcast world since you were in college, you're young yet, only twenty-eight, and Pearson is a big company. You'll have to wait years there to get the kind of responsibility I'm offering, and you know it." He reached for her hand again, squeezing it lightly. "It's a great offer, Deborah. Think about it. Running Brook is established enough that it has name recognition in the direct-to-DVD market so you wouldn't have to start at ground zero, yet it's new enough for you to make your mark both on it and with it. I'd even like you to collaborate on television and film projects with other MEEG entities." He gave her hand a quick squeeze, released it, and sat back in his chair, the twinkle in his eyes gone.

Deborah tried to stare him down, but his eyes had turned to that innocent pleading that reminded her so much of her brother Michael when he wanted her to agree to one of his outrageous schemes. She looked away, toward the piano where a balding man fingered the keys to a jazz oldie.

"I know it's too late for me to play Daddy, Deborah," he said, causing her to turn back to him, "but I hoped we could at least become friends."

Friends, she thought. I have enough friends. I could still use a father, she admitted to herself. How she hated that weakness! "So you want me to work for you so we can become friends?"

"I want you to work *with* me so we can continue to get to know each other. I've enjoyed spending time with you these last few months, and I sensed you felt the same. I'd also like to think you could learn a few things from a fossil like me."

She couldn't help but smile at that comment. Abraham Martin had been described in a lot of ways—entrepreneurial genius and entertainment trendsetter were two that came to mind—but never had anyone referred to him as a fossil.

"That's better," he said. "I love it when you smile."

Deborah could feel herself being swept back under the spell he'd begun weaving around her since the day they'd had lunch together four months ago, the first time she'd been face-to-face with her father. "We can't go back, Abraham," she said. "It's too late."

He shook his head. "It's not too late. Not as long as you have breath in your body and I have breath in mine. We've lost a lot of years, all my doing," he said. "But we don't have to lose another day. You're my daughter, and my business is your business. I'm not just offering you a job, Deborah. I'm offering you your rightful place as my child and heir."

Chapter Two

Y ou've got to talk to Michael, Mama Leah," Josette said in the whiny high-pitched tone that made Leah's skin crawl. They sat facing each other on the extra-long full-sized bed in the bedroom where Michael had grown up. "He's changing. He's started keeping late hours and he's evasive when I ask him about what he's doing. He's cheating on me," she said. "I just know it."

Leah got up from the bed on the pretense of getting more tea. On days like today, she wished her son and Josette had never met, much less married. Raised by overly indulgent grandparents, her daughter-in-law gave new meaning to the word spoiled. Josette was a sweet girl, but Leah could only tolerate small doses of her when she was in complaint mode, as she was today.

Leah took her time dumping the tea in her cup in the sink in the adjoining bathroom, which had once been shared by her son and daughter but now, with its sweet scent of air freshener and the floral towels on the racks, only bore signs of her daughter. When she could stall no more, she returned to the bedroom and refilled her cup with fresh tea from the carafe she'd brought up earlier and set on Michael's old dresser.

Taking a deep breath, she turned back to her daughter-in-law. "What can I say to Michael, Josette? I've already talked to him, and he says he's not seeing anyone. He's just working longer hours these days."

"It's more than that," Josette said, lifting damp eyes to Leah. "He's hiding something from me. I know he is." She rubbed her hand over her protruding belly. "I'd leave him if I weren't pregnant. I might leave him anyway."

Thinking of her unborn grandchild, Leah pushed away her frustration, returned to the bed and sat next to Josette. "You don't mean that," she said, brushing her hand down Josette's silky black hair. "You love Michael and he loves you." At least, she hoped he did.

Still rubbing her belly, Josette said, "I used to think he did, but now I'm not sure. How could he love me and neglect to tell me something as important as who his biological father is? Why couldn't he trust me with that information? If you love a woman, you trust her. You don't keep secrets from her the way Michael has since the beginning of our marriage. Michael has never trusted me, and now I don't trust him."

Leah closed her eyes and said a quick silent prayer. God help her, but she'd wondered the same thing since she first learned that Michael hadn't told his bride-to-be that *the* Abraham Martin was his father. She blamed herself. When they were young she began telling them that their father's identity had to be kept secret. Now she wondered why she'd burdened them that way. How she wished she could change the decisions she'd made in the past! "It's complicated, Josette. Abraham was never a father to them, not really."

Josette lifted damp, light brown eyes to her. "Why didn't you say something?" she asked, disappointment filling her voice.

Leah sighed. She had no excuse. Once again she'd allowed Michael to sweet-talk her concerns away. "I don't know, Josette. Michael's animosity toward Abraham had grown over the years to the point where the man's name couldn't be mentioned without starting a war of words. Then you came along and Michael seemed to mellow a bit. The two of you were so happy together. It was as if starting his own family was helping him to deal with his feelings for Abraham."

"We *were* happy," Josette said. "I thought we were soul mates. I bared my heart to Michael and thought he had done the same with me. Then I learn there is a whole other part of him that he didn't even share with me. How is that supposed to make me feel? What else is he keeping from me?"

Leah didn't know what to say. Her oldest child was becoming a stranger to her. "Don't worry yourself so, Josette. It's not good for the baby for you to get upset."

"I know, but I can't help it. I'm having a baby in less than five months, and my husband is seeing another woman." She dropped her face to her hands and began to weep. "What am I going to do?" she muttered.

Leah prayed for wisdom. She pulled her daughter-in-law to her side and rocked her gently. "Everything's going to be all right," she said. "I'll talk to Michael. You get some rest."

Leah pulled back the covers and eased her daughter-in-law under them. She kissed her brow and tucked her in as she had done with Michael when he was a boy. "I love you, Josette. Now get some rest."

Josette was asleep before Leah picked up the tray with the tea and closed the bedroom door. The front door opened as she reached the bottom stair, and Deborah burst into the foyer. Her youngest child didn't enter a room, she claimed it with an energy that belied her petite frame.

"You're home early," Leah said to her daughter.

Deborah kicked off her Crocs and hung her shoulder bag on the coat tree. "I needed a break."

"Rough day?" Leah asked, glad her daughter had taken off those ugly shoes, which in no way complemented the smart tailored pantsuit.

"Understatement of the year." Deborah pressed a kiss on her mother's cheek. "House guest?" she asked, inclining her head toward the tray.

Leah headed toward the kitchen, with Deborah following her. "Josette."

"Oh," Deborah said, taking a seat at the oak dinette table Michael had bought for the family when he graduated from college and got his first job. The new furniture had been a big deal for them.

Leah placed the tray on the kitchen counter. "Yes, 'oh.'"

"So she's left Michael again?"

Leah pulled a pitcher from the refrigerator, poured two glasses of lemonade, and handed one to Deborah. "Seems that way."

Deborah took the glass, nodding her thanks. "What does that make—four times in the last four months?"

"I've lost count. She'll be back home with him as soon as he comes and gets her. It's become a ritual now. I think she leaves to get his attention."

Deborah took a long swallow of lemonade. "I could strangle that boy, Mama. Josette is the best thing that's happened to him, and he's too stupid to realize it. I don't blame her. I'd leave him, too. Unlike her, though, I'd go farther away than his mother's house and I wouldn't sit around waiting for him to come get me. I'd leave him for good."

"Don't talk like that, Deborah. You know your brother's been going through a rough patch recently."

Deborah rolled her eyes. "Yeah, he's been going through it since he hit puberty. He's a thirty-year-old man, Mama. He needs to grow up. We aren't the only kids to grow up without a father. That excuse stopped working years ago. You don't see me acting the fool the way he does, do you?"

Leah squeezed her daughter's shoulder. "No, you're the good child. You always have been."

"Mama, don't say that. You're making excuses for Michael. Abraham has reached out to us, but Michael won't reciprocate. I don't know what he wants from the man."

Leah could see that the conversation was going nowhere. She sat down across from her daughter. "Your lunch with Abraham must have gone well."

Deborah rubbed her fingers down the side of her glass. "It was okay."

"Just okay?" Leah coaxed.

"He bought me a production company, Mama," Deborah said, awe in her voice. "He bought me a production company. Can you believe it?"

Leah gave her a big smile, wanting to be happy for her daughter, but her thoughts quickly turned to her son and how he might react to the news. Her children had always been close, and she hoped Abraham's largesse toward Deborah wouldn't change their relationship. But she worried about it because anything involving Abraham seemed to set Michael off. His sister's good news could very likely send him into the stratosphere.

Chapter Three

Isaac Martin waited for his mother in the back of the church. She had just dismissed the weekly mid-morning Bible study group that she led. When she saw him, she smiled and headed his way, but Reverend Reeves stopped her and pulled her aside to chat for a moment. Several other folks stopped her before she reached him. In the meantime, he greeted those who saw him. Since this was his home church, he knew practically everybody. He hoped Reverend Reeves didn't corner him today. His church attendance had dropped off significantly in the last four months and he knew the pastor had noticed.

When his mother finally reached him, she lifted her cheek for the kiss he always had for her. "Still the life of the party, huh, Mom?" he teased.

Saralyn Martin gave him a 100-watt smile that made her look more like his sister than his mother. "I see you had your share of admirers."

He held up his ring finger and pointed to the ring. "I don't have admirers anymore," he said. "I'm married, remember?"

She slapped him on the arm with one of her recently manicured hands. "Nobody likes a smart aleck, son."

He laughed. "So where do you want to go for lunch?"

"Honey, I'm sorry but I can't go to lunch today. I need to get back to the office."

He lifted a brow. "The office? Since when did you start going into the office? I thought charity events and cocktail parties took up all your time these days."

"Except for this Bible study class, I've had to clear my social calendar," she said. "Since you decided you were no longer interested in the family business, I figured somebody had to look out for your interests. That somebody is me."

"Don't start, Mom."

"I'm not starting anything," she said. "I'm telling you the truth. You shouldn't have left your position at MEEG. That company is yours and you belong there, no matter what your father has done. Don't forget that my father—your grandfather—started that company."

Isaac hadn't forgotten. He also knew that Ellis News was only a minor cog in the wheel that was now Martin-Ellis Entertainment Group. His father had turned a mom-and-pop newspaper into a multi-million-dollar entertainment conglomerate consisting of a couple of magazines, a film and television production company, and a television station. "Don't start, Mom," he said again. "I didn't come here to talk about him."

"I'm not talking about him," she said, "I'm talking about you. You're letting your disappointment in your father cloud your judgment. MEEG is yours. You shouldn't be working for somebody else. It's not right."

Isaac sighed. The position as VP of Special Products at Infinity Games wasn't his ideal job, but it was a soft landing while he decided what he wanted to do long-term. "It's right for me, Mom. I can't live in his shadow anymore. I don't want to be with him or be like him. I have to become my own man."

"By working for somebody else? That makes no sense. You come from a long line of entrepreneurs, men and women who took pride in building their own, not taking scraps from somebody else. Where did you get your ideas about work? You certainly didn't get them from me, your father, or your grandfather."

Isaac didn't deny the entrepreneurial bent that flowed through his veins, but after learning about his father's other children, he'd needed a break from the man, so he took the first decent opportunity that presented itself. With Infinity, he learned about gaming, an entertainment area that MEEG had yet to explore. Besides, working with his father and trying to meet his excessively high expectations had grown more stressful each day. He'd found himself popping antacids like there was no tomorrow. "You're determined to argue with me, aren't you?" he asked his mother.

She tucked her arm through his and guided them toward the sanctuary's exit doors. "I'm determined to get you to see what's right. There's a difference."

Isaac threw back his head and laughed. "You're the perfect match for Dad. I have to give you that."

She sobered and her steps faltered. "I used to think so."

He hugged her to his side. "I'm sorry, Mom," he said, mentally berating himself for being so insensitive. "I know this hasn't been a walk in the park for you." Though his mother had long known about his father's infidelities, she'd been humiliated by his recent efforts to embrace his outside children.

"No, it hasn't," she said. "But you don't see me walking away from all I've worked for. Now is not the time to be emotional."

Isaac stared at his mother. She looked all prim and proper in her pale pink designer suit and matching heels, but her backbone was as solid and unyielding as the diamonds that adorned her ears, neck, and wrists. "I don't know how you do it."

"You're not a woman," she said. "If women fell apart every time a man did something stupid, that's all we'd do. No, women have to be strong. When the man falls, we have to keep standing. Otherwise, there would be no family."

"Okay, Mom," he said. He could feel her winding up for a lecture and he wanted to cut her off before she got started.

"Okay, nothing. Yes, I'm angry with your father for his betrayal. I'm angered by the insensitivity to our feelings he's showing with his 'do the right thing' campaign. I hate what he's done to this family and I'm not sure I'll be able to forgive him anytime soon. But what he's done doesn't take away from what we've built together. That company is as much yours as it is your father's. Now is not the time to walk away, Isaac. I don't know where your father's head is these days but something tells me we're both going to find out soon, and I don't think we're going to like what we hear. You need to stake your claim before Abraham starts dividing up the pie. Can you see yourself sharing MEEG with those interlopers, working side by side with them? I'd die first."

"Since I'm not working at MEEG any longer, it doesn't really matter to me," Isaac said. "That's a battle I won't have to fight." He wanted, and needed, peace in his life and his work. He knew that now. Let his half siblings have MEEG and the drama that was Abraham Martin.

His mother stopped walking and stared at him. "Now that's the kind of crazy talk that keeps me awake at night. You've got to wake up and smell the coffee, son. We're not just talking about a job here; we're talking about your birthright, your heritage. Don't be a slouch like Esau and give yours away." She started walking again. "I blame your father for all of this. Why stir the pot after all these years? Our lives were going along fine the way things were. Now he's bringing the infidels in among us."

"You make them sound like the enemy."

"In a way, they are. That woman had no respect for my marriage. She didn't have one child with your father, she had two."

Isaac could feel his mother's pain, and his anger at his father grew. How could the man he'd held in such esteem all his life, the man who always spoke of the honor in being a husband and father, mistreat his mother this way, a woman who'd always stood by him? He thought about his own wife and wondered if he could ever do the same to her. He tossed the thought aside as soon as it formed in his mind. He'd never hurt Rebecca the way his father had hurt his mother. He hugged his mother to his side. "Let's go pick up some lunch."

She looked up at him. "You'll come back to the office and eat with me?"

He chuckled. "Yeah, Mom, I will."

"Good," she said, with that bright smile she gave when she got her way. "I need your advice on a couple of things."

Isaac knew very well that his mother didn't need his advice. She had just executed the first step in her efforts to recruit him back to MEEG. He didn't have the heart to tell her that her efforts would not yield the results she wanted. He didn't see himself going back to MEEG, not now, maybe not ever. And not even his mother, the brilliantly manipulative Saralyn "I always get my way" Martin, could change that.

Chapter Four

That's it," Michael Thomas told his staff of fifteen as he folded his portfolio closed. He watched as they left the conference room, giving himself props for having had the insight to bring each of them on board. The team he'd assembled was hungry, as hungry as he was, and their productivity showed it.

He got up, tucked his portfolio under his arm and made his way back to his corner office with its view of the Atlanta cityscape. Every time he walked into this office and looked out those windows, he felt good about what he'd accomplished. The Thomas Management Group was not yet where he wanted it to be, but he was way ahead of his own ambitious schedule. He'd been hustling music groups since he was a teenager. The hustling had continued through four years of college, where he honed the skills he already had and picked up some valuable new ones to round out his repertoire. He landed his first major record deal two months before his college graduation, and they'd continued to fall since then. In no time at all he'd have everything he wanted, everything he deserved. And he'd done it all without a rich daddy to back him up.

He glanced at the profile of the MEEG building clearly visible from his office. That building represented all that he wanted and would someday have. Right now he had to look at Abraham Martin's midtown empire from the windows of his much less costly offices on Atlanta's historic Auburn Avenue. But one of these days he'd own the MEEG building or one even better.

"Knock, knock," a feminine voice called from behind him.

He turned and saw Rebecca Martin standing in his doorway. He still hadn't gotten used to her with short hair. Six years ago, when he first met her, a wannabe singer with more heart than talent, she'd had long neat "home girl" braids that fell midway down her back. Not that the short, above-the-ear cut she sported now didn't work for her. It did. In fact, the new 'do was perfect for her new persona as public relations executive and wife to the son of one of the city's major players. But it made her look a lot softer than he knew she was. He waved her in.

"Close the door behind you," he said, walking toward the couch in the corner of the room so they'd have more intimate seating. He couldn't help but smile when she sat in the club chair instead. He sat on the couch alone. "It's been a long time, Becca," he said. "You're looking good. It seems money agrees with you."

She met his eyes for the first time. "This is not a social call, Michael," she said. "My wedding anniversary is in a few weeks. Don't send us another gift."

He grinned at her. "Why should I stop now? I've been sending them since you got married three years ago."

She smirked. "And I've returned every one of them."

He loved it when she had to fight to keep her fiery personality in check. He knew without a doubt that she wanted to curse him up one side and down the other. He also knew that she wouldn't do it, not here, not now. No, he'd have to get her alone, away from everybody they knew, before she would cut loose. He wondered if he could coax her into a "for old times' sake" tryst for later this week.

"Don't send another one," she repeated, her voice crisp and demanding.

He leaned toward her, put his hand on her knee. "Afraid your hubby won't approve?"

She pushed his hand away and stood, folding her arms across her stomach. "Are you trying to hurt me, Michael, or is it Isaac you want to hurt?"

"You've got me all wrong," Michael said, spreading his arms in supplication. "I don't want to hurt my older brother. The gifts are my way of showing my appreciation for you. I want my big brother to know what a prize he has in you so he'll value you the way I did."

She turned hot eyes on him. "I love him, Michael. I really love Isaac, and he loves me."

Michael met her eyes with his own. "You loved me once."

She looked away. "That was a long time ago. A very long time ago."

"Time is relative," he said with a shrug. "What will good ol' Isaac think when he learns of our history? Something tells me he won't be too happy."

She turned back to him. "Why do you hate him so, Michael? He hasn't done anything to you. He's not responsible for his father's mistakes."

"I don't hate him," Michael declared. "He's nothing to me, other than my half brother, of course. You're the one I care about."

She shook her head. "I've changed, Michael. I'm no longer that woman who would do anything to please you. I'm in love for the first time in my life. Isaac's a good man, like you in some ways."

"Is that why you fell in love with him, because he's a lot like me? I'm sure he'd love to know that."

Her eyes blazed. "You know that's not what I mean." She dropped her hands from her stomach. "Look, this argument is getting us nowhere. I want the anniversary gifts to stop. Your message with them is loud and clear now that I know Isaac's your half brother. Do you get some perverse satisfaction out of knowing you had me before he did?"

He grinned at her. "I wouldn't call it perverse. It's just nice to know that I beat big brother to the table for once."

She shook her head. "I don't know why I came here. I should have known you wouldn't be reasonable."

Michael weighed his options. Sending the gifts had given him some pleasure, and he already had one picked out for this year. He'd send it and then stop. What would be the point now that Rebecca and Isaac both knew he was Abraham's outside son? Yes, this last gift would drive home his message to Isaac. "So are you planning to tell Isaac about our history?"

"That's none of your business."

"Maybe I could tell him for you," he threatened.

"I'm not the only one with secrets, Michael," she threw back at him. "I could give your mother and Deborah an earful. I don't think they'd be too happy to know about the gifts. And I don't think your pregnant wife would be too pleased to know that our relationship continued even after you said your vows, which were a joke, by the way."

He had to grin. Rebecca had been more than his match. She was a pragmatist, like he was. When she'd accepted that she would never become a singing sensation, she dedicated herself to the study of business and became a heck of a PR person. He wondered again how he'd let her get away. "Okay," he said. "I'll keep your secrets, for now, and you'll keep mine. For now."

With a slight nod of acknowledgment, she headed out the door.

He watched her feminine stroll through the glass walls of his office. "I can't believe I let that go," he murmured to himself.

Chapter Five

Leah felt his presence before she saw him ease into a seat in the back of her classroom as her students were leaving. She kept her attention on the student who'd come up to ask a question.

"Make sense?" she asked the student.

He nodded. "Thanks, Miss Thomas."

"No problem," she said. "See you next week."

"See ya." The young man picked up his already full backpack from the floor and stuffed his literature book and tablet in it. Then he hoisted the backpack over his shoulder and made his way toward the door. A tall, darkly handsome Abraham Martin passed him on his way to her. Though she and Abraham hadn't been in the same room in almost thirty years, she'd seen his face numerous times over the years in the news and on the covers of business and celebrity magazines. *Essence* had recently done an article on the Martins and the Martin Estate that she had devoured from cover to cover. He, Saralyn, and Isaac were a beautiful family.

"What brings you by?" she asked when he reached her, thinking of nothing else to say. She forced the memories from the past to remain there. She was a community college teacher with a master's degree, not some starry-eyed teenager too blinded by love to see the truth even after it had slapped her in the face a couple of times.

"I want to talk to you," he said, studying her as she looked at him.

God help her, but she wondered how he thought she'd fared over the years. She considered herself a good-looking woman who kept in shape, but she knew she was not in the same league with the women who surrounded Abraham everyday. "About?" she asked, as she mentally fought off the feelings of inferiority that seemed to engulf her.

"Our children," he said as simply.

Her knees buckled. She braced herself on the table next to her and slid into one of the student chairs. *Our children,* he'd said. Oh, what power those words had; what memories they brought back. She couldn't hold back the flood that assaulted her full-force. Instead of thirty years ago, it was yesterday. And she was a young girl in the throes of what she thought was a perfect love.

He sat in the chair next to her. "How are you?" he asked.

She wasn't sure if he meant in general or now because he was here. She answered the former. "Life is good," she said. "How about you?"

"In some ways, things could be better. In others, they've never been better."

She smiled a bit. "At least, you have the good to balance the bad."

"That's one way of looking at it. You always were the optimist."

She sobered at that. "I think naive is a better description."

He cleared his throat. "I'm sorry, Leah," he said. "I'm so sorry."

The words didn't penetrate, so she couldn't accept his apology. "Because you finally reaped what you sowed?"

He shook his head. "For what I did to you and our children, for the position I put you all in."

She shrugged. "You kept up your end of the bargain," she said. "You didn't let us go homeless or hungry."

"It wasn't enough. I could have done more, should have done more. They needed more than money. They needed me. I realize that now."

She cast an accusing glare at him.

"I know," he said. "You tried to tell me, but I wouldn't listen. I was torn between you and Saralyn. You were telling me one thing and she was telling me something else. I didn't know what to do to keep all the plates spinning. I made the best decision I could."

She folded her arms across her chest. "I don't accept that, Abraham. You made the easiest decision for yourself. You didn't think about Michael or Deborah or me. You showed us what we meant to you."

Leah felt his betrayal anew. She'd been a fool for this man twice. He'd been her first love, and she was devastated to learn he'd cheated on her with Saralyn and intended to marry her because she was pregnant with his child. Still reeling from his news, she'd learned that she, too, was pregnant. Instead of telling him, she'd gone away to stay with relatives until she had the baby. By the time she returned to Atlanta with his son, he was married and had a son with Saralyn, four months older than her own Michael.

"You didn't play fair with me either, Leah. You should have told me you were pregnant."

"What difference would it have made? Would you have ended your engagement to Saralyn and married me instead?"

When he didn't answer, she said, "At least be honest about it.

Saralyn was a catch. I shared your ambitions, wanted for you everything you wanted for yourself, but with me, we'd have to start at the bottom. Saralyn gave you a leg up with that small newspaper her parents owned. It wasn't much but it was a foundation from which you could build. And you did. Mightily. Congratulations."

The harshness of her words surprised her, and it must have surprised him as well because they sat silently for a few long minutes before he spoke. "I did love you, Leah," he said.

She shut her eyes against his words, words that had led to a second pregnancy for them and a second child, this time a daughter.

"I know," she said. "I've heard it all before. You loved me *and* Saralyn. Well, good for you."

He sighed. "I can't change the past, Leah, but I want to change how we go forward from here. I want to get to know Deborah and Michael."

Leah took a deep breath. "It's what I've always wanted, Abraham, but it may be too late. I just don't know."

"Deborah's been meeting me for lunch for the past few months. She's told you?"

Leah nodded.

He smiled. "She reminds me so much of my mother. I only wish——" He stopped, closed his eyes.

"I wish both of them had known Miss Iris," Leah said. "I was tempted a few times to tell her about them, but I never did. A part of me always thought she knew or suspected, but chose to ignore us. I couldn't risk finding out she didn't want to know them. Your rejection had been hard enough. I couldn't go through another."

"It's not your fault," he said, tugging at his salt and pepper mustache. "It's mine. It's all mine, and I'll go to my grave with the regret from it. I did so many things wrong, told so many lies, not just to you and Saralyn, but also to myself. I wanted what I wanted and everybody else be damned."

"Good traits for business," she said, feeling compassion for him despite herself. It was probably because she saw her son's face in his. "Not so good for relationships."

"Don't I know it."

She felt the past hurts recede. "How are things with your wife and son?"

"Better with Saralyn than with Isaac. I'm such a disappointment to him. I don't know if he's ever going to forgive me."

"It's hard with boys. Girls are easier."

"Do you think Michael will ever soften toward me, give me a chance?"

"To be honest, I don't see it right now. I didn't realize the degree of his anger, and I should have. It's been there a long time. I don't know if he can get beyond it. Right now he doesn't want to. His anger is what fuels him." She smiled. "He's like you in that way. He's ambitious and willing to do whatever it takes to achieve his goals. Unfortunately, his personal life suffers because of it."

"His wife's pregnant. We're going to be grandparents." When she lifted a brow, he added, "Deborah mentioned it to me. Don't worry. I make it a point not to ask her about Michael. I don't want to put her in the middle of my problems with him. Because they're so close, he comes up sometimes in her conversations. She shares bits and pieces about him and you, about the past and what's happening now. And I try to share myself, my early days with her. It's not a one-way street."

"I didn't say it was. I know you're sincere in wanting to get to know Deborah."

"Does she know it?" he asked, an uncertainty in his voice that tugged at her heart.

"Some days, but she's not ready to trust you fully yet. She doesn't want to be hurt."

"I won't hurt her," he said.

"I hope not. She's a strong woman, Abraham, but a part of her is still that little girl looking for Daddy's love. Be careful with her heart."

He nodded. "I want her to come work with me. Did she tell you?"

"She told me you bought her a company!"

He chuckled. "It was a small production company, but it's perfect for her." He told her about Running Brook. "I hope she takes me up on it."

"That's between you and her," Leah said. "I'm not going to get in the middle of it. I've given her my opinion, but the decision is hers."

He stiffened. "What was your opinion?"

"I told her to give you a chance."

His shoulders relaxed. "Thanks for that."

"I didn't do it for you. I did it for her. I'm trusting you with her heart, and I hope you're up to the challenge. In the past, trusting you hasn't worked out too well for me. I'm praying that you're different now, that you'll be different with your children than you were with me."

"I won't hurt them, Leah. I promise you that. In fact, that's why I wanted to talk to you. I've shaken things up at MEEG so that there's a more equitable representation among my three children. I think Deborah will be all right with my plans, and I feel I can trust her with a seat on the MEEG board of directors."

"You can," Leah said, surprised and pleased at his generosity. It's about time, she thought.

"I'm not so sure about Michael," he continued. "I want to give him a seat on the board, too, but I can't under the current circumstances. I didn't want my relationship with him to be all about money or business, but that seems to be where we are. I wanted to get to know him, learn about his interests, and together identify the right fit for him at MEEG, much like I've done with Deborah. But Michael's rejected every overture I've made to talk to him, to get to know him. He's rejected lunch and dinner invitations as well as invitations to meet and talk. He's made it perfectly clear what he thinks of me. I'm not sure he wouldn't use the position to make problems for me."

Leah sighed. "I wish I could disagree with you, but I can't. Michael's very angry these days. I thought he was getting past it when he got married, but it all came back when you decided to publicly acknowledge him and Deborah as your children. I don't know what to do."

"It's not your fault," he said, reaching out and touching her cheek.

She pulled back and his hand fell away. "It's not *all* my fault," she corrected. "I was twenty, a grown woman, when we were together. We made decisions, you and I, decisions that have brought our children and us to this point. I'm their mother so I accept the bulk of the responsibility. I should have made better decisions, should have put them before myself."

They were silent again.

Abraham broke the silence. "What I want to do is give you Michael's seat until such time that he is ready to assume it himself."

"You can't—"

He lifted his palm to her. "Hear me out. This will be a temporary arrangement. The seat will be transferred to Michael when you, Deborah, and I feel he's ready for it."

Leah absorbed his plan. "Me and Deborah?"

He nodded. "I want to do right by Michael. I want the decision of his readiness to be made by the three of us."

"Why?"

"Because I trust you and Deborah."

Leah acknowledged his compliment with a slight nod. "What about Saralyn? What does she think about these additions to the board?"

He sighed again. "I haven't told her yet, but I will. She's not going to like it, but there's nothing I can do about that. She's hurt, as she should be, so I can't trust her to look out for Michael's interests. I hope I can trust you. Can I?"

Leah thought about it. "Would Michael know about your plans for the board seat?" she asked.

He nodded. "And he's probably going to exert pressure on you and Deborah to hand it over to him sooner rather than later. If you and Deborah both decide he's ready, then it's done. If one of you resists, nothing can happen. I'm hoping that the three of us together can stand up to Michael, wait for the right time, if and when it comes."

"That's a lot of faith you're putting in me and Deborah."

"It's about time, don't you think?"

Chapter Six

A few days later Rebecca sat on the plush couch in her in-laws palatial living room and watched her six-foot-plus husband pace the natural hardwood floor. "You're making me tired, Isaac." She patted the space next to her. "Sit down and relax. Your pacing is not going to make this evening move faster."

He stopped pacing and turned to her. The Atlanta skyline visible from the floor-to-ceiling windows of the penthouse apartment framed his silhouette. "This is so like him, " Isaac said. "He says he'll be here at seven sharp and then he's late. He's the most selfish man I know."

Rebecca had heard it all before. Isaac's ranting about his father had been going on since he found out about the older man's other children. It had been hard news for him to hear, and given the way Isaac looked up to his father, some disappointment was expected. But she hadn't thought it would go on this long. To be honest, she thought he was carrying things too far, and making himself sick in the process. He'd gone to the doctor a few times recently for what she guessed were stress-induced maladies—headaches, nausea, and the like. When she asked about the visits, he just said the doctor had given him some pills to help him relax.

"He may be selfish, but he's also your father," she told him.

"And? Are the rules different for Abraham Martin?"

She sighed. Isaac was a good man, but sometimes he could be unrealistic in his expectations of people, as unrealistic as he accused his father of being. The standards he set for people were high, and if they didn't meet them, he easily cut them out of his life. She feared the same would happen to her if he found out about her history with Michael. "What if we have a child, Isaac, and you disappoint that child in some way? Wouldn't you want forgiveness?"

Isaac shook off her question. "I'd never lie to my child the way my father lied to us. I'd never treat children of mine the way he's treated his children. He's not the man I thought he was, definitely not the man I want for a role model."

"You don't have to be him to forgive him, Isaac. You just have to love him. He made a mistake a long time ago and lied about it. He's not the first man to have outside children, and unfortunately he won't be the last."

Isaac was saved from responding when his mother returned to the room. Rebecca was always struck by the way Saralyn Martin swept into a room like a queen coming before her subjects. As usual, the older woman was perfectly dressed and coiffed, making Rebecca feel like a slug in her simple black sheath. She had never seen her mother-in-law when she didn't look like she'd stepped out of the pages of a fashion magazine. The red sequined pants ensemble that she wore tonight made her look ready for a night on the town. Her trademark diamonds were in place on her ears, neck, and wrist. Rebecca suspected that she wore Jimmy Choo slides on her feet.

"Your father should be back any minute now," Saralyn was saying. "He went for a short walk." She cast a sideways glance at her son. "Maybe you could go meet him?"

Isaac shook his head. "Maybe not." He looked at his watch. "If he's not back in the next ten minutes, I'm taking you two beautiful women to dinner. He can eat alone."

"That's no way to be—" his mother began, but the sound of the front door opening cut her off. "Abraham?" she called.

"It's me," he answered.

Rebecca smiled. Who else would be coming in the house, a burglar? She scooted over to make room for Isaac when he rushed to sit next to her. Her husband was behaving like a spoiled child.

"I'm sorry I'm late," Abraham said when he entered the room. He bent to kiss his wife, and she turned, giving him her cheek instead of her lips. All was not well between the in-laws.

"You're not that late, Dad," Rebecca told him as leaned down and bussed her cheek. He extended his hand to Isaac, who took it after she nudged him. Abraham noticed and gave her a smile of thanks.

"We're here just as you ordered," Isaac said before Abraham could get settled in his favorite chair.

"And I appreciate it, son." Abraham cleared his throat. "You're all probably wondering why I called you here."

"Of course we are," Isaac said. "The last time we had a meeting like this we found out you had two outside children. I can't even imagine what kind of bombshell you want to drop this time. Please don't tell us it's another set of kids."

Rebecca watched as Abraham seemed to sink into himself at Isaac's words, his normally larger than life persona dimmed by the weight of his son's anger.

"You're being rude, Isaac," his mother said.

"That's all right, Sara," Abraham said.

Though Abraham smiled, Rebecca easily read the weariness in

his eyes. She cast a sideways glance at Isaac to see if he saw what she saw. Her husband's face betrayed nothing of his feelings.

"I'm used to his insolence by now," Abraham continued, sitting up a bit straighter. "He's behaving like he did when he was nine. I'll treat him accordingly."

Rebecca felt Isaac stiffen beside her. She didn't feel sorry for him, though, because she knew Abraham was right.

"I'm in the room," Isaac reminded them.

Abraham looked away from his wife and in Isaac and Rebecca's direction. "I've made some changes at MEEG," he said.

"What kind of changes?" his wife asked, concern high in her voice. "Shouldn't you have discussed these changes with me before calling a family meeting? My father started that business. You can't go around making decisions without me."

He turned to his wife. "I love you, Saralyn," he said, "but I didn't talk with you about this because I knew you'd try to talk me out of it. I can't let you guilt me into doing what you want, not this time."

"Don't blame Mom for your lies," Isaac said, leaning forward and interrupting. "She's not the one with the outside children. You are."

Rebecca watched as weariness made Abraham sink back in his chair again. She marveled that neither Isaac nor Saralyn saw the toll all this was having on him.

"I'm not casting blame, Isaac," Abraham said. "I'm stating facts. Yes, we're in the situation because I betrayed my marriage vows and didn't accept responsibility the way a man should. I've been a terrible example of manhood for you, but I'm trying to do the right thing now. And the right thing is for my other children to have a part in MEEG. It's their heritage as much as it's yours."

Saralyn jumped up out of her seat. "You can't mean it, Abraham. You're not bringing those people into my father's company."

Abraham looked up at his wife, keeping his calm. "Don't worry.

My children won't take what was your father's. The newspaper will always be yours to do with what you want, but the rest of MEEG is ours, and I have a controlling interest in that portion."

"But—" she began.

He shook his head. "There are no buts," he said. "It's been thirty years, Saralyn. I've treated those children—*my* children—as if they didn't even exist for too long."

"Please," Saralyn said, waving a bejeweled hand in his direction. "We've supported them, given them more than we should have." She thumped her chest. "I know. I wrote the check each month."

Rebecca watched as Abraham took a deep breath, let it out, resolute.

"I know how you feel," he told Saralyn, "and I accept your feelings, but I can't let them stop me from doing right by my children. Not this time."

"Stop blaming Mom," Isaac repeated. Rebecca put her hand on his arm when he would have stood. She knew that would only escalate the argument.

"Are you accusing me of something?" Saralyn screamed. "What? For wanting to keep my family intact? For not wanting that woman or those kids to taint this family? Well, if you are, I'm not apologizing for it. I didn't cheat. You did." She dropped back down in her chair, defeated. "You did."

Brushing off Rebecca's hand, Isaac got up and went to his mother. He put an arm around her shoulder as he glared at his father. "I hope this family meeting is going the way you planned."

Rebecca felt sorry for her father-in-law. "You're not helping the situation, Isaac," she shot at him.

Abraham gave her another grim smile, obviously appreciative of her support. "I wanted to let you all know of the changes that would be happening at MEEG. I've asked Deborah to head a new direct-to-DVD production company and she's agreed. She'll be starting at MEEG on Monday."

He might as well have said, "I'm blowing up the house," for all the wailing Saralyn did. Rebecca saw where Isaac got his flair for histrionics. She glanced at Abraham and compassion for him filled her. He was only trying to correct his mistakes, but he got no reward for it. She was glad Deborah was welcoming his offer, because she knew Michael's sole goal in life was to give his father nothing but hell.

Chapter Seven

"T hat was a great meal, Mama," Michael said to his mother later that night as he pushed back his chair and rubbed his belly. Deborah watched him as he eyed the leftover ham, greens, and potato salad. "Babe," he said to his wife, "we'd better get us a couple of doggie bags. No sense letting all this good food go to waste."

Josette chuckled. "This isn't a restaurant, Michael. Mama Leah and Deborah can eat off this food for the rest of the week."

Deborah checked her watch, cleared her throat to get her mother's attention, and shook her head. Her signal told her mother they needed to keep Michael at the table awhile longer.

"The meal isn't finished yet, Michael," her mother said. "We still have dessert."

"I can't eat another bite," Michael said, rubbing his stomach again. "But we can pack it up and take it home, along with the leftovers."

Deborah shot a glance at Josette, who was also clued in to the evening's plans. "I still have room for dessert," she piped in. "Remember I'm eating for two."

Michael smiled at her. "Yeah, you are."

"Don't make me eat alone and feel greedy, Michael," Josette coaxed. "Take some dessert, too."

Michael looked at his sister. "See how they gang up on me, sis. I think they want me to get a belly, too."

Deborah laughed at her brother, and her mother and sister-in-law joined in. Abraham should be arriving any minute now. Their best bet was to have Michael at the table when he got there. Otherwise, she feared her brother would simply leave.

"You've never had a weight problem," Deborah told her brother, putting a hand on her full hips. "And I've always hated you for that." She turned to her mother. "What's for dessert anyway, Mama?"

"Michael's favorite," she said. "Banana pudding."

Deborah rolled her eyes. "You have a pregnant woman here and you're preparing dessert for the expectant father? What kind of grandmother are you going to be?"

Josette laughed. "You know I love banana pudding, too, Deborah. And Mama Leah is going to be the best grandmother. I just know it."

"Stop trying to cause trouble, sis. You're just mad because Mama didn't fix your favorite, red velvet cake."

Deborah pouted. "I'm feeling sorta left out here, Mama."

Leah pushed her chair back from the table, bumping the wall as she did. The dining room wasn't that big. "No need for that. Red velvet cake is on the menu for Sunday after church."

When her mother left the dining room to get the dessert, Deborah stuck out her tongue at her brother.

He laughed. "Girl, you need to grow up." He turned to his wife. "Did you see that, sweetie? That grown woman stuck her tongue out at me."

Josette smiled. "See no evil, speak no evil."

Deborah held out her hand to slap Josette five. "Yeah, sister," she said as their palms touched. "We women have to stick together against the men of the world."

"Watch out, sis," Michael joked. "You're the only woman at this table without a man."

Deborah pretended outrage. "No, you didn't go there."

"Oh, yes, I did." He laughed. "Where do you find your men, anyway—the nursing home? You need to let me introduce you to some men our age. You wear out those old geezers you've been dating. That's why they don't last long."

"Mama," Deborah called out, refusing to be baited. "Michael's picking on me."

"I'm not picking on you. I'm serious. I know a lot of guys who would love to go out with you." He glanced at Josette. "Isn't that right?"

"I prefer men to boys, Michael," Deborah said before Josette could answer. "So I'll find my own dates, thank you very much."

Michael shrugged. "Do you think you can find one under fifty? Maybe if you did, Josette and I could double-date with you sometime."

Michael laughed again and Deborah just rolled her eyes.

Leah reentered the room then, carrying a tray with four bowls and shaking her head. "You two act like you're five sometimes. Josette, I hope Michael doesn't act this way at home. You don't want to have two babies on your hands."

Deborah laughed but Josette said nothing. Deborah could imagine what she was thinking.

"I know y'all see me sitting here," Michael reminded her.

Leah served them each a bowl and kept one for herself. After she'd taken her seat, she said, "I call 'em like I see 'em."

"We never should have given women the right to vote," Michael muttered as he dived into his banana pudding. The women laughed and dug into theirs as well.

"This is delicious, Mama," Michael said. "Maybe it's okay if you vote."

Deborah glanced at her watch again. Abraham was running late. She wondered why he hadn't called.

"Why do you keep looking at your watch, sis?" Michael asked. "Got a late date?"

Deborah glanced at her mother before answering. "Something like that."

Michael put down his fork and gave Deborah his full attention. "I didn't know the guys you dated stayed up this late. Maybe he's fallen asleep. You'd better call him and wake him up."

Deborah shot her mother another quick glance, while Michael laughed at his own wit.

Michael turned to Josette. "Little sister's been holding out on me. Did you know about this new guy?" When Josette just shrugged, he turned to his mother. "Did you know, too?"

Leah nodded.

"So why am I the last to know?" he asked Deborah. "You afraid I won't approve?"

"Something like that."

"Well, come on. Who is this new man and how old is he?"

"It's Abraham Martin," Deborah blurted out. "He's coming over after dinner."

Michael seared each woman at the table with a hot glare. "You all set me up."

"Don't be so dramatic, Michael," Leah said. "Nobody set you up. Abraham wants to talk with the four of us and we knew you'd balk at the idea."

Michael got up from the table and reached out his hand for Josette. "Let's go, honey."

She shook her head. "Stay and hear the man out, Michael. What's it gonna hurt?"

He turned to his mother. "So now you've got my wife defying me."

"Please, Michael," Deborah injected. "Nobody's defying you. We're only trying to get past your stubbornness."

He poked a finger at his chest. "Me? Stubborn? Because I won't fawn over a man who refused to acknowledge us as his children for thirty years? You've got to be kidding me."

"Sit down, Michael," Leah said. "And calm down. I'm asking you to do this for me, not for Abraham. For me."

Deborah knew her mother had secured the deal. Michael would stay for her, but only for her.

"You don't ask much, do you?" he muttered, dropping back down in his chair.

"No, I don't."

The phone rang then. "Let me get that," Leah said.

"Don't, Mama," Deborah said. "I'll get it. It's probably Abraham explaining why he's late."

"More like explaining why he's not going to show," Michael muttered as Deborah headed to the kitchen to get the phone.

Disappointment settled in when the voice she heard was not her father's. "May I speak to Deborah Thomas?"

"This is Deborah," she answered.

"This is Alan Weems. I'm Abraham Martin's attorney. I'm sorry to tell you this, Miss Thomas, but your father has been in an automobile accident. He's been taken to the Emergency Room at DeKalb General Medical Center."

Chapter Eight

Saralyn sat huddled with her son and daughter-in-law in the Emergency Room waiting area. "He has to be all right," she repeated. "He has to be."

"Dad's strong, Mom," Isaac reminded her.

Saralyn had to fight to keep panic from overwhelming her. Despite their problems, she and Abraham had been married for thirty years, most of those very good years. She didn't want him to die, not tonight, not after they'd had such an awful fight. She blamed Leah and those kids for this. They were the ones who had him all stressed out.

"Mrs. Martin."

The three of them stood together at the sound of her name. Isaac held tight to one of her hands, and Rebecca held tight to the other. Saralyn took their strength and braced herself for the news the doctor would give. "I'm Mrs. Martin," she said to the doctor, who seemed to be even younger than Isaac.

"Your husband is awake and wants to talk to you."

She breathed a sigh of relief. "He's okay?"

"He has some internal injuries resulting from the accident," the doctor answered. "We won't be sure of the extent until we get the test results back. We think he had a heart attack and that caused him to lose control of the car. He's awake now and he's lucid. That's very good news."

"A heart attack?" Isaac echoed. "Dad?"

The doctor nodded.

"Mr. Martin's condition is listed as critical but stable. He needs his rest but he's adamant about seeing Mrs. Martin."

"What about me?" Isaac asked. "I'm his son."

"I'm sorry," the doctor said. "Your father needs his rest. Let your mother go in and we'll see where we are."

The doctor turned and Saralyn followed after him. She heard Rebecca comforting Isaac and was glad her daughter-in-law was there for him. She hadn't always felt that way, she realized, in the time the two had been married. To her mind, Rebecca had a bit too much "street" in her to be a good match for Isaac.

She braced herself when the doctor opened the door to Abraham's room. Her husband seemed to have bandages all over his face, arm, and chest. One leg, also bandaged, was lifted in a sling. She bit back her fear and rushed to his bed. "Abraham," she whispered in case he was asleep. "I'm here, Abe."

His eyes fluttered open in his ashen face.

"My sweet Saralyn," he murmured.

She picked up his hand and pressed it to her cheek. "I'm here, hon."

He gave a wobbly smile that she knew masked his pain. "You've . . . always been there . . . for me," he said. "I'm so sorry, Sara. So sorry. Didn't mean . . . to hurt you."

Tears filled her eyes as they filled his. "It's all right, Abe. Don't think about that now. Just concentrate on getting better."

"I love you, Saralyn." The words sounded as if they came from down a well. "I've always loved you."

She let her tears fall. "I know. I love you, too."

"Please forgive me. I know God has forgiven me, but I need you to forgive me. Can you do that?"

She wiped her tears with her free hand. "I forgive you, Abraham."

He sighed, coughed. "Thank you."

She pressed her face to the back of his hand. "No need to thank me. I love you. I was always going to forgive you."

"You're a good woman, Saralyn," he said. "Too good for me."

"Don't say that," she chided. "You're the only man for me. Always have been, always will be."

"No, no." His grip on her hand increased and he winced in pain. "If I don't make it, I want you to find someone else. Young."

"Shh," she told him. "Don't think like that. You're going to be fine."

He grunted. "I need to see . . . children," he said.

"Isaac and Rebecca are outside. I'll get them."

When she would have pulled away, he squeezed her hand and kept her at his side. "All children," he said on a grimace.

Saralyn felt as though her heart froze. Even now, when he feared he was dying, he thought of them. How could he expect her to bring them to his side?

"I don't know how to reach them," she said.

"Please, Saralyn. Do this one thing for me."

She tried to give him a smile but her heart hurt too much. "Okay," she said. "I'll do this for you. Now let me go get Rebecca and Isaac."

"Thank you, Saralyn. You're a good woman. I don't deserve you."

You surely don't, Saralyn thought as she made her way back to the waiting room, where Isaac and Rebecca rushed to her.

"How is he?" Isaac asked. "Can I see him? I need to see him."

Saralyn touched her son's cheek. "He wants to see you two as well, so go on back there. His body is pretty battered but his voice is strong. He's going to be fine."

"Thanks, Mom," Isaac said. He pulled her to him for a long embrace, then reached out for Rebecca's hand, and the two of them rushed to his father's room.

Saralyn pulled her cell phone out of her purse and punched in 411. She pressed the Off button before the ringing began. She wasn't going to call them tonight. Tonight was for family. She'd call them tomorrow.

Chapter Nine

Leah held tight to her daughter's shaking hand and strode beside her toward the Emergency Room waiting area. She prayed the Lord wouldn't take Abraham away before Deborah and Michael had more time with him. She glanced at her daughter. Deborah's tightly clenched jaw told where her thoughts were.

"Abraham's strong," Leah said. "Remember that."

Deborah nodded and kept walking. She didn't speak until they reached the reception desk. "We're here to see Abraham Martin," she said. Then she added, "He's my father."

Leah tightened her hold on her daughter's hand.

"Take a seat back there." The woman pointed to an area around the corner from her desk. "And wait with the rest of the family."

Deborah took a deep breath and then turned to her mother. "Do you think we should? I mean—"

Leah cut her off. "Of course we should. You're his daughter. Maybe it would be better if I stayed out here, though."

Deborah shook her head. "No, I don't want to go back there alone. I need you with me."

Leah nodded her okay. "Let's go, then."

Deborah straightened her back and headed in the direction the receptionist had pointed. "I wish Michael had come with us," she said. "He should be here, too."

"He should, but we can't worry about that now." Leah was angrier with her son than she'd ever been. He'd flat-out refused to come with his sister, leaving that task to her. Her kids deserved to be here. She was the outsider.

Leah saw Saralyn as soon as they turned the corner. She was slumped back in a chair near the window, her head resting against its back, her eyes closed. A cup of coffee sat on the table in front of her. What to do? Leah wondered. She glanced at Deborah, who shrugged and took the first chair they reached. Leah sat next to her.

They sat quietly, as if afraid to wake a sleeping princess whose face they'd seen many times over the years in magazines and newspapers. Leah couldn't help but study her, though. Saralyn indeed looked like a princess. Leah knew the jewels in her ears were real and her fancy pants ensemble expensive. She looked down at her own outfit—simple tan slacks and a crisp white shirt—and felt lacking. She forced herself to look away from Saralyn.

All three of them jumped in surprise when a nurse poked her head around the corner and said, "Jones family."

Saralyn looked at them, apparently thinking they were the Joneses. They shook their heads and the nurse turned away, muttering, "I wonder where they went."

Leah shared another glance with Deborah. She knew they were both thinking the same thing. Saralyn didn't know who they were. This was awkward. It served as a reminder of how little impact she and her children had on Abraham's family. His wife didn't recognize them. That hurt. Badly. Leah gave Deborah's hand another reassuring squeeze. Saralyn resumed her previous sleeping position.

"When do you think they'll tell us something?" Deborah whispered.

"I don't know," Leah said. She glanced toward Saralyn. "We can ask her."

Deborah shook her head. "Let's wait for the doctor."

Leah nodded. "Do you want something to drink?"

"Not really. You?"

"No, I'm fine."

"We'll wait, then."

"And hold good thoughts."

"And hold good thoughts. He has to be all right, Mama. I can't lose him now after only just finding him. We need more time. I want more time with him."

"I know you do, sweetie, and he knows it, too."

Saralyn suddenly sat upright and glared at them. "What did you say? Who are you? Who are you here to see?" Apparently, the princess hadn't been sleeping at all.

Deborah cleared her throat. "I'm Deborah Thomas and this is my mother." She inched her chin up. "We're here to see my father."

Saralyn jumped up from her seat. "How dare you?" she screamed. "How dare you show up here?"

"Hold on a minute, Saralyn—" Leah began.

"That's Mrs. Martin to you," Saralyn spat out.

Before Leah could respond, Deborah said, "Mrs. Martin, I'm only here to see my father."

"Father? Now that's rich. He's never been a father to you, more like an ATM."

Leah flinched as though she'd been gut-punched. "There's no

need to make this ugly, Saralyn," she said, stressing the name. "Deborah has as much right to be here as you do. This is an awkward situation for all of us."

Saralyn looked at her with disdain. "Who are you to tell me about rights? Were you right to sleep with my husband?"

Leah recoiled from the question. She had no answer. The guilt from the past overtook her and she was left defenseless.

Deborah spoke up again, this time forcefully. "Look, Mrs. Martin, I understand your feelings. My mother and I mean you no disrespect, but we also won't be disrespected by you. Abraham Martin is my father and nothing you say will change that. So let's sit here together like the civilized people we are. My only concern right now is my father."

"Civilized?" Saralyn began. "You're going to talk to me about civilized?"

"What's going on here?" a male voice asked.

All three women turned toward the voice. Leah was immediately struck with how much Isaac resembled Michael. They were both well over six feet. Michael had a dark complexion, like Abraham, while Isaac's lighter complexion was like his mother's. The nose, mouth, and ears were all Abraham. They were as evident in Michael as they were in Isaac. She wondered how anyone could not guess that the two men were related. Maybe it was her mother's eyes that gave her such clarity. She wondered what Saralyn would see when she looked at the two boys.

"Mom, what are you doing?" Isaac asked.

"Get these women out of here, Isaac, before I do something I'm going to regret."

Isaac wiped his hand down his face and then looked at Leah and Deborah. "Look, he's asking for you," he said to Deborah. "You should go on back."

"What are you saying, Isaac?" Saralyn demanded. "Don't you know who she is?"

"Calm down, Mom," he said, taking a deep breath. "Of course I know who she is. Dad's asking for her and her brother."

Leah knew that the evening had taken its toll on Isaac. He was mentally drained. He had that hollow look in his eyes that Michael got when his emotions were on overload. The mother in her wanted to comfort him. She fought down the urge.

Isaac turned back to Deborah. "Is Michael here?"

She shook her head.

"Does he know?"

Deborah nodded. "He chose not to come."

Saralyn snorted. "At least one of you has good sense."

"You should go on back," Isaac told Deborah again.

"How is he?" she asked, biting her lower lip. She, too, was reaching her emotional limits.

"He's in some pain. They're still running tests. They say he had a heart attack and that led to the accident."

Deborah nodded. Then she looked at her mother. "Come with me."

Leah shook her head. She wanted to support her daughter, but some boundaries had to be set. "It's not my place. You can handle it."

Deborah glared at Saralyn as if to say, *Leave my mama alone,* and then she turned and headed to Abraham's room.

Chapter Ten

Saralyn picked up her coffee cup and glared at her son. "If she stays," she said, inclining her head in Leah's direction, "I'm leaving."

"Mom—" Isaac began. He was too tired and too scared to deal with his mother's antics. Not when his father could be dying.

Leah stood. "I'm going to get some coffee from the cafeteria," she said to Isaac. "If Deborah returns before I get back, will you tell her where I've gone?"

Isaac nodded. "Thank you," he said. He would have said more but he knew additional words would only raise his mother's ire.

"No need to thank me," Leah said. "This is a difficult situation for all of us."

"So the whore is having a difficult time!" Saralyn said. "Please."

"Mom!" Isaac said, turning to her as Leah left the room. "What is wrong with you?"

Saralyn crossed her legs and folded her arms. Isaac recognized the position. His mother had staked out her point of view and wasn't going to budge. "What's wrong with me?" she asked. "What's wrong with me? What's wrong with you? Why are you being so nice to those people? They're like vultures, coming here to clean your father's bones."

Isaac sat down next to her. "You've got to get a handle on yourself, Mom. Dad wants them here. He said you were going to call them. Why did you call them and then treat them this way?"

"I didn't call them," she said.

"But Dad said—"

"Your father expects too much from me. I didn't call them. I was going to do it tomorrow."

"Then who?"

She shrugged. "Probably Alan. I'll have a word with him tomorrow. Sometimes he oversteps his role as the MEEG attorney. He had no right to invite those people to come down here."

Isaac took a deep breath and tried to understand his mother's position. "Alan did the right thing. Dad thinks he may die, Mom. He wants to see them in case he does. Can you give him that?"

His mother laughed an empty, cynical laugh. "So the tide has turned. Now you're taking your father's side?"

Isaac shook his head. His frustration with his mother was quickly turning into disappointment and disillusion. Where was her compassion? "It's not about sides. It's about my father lying back there in that bed, unsure if he's going to live to see tomorrow. I had to put my anger and disappointment on hold. I don't want to lose him, Mom. He could die."

His mother reached for him, pulled him into her arms. "I'm so sorry, darling. I know you love your father. You have every right to be concerned about him."

"He's afraid, Mom," he said. "He's afraid he's going to die before he makes things right with all of us."

"Your father's not going to die," she said, as if saying it made it so.

Isaac wasn't so sure. "He wants to see Michael. Do you think I should contact him?"

"Didn't his sister say he didn't want to come?"

Isaac nodded.

"Then leave it alone. If he wanted to be here, he'd be here."

"This is not about him, Mom. It's about Dad."

She pulled away from him. "Do what you feel you have to do, Isaac, but don't forget that the boy has every reason to hate you. If you reach out, don't be surprised if you lose a limb."

Isaac considered his mother's words and knew she was right. He didn't want to contact Michael, but he did want to honor his father's wishes. "Maybe I'll talk to his mother. What do you think?"

"Do what you want, Isaac. I say leave those people alone, but do what you want."

Isaac knew he was hurting his mother, but he didn't think he could live with himself if his father died and he hadn't tried to convince Michael to see him. He stood and pressed a kiss against his mother's forehead. "I love you, Mom."

"I know, son," she said. "Just be careful."

"I will," he said. Then he left the waiting area and headed for the cafeteria to find Deborah's mother.

He didn't have to go far. She hadn't gone to the cafeteria after all. She was seated out in the main waiting room, in front of the reception desk.

He walked over to her. "Missus . . . ah, Miss . . . ah—"

"Just call me Leah," she said.

He cleared his throat. Though he tried to keep his thoughts in the present, he was unsuccessful. He wondered why his father had chosen this plain, seemingly unassuming woman when he'd had the beautiful and vivacious Saralyn. "Leah, my father is asking for

Michael. I know Deborah said he didn't want to come, but is there any chance you can convince him? Dad really wants to see him."

She began wringing her hands. "Michael is so stubborn. No, I don't think I'll be able to convince him."

"What if I got in touch with him?"

She met his eyes. "You?"

Isaac nodded. "I'd try," he said. "For my father."

She hesitated, and Isaac wondered what she was thinking. "He should be home now," she said finally. She pulled out a pad and scribbled on it. "Here's his number. Good luck."

Chapter Eleven

Did I doze off?" Abraham asked Deborah, who was perched on a chair next to his bed.

She stood and leaned on the bed railing. "For a few moments." She bit her lip to keep from crying. Her father, who had been full of strength and vigor at their last lunch together, now lay weak and ashen in a hospital bed. He seemed to have aged more than ten years in that short time.

He groaned. "Sorry, I'm tired."

"That's okay. I can leave so you can sleep."

His eyes fluttered closed and then opened. "No, stay. Talk to me."

"What do you want to talk about?" He grimaced, and she winced, feeling his pain. "Do you want me to ask the nurse for more medicine?"

"You mean Nurse Ratchet? No way." He tried to laugh but it came out as a cough.

She hurt for him, for her and for the time she had missed with him. She was also angry. Why did he wait so late to come into her life?

"Your brother?" he asked.

She pushed her anger aside. "He couldn't make it," she said, not wanting to blurt out the truth.

"Don't sugarcoat it," he said. "He didn't want to come, did he?"

Anger rose anew in her. This time it was directed at Michael. Sometimes her brother took his selfishness too far. Tonight was one of those times. "I'm sorry," she said to Abraham.

"Don't be sorry. I don't too much blame him." He coughed again. "I'd probably feel the same way if I were in his shoes." He tried to smile but it turned into another grimace. "Thank God your heart is softer than both of ours. You're my girl, aren't you, Deborah?"

She smiled back him. "I sure am."

He teared up. "So sorry for the past . . . " he began.

"Don't worry about the past. Be glad we have today. I am." She wiped his tears with her fingers, the first time she'd touched his face this way. The hairs on his face tickled her hand. This was her father! "I don't want to lose you, Dad. I need more time to get to know you."

He smiled, this time a real one, and it made her smile back.

"Something good came out of this," he said. "First time you called me Dad. I hope I'm not dead and in heaven."

She chuckled. "You're not dead," she said, her eyes filling with happy tears. "First time I've said the words to you, but I've practiced them a lot."

"Your mother did a good job with you. She could have made you hate me."

She shook her head. "She never wanted that."

"Good woman."

Deborah had so many questions she wanted to ask him. Did he ever love her mother? Why did he cheat on his wife? Did he love his wife? How could he ignore her and her brother all those years? All questions she had to put on hold now. Questions she might never get to ask.

"Need your help," he said.

"Whatever you need."

"Take care of the family. Isaac's angry with me, Michael hates me, and Saralyn hates everybody but Isaac." He winced. "You're going to have to hold them together. Make a family."

"I'm not sure—"

"You can do it," he said. "It'll be hard, but you can do it."

"But—"

"Just say you'll try."

Deborah thought about it, but knew she really had no choice. The pleading in his eyes ensnared her heart. She couldn't deny him—not now. "I'll try."

"Good girl," he said. Then he yawned. "Sleepy."

She rubbed her hand over his head, now taking every opportunity to touch him. "Go to sleep," she said. "I'll sit here quietly until you do."

Then she sat silently next to her father's bed, praying he would get better. Strange that she had gone all these years without a father and now it would be hard to go on without him.

Chapter Twelve

I t's better than I thought," Josette overheard Michael say on the phone as she walked into the kitchen of their recently reno-vated Cape Code in Atlanta's Buckhead suburb. She had been dying to move out here, even though the price tag pushed them to the limits of their budget. Good for business, she'd told him when he balked. Those three words had sold him.

"Sounds to me like the old man is going to be out of commis-sion for a while," he said into the phone. He smiled at her as she opened the stainless steel refrigerator and pulled out a carton of milk. "Let's talk more about this tomorrow," he said, hanging up.

"What was that about?" she asked.

When she reached up to get a glass from the cabinet, he came up behind her, put his arms around her waist and pulled her close. Kissing her neck, he whispered, "Ready for bed?"

"Almost," she said, sinking into his embrace even though she realized he was trying to turn her attention from his telephone call. This wasn't the first time he'd abruptly ended a call when she entered the room. It made her suspicious.

"Let me get the glass." He reached over her head, not releasing her, and brought down the glass for her. "You have a man to do these things for you," he whispered, "so take advantage." He cuddled closer behind her. "I plan to take advantage of you later on." Still holding her body tight against his, he poured the milk and handed it to her.

She loved him when he was like this with her, so affectionate, so protective. The doorbell rang as the first swallow of milk went down. "Who could that be?" she asked.

"Ignore it," Michael muttered, dotting kisses down her neck.

She wanted to follow his lead, but her head prevailed over her heart. "We can't. It could be your mother or Deborah with news about your father."

She felt him stiffen. "All the more reason to ignore it."

When the bell rang again, Josette pulled out of Michael's arms. "We have to answer the door, Michael."

He tapped his middle finger against her nose. "Party pooper."

She chuckled. "You're a trip." She held out her hand to him. "Come with me," she said.

He waited until the bell rang the third time before he took her hand. "Maybe they'll be gone when we get to the door and we can head straight upstairs."

Josette was still laughing at her husband when she opened the front door. Her laughter stopped abruptly when she saw a disheveled and weary-eyed Isaac standing in the doorway. "Isaac?"

Behind her, Michael said, "Told you we shouldn't have opened the door."

Ignoring her husband's rudeness, Josette asked, "Is this about Mr. Martin?"

Isaac nodded. "He wants to see your husband." To Michael, he said, "He's asking for you."

Michael folded his arms across his chest. "And?"

Isaac sighed. "Look, I don't want to be here anymore than you want me to be here, but our father wants to see you. The least you can do is honor his request."

Dropping his folded arms, Michael laughed. "You're kidding me, right? You didn't just ask me to honor our father's request? Are you talking about the father who failed to acknowledge me for thirty years? I can't believe you're asking me to honor anything from him. What honor has he shown me, my sister, or my mother?"

With those words, he stalked away from the door. Josette heard his footsteps going up the stairs. "I'm sorry," she told Isaac, with a wobbly smile. This was their first face-to-face meeting, and she was struck by how much he and Michael looked alike. She'd seen the resemblance in photos, but seeing him up close like this made it more vivid. "There's no getting through to him when it comes to Mr. Martin. Leah and Deborah tried to get him to go to the hospital. If Leah couldn't convince him, nobody can."

"I don't know what to do," Isaac confessed. "Dad's talking like he's dying—"

"Has his condition worsened?"

Isaac wiped his hands down his face. "Not according to the doctors, but Dad's telling a different story. This pessimism is so unlike him. He's a fighter, but it seems he's giving up."

Josette felt Isaac's pain and wished again that Michael would try harder with him. They would both benefit. "I'll try again with Michael," she said. "But I don't want you to get your hopes up. He's pretty rigid when it comes to Mr. Martin."

"I know," Isaac said, "but thanks for offering to try. That's all you can do. That's all any of us can do." He shoved his hands in his pockets. "Well, I'll be leaving. Thanks for everything."

Josette closed the door and mounted the steps to their bedroom with a heavy heart. Every thought of Michael's hatred for his father was accompanied with the question of how much that hate was affecting their marriage.

He was stretched out on their king-sized bed, talking on the phone, when she entered the bedroom. He hung up, again obviously not wanting her to hear his conversation. She hated this secrecy and the suspicions it aroused in her.

"Can you believe that guy?" Michael asked. "Coming here and asking me something like that?"

"What I can't believe is you," she said, angered because he was hiding something from her. "All the man wants is to see you."

Michael leaned on his side so he faced her. "Well, he had thirty years to see me and didn't. I'm not going to give him the satisfaction of asking me to forgive him. All he wants to do is clear his guilty conscience. Once again, Abraham Martin is only concerned with Abraham Martin."

"You're certainly his son," Josette said. She turned toward the dresser and began removing her earrings.

"What do you mean by that?"

She turned back to him after removing both earrings and her necklace. "I mean you're repeating his mistakes." She perched on the side of the bed. "Don't you see, Michael? You've set yourself on a path to ignore your father, the same way he set himself on a path to ignore you. He was wrong then and you're wrong now."

"You can't seriously be comparing me to him. There is no comparison in how he treated us and the way I'm treating him. No comparison at all."

She sighed. "I know you don't see one, but it's there. Answer me this, Michael. Do you love me?"

He looked directly into her eyes. "Of course I love you. That's a stupid question. Don't I show my love all the time? See, now he's got you questioning my love."

She shook her head. "Not him. You. Why didn't you tell me that Abraham Martin was your father before we got married?"

"There was nothing to tell. That old man was never a father to me."

"That's not good enough," she said, needing a better explanation.

He reached up, pulled her down to lie flat against him and began to massage her pregnant belly. "Because I didn't want you to marry me for money you thought I might inherit one day," he said with a grin. "Now stop asking these crazy questions. You're going to make our baby dizzy."

Josette allowed him to coax her out of her upset. She settled against him. "Will you do one thing for me, Michael?"

He pressed a kiss against her forehead. "Don't ask me to go see the old man, because I'm not. Anything else and you've got it."

"Please reconsider your plans for revenge against your father."

"What plans?"

"Don't deny them. Not tonight. Not now. I've overheard enough of your phone conversations to know you're plotting something. All I ask is that you reconsider your plans. Think about how they'll affect your mother and Deborah. Think about how they'll affect our baby and us. Don't let your animosity toward your father cause you to hurt the people you claim to love. I beg you."

Chapter Thirteen

Rebecca lay in the antique four-poster bed she shared with her husband, staring out at the Atlanta skyline from the floor-to-ceiling windows of their midtown Atlanta condo. She loved the view, and everything about the condo, which had been a gift from Isaac's parents. On any other night she'd lose herself in the starry sky and her concerns would fade away.

Not tonight. Her mind was too crowded, her heart too anxious. She loved Isaac more than she thought she could love a man, and she knew he loved her. She just hoped he loved her enough to forgive her.

"Well, I did try," Isaac said, flicking off the light to the master bathroom. He yawned as he headed toward the bed. "That's all I can do. Maybe Michael will change his mind."

Rebecca pulled back the duvet bedcover so he could join her. He'd had a long, stressful day, and she knew he needed to rest.

"Don't count on it," she said. "Michael's deep-seated resentment toward your father is not going to change overnight."

He sank down in the bed and pulled her close to him. "Maybe you're right, but it means so much to Dad. Maybe I should try harder with Michael."

She wrapped her arms around his middle, needing a greater connection with him. "I think you should stay as far away from Michael as possible. He's not to be trusted."

He kissed her forehead. "You're starting to sound like my mother."

"Well, I agree with her on some things. For one, I think you should go back to MEEG, especially now that your father is ill. We still don't know how long he's going to be out of commission."

"Mom's there," Isaac said. "And you're there. Certainly MEEG can get along with one missing Martin."

"But you need to be there, too," she said. "Your mother's right. MEEG is your birthright. You can't just give it up."

He rubbed his temples, a sure sign that he was stressed out. "Using that logic, it's as much Michael's and Deborah's birthright as it is mine."

Rebecca thought about the anniversary gifts Michael had sent them over the years. Though she hadn't known it at the time, those gifts had been nothing but jabs at Isaac. "Michael wants to hurt you, Isaac. He wants you to pay for being the cherished son of Abraham Martin."

He kissed her softly on her lips. "Where do you get that from? From where I sit, all he's done is tell Dad to stay out of his life. I can't much blame him for that. Besides, things have changed now. Dad's sick. The family needs to rally around him. Whether we like it or not, that family includes Michael."

Michael's threats when she visited his office played in Rebecca's mind. She didn't want Isaac to let down his guard where Michael was concerned, and only knew of one way to convince him that present circumstances demanded he take charge. "Do you love me, Isaac?" she asked, knowing she was about to put that love to the test.

He brushed a kiss on the top of her head. "You know I do."

She looked up into his face, needing reassurance of his answer. "I mean really love me?"

"What's this about?" he asked, his brow lined with concern.

She turned away from him, unsure she could say the words she needed to say. "When you found out your father had been lying to you for years, you turned your back on him. And you're only turning back to him now that he's ill. What if I did something you didn't like? Would you turn your back on me?"

He tightened his arms around her. "Okay, these hypothetical questions aren't helping. You're not going to do anything that will make me turn away from you."

"What if I already have?"

He tipped her chin up. "What have you done?"

"It's not what I've done. It's what I've haven't told you." She took a deep breath. "Michael sent us a wedding gift, and he's been sending us a gift on our anniversary every year."

His eyes widened and he pulled back from her. "What? Why would he do that?"

She bit down on her lower lip. "I think he did it as some secret joke on us. Michael and I were in a relationship a couple of years before I met you, though it wasn't anything serious. I think he sent the gifts because he knew something that neither of us knew at the time: that you and he were half brothers."

Her heart ached at the confusion in his eyes. "That's sick."

She shook her head. "That's Michael. And that's why you have to be careful of him. He wants to hurt you Isaac. That's why—"

He didn't let her finish. "Why didn't you tell me about these gifts?"

He looked at her as if he didn't know who she was. "There was nothing to tell," she said. "Michael was an old boyfriend trying to reach into my current life. I didn't want him to, so I sent the gifts back unopened."

"You still should have told me," he said, shaking his head.

She sat on her knees on the bed and pleaded with him. "I know that now."

He rubbed his hand across his head. "Do you still have feelings for him?"

She looked down at her hands and then back up at him. "No way. As I said, it was never serious. I was young and thought I was the next Mary J. Blige. He thought he was the next Sean Combs. We both were looking for something other than love in the relationship. It ended when we realized we couldn't advance each other's careers."

Isaac rolled away from her and got up from the bed. He looked down at her. "You slept with him to advance your career? Is that why you slept with me?"

Rebecca's mouth dropped open. "You can't believe that. I love you, Isaac. What was between Michael and me was nothing compared to what we have. I love you."

"So you say," he said. "Your words would be easier to believe if you'd told me about Michael and the gifts from the start. Now they sound like an excuse, a weak excuse."

"You have to believe me," she said.

Isaac's mouth opened but no words came out. He turned, then, and stormed out of their bedroom, slamming the door behind him.

Rebecca folded over and began to weep. She prayed she hadn't ruined her marriage, but somewhere deep inside, she knew she had.

Chapter Fourteen

Go to bed, Deborah," Leah said.

Deborah had sprawled out on the lovingly worn sofa in the family room, and Leah sat curled up in her favorite club chair. Had Michael been there lazing in the recliner next to the sofa, the family picture would have been complete. The three of them had spent many a night in this room watching television or engaged in some lively conversation.

"I'm exhausted, too tired to move."

"I know you are, baby. You've had a rough day."

Hearing the concern in her mother's voice, Deborah reached for her hand. "So have you. Thanks for going to the hospital with me, Mama."

"No need to thank me. I didn't want you to be there alone."

"I know, but I didn't anticipate the treatment you got from Saralyn." She turned up her nose and raised her voice an octave. "Oh, excuse me, Mrs. Martin."

Leah chuckled. "Don't let her get to you. You had a right to be there."

"You're my mother. You had a right to be there as well."

Leah dropped her daughter's hand and settled back in her chair. "I love you for saying that, and on one level you're right, but you can understand why Saralyn didn't want me there, can't you?"

"Because of something that happened twenty-eight, thirty years ago?" Deborah shook her head. "She needs to get over it."

"The kind of betrayal she experienced has a long half-life. I'm a reminder of a time in her marriage she'd rather forget. To be honest, I'd rather forget it, too."

"Well, I think she was out of line. Dad is going to have to put her in check when he gets out of the hospital. She'd better be glad—" Her mother's broad smile made her stop talking. "What?" she asked.

"You called Abraham 'Dad.' "

"I know," she said. "It just came out when I was talking to him in his hospital room."

"How does it feel to say it?"

"Good," she said. "Natural." Deborah noticed tears streaming down her mother's face. She sat up and faced her. "What?"

"I'm so sorry, Deborah."

"You have nothing to be sorry for."

She wiped her tears. "Yes, I do, and you know it. It's my fault—*partly* my fault—that Abraham hasn't been in your life. What was I thinking to go along with an agreement that kept him out of your lives? The little money they sent us was not enough reason. You and Michael needed your father."

Deborah had wondered at her mother's decisions but had never been bold enough to ask her about them. "What happened between you and Abraham, Mama? You've never really told us, and I haven't wanted to ask because it seemed painful for you to discuss."

"I know," she said. "And I've known you were curious. I just didn't know how to talk to you two about it. I wanted you and Michael to look up to me, and the story of my relationship with Abraham hardly paints me as a woman worth looking up to."

"Don't think like that, Mama. There's nothing you could tell me that would make me love you or respect you less. Me or Michael. You played the cards you were dealt. One thing I really appreciate is that you never painted Abraham as the bad guy, and you could have. If you had, I probably wouldn't be able to accept him now. You left room in my heart for a relationship with him to grow. I thank you for that."

Leah squeezed her daughter's hand. "I've always hoped there'd come a time when you could get to know him. You and Michael both. Things aren't working like I'd hoped with Michael, though."

"I think it's different for him because he's a man. It's been especially hard for Michael to have had no relationship with Abraham, while Abraham has lavished everything on Isaac. Maybe I'd feel the same if he had another daughter. I don't know."

"All I can say, Deborah, is I hope you make better choices in your life than I have, that you keep your head when you fall in love. Don't always trust your heart. It can fool you sometimes."

"Tell me, Mama. I want to know about you and Abraham. What happened?"

Leah gave a wry smile. "I fell in love with a man who wasn't ready to be in love."

"What does that mean?"

"I think Abraham loved me, in his way, but he loved other things more."

"Saralyn?"

"And what she represented. Abraham was always a big dreamer. I saw myself working side by side with him making those dreams come true. But Saralyn represented the dream. She and her family were much farther along the road to Abraham's dream destination than either his family or mine."

"So you don't think he married her for love?"

"I didn't say that. Of course he loved her, loves her still. But back then I think Abraham loved himself more than he loved anything or anyone else. How else could he make the decisions he did where you and your brother were concerned? He's a better man today than he was then, I think. He's learned something from life's lessons."

"I don't know how to ask this . . . " Deborah murmured.

"Just ask, sweetie. We've started this. We may as well finish it."

Deborah took a deep breath, then let it out slowly. "Okay, you had two babies with Abraham. Michael and Isaac are about the same age and I'm two years younger. What happened?"

Leah winced as if in pain. "It's something straight out of the tabloids. Abraham was dating both Saralyn and me at the same time, though neither of us knew, and he got both of us pregnant. Unfortunately for me, I didn't find out I was pregnant until after Abraham told me he was going to marry Saralyn because she was pregnant. When I found out about my condition, I had too much pride to tell him. Saralyn had beat me to the pregnancy line by about four months." She shrugged. "What could he do anyway?"

"So what did you do?"

"I spent a year with some relatives in Ohio. I had planned to live there, but my mother got sick and I had to come back home. Abraham found out about the baby and we started up again."

"Even though you knew he was married?"

She nodded. "I told you the story doesn't make me sound like a good person. I knew he was married, but my heart was still his. It remained his until the day I found out I was pregnant with you. Something happened to me that day, Deborah. It was as though a lightbulb went off and I clearly saw who I was and what I was doing. I didn't like what I saw at all."

"So you ended it?"

Leah gave a wry smile. "Relationships don't end in such a clear-cut manner, sweetie. I said the words but the relationship had been over since the day Abraham decided to marry Saralyn. I just refused to accept it."

"So what happened when you told him about me—being pregnant with me, I mean?"

"He was dumbfounded. Before you even ask, no, he didn't ask me to terminate. He was shell-shocked because Saralyn was pregnant again, too." Leah lowered her eyes. "I wouldn't believe this if I hadn't lived it, but sadly it's true. Again, Abraham had two women pregnant, the same two women."

"Man," Deborah said, "I had no idea."

"It's not something we talk about. Saralyn found out about my pregnancy and had a miscarriage. Though neither of us spoke of it, I think both Abraham and I felt responsible. Saralyn demanded that he cut all ties with us. I didn't blame her. Abraham agreed, but told her he had to support us financially as best he could. Saralyn didn't like it but she went along with it."

Deborah thought about the harsh words Saralyn had spoken and felt a bit of compassion for her. "No wonder she hates us—me, especially. Why didn't you tell me, Mama?"

Leah studied her hands. "Because it's hard to think about that time in my life, even harder to talk about. I told you it wasn't a pretty story."

"No, it's not," Deborah agreed. She had a lot of new information to process. It would take some time to make sense out of it all.

"Do you hate me?" Leah asked.

Deborah met her mother's eyes, saw the fear there. "I could never hate you."

"But what I've told you makes you think less of me. I know it does."

Deborah thought about it before she answered. Her mother had been honest with her, so Deborah felt she deserved honesty in return. "I'm glad you waited to tell me the details. I don't think I could have handled all this as a teenager. I'm also glad you waited until after I had a chance to get to know Abraham some. I'm not sure how knowing these details would have affected my reaction to his outreach. I do know that I'm glad for the chance to get to know him. And I'm glad you're my mother. You made some bad decisions, Mama, but you made up for them. You went off and made a career for yourself and you raised two good kids. Well, one good kid and one great kid. I'm the great kid."

Leah smiled, as Deborah had hoped she would. "I love you, sweetie."

"I love you, too, Mama," Deborah said, standing up to embrace her mother. Only now did she realize the full gravity of Abraham's request that she try to put the family together. There was a lot of history and a lot of hurt on both sides. She didn't know if she was up to the task.

Chapter Fifteen

Rebecca stood outside her father-in-law's office on the twelfth floor of the MEEG Building in downtown Atlanta. She braced herself to come face-to-face with her husband for the first time since her confession last night. Isaac had become so angry with her that he had left their bed and spent the night in one of their guest rooms. Then this morning he'd left before she awakened. She knew she had work to do to repair his trust in her. He was on the phone when she walked in, so she took a seat in front of the massive mahogany desk with inlaid granite top that had Abraham's masculine stamp all over it.

"I've got it," Isaac said into the phone. "We'll have a company-wide meeting at noon to update everybody on Dad's condition and to reassure them that the company will operate as usual while he's in the hospital. Thanks for getting on this so quickly, Alan."

Isaac hung up the phone and jotted something on the calendar in front of him before looking at her. "You should be at the companywide meeting," he said. "It's important that we present a unified front."

"I'll be there."

He drummed his fingers on the desk. "Was there something you wanted?"

She leaned forward. "I wanted to talk to you about last night."

He flipped through his dad's desk calendar, refusing to look at her. "I think you said enough last night."

She shook her head. "We didn't talk," she said. "You stormed out of our bed and our bedroom and refused to speak to me."

He finally lifted his eyes to hers. Her heart ached at the weariness she saw there. He hadn't gotten much sleep last night, either. "I didn't trust myself to talk to you," he told her. "I still don't. The thoughts I'm thinking, believe me, you don't want to hear."

"I know you're hurt, Isaac, but believe me, if I had known Michael was your half brother, I would have told you. This whole thing is only an issue because we both found out about your relationship to Michael. Otherwise, he'd just be some old boyfriend who didn't matter to either of us."

"Well, he's not just some old boyfriend." He pressed his hands, palms down, on the desk and leaned toward her. "And all this time he's been thumbing his nose at me and I had no idea."

"I'm sorry, Isaac, but I didn't know."

He leaned back in his chair, took a deep breath. "But if you had told me about the gifts, I would have looked into it and maybe learned about my dear brother long before now."

"We're going to get past this, right?" she asked, praying for an affirmative answer.

"I don't know." Isaac steepled his fingers across the bridge of his nose. "I know it shouldn't matter, but it does. One of the downsides of being born into a family with money is that you always wonder about the motives of the people you meet. I never had those questions with you, but I do now. When you tell me that your relationship with Michael was based on what you thought he could do to advance your career, I have to wonder if our relationship is any different. Being married to me has certainly helped your career."

Rebecca felt like a battered boxer in the ring with a much more talented opponent. "How can you even say that to me?" she asked. "I love you, Isaac. I've always loved you. You have to know that."

He shook his head. "Let's not get into it now. There's too much going on with Dad. We'll get through this storm and then we'll deal with our marriage. In the meantime, in public we'll act as if everything is all right. I don't want to add to my mother's stress. She'd be in a bed beside Dad if she knew about your history with Michael and those gifts he's been sending. I can't do that to her."

Rebecca accepted this punishment, though she didn't think it was fair. "I understand. I'll do whatever it takes."

"Thanks. Right now what I need is for you to cover for Mom, take over her PR responsibilities so she can focus on Dad. You should probably head over to the hospital after the companywide meeting and talk with her."

"Aren't you going too?"

He rubbed his temples as if he had a headache. "I stopped by to check on her and Dad on the way over this morning."

"How is he?"

"The injuries from the accident aren't serious, but they're worried about his heart. They want to run more tests. He's in a lot of pain and they can't figure out the cause."

"So we probably won't see each other until dinner. I'll pick up something and we'll eat with your mother at the hospital. I'm sure she won't want to leave."

He shook his head. "That won't be necessary. I told Mom you had to work tonight, so she isn't expecting you for dinner. You can see her and Dad when you meet her to discuss work."

Her heart ached. "So that's how it's going to be, huh? You're shutting me out."

He met her gaze. "I'm doing the best I can, Rebecca. I can put on a front for a few hours at work but I can't do it for an extended time around my mother. She's not stupid. She would know something wasn't right between us and she would worry. I don't want that."

"I don't want it either, Isaac, but surely your mother will realize that we're rarely together."

"We'll just attribute it to work. I'll be busy here at the office trying to catch up anyway, so we won't really be lying to her."

"Yes, we will. We won't be telling her the full truth."

He met her eyes, his full of accusation. "Well, then that shouldn't be a problem for you, should it? You've had a lot of practice at it."

Those words stung and she had no comeback. The ringing phone saved her from having to respond. What had she done to her marriage? What would she have to do to save it? The questions filled her mind and she had no answers.

"Calm down, Mom," Isaac said as he stood, the phone to his ear. "We're on our way to the hospital now."

"What is it?" she asked when he hung up.

"They've put Dad into a coma," he said, rushing for the door.

"Oh no!" Rebecca said, running to catch up.

Chapter Sixteen

Isaac saw the dapper Alan Weems, MEEG's lead counsel, as soon as he stepped off the hospital elevator wearing his signature Cardin double-breasted suit. The older man, a longtime family friend, greeted his mother first. "I'm so sorry, Saralyn," he said, pressing a kiss on her makeup-free cheek.

"Thank you, Alan. We're going to be counting on you a lot during the next few days and weeks of uncertainty."

"I won't let you down. I promise you."

She nodded. "I know you won't." She stood slowly, seeming much older than her forty-eight years. She normally looked much younger than her age, but she had been at the hospital all night so she appeared far from her typically perfect self. "I'm going to go sit with Abraham and leave this meeting to the next generation of Martins." She looked at Isaac. "It's your time now, son. Don't let me or your father down."

"I won't, Mom," he said, pressing a kiss against her cheek.

She embraced Rebecca. "I'm counting on you, too," she told her. "We're going to need your PR expertise in the office, but Isaac is going to need you even more as his helpmeet. Stand strong with him, Rebecca. He's going to need the safe haven that you provide."

"Yes, ma'am," she said. "I'm behind Isaac one hundred percent. I always have been and I always will be. You don't have to worry about that."

"I know," she said, squeezing Rebecca's hand. She added for the attorney, "Thanks again, Alan."

"You take care of yourself, Saralyn," he said, "and give my best to Abraham."

She nodded and then turned toward her husband's hospital room.

"She's holding up well," Alan observed. "What are the doctors saying this morning?"

"Not much," Isaac said. "They induced the coma to deal with his pain, and they'll keep him in it until they find out the cause. It's an awful situation. Dad didn't deserve this."

Alan placed a hand on Isaac's shoulder. "Your father's a strong man, Isaac. He'll beat this, whatever it is."

"I certainly hope so."

Rebecca came and stood next to Isaac. Though he was still angry with her, he appreciated her presence. Until now he hadn't considered how small his family really was—him, Rebecca, Mom, and Dad. Deborah and Michael were a distant afterthought.

"There's no good time for this, but we need to talk business," Alan said. "With the change in Abraham's status, I've postponed the companywide meeting. Our more immediate need is for a press conference."

"Can't this wait a few days?" Rebecca asked, rubbing her hand across Isaac's back. "We're still in shock."

Alan shook his head. "I'm afraid not. MEEG is not going to stand still because Abraham is out of commission. We need to mobilize now so that the company doesn't suffer a loss of momentum." He turned to face Isaac. "Your father has several deals going, and his partners need to be reassured that MEEG can and will stand by those deals. You're going to have to convince them of that, Isaac. They're going to be looking for a voice from the family, and that's you. It's what your father wanted, what he ordered."

Isaac nodded. "I know and I'm ready. Just bring me up to date on the outstanding projects."

"We can start that tomorrow. I'll be in your office first thing— say eight o'clock?"

"That's fine," he said, reaching for Rebecca's hand in a show of solidarity that she knew was simple play-acting. "We'll be there."

"Good. There is one order of business that we need to take care of today, though."

"What's that?" Rebecca asked.

"The board of directors."

"Now that Dad's out of commission, the board consists of you, Mom, and me," Isaac said.

"That used to be the composition," Alan said. "Before his accident, your father added two members: Leah and Deborah Thomas."

"You're kidding me," Isaac said. He didn't want to even think about his mother's reaction to this news. He sat in the chair nearest him. Rebecca and Alan followed, taking seats on either side of him. "When did Dad do this? I knew he'd offered Deborah a job and that she'd taken it, but he didn't mention anything about the board."

"He was supposed to tell you and them the night of the accident. I know why he didn't tell them, but I'm not sure why he didn't tell you."

"He tried," Rebecca said, "but the conversation deteriorated pretty quickly."

"I understand," Alan said. "Abraham didn't think the news would go over well."

"Then why did he do it?" Isaac asked, thinking how much his world had shifted in the last four months. He rubbed his temple as he felt another stress headache coming on.

"His only explanation to me was that they are his children."

"Leah is not his child," Isaac said, angry on his mother's behalf. "She's his former mistress. Putting her on the board is a slap in my mother's face. How could he disrespect her this way?"

Alan put a hand on Isaac's forearm. "It wasn't about disrespecting your mother. It's that he didn't trust Michael Thomas. His mother is on the board in his stead."

At the mention of Michael's name, Isaac met his wife's gaze. "At least Dad is rational where Michael is concerned," he said to Alan. "But I still don't like the idea of Leah and Deborah with seats on the board."

"I'm sorry, but it's a done deal. When I leave here, I'm meeting with the two women. They need to be at the press conference."

Isaac shook his head. "No way," he said. "Their presence will only add more uncertainty to an already uncertain situation."

"But your father—"

Isaac met the older man's gaze. "My father's in a coma and I'm running MEEG. I'm not going against his wishes. If he put them on the board, they're on the board, but we don't make that announcement at the press conference or at the companywide meeting. We do it down the road in a month or so. If Dad's back at the helm by then, all well and good, then he can make the announcement. If he's not, then people will have become used to his absence and the announcement won't generate much interest."

"If that's the way you want it."

Isaac nodded. "That's the way I want it."

"We need to have a board meeting in the next day or so."

"Let's talk about that tomorrow morning. Right now, I need to spend some time with my family."

Alan checked his watch. "One more thing. Have you told Leah and her family about the change in Abraham's condition?"

Isaac shook his head. "Mom wouldn't hear of it."

"I know this is hard for her, Isaac, but you're going to have to make room for your half brother and half sister. It's what Abraham would want. It's the right thing to do."

Isaac winced at the terms "half brother" and "half sister." Deborah and Michael weren't only Abraham's children, they were also his brother and sister. He pushed away the childhood memory of himself asking his mother for a baby brother or sister. "I know you're right, Alan, but she's my mother and this is killing her. She has to come first."

"Look," Alan said, "I'll let Leah and Deborah know when I go over there, and we'll work out a visiting schedule of some sort. Talk to your mother. She can't make those kids go away."

"I'll try but you should talk to her, too. You'll probably have more sway with her. She trusts you."

"Good enough," Alan said. "I'll come back here around lunch and force her to get something to eat. While we're eating, Leah and Deborah can visit with Abraham. I'm pretty sure Michael won't be visiting, so he won't be a problem."

"I understand about Deborah and Michael, but I don't see why Leah has to be here. You weren't here the other day when she and Mom came face-to-face. It wasn't pretty. Mom lost it."

Sighing, Alan stood. "This entire situation is a mess, isn't it? I'll speak with Deborah and Leah. We'll work something out."

Isaac stood and extended his hand. "Thanks, Alan. I know Dad trusted you and counted on you. I'll be counting on you a lot as we go through this transition."

"I'm ready to assist you in any way I can."

"Good. I'll see you tomorrow."

With that, Alan left.

"You did good," Rebecca said. "I'm so proud of you."

"Don't be proud yet," Isaac said. "Anybody can talk a good game, as you well know."

Rebecca flinched at his words, and he knew they had hit their target. Unwilling to offer her any comfort, he left her alone and headed for his father's room.

Chapter Seventeen

Deborah glanced at her watch again. Alan Weems was a long-winded guy. Handsome, but long-winded. Why didn't he just get to the point? She wanted to get to the hospital to see Abraham. She'd called this morning to check on his condition only to learn that the doctors had put him in an induced coma. While she knew there was nothing she could do, she wanted to be with him. Instead, here she sat on her living room couch while this attorney droned on and on.

"So in addition to your new job as head of Running Brook Productions," he said to her, "you also have a seat on the board of directors of MEEG, along with your mother."

"What?" Deborah asked, jerking upright in her chair. "Abraham didn't tell me anything about this."

"He was going to tell you the night of his accident," Alan explained.

"He's right, Deborah," her mother chimed in. "Abraham told me so himself."

"When did you talk to him?" she asked her mother.

"A few days ago. He came by my classroom at the community college. He wanted to run the idea by me before he approached you and Michael."

Deborah turned back to Alan, unsure how she felt about her mother and Abraham having secret talks about them. "Okay, there's a place for me and Mama. What about Michael?"

Alan sat forward in his chair and faced them. "Well, Deborah, your father doesn't trust Michael to act in MEEG's best interests, so he doesn't have a seat on the board at this time."

"That's not fair," Deborah said. "Abraham needs to earn Michael's trust. It's not fair to leave him out."

Her mother placed her hands on Deborah's. "He hasn't left Michael out exactly," she explained. "I'm holding his seat on the board."

"I don't understand."

"Abraham has made a place for Michael, but I'm holding it until Michael is ready for it."

Deborah snorted. "And who decides when Michael is ready?"

"I have Abraham's proxy, since he's incapacitated, so the three of us will decide," Alan said. "I understand and appreciate your inclination to look out for your brother's best interests, but you have to trust that Abraham will do right by him."

"Why should I trust him where Michael is concerned?" Deborah asked, jumping up from her chair. "Maybe Abraham feels he has one son and doesn't need another."

"Deborah," her mother chided. "You know that's not true."

Deborah sighed deeply. This was all happening too fast. Her father had come into her life. He bought her a company. Then he had an accident, was hospitalized and placed in a coma. And now she'd learned that he put her on his board of directors. How could so many good things and bad things happen at the same time? Why couldn't things be all good?

"I'm sorry, Mama," she said, sitting back down. "You're right." She turned to the attorney. "Forgive me, Mr. Weems. So much is happening so fast. It's all a bit overwhelming."

Alan gave her a smile that showed his perfect white teeth. He was indeed a handsome man. In fact, he was the spitting image of the gorgeous black guy who played the president on that TV show 24. She guessed his age to be late forties, early fifties. "I know this has to be a difficult time for you," he said. "Believe me when I tell you that Abraham wanted things to go smoothly for you. His accident upset his plans."

Leah gave a dry laugh. "Not even Abraham can control everything."

"He certainly makes a great effort, though," Alan said. "That's one of the keys to his success."

"He was that way when we were kids. I knew he'd never change."

Deborah heard a wistfulness in her mother's voice she hadn't heard before. She wondered if her mother still had feelings for Abraham. What if she'd never stopped loving him?

"I've know him for twenty-five years," Alan said, "and I can tell you that he hasn't changed much in that time. If anything, his basic characteristics have only grown stronger with age."

Leah laughed outright. "So you're saying he's become more controlling with age?"

"You didn't hear it from me," Alan said good-naturedly.

The attorney's long-term relationship with Abraham caught Deborah's interest. Maybe this man could help her learn about her father. She needed that, now that Abraham was in a coma.

Alan cleared his throat. "I know you two want to get to the hospital, but there's one other thing I'd like to talk to you about."

"What?" Leah asked, concern in her voice.

"Saralyn."

"Oh," Leah and Deborah said at the same time.

"I want to preface what I'm about to say with this: You have every right to be at Abraham's side while he's ill. It's what he would want."

"I hear the 'but' coming," Deborah said.

"Yes," Alan said, meeting her eyes. "Saralyn is the 'but.' This situation is difficult for all of you, I know, but I still need to ask you to do a favor—not for Saralyn, but for Abraham."

"What is it?" Deborah asked warily.

Leah stiffened. "I hope you're not going to ask Deborah to stop visiting her father."

Alan shook his head. "I'd never do that," he said. "I only ask that for the immediate future you plan your hospital visits around Saralyn's so you aren't there at the same time."

"Something tells me that Saralyn's idea of coordination would be for us to never show up," Deborah said. "Maybe you should be talking to her."

"I'm scheduled to meet with her for lunch today and we're going to have a long talk. My idea is that you plan to be at the hospital when Saralyn isn't there. In return, she promises to make herself scarce the times you're there and to keep you updated on any changes in Abraham's condition."

"Somehow I don't see her agreeing to that," Deborah said.

"She'll agree," Alan said with confidence. "She doesn't have much choice. You're Abraham's acknowledged daughter. As I said, you and your brother have as much right to be there as she and Isaac do."

"What about Mama?" she asked. "She's family. I want her there with me."

Leah hugged her daughter's shoulders. "I'll go with you some-times, sweetheart," she said. "But it's not really my place to be there. My presence would only make the situation more difficult for you."

Deborah felt a weight settle on her chest. Too much was happening too fast. "But what if I need you?"

"Then I'll be there just as I am whenever you need me. But I'm sure you're going to find you won't need me as much as you think you will. Besides, you need time with Abraham and to get to know your half brother. My presence will only hinder your building those relationships."

"But—"

"No buts," Leah said. "I'm right and you know it." She turned to the attorney. "We agree to your plan, Mr. Weems. As long as Saralyn agrees to keep Deborah up-to-date on changes in her father's condition, she'll schedule her visits so that she doesn't overlap with Saralyn."

"I appreciate it," Mr. Weems said. He turned to Deborah. "I'm taking Saralyn to lunch, so you're welcome to ride over to the hospital with me and visit with Abraham while she and I dine. Afterward, I can bring you back here or I can drive you over and show you your new office at MEEG."

Deborah looked at him. She knew she could drive herself over, but she welcomed some time with this man who knew her father so well. "I'd like that," she said, "the ride to the hospital and the visit to MEEG, if you're sure it won't put you out."

"It'll be my pleasure," Alan said. "I'd like to get to know Abraham's daughter."

And Abraham's daughter would like to get to know you, she thought. "It's a date—I mean a deal—then."

Chapter Eighteen

L eah drove around in her eight-year-old Nissan for half an hour before deciding to go to the one place she wanted to be. She took a deep breath and turned onto Sycamore Street. When she reached the fourth house, she opened her purse and pulled out the garage door opener she rarely used. She pressed the button and the door went up. The late model white Benz parked there confirmed that he was home. She breathed deeply and pulled her car in next to his. The door to the kitchen opened just as she pressed the button to lower the garage door, and she saw him standing there, a slight, balding man sporting thick professor glasses.

When the garage door was closed, she got out of her car and walked directly into his arms. "I've missed you," he whispered, holding her close. "I've missed you a lot."

She lifted her face for his kiss and then lost herself in it.

When it ended, he smiled down at her and said, "I guess you missed me, too."

He'd worked his magic and made her laugh. How had she been so lucky to find him? "It's only been a couple of days."

"Seems like weeks to me," he said, leading her into the house. "I was about to fix lunch. Are you hungry?"

She shook her head. Before she could explain, tears filled her eyes and she began to cry.

"What's wrong?" he asked, pulling her close. "Tell me what's wrong so I can help."

She opened her mouth to speak, but the words wouldn't come. She held him tightly, reveling in the comfort he provided. He was so good to her. She didn't deserve him, not really, but neither could she give him up.

"It's going to be all right," he said, leading her to the upholstered couch in his living room. He sat down on the couch, pulled her down with him, and continued to hold her close. "It's going to be all right."

Her tears and soft weeping continued until she emptied herself of them.

He tipped her chin up. "Feel better?"

She nodded. "I'm sorry for crying all over you."

He pressed a kiss against her forehead. "I'd rather you cry all over me than all over some other man."

She chuckled. "No other man would put up with me."

"Then I guess that makes me one blessed man. You know, I pray for you and thank God for you every day. You're a blessing to me, Leah."

The words were hard for Leah to hear. A chance meeting at a reception for a visiting lecturer at the community college had led to a relationship that fulfilled her in more ways than she could name. It still amazed her that Melvin Reeves was in her life when he could have any woman he wanted. She knew for a fact that several single women in his church were convinced that he'd one day be their husband. Maybe one of them would be his wife someday. But for now, he was hers. "You're the blessing, Reverend."

He tapped her nose with his finger. "That's Reverend Doctor to you."

She laughed again.

"I love to hear you laugh," he said. "The sound fills my heart and makes me happy. I never thought I'd feel this way about a woman again, but you changed that for me."

"You make me happy, too. That's why I had to come over. I needed to hear your voice, feel your arms around me."

He squeezed her shoulders. "Tell me what had you so upset."

"Abraham."

"Has he taken a turn for the worse? I was there with Saralyn this morning when she got the news about the doctors inducing the coma."

She shook her head. "Not really. It's me. I feel so guilty, Melvin. My children are hurting and it's all my fault."

"You can't blame yourself," he told her. "You made some mistakes a long time ago. God has forgiven you, now you need to forgive yourself."

"I was on my way to doing that until Abraham burst into our lives again. He's turned everything upside down, brought back a lot of painful memories."

"I thought you were glad he'd finally acknowledged your kids."

She eased out of his arms and got up from the couch. She couldn't have this discussion sitting down. "Of course I'm glad. It's about time. But I'm also angry that it took him so long. My feelings are all over the place." She tucked her hands in the pockets of her jeans. "Why does life have to be so complicated?"

"Because we have free will, which is a double-edged sword. We're free to make good and bad decisions. In exchange, we have to suffer the consequences of those decisions."

"Sometimes I think God is laughing at us."

Melvin shook his head. "Never. He's crying with you. He doesn't like to see you suffer. That's why He always makes sure your suffering is not in vain. You'll benefit from it or someone else will."

"I understand that, but why do my kids have to suffer the consequences of my actions? They're innocent."

Melvin got up and walked to her, pulling her into his arms again. "That's why you have to trust Him. There's one thing you can be sure of: As much as you love your kids, God loves them more. That knowledge should comfort you."

"I know it should, and most times it does. But when I see them suffer and know that my decisions caused it, it's hard. It's real hard."

"That's why I'm here, so that you can lean on me during the difficult times. I'm God's gift to you."

"I know," she said, her eyes filling with tears. "I know there are other women better for you than me, but I'm so happy that you're in my life."

"There is no other woman for me, Leah, and I want to shout it to the world. How many times do I have to tell you?"

She wished she could be as open with their relationship as he wanted her to be, but for now she was much more comfortable keeping it a secret. She hadn't even told Deborah or Michael. "People would talk," she told him.

He snorted. "People always talk. That's a given. Talk doesn't bother me, and it shouldn't bother you."

"You're a preacher," she said. "You need a woman who's above reproach, as the Bible says."

He chuckled. "You're above reproach."

She pulled out of his arms. "You know what I mean. You need a woman without a past, especially a past like mine. Melvin, I have two kids and have never been married."

"So? That was then; this is now. You can't live in the past. You can't keep beating yourself up about it."

This was a conversation they'd had many times. He was patient with her, but she wondered how long his patience would endure. "Once the women in your church find out you're seeing me, they're going to beat up on you."

He pulled her close again. "I'm tough. I can take it. "

She met his eyes. "Can you take Saralyn Martin? She'll enjoy running my name down to your congregation."

"Let me handle Sister Martin."

Saralyn and Abraham were big shots at Faith Community, where Melvin pastored, and they wielded a great deal of influence. If her relationship with Melvin became common knowledge, she had no doubt Saralyn would use it against him. She'd either try to ruin the relationship or try to get Melvin kicked out of his job. Maybe she'd try both. Looking at Melvin and the naive smile he wore, Leah decided to change the subject. "Now that I'm feeling better, I'm getting hungry. Still wanna fix me lunch?"

He met her eyes. "You're going to have to stop hiding one day, Leah. You insult God when you reject His forgiveness. And you insult me when you think gossip will change my feelings for you. That'll never happen."

"I know," she said, but she really didn't know. "Now let's go eat."

Chapter Nineteen

Deborah sat in her plush leather desk chair in her twelfth floor office in the MEEG Building in downtown Atlanta. The first floor lobby, while lush, gave no hint of the luxury found on this floor. She'd first come to this building when she and Michael were in high school. Both of them were curious about their absentee father and thought a trip to his building would offer some insight. They had read about MEEG in the papers and in the magazines their mother tried unsuccessfully to hide from them. She'd returned from the trip in awe of the wealth her father had amassed. Michael returned angry at what he considered the scraps Abraham tossed their way when he obviously had so much more.

As she sat taking in her surroundings, from the gold nameplate on her massive mahogany desk, to what she suspected was museum-quality art on the walls, to the magnificent view of the

Atlanta skyline through the floor-to-ceiling windows, she couldn't help but acknowledge that Michael had been right to be angry.

While they had not been poor growing up, neither had they been well-off. Sure, Abraham provided money, but both she and Michael had needed scholarships and loans to get their degrees. They'd both gone to Georgia State in downtown Atlanta and lived at home to keep expenses low. Looking at the opulence that was MEEG, she had no doubt that Abraham could have easily paid their full ride. Why hadn't he?

A knock at her door got her attention, and she looked up to see a smiling Alan standing in her doorway. "How do your like your office?" he asked.

To be honest, she thought it was a bit of overkill. "Let's just say it's a few stories, not steps, up from my cubicle at Pearson Entertainment. I'll have to invite some of my old colleagues over here so they can see how the rich live."

Alan walked fully into the room and slid easily into the guest chair in front of her desk. "What can I say? Abraham and Saralyn believe in going first class all the way."

Except when it came to us, she thought. "So I see. It's going to take some getting used to."

He chuckled. "Believe me, it won't take that long. Did you get everything taken care of in Human Resources?"

She nodded. "Very efficient group. I didn't have any problems. I'm now an official MEEG employee."

"Don't be modest," he said. "You're more than that. You own a part of this company, or you will one day."

She shook her head. "I still can't believe that. After all these years, Abraham remembers he has two other children. It doesn't make sense."

"I don't know," Alan said. "Sometimes a man reaches a point where he has to take stock of his life. When he doesn't like what he sees, he tries to right some of his wrongs."

Alan's choice of words stung. Somehow they made her and Michael seem like the wrongs, when Abraham's desertion was the real wrong. "Is that what you think Abraham is doing?"

He nodded. "Don't you?"

A part of her hoped that it was more than duty driving him. She wanted to believe that he cared for her and Michael. Maybe it was wishful thinking. "You said you've known him for twenty-five years. Did you know about us?"

He shook his head. "Not until earlier this year."

So Abraham had kept them a secret from the people who'd known him longest. That knowledge made her heart ache, if only a little.

"I'm sorry," Alan said. "I shouldn't have been so matter-of-fact about it."

Deborah realized then she was wearing her emotions on her sleeves. She'd have to watch that in the future. "You don't have to be sorry. How did you end up working for Abraham?" she asked, seeking to change the subject.

"It's a long story."

"I've got time," she said with a grin. "I'm the boss's daughter."

He chuckled. "You're going to be a breath of fresh air around here. I'm glad to have you on board."

"Thank you," she said, "but you haven't answered my question."

"Pretty and sharp, too."

Deborah lifted her brow at the "pretty" as she wondered if Alan was flirting with her. Not that she'd mind. In fact, he was just her type. She glanced at his left hand. No ring, but that didn't mean anything. "Are you married, Alan?"

"No, why do you ask?"

"Because I think you're flirting with me. Are you?"

"Would you mind it if I were?"

She wasn't ready to answer that one yet. "It would depend

on why you're flirting with me. You still haven't answered my question."

He chuckled again. "Abraham may not have raised you, but you definitely have his genes. Like you, he gets what he wants."

She leaned back in her chair. "Does that mean you're going to answer my question?"

"Do I have a choice?"

"I guess not."

"Your father and I were classmates at Morehouse. He looked me up when his business began growing and made me an offer I couldn't refuse. I've been with him ever since."

"You must be good at what you do."

"The best."

She laughed. "And modest, too."

"That's something else you'll learn about your father. Modesty is not a trait he possesses nor is it one he respects. He's self-confident to the point of being arrogant, and respects self-confidence in others."

"I'll have to remember that."

"You won't have a problem. Abraham would not have bought Running Brook and put you in charge if you didn't have traits he respected, daughter or no daughter. It's not in his DNA. Ask your half brother, Isaac. Abraham is a hard taskmaster and he has high expectations."

"I have a lot to learn about him, don't I?" she asked, praying that she'd have the opportunity.

"Don't worry about Abraham," he told her, as if reading her mind. "He'll probably be kicking around here long after you and I are gone. He gives new meaning to tough."

"There's so much about him I don't know," she confessed. "And I want to know everything. You've known him a long time. What kind of a man is he?"

Alan leaned forward and rested his palms on his knees. "I think you already know the kind of man he is. He's driven. He'd have to be to build MEEG. He can be selfish. He'd have to be to have ignored you and your brother all these years. What kind of man is he? He's human, with all the flaws and frailties we humans have. Sometimes he does the right thing; other times, he does the wrong thing. To his credit, he's a man who admits his mistakes when faced with them. He's just a man, Deborah. Take what he has to offer, but don't expect more than he gives. He'll undoubtedly disappoint you, but then so would any man. Rarely do fathers live up to the expectations of their daughters." He sat back in his chair and studied her. "Did that answer your question?"

Deborah nodded. "Thank you."

"No problem," Alan said, standing. "Why don't I take you home and you can get a fresh start in the morning. I've arranged for you to meet with the current Running Brook team at ten A.M. They're a good group but you're not going to want to keep them all. We can talk about all that tomorrow. You've had a full day."

Deborah dutifully followed him out of her office. Alan had answered some of her questions but raised many more. There was still much she wanted to know about Abraham, and she also wanted to know about Alan. But she'd have to wait until another time to ask. She didn't want to scare him off by asking too much too soon.

Chapter Twenty

Deborah knocked on her brother's front door. After learning that Alan lived in Buckhead, she called to make sure Michael was home and then asked Alan to drop her off at Michael's house. She wanted to tell him what Abraham had done, rather than leaving it to the lawyer. Her brother answered on the third knock.

"Took you a long time to answer," she said when he opened the door wearing sweats and a T-shirt. "You may want to consider increasing the number of days you exercise each week."

He kissed her cheek. "Please. You can't give me exercise tips. When was the last time you made it to the gym?"

She followed her brother down the stairs to the recreation room, where the fifty-inch plasma was blasting some sports talk show. She kicked off her shoes, tossed her bag on the first chair she saw, then raced to her brother's favorite recliner.

"Beat you," she said, falling into the chair.

Michael laughed. "Girl, you need to grow up." He went over to the minirefrigerator and pulled out two bottles of water. He tossed one to her and then walked over and sat on the end of the weight bench. "So, what brings you by?"

She twisted the cap off the water and took a sip. "Can't a sister visit a brother without having a reason? I wanted to see you."

"Right," he said, taking a swig of his water. "I know you went down to MEEG today. How was it?"

"So you've talked to Mama, then? What else did she tell you?" Maybe her mother had told him the news and she'd be spared the duty.

He put down his bottled water and picked up two dumbbells. "She just said you were starting your big-time job at dear old dad's company today. So how was it?"

"It was all right."

He did a couple of bicep curls. "Tell the truth, girl. I know it had to have been a trip. Do you remember when we went down there when we were kids?"

"Yeah. Well, if you thought the lobby was something, you should see the twelfth floor offices. I knew Abraham had money, a lot of money, and that MEEG was a huge business with a lot of different holdings, but I guess it really didn't sink in until I saw that floor. You know, it's one thing to think someone is rich; it's a whole other thing to see how the rich live. It's a different world, literally."

"Yeah, the old man is loaded, but you'd never know it from the crumbs he gave us."

"I hate to say it, but you're right."

Michael lay flat on his back on the bench and continued his bicep curls. "Yeah, I'm right. I've been right about him all along. That man doesn't care a thing for us. He just wants to ease his conscience now that he's getting older. It'll be a cold day in hell before he uses me for that purpose."

"Are you angry with me for spending time with him, for taking the job?"

Michael rested his dumbbells on the floor, sat up, and looked at his sister. "I'm not going to lie," he told her. "I was angry with you at first, but now it doesn't matter. I say get as much out of the old dog as you can. He owes us. Big-time."

Deborah didn't believe Abraham owed them, but she did feel that he could have done better by them. "Maybe he's starting to pay us back," she said, deciding to jump right to the main issue. "Did Mama tell you that he gave us seats on his board of directors?"

"What? You and mama are on his board? I don't believe it."

"I couldn't believe it either, but it's true. We found out this morning."

"Apparently, he didn't think enough of me to add me to his board. What a poor excuse for a man. He knows I'd outperform that pansy boy of his, Isaac. Well, Abraham never did anything for me in the past, and I don't need him to do anything for me now. I can make my own way. Forget Abraham Martin."

Though he'd never admit it, Deborah knew Abraham's slight hurt her brother. "It's not as bad as you think, Mike. Abraham did think of you. Mom's seat on the board is really yours."

"What kind of crap talk is that? If the seat were mine, I'd be sitting in it. You've got to stop believing everything that old man tells you."

Deborah hated when Michael talked about Abraham this way. It seemed to make light of her feelings for her father. "It's true. Abraham doesn't trust you to have control in MEEG. He thinks you'll do something to damage the company because you hate him so much."

Michael snorted. "Maybe the old man isn't as stupid as he looks. I'd love nothing more than to bring him down."

"But the company is our legacy now, too, Michael. Why would you want to bring it down?"

"I didn't say I'd bring the company down. I said I'd bring Abraham down."

Deborah didn't see the difference but she saw no value in pursuing the topic. "Anyway, Mama and I go to our first board meeting on Friday."

"That ought to be interesting," he said. "Maybe I'll drop in."

Deborah's antennae of concern shot up. "But you're not on the board yet."

Michael shrugged. "What are they going to do? Kick me out? I doubt it. I am Old Boy's son, in case you've forgotten."

Deborah hoped Michael was joking, but she couldn't be sure. She decided to change the subject. "Have you been to see him?"

He shook his head. "Why would I do that?"

"You should have gone before they put him in the coma. You're going to regret you didn't if he doesn't wake up."

"Oh, he's going to wake up, all right. That old man won't go down that easy."

"I hope so." She got up, walked over, and sat next to her brother on the bench. "I don't know how I feel about him, Michael. Sometimes I'm just happy to have a dad in my life. Then when I think about how he's treated us, I'm angry." She leaned her head on her brother's shoulder. "I'm pretty messed up, aren't I?"

Michael pressed his hand against her head. "Both of us could probably do with some time on a psychiatrist's couch. How could we not be messed up, given how we grew up?"

"But Mama did a good job with us, even if Abraham wasn't around."

"That's the thing, sis," he told her. "Abraham was around. He was always there. He just wasn't with us. Sometimes I think we would have been better off if we hadn't known who he was."

Deborah considered her brother's words and wondered what her life would have been like had she not known all these years that Abraham was her father. "I don't know."

He chuckled. "You'd probably still be dating older men."

She raised her head and slapped him on the shoulder. "Enough with the psychoanalysis." Her brother was right, though. She didn't need a psychology degree to know that her affinity for older men was somehow tied into having an absentee father. She just accepted it as who she was. But Michael had his own demons. "How's Josette and where is she?" she asked.

"Nice segue, sis. My wife is fine. She's out doing baby shopping, which seems to be how she spends most of her time."

"Be honest, Michael. You can't lie to me, either. How are you two? Josette thinks you're having an affair. Are you?"

He shook his head. "No. How many times do I have to answer that question? I'm in the music business. A lot of my work happens in bars and clubs in the late night, early morning hours. What about that is so hard to understand?"

Deborah wasn't sure she believed him. "Just don't do to Josette and your baby what Abraham did to us. Be a better man to your family than he was to his."

Chapter Twenty-One

Banished from the hospital by her husband, Rebecca sat flipping through magazines in her living room when she heard the door open, followed by the voices of her husband and mother-in-law. She patted her hair in place before heading toward the door. She wanted to look her best for her husband. She was leaving no stone unturned in her quest to win back his trust.

"I can stay at my own place," she heard her mother-in-law say. "You don't need to babysit me. I'm a big girl."

"I know you are," Isaac said. "I'd just feel better if you're here with us."

Rebecca met Isaac's eyes when she reached them in the foyer. There was no welcome in them. She smiled anyway. "We're glad to have you with us, Saralyn. Besides, having us all together makes it easier for the hospital to reach us if they need to."

Saralyn yawned, belatedly covering her mouth. "Well, I'm too tired to argue. Just point me to the bed and I'll be out of your way."

"Are you hungry?" Rebecca asked. "I prepared a light snack just in case."

"All I want right now is a bed."

"I put clean linens in the front guest room," she told her mother-in-law, "and left a tray of fruit, cheese, water, and juice on the dresser, in case you change your mind about eating. I also went down to your apartment and picked up a change of clothes for you, something to sleep in, and your makeup case. It's all in your room."

Saralyn leaned over and kissed her cheek. "You're a good daughter-in-law, Rebecca. Isaac is very fortunate to have found you." Then she turned and gave Isaac a similar kiss. "Good night, you two," she said, heading off toward the guest bedroom.

"She's wore-out," Isaac said, his eyes following his mother down the hallway.

"A good night's sleep will serve her well. She'll be fine in the morning."

Isaac pulled his already loosened tie from around his neck. "She won't be fine until Dad gets better. Their marriage wasn't perfect by any means, but they've been together for thirty years. If he doesn't pull through, I don't know what she'll do."

Hesitantly, Rebecca reached out and touched his arm. She was heartened when he didn't recoil at her touch. "Abraham's going to be back and as good as new before we know it. We have to believe that, Isaac. We have to have faith."

She read the stress in his tired expression and wanted to pull him into her arms. She searched his face for some sign that an embrace would be welcomed, but he turned away from her. "Are you hungry?" she asked.

He shook his head. "I'm tired. I guess I'll go to bed, too."

She wasn't sure where he meant to sleep and she wasn't sure how to ask.

He stepped close to her and whispered, "Since Mom is here, I'd like for us to pretend that nothing is wrong between us. I don't want her to worry."

His words hurt. "So you'll be sleeping in our bed tonight, with me?"

He met her eyes. "Only because my mother is here. We're not even close to fixing what's wrong between us," he said. "I don't want you to be confused by this show we're putting on."

"Oh, I understand," she said, fighting back the defeat that seemed to surround her. "You're being very clear."

"You can't be angry with me," he said, eyes wide with surprise.

"Of course I'm angry," she said, folding her arms around her chest. "You're being unreasonable. Michael is just some man from my past. I had no idea he was your half brother."

He lifted his arms in exasperation. "There's more to it than that. He's a man you slept with to further your career, a man who happens to be my half brother."

Rebecca looked away. Though she'd asked for this conversation, she didn't relish having it. "I can't change the past, Isaac."

"And I can't change the uncertainty I feel about you and our marriage."

She glanced down the hallway, his words breaking her heart. "If you don't want your mother to hear us arguing, you'd better keep your voice down."

He took a deep breath. "I have one question. Did you really not know he was my half brother?"

She recoiled from him. "Of course I didn't. How can you even think that of me? I know you're angry, Isaac, but now you're just being cruel."

His eyes darkened. "We look a lot alike," he said. "How could you miss the resemblance? Are you saying you never noticed it?"

Rebecca wished she could lie. "Sure, I recognized similarities in you, but that didn't mean anything. Like most women, there is a type of man that I find attractive. You and Michael both have that look."

"Yeah, right."

"I'm not lying," she pleaded. "Why would I lie?"

"That's what happens when trust goes," he said, turning away from her. "Everything sounds like a lie." He cleared his throat. "You should start looking for someplace to live. I want you out of here as soon as Dad's better."

Rebecca absorbed his words like a body blow. "You don't mean it."

He turned back to her, fire in his eyes. "Yes, I do mean it. And I want you out of the MEEG Building, starting tomorrow. Gail Rivers can take over mom's PR duties and yours. She'd probably be next in line for the top job anyway if you weren't married to the owner's son."

"You're going too far, Isaac."

He shook his head. "I only wish I could get you out tonight. Don't you see that I can't trust you?"

"Of course you can trust me. You wouldn't have any of this to hold against me if I hadn't told you about Michael and those gifts. And I told you so that you'd know how he really feels about you. I was trying to protect you, Isaac. If there is anybody you can trust, it's me. I've always had your back."

He studied her. "You know, a part of me believes you're sincere, but I can't even trust my feelings for you."

"Yes, you can," she said, tears streaming down her cheeks.

He brushed his hand across his head. "I can't keep talking about this," he said. "I'm tired and I'm worried about my father. I don't have energy for anything else."

"Not even our marriage?"

He snorted. "What marriage?" Then he turned and headed in the direction of their bedroom.

Chapter Twenty-Two

Michael Thomas strode into the hospital after midnight. The hallways were quiet, just as he suspected they would be. Abraham's room was out of direct eyesight of the nurses' station so he had no problem simply walking into the room. He hesitated a moment near the door as he looked at the older man in the bed, his father.

He shook his head. No, not his father, but the man who had impregnated his mother and paid the price with steady but measly duty checks. He walked closer to the bed. The light from the machines monitoring Abraham's vitals cast enough light for Michael to clearly see his nose and his chin in the older man's face. It hurt to look into the face of the man he hated and see himself. It almost made him hate himself.

Almost. The irony of it was that, with his dark complexion, he looked more like Abraham than the cherished son, Isaac, did.

Isaac looked more like his mother, took his complexion from her. He wondered if that drove the old man crazy. He hoped it did.

"You better not die, old man," he whispered through tight lips. "You better wake up so you can see me when I bring you down. You're going to pay for every tear my mother cried, for every time my sister wished for a father who wasn't there, and for every moment you loved your other son and refused to acknowledge me. What goes around, comes around. You reap what you sow. Vengeance is mine—Michael Thomas's—and I will repay. You can count on it."

Michael stood back from the bed, folded his arms across his chest, and stared at the old man. He exerted all his energies willing him to wake up. Nothing would have made him happier than to have the old man wake up so he could repeat everything he'd just said to his face.

He waited. And waited. And waited.

"Not tonight," Michael said. "But one of these nights you're going to wake up, and I promise you, I'll have a big surprise waiting for you. Count on it."

With those words, he turned and left the hospital.

Death had better not try to cheat him, he thought. Abraham Martin had a debt to pay, and he was going to pay it.

Chapter Twenty-Three

Josette looked at herself in the bathroom mirror. She looked like Rudolph, the red-nosed reindeer. She plucked a tissue from the box on her vanity and blew her nose. Again. It seemed all she'd been doing that evening was crying and blowing. She tossed the tissue into the wastebasket.

Why was she letting Michael treat her this way? It was after midnight. He wasn't home and he hadn't called. He could deny it all he wanted, but she was certain he was cheating on her. What else could explain his long, long nights? She'd never believe that work required this much late night entertainment.

She rubbed her hand across her bulging belly. "What have I done to you, baby girl?" she whispered. "What kind of father have I given you?"

She flipped off the light in the bathroom and headed for the bed. After pulling back the covers, she slid in and turned off the bedside light. Her tears began to fall again, and she let them fall unheeded.

She awoke when the bed sagged next to her. Her husband had finally dragged himself home. She sniffed to detect any hint of another woman's perfume. Nothing. She should have known he was smarter than that.

A part of her wanted to ignore him, to pretend she was asleep. That part lost. She reached up, switched on the lamp, and turned to him. "You finally made it home, huh?" she said to his back.

He glanced over his shoulder at her. "Don't start," he said.

"You started it," she said. "I'm finishing it."

He jerked off his tie and stood. "I don't know what you're talking about."

She watched as he kicked off his shoes and tossed his tie on the chair near the closet. His shirt and pants quickly followed. Then he was in bed next to her. He had the nerve to yawn.

"Tired, huh?" she asked.

He yawned again. "I had a long day."

"I noticed."

He turned exasperated eyes to her. "I'm not going to argue with you."

Her heart sank at his words because she knew they were true. He didn't care enough about her feelings to calm her fears by answering her questions. "If you want out of this marriage, just say so, Michael."

"Now you're talking crazy," he said, dismissing her as if she were a child.

"You're crazy if you think I don't know what's going on."

He turned on his side and faced her. "What do you think is going on?"

"I think you're having an affair."

He laughed. "I don't have time for an affair. I work too hard and too long."

She felt those words as if he'd stomped on her heart. "That's the only thing stopping you—you don't have time?"

"You're twisting my words," he said. "Those pregnancy hormones of yours are all out of whack. You'd better talk to your doctor about them."

"If you're not having an affair, why were you so late? Why are you always late?"

"Work."

She didn't believe him. She'd called his office. "You're a liar," she said. "And a bad one." She turned away from him, flicked off her lamp, and sank down in the covers. "You're Abraham Martin's son, all right."

That got his attention. He rolled over to her. She felt his breath on her neck but she didn't turn. "What did you say?" he asked.

"You heard me."

"I'm sure I didn't hear you because I know you didn't say what I thought you said."

Josette savored the taste of victory. She'd found a button to push. "I said that you're Abraham Martin's son, all right. You're doing to me what he did to his wife. Cheating must be in your blood."

He grabbed her shoulder and turned her flat on her back so that she faced him. "I'm nothing like him," he said through clenched teeth. "Nothing."

"Keep telling yourself that," she said. She glanced at his hand on her shoulder. "And don't manhandle me again." She turned back on her side, away from him. She could still feel him seething behind her. She didn't care. She'd finally turned the tables on him. She liked the feeling it gave her.

"I'm not like him," Michael said again. Then she heard him turn away and settle himself in the bed.

Her joy at winning tonight's battle subsided quickly as she realized that she was still losing the war.

Chapter Twenty-Four

Leah stood, unmoving, outside the MEEG Building and stared at the smoked glass revolving doors. This building represented the life she and her children could have had if Abraham had made her his wife. Now here she was preparing to take her son's place at a MEEG board meeting. She felt her knees weaken. She knew she needed to recover before she entered. She didn't want Deborah to see her this way.

Slowly, she made her way over to one of the marble benches that dotted the garden park in front of the building. She eased herself down on the first bench and practiced the breathing exercise that she used to ward off panic attacks. It had been a long time since she'd needed to do this. The last time had been right before she defended her master's thesis. She was more anxious now than she was then.

She exhaled and began to feel the calmness settle around her. She blamed Abraham for this. Her anxiety attacks had started after Deborah was born, when she realized that she was going to have to raise two children alone, even though their father lived close by. She'd had to take things day by day, and still found herself oftentimes overwhelmed by the challenges she faced.

How was she going to raise two children, when she was twenty and barely an adult herself? she'd worried. Abraham's money had kept them off welfare, but not much more than that. He never felt compelled to see that their children's fortunes increased with his. No, it was as though what he gave them was no more than the minimum payment on a revolving credit card balance. She gave him points for paying faithfully each month, but the sheer grandness of the building in front of her showed clearly that what he'd given them was a pittance compared to what he had. That the original three hundred dollars per month had grown to two thousand by the time her kids graduated college seemed inconsequential.

She took another deep breath. It did her no good to go down that road again. She'd had to forgive Abraham a long time ago in order to be a good mother to her children. She wanted them happy and she knew a mother raging about an absentee father would only do them harm. So she'd prayed and tried to move on with her life. She hadn't done too badly with Michael and Deborah, either. Or she thought she hadn't until recently.

She shook her head back and forth a couple of times to shake off the negative thoughts. Taking a final deep breath, she stood and walked determinedly to the revolving doors that had initially paralyzed her. She pasted a smile on her face as she strode through the doors of what was now her children's heritage.

"Good morning, ma'am," the security guard said when she reached the grand 360-degree, marble-topped front desk. "May I help you?"

"I'm here to see Deborah Thomas," she said. "I'm her mother, Leah Thomas."

The guard punched a few keys on the keyboard and looked at the screen that was facing him on the counter. Then he picked up the phone and dialed. "Ms. Thomas," he said a short while later. "Your mother is here to see you."

Leah watched as the security guard nodded. Then he hung up the phone. "I'm going to need you to sign in, Mrs. Thomas," he said.

Leah didn't bother to correct him. She merely entered her signature on the electronic signature pad. When she was finished, the security guard opened a drawer under the counter and pulled out a visitor's badge that he handed to her. "You have to wear the badge at all times," he told her. "And you have to return it before you leave the building."

"Thanks," she said, taking the badge and clipping it to the lapel of her suit jacket.

"To get to your daughter's office, take the elevators to the twelfth floor. Her name and room number will be on the wall facing you when the elevator doors open. Welcome to MEEG."

"Thank you," Leah said, impressed with the operation Abraham had set up here, despite herself. She turned toward the elevators and was pleasantly surprised to see Deborah's smiling face when the doors opened.

Deborah stepped off the elevator. "You're looking good, Mama," she said.

Leah looked down at the two-piece navy suit that she rarely wore. Teaching at the community college required a much more casual look than the outfit she sported now, but she'd felt the need to dress for the occasion. "I didn't want to embarrass you," she told her daughter.

Deborah's smile disappeared. "Don't say that, Mama," she said. "Don't even think it. Try not to let this impressive building intimidate you. You belong here as much as I do."

Leah patted her daughter's cheek. "Calm down, sweetie," she said. "I was teasing."

Deborah pressed the button for the elevator, whose doors had closed. "Sorry," she said. "I'm being too sensitive."

"That's okay," Leah said when the elevator doors opened. She followed her daughter in. "This is new for all of us."

Deborah pressed the button for the twelfth floor. "Now that's the understatement of the year." She glanced sideways at her mother. "Michael and I never told you, but we came down here when we were in high school, just to see what it was like."

Leah's heart ached. "Oh, sweetie."

Deborah shook her head. "It was childish curiosity, Mama. We had to check the place out. Once, Michael even drove us by the Martin estate in Forest Park, but the house was hidden in a thickly wooded area so we didn't see much."

"I never knew," Leah said. "I should have guessed, though. Why didn't you tell me?"

Deborah shrugged. "We thought it would hurt you."

Leah fought the onslaught of another panic attack. As their mother, she'd tried to protect her children, and all the while they were protecting her. What a burden that must have been for them! What had it done to their childhoods? She'd thought they were happy and healthy but maybe she was only seeing what she wanted to see. What had she done to her precious offspring?

Chapter Twenty-Five

W hat are you doing here?" Isaac asked when he turned from the paperwork he was studying to find Rebecca standing in the doorway of the MEEG boardroom. "I thought we agreed that you were not welcome here any longer."

Rebecca hid her pain behind a false bravado. She needed the false front to fight for her marriage, since Isaac seemed determined to end it. She couldn't let him see weakness. She had to be resolute in her determination.

"We didn't agree on anything," she said, holding her head high as she marched to the table and slid into the chair next to his. "As long as I'm your wife, my place is beside you, and that's where I'm going to be." Her mask slipped a bit. "I love you, Isaac," she said. "I'd never do anything to hurt you. I told you the truth about me and Michael because I love you, and because you needed to know the lengths he'd go to hurt you."

Isaac turned cold eyes on her. "You don't want me to call security."

She shrugged. "Call them, but you'd better tell your mother our marriage is over first."

Isaac opened his mouth and then closed it again. Rebecca read his action, or inaction, as his acceptance of her presence at the board meeting. She wanted to tell him again that she loved him, but knew that words would not work. She'd have to show him. So, instead of pleading her case, she sat quietly next to him and waited for the other board members to arrive.

Saralyn sailed in first. She looked as though she'd stepped off a Paris runway in her fuchsia suit dress with matching shoes and hat. Rebecca wondered, as she often did, how the woman managed to pull it off. Self-conscious, she brushed her hands down the simple burgundy sheath she'd chosen because it was one of Isaac's favorites. Unfortunately, he hadn't even noticed.

"Good morning, children," Saralyn said, filling the room with her presence. She pressed a kiss against Isaac's cheek and then against Rebecca's.

"You're in good spirits this morning," Isaac said, surprise evident in his voice. Rebecca was surprised, too, since she knew that Saralyn hated the changes Abraham had made to the board.

"I'm doing what a woman has to do," Saralyn said, removing her hat. "We have to take care of things in your father's absence." She placed her hat on the table in front of the chair where she usually sat, which was to the right of Abraham's chair at the head of the twenty-foot mesquite conference table with granite inlay.

Rebecca wondered what Saralyn had up her sleeve. Her mother-in-law was used to things going her way, and right now they weren't.

Casually, Saralyn fingered her long tresses until they lay perfectly across her shoulders. Then she moved to stand next to Abraham's chair. "You should sit here," she said to Isaac, pointing at the chair Abraham had vacated only recently.

Isaac, who sat in his usual chair to the immediate right of his father's, said, "I'm more comfortable where I am. Let's leave Dad's chair vacant until he gets back."

Saralyn turned toward Rebecca. "Please talk to your husband, darling. He doesn't seem to understand that impressions are everything. We need to let those Thomas interlopers know where they stand from day one. That way there's no confusion."

Rebecca had to smile. Saralyn did not disappoint. She turned to her husband. "Saralyn's right, Isaac. For all intents and purposes, you're Abraham until Abraham can be here himself. He'd want you in his chair."

Isaac flashed those cold eyes at her again and she flinched.

"Look, you two," Saralyn said, glancing from one of them to the other, "I don't know what that look was about but I do know that this is not the time for you two to engage in some petty bickering between yourselves. We need to be united now more than ever. You're going to have to put your marital squabbles on hold. We don't have time for them." She gave them each a pointed stare. "Can I count on you two?"

"Yes," Rebecca answered first, avoiding Isaac's eyes.

"Son." Saralyn tapped her fingers on Abraham's chair. "I'm waiting."

"You know you can count on me, Mom," he said.

She nodded. "Good. Then get your rear out of that seat and into this one. We all need to be situated before the others arrive." After Isaac moved to his designated chair, Saralyn pointed to the one he had vacated. "You sit there, Rebecca."

After Rebecca had done as directed, Saralyn glided into her own chair. "Now we're ready to face the world and our enemies."

Isaac looked at his mother. "Dad invited these 'enemies' to the table, Mom. We can't keep them away."

"Don't remind me," Saralyn said. "There were other ways your father could have assuaged his guilt. Why didn't he just write them a check, a big, big check? I think that would have satisfied them. There was no reason for him to bring them into our lives, our business. He was wrong to do it."

Rebecca glanced at her husband to see what he was thinking.

"According to Alan," Isaac said, "there's nothing we can do."

Saralyn frowned. "Alan's not the only attorney in Atlanta. If we don't like his answers, we'll find another attorney with better answers. Your father never took no for an answer, and neither should we."

Rebecca thought Saralyn made a good point. She didn't know about the other Thomases, but she knew she didn't trust Michael. His hatred of Isaac was too deep. She'd never feel safe with him in their lives.

Before Isaac could respond to his mother, the door to the boardroom opened and in walked Michael. "Good morning," he said, as if his presence were expected and welcome. "I'm Michael Thomas," he said, extending his hand first to Saralyn.

"You don't belong here," she said with disdain, not taking his hand.

"Nice to meet you, too, Mrs. Martin," Michael said, not missing a beat. Then he turned his attention to Rebecca. "I know it's early, but happy anniversary," he said with a wink. "I hope you like this year's gift better than you liked last year's."

Isaac jumped out of his chair. "How dare you?" he said, standing nose-to-nose with Michael.

Michael didn't back up an inch. "How dare I what? Be your bastard brother?" He glanced at Saralyn. "Or enter your adulterous husband's building?" He then turned back to Rebecca, who shot fiery darts at him with her eyes. "Or maybe you're daring me to seduce your sweet wife again?"

Isaac raised his hand—

Saralyn and Rebecca came up out of their chairs. "No," they yelled at the same time.

Chapter Twenty-Six

Smiling, Michael rubbed his jaw. "So big brother has an awesome right hook," he said to Isaac. "Not bad." His smile turned ruthless. "Maybe I should be the one to call security. I believe you just assaulted me." For effect, he let his eyes roam the room. "All of this could be mine someday, thanks to you." He clapped his hand against his forehead. "What am I saying? This *will* be mine someday."

"Over my dead body," Saralyn piped in.

Isaac shot his mother a glare. "This is between him and me," he told her. "Stay out of it, Mother."

Michael glanced in her direction. "Yes, Stepmom," he said to the woman whose outfit had to cost more than his mother's entire wardrobe. "Stay out of it."

Rebecca stepped between the two men. "You both need to take a step back." When neither man moved, she added, "Literally."

Michael grinned at her. "I like it when you go all home girl on me, Rebecca," he said to irk her. "It gets me hot." He turned to Isaac to get in another jab. "She's perfect isn't she—a perfect lady during the day and a perfect freak at night?"

Isaac raised his fists again. "You—"

"Isaac, no!" both women screamed as Isaac quickly pushed Rebecca out of the way and lunged at Michael. Caught off balance, Michael fell to floor with Isaac on top of him, the women yelling for them to stop. Rebecca grabbed Isaac by the collar in an attempt to pull him off Michael. Saralyn stood with her arms folded, apparently happy to see her son get the best of her stepson.

The conference door shot open.

"Michael!"

"Stop it now!"

"What's going on here?"

Michael recognized the voices of his mother and sister. He turned and saw them standing in the doorway, mouths open, aghast at what they were seeing. The MEEG attorney, Alan Weems, stood with them.

"This is not what Abraham wanted," Alan said, taking control of the situation by first pushing Rebecca away from Isaac and then pulling Isaac off Michael. Then he extended his hand and helped Michael up from the floor. He looked at the two brothers. "You're behaving like children," he told them. "This room is not soundproof. Everybody along this hallway could hear you. I can only imagine what they're thinking."

Michael straightened his clothes. "I thought you rich people were more in control of your emotions and actions than poor working stiffs like me." He shrugged, rubbing his jaw again. "I guess I was wrong."

"That's enough, Michael," his mother said, her voice full of disappointment. He hated when she used that tone. "You shouldn't be here."

Michael turned to her. "Why not, Mama?" he said, angry with what he interpreted as her putting Abraham's wishes above her children's needs . . . again. "I'm Abraham's son. I have as much right to be here as the rest of you."

"You have no rights," Saralyn said. "If it were left to me, none of you would be here. I have no idea what Abraham was thinking. This will never work."

"Everybody needs to take a deep breath," Alan said. "This has to work," he said to Saralyn. "It's what Abraham wanted."

She folded her arms across her chest. "This company has other priorities beyond what Abraham wants," she declared.

Alan nodded. "You're right." He glanced at each person in the room. "Why don't we all take a seat?"

"He shouldn't be here," Saralyn said, pointing at Michael.

Alan ignored her. "Everybody please take a seat. We can and will conduct this meeting professionally and in an orderly fashion."

Seeing Isaac take the seat at the head of the table, Michael proceeded to the chair at the opposite end, facing him. Two could play this game. Rebecca and Saralyn sat on either side of Isaac. His mother and Deborah sat on either side of him. That sides had been chosen was clear from the seating arrangements. There were three empty chairs between Saralyn and Deborah, and three between Rebecca and his mother.

Alan, the mediator, chose the middle ground. He took the center chair on the side with Saralyn and Deborah. "Look," he said, as he glanced around the table, "this is not an ideal situation for any of us, but it's our reality until Abraham returns to the helm. You all may not like each other, but if you care anything about this company, you will find a way to work together."

"I'm not sure I agree with that," Saralyn said. "We know this company inside and out. We don't need them. And he"—she pointed to Michael—"doesn't even belong here."

Michael leaned back in his chair and propped one leg over the other. "Seems somebody is forgetting etiquette class."

"Michael—" his mother chided.

He shrugged as if he didn't know what he'd done to incur her wrath.

"What are you going to do, Saralyn?" Alan asked, so clearly exasperated he didn't even wait for an answer. "There's nothing you can do if you care about this company. Any infighting at this point with Abraham out of commission will be read as instability by our business partners and our competitors. Do you want that?"

"But—"

Isaac covered his mother's hand with his own. "He's right, Mom. It doesn't matter how we feel about each other. We have to present a united front. The vultures will swoop in at any sign of weakness. We all lose if that happens."

Saralyn sat back in her chair, quieted for now. Rebecca said nothing. Michael surmised that, like him, she didn't have a vote in what went on.

"Now that we've settled that issue," Alan said, "let's move on to the business at hand."

Michael watched the faces of the folks present at the table more than he listened to the attorney. Saralyn Martin was everything he hated in a woman. She thought she was better than him and his family. She especially thought herself better than his mother. She and Abraham would have to pay for that attitude.

Isaac, on the other hand, had impressed him. He rubbed his chin again. His older brother could land a punch. Not bad for a man who'd been born with a silver spoon in his mouth. Isaac was made of sterner stuff than he'd thought. Michael glanced at Rebecca, who paid him no attention. No, she kept her attention on Isaac. She'd fought for her man, so maybe she really did love him. And Isaac's reaction to his taunts suggested that he loved Rebecca as well, though there was something in the way he refused to look at her that made Michael think there might be a problem in paradise.

He spent the rest of the meeting contemplating ways to exploit the problems in Isaac and Rebecca's marriage to his advantage.

Chapter Twenty-Seven

Josette stepped off the hospital elevator, unsure she was doing the right thing but positive something had to be done. If she weren't pregnant, she could let things slide, but she was going to be a mother, and mothers couldn't afford inaction. Not if they loved their children. She rubbed her hand across her tummy. And she desperately loved her child. If she didn't, she would have walked away from her marriage to Michael as soon as she'd learned of his relationship with Abraham and Isaac. But the child growing inside her kept her from making rash decisions. Yes, her emotions were all over the place, but somehow she was grounded enough to know that fighting for her marriage was the right thing to do.

There had been something about Michael that attracted her. She wasn't so superficial as to fall for him because he'd romanced her. No, there was a vulnerability in him that she saw from the first. Of course, he'd tried to hide it. But she felt closest to him then.

Those times when his vulnerability showed had been infrequent since his kinship with Abraham became public knowledge.

She walked to the reception desk. "I'm here to see patient Abraham Martin. I'm his daughter-in-law." That was the truth.

"He's in intensive care," the nurse at the desk said. "That's on the fourth floor. Take the elevator around the corner."

Josette rubbed her stomach as she made her way to the elevator and up to Abraham's floor. The nurse there directed her to his room. Josette stood at his door looking at him. It seemed that he was asleep, and she guessed he was. A coma was a deep sleep, wasn't it?

She walked over to the bed and pressed a kiss on Abraham's forehead. "Hi, Grandpa," she said. She reached behind her, pulled a chair up close to the bed and eased down into it. As she sat before the sleeping Abraham, she began to weep quietly. This man was her father-in-law, her unborn child's grandfather, and her husband hadn't bothered to tell her.

When her tears finally subsided, she felt a little better. "Abraham," she said, "I need you to wake up. Your first grandchild needs you to wake up. You started something when you acknowledged Michael and Deborah as your children, and you need to wake up so you can finish it. Things are not going well without you. Though he'd never admit it, Michael is a wreck. I'm afraid he's going to repeat your mistakes."

She looked up at Abraham, hoping her declaration would awaken him. She found him still sleeping. "I'm a wreck, too, and it's all your fault. Why did you treat your children so badly?" She grabbed his hand and squeezed it. "You have to get better, Abraham, so you can fix this mess. Michael is bound and determined to make you pay for your indifference to him and Deborah. He's crashing your board meeting this morning. He wanted me to join him but I refused. I can't take the drama. The baby can't take it."

She brushed away the tears that streamed down her face. "I

don't want to leave Michael," she said, "but it's like he's pushing me away intentionally. One day he's going to wake up, and the baby and I will be gone. Maybe that's what he wants. Maybe he feels he doesn't deserve to have a family. Maybe he doesn't know how to be a husband and father, since you were never there. That's why you have to get better, Abraham. You weren't there to teach Michael how to be a man when he was a boy, so now you have to help him learn it as an adult.

"He's going to fight you all the way, but you owe me and you owe him. I'll never do to my child what you did to Michael. I don't see how you could do it—walk away from your son. It's hard for me to reconcile that man in the magazines all buddy-buddy with Isaac with the man who refused to acknowledge a son and daughter for thirty years." She gave a bitter laugh. "What kind of man does that make you?"

Josette sat back in her chair. She realized she was directing all the anger she felt toward Michael onto Abraham. He did share some of the blame for the problems in her life, but Michael was a grown man. He had to deal with being a husband and father regardless of how his relationship with Abraham progressed. Maybe she should be having this conversation with him.

Chapter Twenty-Eight

Deborah tried to present a calm demeanor, when she actually felt anything but calm. Saralyn Martin was a piece of work, sitting through the entire meeting staring at her, Michael, and her mother as though they were gum stuck to the bottom of her new Gucci pumps. If nothing else, the woman's attitude made her glad Abraham had not reached out to them when they were children. The hatred coming from this woman would devastate a child.

Deborah glanced at her mother and was proud. Leah Thomas held her head high and wore a serene expression on her face. Saralyn Martin might have more money and live a more glamorous lifestyle, but her mother had more class, hands down. Saralyn Martin lacked the simple "home training" that her mother had instilled in her and her brother.

Well, she had to be honest. Michael seemed to have forgotten a bit of his "home training," otherwise she, her mother, and

Alan would not have found him tussling on the floor when they entered the boardroom. Talk about embarrassing! She could kill Michael for acting a fool in front of these people. He was only showing them what they expected to see.

"We all have our parts to do," Alan was saying. "And we have to support each other."

"I think what you mean, Alan, is that we all have to rally around Isaac now that he's stepped in for *his* father," Saralyn said, stressing the *his* to exclude Abraham's other children. Deborah couldn't help but roll her eyes. The woman was pathetic.

"True," Alan said. "Isaac is at the helm of MEEG until Abraham gets back. And his job is to keep the ship on its current course, not change it. This is a temporary change of leadership, not a final one."

"I understand, Alan," Isaac said. "I wouldn't want it any other way."

Deborah had been studying her half brother throughout the meeting but hadn't gotten a good read on him. All she could surmise was that he and Michael must have inherited their temperaments from Abraham, since both of them had been tussling on the floor.

"Now for our final order of business," Alan said. "I've shared Abraham's wishes with all of you. The board needs to approve Isaac's installment as temporary president and CEO. We can do this by a voice vote."

"Hold on a minute," Michael said. "If the board has to vote, does the board also have the right to submit additional nominees?"

"Legally, yes," Alan said, "but practically no. There are six votes on the board. I hold Abraham's proxy, and I also have my own vote. Saralyn has a vote, Isaac has a vote, and your mother and sister have a vote. Thus, it'll only take three votes to gain the approval. I'm casting my vote and Abraham's proxy in accordance with his wishes, and I'm certain that Saralyn and Isaac will, too." He looked at them. "Am I right?"

Saralyn stood. "Let's stop playing games, Alan. There's no need for a vote. There are four of us and two of them. We don't need their approval. They should be happy to be in the room." She shot a hot glance at Michael. "And Mr. Big Mouth over there doesn't even have a vote, so I don't want to see him at another meeting."

"Who are you calling Big Mouth?" Michael shouted, nostrils flaring.

His mother stopped further input from him with a stern, "Michael!"

"You can't do that," Deborah said, jumping in before she could stop herself. Michael shouldn't have come, but Saralyn had no right to treat him with such disdain. "If Isaac's wife can be here, then I don't see why my brother can't. He is, after all, Abraham's son." Deborah took a huge dose of satisfaction when she saw Saralyn blanch. She opened her mouth to say more, but her mother shook her head and mouthed, *That's enough.* Her "home training" demanded that she obey.

"In case you weren't listening," Saralyn said, "we have four votes, including Abraham's, and you have two. I can do whatever I want."

"Mother," Isaac said, a warning in his tone.

Saralyn looked at her son. "I'll see you in your office in ten minutes." With that, she picked up her hat, put it on, and strode out of the boardroom.

Alan cleared his throat. "We're about finished here. I'll be working closely with Isaac to make sure the ongoing projects outlined today run smoothly. In addition, I'll be assisting Deborah as she gets up to speed with Running Brook."

"Just keep me updated," Isaac said, looking at her for the first time.

Deborah wondered if he wanted updates because it was her project, but it didn't matter. "Of course," she said, deciding not to give in to her insecurities.

He nodded. "I'll have my secretary set something up over the next week or so."

Deborah nodded. What he proposed seemed fair to her. He was the boss, after all.

"You don't have to look over my sister's shoulder, Isaac," Michael said. "She's more than competent at what she does. She's had to work for everything she's ever gotten." His unspoken *unlike you* was heard loud and clear.

Her brother was anything but subtle, Deborah thought. "It's all right, Michael. I can defend myself." She turned to Isaac. "You're well within your rights to ask for updates. I think they'll be good for both of us. We haven't worked together before so the updates will be a chance for us to get a feel for each other's work styles. I don't have a problem with it at all. I think it's a great idea."

"Good," Isaac said.

Alan gave her a smile that told her he was proud of the way she'd handled the brewing controversy. "Well, that's it for today's meeting," he said.

Isaac and Rebecca hustled out of the room. Deborah guessed they were going to meet Saralyn in Isaac's office.

"Good riddance," Michael said when the door closed behind them.

"Michael Thomas," his mother said. "What did you think you were doing? I know you have better manners than you showed today."

Michael pressed a kiss on her cheek. "It was business, Mama. Sometimes it gets dirty. It can't be helped."

Leah didn't look as though she agreed.

"Don't worry about it, Mrs. Thomas," Alan said. "This was a

tame board meeting compared to some others we've had. Abraham likes—how can I put this—engagement."

Deborah laughed. "Always the diplomat, huh, Alan?"

"Somebody has to be the voice of reason. Hot blood runs through those Martin veins." He turned to Michael. "Abraham would have enjoyed sparring with you today."

"The old man wouldn't be a match for me," Michael said. "Besides, if he'd wanted an equal sparring partner, I'd be on the board."

"He has a point, Alan," Deborah said. "Let's hear the diplomat's response."

Alan smiled at her again and she smiled back. "I'd rather have that discussion with Michael man-to-man, over lunch." He turned to Michael. "I'm free today. How's your schedule?"

"I always have time to gain insight into how the old man thinks, if he thinks."

"Michael!"

"Sorry, Mama," Michael said. "I seem to be on a roll."

"Well, you need to get off, and quickly."

Deborah stood staring at Alan. "What?" he asked.

"I can't believe you're such a sexist—a man-to-man meeting? This is not the fifties. Women *do* think."

Michael chuckled. "Down, girl," he said. "Alan probably knows our conversation might get heated. Isn't that right, Alan?"

"It is," he answered, keeping his eyes on Deborah. "Otherwise, there'd be no contest. I'd choose you for a lunch date over your brother any day."

Deborah couldn't believe Alan was flirting with her with her mother and brother present. She brushed off his words. "Always the diplomat." She turned to her mother. "Why don't we do a girls' lunch?" she offered. "We don't need men, do we?"

"Speak for yourself, darling," Leah said. Both men laughed.

Alan checked his watch. "It's about noon," he said to Michael. "Are you ready to eat?"

Michael nodded. "I'm ready to have this conversation. I don't need food."

"Well, I do," Alan said. He turned to Leah. "It was good seeing you again," he said. "I hope you weren't too overwhelmed."

"It was fine," she said. "I'm used to unruly children."

Alan smiled. "Deborah, I'll see you at the three o'clock production meeting."

"I'll be there," she said.

After the men left the room, Leah turned to her daughter. "What's going on with you and Alan?"

Chapter Twenty-Nine

Michael followed Alan down the hallway from the board-room to Alan's office, his feet almost swallowed by the plush carpet. He tried not to be too impressed with what Abraham Martin had accomplished in his life but it was hard not to be, with all the awards and recognitions lining the hallway wall. He even caught a glimpse of the old man standing with Barack Obama. Still, Michael was determined to outdo him.

He followed Alan into his office and closed the door behind him. Instead of settling himself into one of the chairs, he lifted a palm and gave Alan a high-five. "I can't believe we pulled it off," he said.

Alan slapped his palm. "We haven't done anything yet," he warned. "We've only executed the first steps of our plan. We have a ways to go."

Michael dropped down on the leather couch in the corner of the office. "That Saralyn is a piece of work, isn't she?"

Alan went to his wet bar and opened a bottle of scotch. He poured two glasses and handed one to Michael. "She's spoiled. Always has been. Started with her father and continued with Abraham. She's used to getting her way." He sat in the club chair across from Michael.

Michael thought of his own mother and how hard she'd worked to give them a decent life. No one had pampered her. He would some day, though. "I bet her son is spoiled, too."

Alan chuckled. "Don't be too sure. From where I was standing, he was on top in that little skirmish between the two of you."

Michael gulped down all of his scotch in one swallow. "I didn't want to hurt the little pansy. I was feeling him out, trying to push his buttons." He grinned at Alan. "It worked."

"Maybe, but we need to cut the physical contact." He tapped his forehead. "We'll achieve our goal with brain power, not brawn. We're going to beat Abraham on the field where he thinks he rules."

"You hate the old man as much as I do," Michael observed. "What did he do to you?" he asked, not expecting an answer. It was a question he'd asked before, without receiving an answer.

"Let's just say your father is a taker. He thinks the world and everyone in it is his for the taking. He holds himself in the highest esteem and everyone else to no esteem."

"What about his wife? He seems to dote on her. A blind man could see the sparkles in her jewelry."

"Abraham likes women . . . *all* women. Saralyn only gets special attention because as his wife she's a reflection of him. Same with the boy. They have to live up to his lofty standards. Be glad that you and your sister didn't grow up under that kind of scrutiny."

Michael wasn't so sure. A boy benefitted from a father's guiding hand. Having a father allowed a boy to be a boy. In a household of women, a boy had to become a man too soon. "So, was it a woman?"

Alan stared at his glass. "Yes, but not in the way you think. It was my sister."

"What happened?" Michael wanted to know.

"What usually happens? It's the same old story. Older married man seduces young, impressionable girl. She falls in love; he doesn't. He ends it; she's devastated."

Michael hated the obvious similarity with his mother. "Did she get pregnant?"

Alan shook her head. "She drove her car into a tree. They called it suicide but I know it was murder. Abraham killed her when he broke her heart."

Michael had no response. When Alan had come to him four months ago with a proposal for a partnership to bring down Abraham Martin, he hadn't needed much coaxing. Alan was an insider at MEEG. He had access to information that they could use against Abraham. "We'll make him pay, Alan."

"I know we will," the attorney said. "It was clear today where the votes are on the board. If Abraham remains in his coma for a while, we may be able to short-cut our way to victory. I'm the deciding vote in his absence."

"How long before we can get everything in place?"

"Six months, tops."

"That's a long time. I doubt he'll be in a coma that long."

Alan shrugged. "He could die."

The words took Michael aback. "You hate him more than I do."

"My sister is dead. Your mother and sister are alive. There's a difference."

Michael realized his partner was right. Then he had a terrible thought. "The old man's car accident," he said, "it was an accident, wasn't it?"

Alan chuckled. "I may hate Abraham Martin but I wouldn't kill him. It wouldn't bring my sister back and it wouldn't hurt Abraham enough. He has to suffer—the way my sister suffered."

Chapter Thirty

You can't let Michael get to you like that, Isaac," Rebecca said, once they were out of the boardroom. "He deliberately goaded you, and you fell for it."

He gave her a cold glance but kept moving. "You don't want to talk to me about Michael right now, Rebecca," he said.

"We have to talk at some point," she said.

"I said everything I needed to say the other night. This marriage is over."

Rebecca stopped, grabbing his arm so he skidded to a halt with her. "Don't you think that's what Michael wants? He knows I love you, and he'll take great joy in breaking us up."

"You should have thought about that before you lied to me."

"I'm sorry, Isaac. How many times do I have to say it?"

He shrugged his arm out of her grasp and resumed walking. "Too little, too late. It's over."

She jogged a couple of steps and fell into pace with him. "You can't toss me out like the morning garbage," she said. "I won't let you."

He chuckled dryly. "You can't stop me."

She was about to say more when they reached his office and he opened the door. She spotted his mother stretched out on his couch, one of her arms resting on her forehead. "This conversation is not over," she whispered.

He walked toward his mother, ignoring Rebecca's whispered words. "Are you all right, Mom?" he asked.

She lowered her arm and sat up. "I'm fine. I just needed to rest my eyes for a minute. I can't put up with any more of those meetings," she said. "Your father was wrong to put us in this situation. What was he thinking?"

"You know as much as I do," he said to his mother. "I would invite you to lunch, but I'm already committed to meet with one of our vendors, though you're welcome to join us."

Saralyn shook her head. "I can't do another meeting today." Glancing at Rebecca, she said, "Rebecca and I can have a nice lunch and then I'll head off to the hospital. You two can join me later for dinner. According to the schedule, Deborah Thomas is supposed to have time with Abraham tonight. God, these people have invaded my life."

Isaac pressed a kiss on his mother's forehead. "You can handle it," he said. "I have faith in you."

She rolled her eyes. "I had faith that you'd never get into a brawl in the boardroom, too, and look what that got me."

"He was asking for it," Isaac said.

"You're a better man than he is, Isaac," his mother said. "I don't care what he does—you have to maintain your composure. When you go off like that, he wins. I don't want it to happen again."

Rebecca slid a sly glance at Isaac to see if he received his mother's words better than he'd taken hers. She was disappointed when his response was a perfunctory nod.

He looked at his watch. "I've got to run," he said. "You two enjoy lunch."

After he left the office and closed the door behind him, Rebecca turned to Saralyn. "So where do you want to go for lunch?"

Saralyn patted the space next to her on the couch. "I can't eat a thing," she said. "You and I need to talk about Isaac."

Rebecca welcomed the discussion. Her mother-in-law seemed to share her thinking in regard to Michael and Isaac. She took the offered seat, saying, "I've never seen Isaac react the way he did today. I told him he shouldn't let Michael get under his skin."

Saralyn crossed her legs and turned sideways to face Rebecca. "Evidently, Michael pushed some hot buttons. He insulted you, Abraham, and me. He had a lot of ammunition and he seemed to use it all."

Rebecca began to grow wary of the way Saralyn was looking at her. She couldn't think of a suitable response.

"To me, it seemed his insult to you is what tripped Isaac's switch," Saralyn said. "Has Michael done or said something inappropriate to you?"

Rebecca shook her head. She didn't want to have this discussion with Saralyn. The woman was too observant. "Michael was just trying to get under Isaac's skin."

"Are you sure there isn't something more?" Saralyn probed. "Michael seemed very specific when he mentioned anniversary gifts and seducing you."

Rebecca looked at the framed artwork above Saralyn's head. "It was all just talk."

Saralyn leaned close and placed her hand on Rebecca's knee. "Isaac is my son, Rebecca, and I know him about as well as any mother knows a son. Idle words from Michael would not have provoked him to physical violence."

"I don't know what Isaac was thinking," she said.

Saralyn studied her. "I'd like to think our relationship has grown since Isaac first brought you home to meet us. It took me a while to warm to you and I'm sorry about that, but I've always been a bit overprotective where he was concerned. I had to make sure that you really loved him."

"I know," Rebecca said. "And I understood."

"From where I sit, you've been a good wife to him. I think you love him."

"I do."

"Yet I can't help but think that whatever is wrong between you and Isaac contributed to his reaction to Michael today."

"I don't know what you mean."

Saralyn met her eyes. "I think you do," she said, "but since you won't be more forthcoming, I'm going to have to ask you straight out. Did you have an affair with Michael? Is that what he meant with his seduction comment to Isaac?"

Rebecca kept her eyes fixed on Saralyn. "I have never cheated on Isaac with Michael," she said, telling the truth but not really answering the question.

Saralyn sat back. "But you have slept with him, haven't you?"

Rebecca looked away. She had no explanation to give Saralyn.

"You don't have to answer. I'm assuming you didn't tell Isaac before you were married."

Rebecca shook her head. "At the time, I had no idea that Michael was his half brother. Why would I tell him? He didn't tell me about all the women he'd slept with." She didn't see any value in telling Saralyn about the anniversary gifts. She needed her mother-in-law on her side.

"You may be right, but you should have told him as soon as you learned that Abraham was Michael's father. When you didn't, you should have kept it to yourself. Forever. That's the cardinal rule of lying to your husband. Once you do it, you have to stick to it. I'm assuming you told Isaac in some grand moment of true confessions."

"I didn't want Michael to hold it over him."

"Don't kid me, Rebecca. I wasn't born an old married lady. I know the games men and women play. You told because you knew Michael would tell him at some point and you wanted to beat him to it."

"Maybe that was part of it," she said. "But you know I love Isaac. Can't you help me make him see that I do?"

Saralyn patted her knee. "You need to face a hard truth, Rebecca. Your marriage to Isaac is over. He's never going to get past this, and frankly, I don't blame him."

Chapter Thirty-One

Deborah shook her head. She couldn't believe how her brother had treated Isaac in the boardroom. She placed her order and handed the menu back to the waitress. "Mama, I think we've got bigger problems than me and Alan. Your son was fighting with his half brother during a business meeting. We've got to do something."

Leah took a sip of iced tea. "Well, he said Isaac threw the first punch."

"Come on, Mama," Deborah said. "You and I both know Isaac didn't jump Michael out of the blue. "

Leah shrugged. "We don't know any such thing."

Deborah could not believe this conversation. "You can't be making excuses for Michael, Mama, not now, not after what he did today."

Leah wiped her fingers down the side of her glass. "I'm not making excuses for him," she said. "I'm trying to see things from his perspective."

Deborah loved her mother but she couldn't hold her tongue any longer. "Maybe we've tried to do that too much, Mama. Maybe all we've done is turn a blind eye to Michael's misdeeds."

"That's not true," Leah said.

Deborah bit her lower lip. "Yes, it is. The most glaring example is how we treated his relationship with Josette. We should have made him tell her that Abraham was his father and Isaac his brother. And if he didn't tell her, we should have. Instead, we went along with it, convincing ourselves that Michael's motives were pure. When is it going to stop, Mama?"

Leah wiped at a tear with a hand. "I don't know what to do. How do you think it makes me feel to see how much my son hates his father?"

Deborah squeezed her mother's hand. "It's not your fault, Mama. It's nobody's fault. It's just the way things are. But if we love Michael—and we do—we have to find a way to help him."

"I've talked to him and talked to him," she said. "My words don't penetrate."

"I know what you mean," Deborah said. "Words aren't working. Everything he's doing goes back to the animosity he feels toward Abraham."

Leah smiled weakly. "Now who's making excuses for him?"

"I don't seem to be able to help myself. I know the rejection he feels. I felt it, too. And I think Abraham was wrong not to put Michael on the board. That was only more rejection. We shouldn't have gone along with it."

The waitress brought their meals and placed them on the table. When she was gone, Leah said, "The proposal made sense when Abraham first put it to me. I think he had good intentions."

Deborah sprinkled salt on her fried potatoes. "Maybe he could have made them work if he weren't in the hospital, but I can safely say that his plan is one big failure."

"What can we do about it?"

"We can give Michael his seat on the board. All we need to do is tell Alan that we think he's ready."

"Do you think he's ready? Abraham was concerned that he might try to sabotage the company."

Deborah picked up her hamburger and took a bite. "What could he do? Saralyn made it perfectly clear that we don't have enough votes to do anything. What harm could come of it?"

"I promised Abraham—"

Deborah stopped her mother. "Mama, we need to think about what's best for Michael, not what's best for Abraham. I think giving him some say in his father's company would go a long ways toward helping him establish some relationship with Abraham. As it stands now, there is no chance for that. He's still an outsider. He probably feels more of an outsider now that I'm working at MEEG and sitting on the board. It's his birthright. He shouldn't have to earn it if Isaac and I didn't have to."

"I'll think about it," Leah said. "It's hard for me to picture Michael and Isaac working side by side, given what happened today."

Deborah chuckled. "It's hard for me to picture it, too, but that's where we are. They're both Abraham's sons. They both have to adapt. This would be a lot easier if Abraham were awake, but we have to work with what we have."

"When did you get so smart?"

"I'm not smart, Mama." She stabbed a fry with her fork. "Abraham told me that he wants me to help bring this family together. I think he'd approve of what we're considering. We're never going to be a family if Michael is on the outside looking in. It won't work and it's not fair."

"I bet this will go over well with Saralyn."

Deborah laughed. "We'll leave the telling to Alan. He'll find the best way to break it to her."

Leah took a bite of her salmon. "Alan's an attractive man."

"Does that mean I'm going to have to fight you for him?"

Leah shook her head. "He's too old for me."

Deborah laughed and flicked a fry at her mother. "No, you didn't say that."

"He seems like a nice man. Your type—smart, established, handsome, older."

"Right on all four counts, but there's nothing to worry about. Yet. We haven't even gone out."

"But you will," Leah said.

"Probably," Deborah said. "I'm taking it slow. Part of the attraction is that he's known Abraham for a long time and he's willing to share those stories with me."

"Be careful," Leah said, "of your own heart and Alan's. There are quite a few broken hearts in your past, sweetheart."

Deborah sighed. "Don't start. If another person tells me I have commitment issues, I think I'll scream." She picked up the dessert menu in the middle of the table. "Enough of the serious talk," she said. "My sweet tooth is calling me."

Chapter Thirty-Two

Why do women always have to clean up after men? Saralyn asked herself as she strode to Deborah's office after lunch. She and the young woman needed to come to a meeting of the minds after that disastrous board meeting. It was obvious to a blind man that Isaac and Michael could not continue together at MEEG. Even though Michael Thomas was not officially on the board, it was apparent he was going to make a nuisance of himself. Somebody had to take charge.

When she reached Deborah's door, she opened it without knocking.

The desk chair faced the wall. When it turned around, she saw Leah sitting there instead of Deborah.

"Where's your daughter?" she asked, not interested in speaking with the woman. She could barely stand to be in the room with her, but desperate times called for desperate measures, as the saying went. She'd tolerate her as a means to an end.

"She's in a meeting."

Saralyn assessed this woman who had been her husband's mistress, and as she had years ago when she learned of the affair, concluded that she was not a worthy opponent. She closed the office door and strode to the desk. Instead of sitting in the chair, she walked around the desk and leaned on its edge, facing Leah.

"What do you want?" Leah asked, rolling back a bit in her chair in a futile effort to regain her personal space.

"I want to talk about that fiasco of a board meeting," she said. "You have to know this idea of Abraham's is not going to work."

"That's your opinion," Leah said, giving away nothing.

Maybe the woman had some skills after all, Saralyn thought. "Look, Leah," she said. "Abraham tried to do the right thing by your children, but he went about it the wrong way. He made it much more complicated than it had to be."

Leah eyed her skeptically. "What do you mean?"

"It would have been much simpler had Abraham written a check. In fact, I'm ready to do that now. Name your price and I'll have the check cut before the day is over."

Leah rolled back some more and then got out of her chair. "You want to pay us off?"

Saralyn followed her with her eyes. "Let's just say I want to make a better arrangement for all of us. You'll get what you want and I'll get what I want."

"And what do you want, Saralyn?"

"I want you and your children out of my life for good. I thought I'd gotten rid of you twenty-eight years ago, and yet here you are. So tell me your number."

"You think you can buy us out of your life, out of Abraham's life?"

Saralyn laughed. "I did it before," she said. "I'll do it again. Though I'm sure I'll have to spend a bit more this time. You went cheaply before."

Leah's eyes widened. "What are you talking about?"

"Don't play innocent with me, Leah," she said. "I'm talking about the checks you received each month when your kids were growing up. Surely, you didn't think Abraham sent them, did you?" Saralyn laughed again. "And here I thought you knew Abraham. Honey, I told Abraham to offer to send you money—it was better than having you go through the child support system—and I personally had those checks sent every month like clockwork. Abraham never gave you another thought until he had his 'come to Jesus' moment after his mother died. He was too busy building his empire to think about the small details of life, which is what you and your children were to him. Don't ever think you were more than that."

"I don't believe you," Leah said. "Sending the money was Abraham's idea."

Saralyn shrugged. "Believe what you want. What matters now is how much the last check should be for. Pick a good number because this will be all you and yours get from us."

"I don't want a check, Saralyn."

"What do you want, Leah?"

"I want my children to have their birthright."

Saralyn laughed again. "Bastard children don't have a birthright. Don't you read your Bible?" She took satisfaction in the pain in Leah's eyes. She focused so much attention on the other woman's eyes that she didn't see Leah's left hand until it was too late. The slap caught her totally off-guard. She rubbed her throbbing cheek but refused to give any other reaction.

"My children are as much Abraham's children as your son," Leah said. "You and Abraham ignored them all their lives and I went along with it, but no more. My children are here, in your life and here at MEEG, as long as they want to be here. You can't buy them off and you can't run them off. I'm sure you'll try, though."

Saralyn smiled at her. "You're no match for me, Leah Thomas.

You never have been. You think I didn't know Abraham was sneaking around with you when we were dating? Please. You were no competition for me then and you're no competition for me now. You know why?" She paused for effect, to let little Leah stew for a bit. "Because you don't know how to handle Abraham. You let him tell you what to do. Unlike you, I told him what to do, and look which one of us he married."

"He only married you because you were pregnant," Leah spat at her.

"You keep thinking that. We both know Abraham was always going to choose me. He was too self-involved to make any other choice. Your only chance to get him was to get pregnant, and I beat you to it."

Leah studied her. Then, with a horrified expression on her face, she said, "You did it on purpose. You got pregnant to trap him."

Saralyn didn't bother to answer. "I did what I had to do to get the man I wanted."

Leah lifted her chin. "But Abraham still came back to me after he found out about Michael."

"I wouldn't boast about that if I were you. All you got out of it was a second bastard child. You still didn't get Abraham."

"I turned him away," she said, "because I had sympathy for you."

Saralyn shook her head. This woman was not allowed to bring up the miscarriage that she had caused. "Don't pity me," she said. "I got what I wanted. Now pick a number. We both know I'm going to win. I always do." Then she got up and stalked to the door. "You know how to reach me," she said, and left the office.

Chapter Thirty-Three

Isaac rubbed the back of his neck as he stepped off the hospital elevator after work the next day. The day had been long, too long. He wanted a day off but didn't see one in the near future. He had to deal with the all-consuming work of MEEG combined with the ultimate dysfunction of his own family.

"Hello, Isaac," a warm, feminine voice said.

He looked up to see Josette standing before him. "What are you doing here?" he asked.

Her lips turned up in a slight smile. "It's nice to see you, too."

"I'm sorry," he said.

"Don't be sorry," she said, a full smile on her face now. "To answer your question, I was here to see your father. Since no one was around, he and I had some quality time. I told him he needed to wake up so he can fix this mess that he's made."

Isaac smiled. "It's good to know that somebody around here is thinking with a clear head. I hope he heard you."

She rubbed her belly. "This little one keeps me sane. I'm not going to lose my mind, even though it feels like it some days." She met his eyes. "Your father is my baby's grandfather and you'll be his uncle. Be honest with me, Isaac. Will you love my child the way an uncle loves a child?"

Isaac didn't answer immediately.

Josette began to weep. "I don't want my child born into a family like this. Had I known everything, maybe I wouldn't have married Michael and I wouldn't be here now. But I did marry him and now I have to make the best of it for my child."

Isaac felt her pain and wanted to ease it. He took her by the elbow and moved her to one of the lounge couches, then sat next to her. "I'm so sorry you and your baby got caught in the middle of this family drama, Josette."

"You could help lessen the drama, Isaac," she said. "All you have to do is give Michael a chance."

Isaac didn't see how that was possible, given this morning's board meeting, but he didn't want to disappoint this distraught pregnant woman. "I'll try," he said.

"Put yourself in his shoes," she said, her eyes pleading with him. "Even though he won't admit it, he's jealous of you and your relationship with your father. He's so focused on what he's missed in life that he doesn't see what he has. This should be the happiest times of our lives, but Michael's so focused on you and your father that he has little energy left for me and the baby."

Isaac didn't have any words of encouragement for her so he smiled and said, "Do you want me to beat some sense into him?"

She chuckled, as he'd hoped she would. "Maybe a good fight would get it all out of his system. Think you can arrange it?"

He lifted his shoulders in a slight shrug. "We already had round one."

She bit her bottom lip. "Oh, no," she said. "I knew he shouldn't have crashed that board meeting."

Not wanting to upset her more, Isaac added, "There was too much testosterone in the room. We needed an outlet for some of it."

"You see, that's what I mean. I don't want my baby around a father and uncle who can't even be in the same room without arguing or coming to blows. I want her to know her grandfather, spend time with him. How can this happen if you and Michael are always fighting?"

Isaac didn't know. Michael had crossed too many boundaries. His actions with Rebecca and the anniversary gifts suggested a pattern that was unlikely to change. He would bet that even now Michael was plotting his next attack. "The good news is that we have a few months before the baby gets here," he said, seizing on the one positive he could find. "A lot can happen in that time."

"That's what I'm praying for," she said. "Your father needs to get better. He could help set things right."

Isaac grunted. "That would be fitting since he's the one who caused the trouble in the first place."

"It really is a mess, isn't it?"

Before Isaac could answer, Rebecca rounded the corner and stopped abruptly. She looked from him to Josette. He could guess what she was thinking. "I hope I'm not interrupting anything," she said. He detected her sarcasm but hoped Josette didn't.

Josette sat up and away from Isaac. "No," she said. "Your husband was only comforting a crying pregnant woman. We tend to get a lot of sympathy." She extended her hand to Rebecca. "I'm Josette Thomas. Michael Thomas is my husband."

Rebecca shook her hand. "Nice to finally meet you," she said. She cast a quick glare at Isaac, then added, "I can always count on my husband to rescue a woman in distress. He's not a man to sit idly by when a woman needs help."

Seeming to sense the tension, Josette stood. "It's time for me to head home," she said. "I'm sure Michael will want to give me the details of the exciting board meeting."

Laughing, Isaac stood, too, ignoring the scowl on his wife's face. "You take care of yourself and that baby. Everything's going to work out."

"From your lips to God's ears," she said. Turning to Rebecca, she said, "You have a keeper here. Maybe together we can end this family feud."

Isaac watched Rebecca watch Josette leave. He was staring at her when she turned back to him. "You two certainly were cozy," Rebecca said, accusation in her voice.

"Tell me you didn't sleep with Michael after he married Josette. Please tell me you had more self-respect than that."

When she looked away before responding, Isaac had his answer. And it hurt. He'd loved Rebecca, truly loved her. But he didn't even know her.

"What matters is that I wasn't sleeping with him when you and I started dating," she said, "and that I've never cheated on you. Have I asked for a rundown on the women you slept with before we met? No, I haven't. And I wouldn't."

"I guess that's a yes, then."

"So what was that I saw with you and Josette? Are you looking for a way to get back at me, Isaac? Seducing Josette would be the perfect knife in the back for both me and Michael."

Isaac shook her head. "Now you're talking crazy. In case you didn't notice, Josette's pregnant—very pregnant. Besides, I barely know the woman."

She bit her lower lip. "Maybe it doesn't matter to you."

"Let me make this clear," he said. "Josette is not part of our problem. Your lies about your relationship with Michael are our problem."

"We can work through it," she pleaded. "Other couples have made it through worse."

He shook his head. "I don't see how we can. It's too close for comfort. The reality is that he's my brother and you've slept with both of us. I don't see how I can get around that. Maybe if you had told me when you found out I could have adjusted, but not now when I have to deal with the act and the lie. It's too much."

"But I love you. Doesn't that count for anything?"

He studied his wife. He tried to summon up the confidence he'd felt in their love, their relationship, but there was nothing there. "You need to see an attorney," he said.

She began shaking her head as if she didn't want to hear what he was saying. "I don't want a divorce," she repeated. "I love you."

A part of him wanted to comfort her, but he didn't want to send mixed signals. "Get an attorney," he said. "I'll be fair."

"Fair—" she began.

"Excuse me," a uniformed nurse that Isaac had met before said, interrupting their conversation. "Mr. Martin, there's been a change in your father's condition."

Chapter Thirty-Four

Deborah sat in the passenger seat of Alan's Benz while he drove them down a winding road in the southern Atlanta suburb of Forest Park. When he'd told her he wanted to take her somewhere, it never occurred to her that it would be to the Martin estate. "Are you taking me where I think you're taking me?" she asked.

He gave her a sideways glance. "You've asked a lot of questions about Abraham, so I thought you might like to see his place. Was I wrong?"

Deborah had mixed emotions. She'd always wondered about this estate, but the idea of seeing it only made her anxious. She remembered the trip she and Michael had made out here and their reluctance to travel down this road to get a good look. Instead, they stopped at the main road and had to imagine what the estate looked like. "You weren't wrong," she said. "It just feels strange."

"How so?"

She looked out the window at the wooded forest lining both sides of the road. "It drives home the differences in our lives, his with Saralyn and Isaac, and mine with Mama and Michael. I'll have to show you where we grew up."

He reached for her hand. "We can turn back," he said. "We don't have to do this."

She shook her head. "No, I want to see it."

"Get ready," he said. "It takes your breath away."

"Oh . . . my . . . God," Deborah said when she saw the expansive two-story stucco, stone, and limestone mansion sitting at the end of the road. The house looked like something from *Lifestyles of the Rich and Famous*. There was an active fountain within the brick herringbone-patterned circular drive. "I never imagined."

"Blame the extravagance on Saralyn. Abraham loved the location. She did the rest." He pulled the car to a stop near the front door. "Want to get out?"

Deborah's curiosity overwhelmed her anxiety. "Of course," she said, unbuckling her seat beat. "Are you sure it's okay for me to be here?"

"Positive," he said. "Abraham and Saralyn spend most of their time in their downtown condo. They come here on weekends and when they're hosting a big event that needs the down home touch."

Deborah stepped out of the car after Alan opened the door for her. "Thank you," she said. "And not just for the car door. Thank you for bringing me here. It was a sensitive and caring thing to do."

Alan pushed one of her braids across her shoulder. "It's the least I can do. An old man like me has to go all out to keep the attention of a beautiful young woman like yourself."

"You're not an old man," she said.

He lifted a brow. "How old are you?"

"A woman doesn't reveal her age," she said. "How old are you?"

"Old enough to be your father," he said. "Fifty-two. Same as Abraham."

"That's not old."

Alan threw back his head and laughed.

"What's so funny?" she asked.

"You," he said. He took her hands in his and pulled her up the marble steps to the mahogany double-entry front doors. "Ready?" he asked. When she nodded, he lifted the gold door knocker.

Shortly, a black woman in her early sixties, wearing a dark gray dress and white apron, opened the door. "Mr. Alan," she said. "I've been waiting for you."

Alan leaned in and kissed her brow. "Thanks for taking care of us."

"It's not a bother. This house needs more activity." She glanced at Deborah. "And who is our guest today?"

"This is Abraham's daughter," he said. "Deborah, this is Mrs. Hall. She's been working for Abraham and Saralyn forever. She runs the place," he added. "They just live here."

Chuckling, Mrs. Hall extended her hand. "Welcome, Miss Deborah," she said. "It's nice to finally meet Mr. Abraham's daughter. You look like him."

"You should see my brother," Deborah managed to say. She was overwhelmed by the majesty of the home. The foyer felt bigger than her mother's whole house. She could see the graceful ironwork of the winding staircase to her left. A rotunda library was to her right. Straight ahead was what she assumed was the great room, and a great room it was. A wall of two-story windows showcased the patio and gardens beyond.

"Well, I look forward to meeting him," Mrs. Hall was saying. She turned to Alan. "Are you ready to eat now or would you like to tour the house first?"

"What do you think?" Alan asked Deborah.

"I don't know," she answered, torn between wanting to explore like a kid and to hide like a burglar. "I'd feel like I'm invading their privacy."

"Let's eat first, Mrs. Hall," he said to the older woman. "I'll show Deborah to the back patio."

Alan took her hand. "There's no need to be nervous. This is your father's house. He's opened his life to you, Deborah. He would approve."

She looked sideways at him. "Would Saralyn?"

"Beautiful and smart," he said, "a lethal combination. Don't worry. We're safe. Saralyn's at the hospital with Abraham."

He led her through the foyer and the great room, on through some double doors and out to the patio. Except it was a patio unlike any she had seen. It ran the length of the house and was separated from the gardens by a short wall about a foot tall that served as seating. She guessed the patio floor was made of travertine, which most people used inside their homes.

"Saralyn has good taste," she muttered, taking in the elegantly set patio table. She'd bet the glasses were crystal and the plates were designer. Lifestyles of the rich and famous, right down to the linen napkins.

Alan pulled out a chair for her and took the one next to it. Deborah couldn't help but compare the extravagance of this home with the humbleness of the places she'd lived while growing up. They lived in a two-bedroom rental house until she was in middle school and her mother had purchased a home. She still remembered the celebration the three of them had the first night in their new but modest house. She and Michael were ecstatic to finally have their own rooms after having shared a room for so long. She thought about how hard her mother had worked to be able to purchase that home, and how proud she'd been to do it. She wondered what Saralyn and Abraham would think of the home that had meant so much to her, her mother, and her brother.

"A penny for your thoughts," Alan said.

She turned her attention to him. "I'm afraid they're not worth that much. I was thinking about how they live here and how I live. They're two very different worlds."

He poured them each a glass of lemonade from the pitcher on the table. "It's natural to wonder what it would have been like to grow up here."

Shaking her head, she picked up her glass. "You know Abraham," she said, leaning toward him. "How could he have all this and not share more of it with us? Sure, he sent us money regularly over the years, but it was nothing compared to this. My mama had to work, and work hard. My brother and I have always worked, too. I'm not saying Abraham should have made sure our lifestyle matched his, but he certainly could have made life much easier for us. And the cost would have been a pittance to him. I don't get it."

"Be happy that you don't get it," Alan said. "It means your mother did a good job with you."

She lifted a brow. "You can say that after Michael's fight in the boardroom yesterday?"

Alan laughed. "Everybody has an off day."

"How kind of you."

"Seriously, though, don't waste your time figuring out why. It's going to take all you have to deal with now."

Deborah wasn't sure how realistic Alan's suggestion was, but she decided to give it a shot, at least for this afternoon. "I'll try," she said, sipping her lemonade.

He reached for her hand. "Let's take a walk through the gardens and down to the pools while we wait for our meal."

She took his hand and let him lead her through the beautiful gardens. "I wanted to talk you about something," she said as they made their way down the marble stairs to the lower gardens.

"Sounds like work."

"There's a fine line between work life and personal life these days."

He chuckled. "Good point. What do you want to talk about?"

She paused when they reached the pools. There were two of them, an Olympic-sized pool and a smaller oval shaped pool. There was also a spa that would seat about twenty people. "Mama and I have decided Michael should take his seat on the board."

He led her around the pools. "May I ask why?"

"We think it was wrong of Abraham to keep him on the outside. I didn't have to prove myself, and neither did Isaac. Why should Michael? It's not fair. Do we have your support?"

He stopped and looked at her. "You don't need my support. Abraham was clear. As long as you and your mother are in agreement, it's done."

They had circled the pools and were now headed back up the stairs to the patio. "That's it? It's that easy?"

"I like easy," he said. "Don't you?"

Before she could answer, Alan's cell phone rang. He dropped her hand. "Excuse me, I need to get this." He stepped away from her and took the call. When he hung up, he said, "We have to get to the hospital. Abraham's out of his coma."

Chapter Thirty-Five

I want that one," Josette said pointing to the white wicker bassinet on the laptop screen. "Don't you love it?"

Leah stood over her daughter-in-law's shoulder. "It's cute, but I like the one next to it better." She pointed to the screen. "What do you think?"

Josette giggled. "Maybe we should get both—one for our house and one for yours."

Leah squeezed Josette's shoulders. "I like how you think."

Josette typed in another search term. "Let's look at strollers. I saw one that would be perfect for jogging."

Leah settled into the dining room chair next to Josette and moved it so she had a good view of the computer screen. She knew they were in for a long and very enjoyable evening of computer window-shopping. "A jogging stroller? You've got to be kidding."

"Kidding about what?" Michael asked, entering the dining room, spatula in hand. "I need more barbecue sauce, Mama. Please tell me you have some. I don't want to have to go to the store again."

Leah pushed back her chair. "There should be some in the pantry. Did you check?"

Michael looked down on his mother and pretended to pat the top of her head with the spatula. "My focus is on the cooking. You women ought to be responsible for something."

"I'm going to pretend I didn't hear that," Josette said.

Michael looked over Josette's shoulder at the screen. "What are you looking at?" he asked her.

Leah got up and went to look for the barbecue sauce. The phone rang as she walked past. She picked it up. "Hello."

"It's me, Mama," her daughter's voice came through the line.

"Oh, hey, Deborah. Michael's barbecuing tonight. Why don't you come over?" she said. To be contrary, she added, "You can bring Alan."

"Mama," she said. "Abraham's out of his coma. Alan and I are on our way to the hospital. Will you meet us there? I'll call Michael."

"Michael's here," she said. "I'll tell him."

"But you'll meet us there?"

Leah held the phone tighter, using both hands. "I'll make sure your brother comes. I don't think I should be there."

"I understand," Deborah said, though she was clearly disappointed. "Tell Michael I need him."

"Will do," Leah said. Then she hung up the phone.

When she returned to the dining room, Michael had taken her seat and was now held captive by Josette. "That was Deborah," she told them.

"Did you tell her to get over here?" Michael asked. "We have more than enough food."

Leah shook her head. "The doctors brought Abraham out of

the coma. Deborah's with Alan and they're on their way to the hospital." She pinned Michael with a stare. "She wants you to meet her there."

Michael shook his head. "No way. You go."

"I shouldn't be there," she said. "You and Deborah are his children. You should go."

"Your mother's right," Josette added.

Michael got up from his chair. "I've got ribs and burgers waiting on me."

Josette reached for his hand to stop him from leaving the room. "You need to go, Michael."

He tried to shake off her hand but she held on. "The man means nothing me, Josette, and I mean nothing to him. I don't belong there."

"Maybe it's time you tried to change that," she pleaded. "Whatever is going on with you and Abraham, he's the grandfather of our unborn child. Our baby deserves to know him, to have a relationship with him. If you won't do it for yourself, do it for the baby."

Leah watched a variety of emotions cross her son's face and prayed he'd make the right decision. "I can't do it," he said. "I can't."

Josette took her hand off Michael's hand. "Okay," she said. "But if you won't do it, I will."

Michael looked at her as though she'd said she was going to kill somebody. "Do what?"

Josette pushed back her chair and stood. "I'm going to the hospital to see Abraham."

"You don't have to do that for me."

Josette picked up her purse and fished out her car keys. "I'm not doing it for you. I'm doing it for our baby and for Deborah. I know she doesn't want to be down there with the Martins by herself. Did you think of that, Michael?"

He looked away. "Deborah's a big girl. She can handle it. Besides, Alan's with her. What's up with that anyway?"

Josette ignored his comment. She looked at Leah. "Are you sure you don't want to come with me?"

"I want to be there for Deborah, but I think there'll be less drama if I stay away." She pulled Josette into a hug. "Thank you, sweetheart, for representing the family. You're so right to think of your baby first." She eyed Michael. "Unlike some people."

Josette pulled out of Leah's embrace. "I'll call you as soon as I have some details."

Leah walked her to the door. "Drive carefully," she said, then stood in the doorway and watched Josette drive away. When Josette was out of sight, Leah closed the door and went looking for Michael. She found him in the backyard at the grill.

"You should have gone, Michael," she said. "If not for Abraham, for Deborah. She's your sister and she needed you."

Michael flipped a burger patty. "Deborah's fine without me," he said. "She's making a place for herself in that family. She'll be fine."

"Deborah's not trading in one family for another. You know that, don't you?"

"Maybe she's trading up to a better family."

Leah slapped her son on the back of his head. "You're talking crazy. You know that, don't you? Deborah loves you," she said. "But that doesn't mean she can't love her father. Don't take that away from her."

"I'm not taking anything away from her."

"Then let my words serve as a warning. Don't make her choose between the two of you."

"Because she'll choose him?"

Leah shook her head. "Because she'll choose you."

"Don't be so sure."

"You don't know how wrong you are. She's very upset because

Abraham didn't give you a seat on the MEEG board. She's talking to Alan tonight about you taking your rightful place there."

"I thought you agreed with Abraham that I couldn't be trusted to have a voice in his business."

She placed her hand on his cheek, hoping to counter some of the bitterness she heard in his voice. "You're my son and I love you, but let's be honest. You haven't given Abraham any reason to trust you."

"If you feel that way, why are you going along with Deborah's idea?"

She pushed out an exasperated sigh. "Because she's right. Isaac didn't have to prove his loyalty to get his seat and neither did she, so why should you? Don't ever doubt how much your sister loves you, Michael, and don't ever put that love to the test. You'll win and lose at the same time. You both will."

Leah pressed a kiss against her son's cheek and left him to think about her words. She had to think on them herself. Her feelings about Abraham had grown very cold since her last conversation with Saralyn. It hurt to know how little he'd concerned himself with her, Michael, and Deborah over the years, even less than she'd thought. She would never let her kids know, and she prayed Saralyn would never tell them either.

Chapter Thirty-Six

The bossy Nurse Ratchet reentered Abraham's hospital room. "There are too many people in here, Mr. Martin," she said. Her voice was stern, but Abraham had learned that she was a pushover. He grinned at her. "Don't try your smooth ways with me," she said. "Just for tonight we're going to break the rules. You can have your whole family in here for the next hour or so but then I'm kicking everybody out. You need your rest. Open up," she said. When he did, she stuck a thermometer in his mouth.

"He needs his rest," the nurse said to Saralyn, Isaac, and Rebecca. The three of them huddled near the foot of the bed, out of her way. "Even if he doesn't think so."

"We understand, Nurse Wilson," Saralyn said. "I'll make sure they're out of here soon. He wanted to see everybody. He can be bull-headed when he wants something."

"You're telling me. I know that and he's been awake less than an hour." Nurse Wilson pulled the thermometer out of his mouth. She recorded his temperature on her PDA. "I'll be back in an hour," she told him. "If you need me before then, press the call button and I'll come running."

Saralyn and Isaac moved closer to the head of the bed after the nurse left. "Are you sure you're feeling okay?" Saralyn asked.

Abraham took her hand in his. "I'm fine," he said. "Stop worrying."

"Dad," Isaac said, standing next to his mother, "you're not exactly fine. Your full memory hasn't come back yet."

"I remember everything up to the accident, and I remember everything since I woke up. I'm not sure I want to remember what happened in between. How's the car?"

"Pretty bad," Isaac said. "You ran off the road and hit a tree—a big tree. It crashed the front end all the way up to the windshield. It's a miracle you're alive."

Abraham nodded. "It's also a miracle I didn't hit anybody. That would have been a tragedy."

"Don't think about it," Saralyn said. "Just focus on getting better."

"I'm a strong old man. I'll be fine."

"You're not old," Rebecca said with a smile.

Abraham could tell her smile wasn't sincere. She stood on the opposite side of the bed from Isaac and Saralyn, which he thought odd. Something was wrong. He'd find out later what it was. He turned to Saralyn and Isaac. "Did one of you call Deborah or Michael to let them know about the change in my condition?"

"I called Alan," Isaac said. "He was supposed to contact them."

"Don't worry about them, Abraham," Saralyn said. "You have all the family you need right here. You've reached out to those children. You can't make them care about you. I don't say that to hurt you, but you need to be realistic in your expectations."

Abraham nodded. He knew Saralyn was right, but he still

wanted to see them. He had some vague memory of Deborah vis-
iting him here in the hospital. "Have they come at all since I've
been here?"

Saralyn stepped away from the bed and Isaac moved up in her
space. "Deborah and her mother came the night of the accident,"
he said, "and Deborah has been here several times since."

"And the boy?" Abraham asked, another vague memory flash-
ing in his mind.

Isaac shook his head. "I'm sorry."

"No need to be sorry, Isaac. Your mother's right. I didn't have
any interest in them for all of their lives so I can't expect them to
be that interested in me. I'll have to settle for what they're willing
to give." He sighed. "Enough of that. Tell me what's going on at
MEEG."

"Abraham," Saralyn warned. "There'll be plenty of time to talk
business in the morning."

Abraham ignored her. He looked at Isaac and waited for an
answer.

"We'll be glad to have you back at the helm."

"So you came back?"

"Of course I did, Dad," Isaac said. "The company needed me."

Isaac's answer gave Abraham hope. "Are you back for good?
Have you forgiven me?"

"I don't know the answer to your first question. All I know is
that I'm back at MEEG until you're ready to resume your role.
As for your last question, that's a little bit harder to answer. I'm
trying to understand, though. That's about the best I can do."

Abraham grabbed his son's hand and looked directly into his
eyes. "If that's true, then my accident was worth it. I'm sorry I've
disappointed you, Isaac. You'll be a better husband and father
than I am. I really believe that."

Abraham saw the quick glance that Isaac shot at Rebecca. That glance told him that all was not well with his son and daughter-in-law. He'd have to see what he could do to fix the problem.

"Saralyn—" he said, but stopped when the door opened and Deborah walked in, followed by Josette and Alan.

"It's about time you got here," he said to them.

Deborah stood at the foot of the bed. "I'm glad you're better," she said.

"Much better now that you're here."

She smiled, and it warmed his heart.

Josette came closer to the bed. "I knew you'd wake up before your grandchild was born," she said. "She's been praying for you."

Abraham vaguely remembered a visit by Josette as well. She looked cheerful enough now but he felt her visit had not been a happy one. "Is everything all right with the baby?"

Josette rubbed her belly. "She's perfect."

"Good," he said. "And thanks for coming to see me."

She nodded. "About Michael—" she began.

"Don't," he said. "I understand. I'm just glad you're here." He glanced around the room at Deborah, Alan, Saralyn, Rebecca, and Isaac. "I'm glad you're all here. There's nothing more important than family. I hope it won't take you all as long to learn that as it took me."

Saralyn came back and took up her position next to the bed. "Okay," she said to Abraham. "You've seen everybody and had your say. Now you should get some rest."

"But I haven't even talked to Alan yet," he said.

"We can talk tomorrow morning, old friend," Alan said. "MEEG is in good hands with Isaac. Your boy is off to a fine start."

Abraham met Isaac's eyes. "I never doubted him."

"Okay," Saralyn said, "everybody out."

Josette leaned over and kissed him on the forehead. Rebecca did the same thing. Isaac and Alan shook his hand. Deborah hung back, as if unsure what to do. He called her over to him.

When she reached him, he beckoned her to come closer. Then he whispered, "I remembered you called me Dad. I liked it."

A smile lit her face, replacing the earlier sadness. "I'm so glad you're better," she said. He smiled, but noticed that Saralyn did not. His perfect family was not as perfect as he'd hoped.

Chapter Thirty-Seven

Michael met Alan during one of their scheduled late night runs/meetings in Piedmont Park. When he saw him round the well-lit bend, he fell in with him. "So how's the old man?" he asked.

"He's fine, good as new, the doctors say. Apparently, as they had hoped, the coma gave him time to heal. They're going to keep him two to three more days for observation before releasing him. He'll be back at MEEG within a couple of weeks at most."

"Do you think he'll go along with the plan my mother and Deborah have to give me the seat on the board?"

Alan stopped and began jogging in place. Michael did the same.

"That one's hard to gauge. Your mother and sister need to talk to him, tell him what they want to do. They may be able to guilt him into going along with it. Of course, I'll do my part to see he goes along."

"Of course."

"We have to be patient, Michael. After Josette has the baby, per the bylaws, she'll get a seat and then we'll control the board. I'll be the deciding seventh vote in all decisions. It's perfect."

"And Abraham won't know what hit him when you vote with me instead of with him."

"I can't wait to see the expression on his face."

Alan resumed his jog, and Michael had no choice but to follow after him.

"I wanted to talk to you about something, Alan."

"What?"

"Are you dating my sister?"

Alan glanced over at him. "I don't think I'd call it dating. She has questions about Abraham and I answer them. I enjoy her company. We've shared a few meals. Do you have a problem with that?"

"Not a problem exactly," Michael said, wiping sweat from his brow. "More like a concern. I don't want to see her hurt."

"I don't plan to hurt her, Michael," he said. "Like I told you, I enjoy her company."

Michael glanced over at him. "You know how you feel about Abraham because of your sister. Well, I'll feel about the same way about you if you hurt Deborah. I don't want her to feel used after our plan unfolds."

Alan stopped running but kept jogging in place. "I get the message, Michael," he said, breathing heavily. "Loud and clear. I'll keep things friendly but professional with Deborah."

Michael stopped and then bent over, hands on knees. "Good."

"You realize," Alan said, "that in order to carry out our plan, you're going to have to lie to your sister and your wife. Something tells me they're not going like it."

"They won't," Michael said, "but they'll forgive me eventually. I can always count on them to stand with me."

Michael started moving again, and this time Alan had to follow him.

Chapter Thirty-Eight

Abraham sat in his hospital bed reading a report that Alan had left for him earlier that morning. He found himself distracted by his wife, who sat in a chair next to his bed flipping through one of her fashion magazines. She had one leg crossed atop the other, the top one moving rapidly back and forth. She was angry, he knew. He also knew she would never admit it unless he asked her. This was the pattern with them, always had been, and always would be. Saralyn had been a spoiled child who grew up to become a pampered wife. It was too late to change the rules governing their relationship now.

Besides, she had always been a good wife to him and an excellent mother to Isaac. She'd been the perfect woman to have on his arm when he needed to impress a business colleague, and the perfect woman to share his bed when he needed to have his ego stroked. He loved her. He knew he always would.

"Okay, Saralyn," he said, closing his file and placing it on his bedside tray. "What's wrong?" She kept flipping through the magazine. "You have my full attention," he said.

She closed the magazine and placed it on her lap. "You know what's wrong," she said. "That part of your memory wasn't affected. What are you going to do about them, Abraham? This plan of yours isn't working."

"We have to give it time, Saralyn," he said, already growing weary of the conversation.

She got up and came to the bed. "The price is too high. You almost lost Isaac over all this. You might lose him still."

"What do you mean?" he asked, knowing his wife was given to hyperbole.

She perched on the side of the bed. "Isaac left MEEG when he found out about Deborah and Michael. He only came back because you were ill and he was needed at the company. I don't see him staying there, not if he has to deal with Michael. The man hates him."

"I'm going to convince Isaac to stay," he said. "Maybe all he needed was a bit more responsibility."

"Don't kid yourself. Did Alan tell you Isaac and Michael got into a fistfight at the board meeting?"

He eyed her skeptically. "You're exaggerating."

"No, I'm not. Our son, who's never been in a fight in his life, was rolling around on the boardroom floor fighting with Michael Thomas. I wouldn't have believed it if I hadn't seen it with my own eyes."

"I can't believe it. Not Isaac."

Saralyn nodded. "That incident should tell you that it's going to be impossible for the two of them to work together. You've got to come up with another plan, Abraham. This one is not going to work."

"What was Michael doing at the board meeting?" he asked. "He's not on the board."

"I tried to make that point, but Alan, Leah, and Deborah basically shut me down. Michael even wanted to nominate himself for acting president and CEO of MEEG in your absence. The nerve of him."

Abraham bit back a smile. He could relate to Michael's audacity, though he'd never tell Saralyn. "What happened?"

"Nothing happened. Alan explained to him that he didn't have a chance in hell of winning against Isaac because Leah and Deborah only had two votes and we had four. That bit of information seemed to put him back in his place."

Abraham wanted her to see that Michael's place was no different from Isaac's but he knew she wouldn't view it that way.

"I don't know what more I can say, Abraham. Obviously, you don't trust the boy or you would have given him a seat instead of giving the seat to his mother. If you don't trust him, I don't want him around."

"I hear what you're saying, Saralyn, and I'll think about it."

"You'd better do more than think about it," she said. "You need to take some action. Have you thought about giving them a settlement of some sort? That would be a quick and easy way to get them out of our lives."

Abraham studied his wife. At times like this he found her selfishness and self-centeredness very unattractive. "I don't want them out of our lives, Saralyn. I want to get to know them."

She eased up from the bed. "You've always accomplished whatever you set your sights on, Abraham, and usually on your own terms. Something tells me things won't work out so smoothly for you this time. You're going to have to make some hard choices."

"What are you saying, Saralyn?"

She folded her arms and looked down at him. "Let me be perfectly clear. You have this unrealistic vision of your two families living together happily ever after. Well, it's not going to happen.

I'm never going to accept Leah and her bastards, and you're wrong for even expecting me to."

"Don't threaten me, Saralyn," he told her. "I don't like threats."

"We've been married thirty years, Isaac, and I've never threatened you and I'm not starting now. I'm only making you aware of the consequences of your actions. Pretty soon you're going to have to choose between me and Isaac and them. You can't have us both."

"Why are you so unwilling to work with me on this?"

"Do you even hear what you're saying? Do you know what you're asking of me?" When he nodded, she added, "Why would you think I'd accept those bastards now when I didn't accept them when they were children?" She picked up her magazine and her purse. "Write them a check, Abraham, and send them on their way so that we can get on with our lives."

He watched as she stalked to the door and snatched it open. When it closed behind her, he began to do what he often saw his mother do but he had never taken up himself: pray. He knew he needed a miracle to get what he wanted.

Chapter Thirty-Nine

Deborah stood at her desk and flipped through the slides she'd copied for her meeting with Isaac. Even though she told herself the meeting wasn't a big deal, she was anxious about it. She felt she needed to prove to him that she was competent for the position Abraham had given her with Running Brook. Even though she wished it wasn't so, it was important that he thought well of her and Michael.

Satisfied that the status of Running Brook was accurately represented in the slides, she put one set in each of the two folders on the desk before her. Taking the folders, she headed out of her office and to Isaac's. Not seeing his secretary, she checked her watch. Two minutes early. Perfect timing. She knocked on his door.

"It's open," Isaac said. "Come on in."

She opened the door and entered his office. Hers looked like a cubbyhole in comparison. She knew from Alan that this was actually Abraham's office. The massive desk drew her attention first—it was twice the size of hers. She didn't want to gawk, but couldn't help sneaking a peek at the photos on his desk. She thought she saw one with him and former President Bill Clinton. The bookcase—actually, a library media unit—was filled with gilt-edged books.

Isaac waved her over to the conference table where he sat, a multitude of files and papers in front of him. When she reached the table, he stood. "Thanks for coming," he said, a welcoming but professional smile on his face.

"No problem. You're the boss, after all." His smile faded a bit. She wanted to take back the words as soon as she said them.

"Have a seat," he said, reseating himself.

She followed his direction.

"This is awkward, isn't it?" he said.

She was taken off guard by the comment. She'd expected him to keep their conversation strictly work-related. "Very awkward."

He studied her for a long minute. "Do you mind if we talk about it?"

She shook her head. She didn't mind but she had no idea where or how to start.

He chuckled. "I don't know how to talk about it."

She smiled. He was trying, and she had to give him credit for that. "It must be harder for you. You grew up an only child. I grew up with Michael."

It was his turn to laugh. "I don't know if I'd agree. Growing up with Michael couldn't have been easy."

Deborah had to walk the tightrope of defending her brother and making excuses for him. "I apologize for what happened at the board meeting. Michael shouldn't have hit you."

"I hit him first," Isaac said. "He provoked me, though."

"I'm sure he did," she said. "I don't know what else to say."

"Our father wants us to be this big happy family but I don't see how that can be, since Michael hates me."

"He doesn't hate you."

"He and my wife Rebecca used to date. Did you know that?"

Deborah shook her head. Michael had gone through a lot of women before he married Josette. He didn't bring many of them home to meet the family.

"Well, they did. Michael sent us a wedding gift and followed that up with anniversary gifts each year. He was taunting me, even before I knew he was my brother. I'd say he hates me."

"I'm so sorry," she said. "I don't know what gets into Michael."

Isaac tossed his pencil on the table and slouched down in his chair. "I don't blame you or him for what happened between your mother and my dad, so why does Michael blame me?"

"Think about it, Isaac," she said. "Put yourself in Michael's shoes. It's easy for you to be magnanimous. You grew up with a father and all of this. We had neither."

He seemed to consider what she said. "Do you hate me, too?"

She gave his question similar consideration. "I don't hate you," she said, "but I hate what you represent."

"And what's that?"

"Someone my father chose to love when he didn't choose to love me."

"Oh, my God." Isaac wiped his hand down his face. "I never looked at it that way."

"Why should you? You've always had Abraham. You probably took—take—his love for granted. You have a sense of entitlement that's been inbred in you, and nobody blames you for it. You're entitled because you're a son. It's different with us. I'm a daughter, but I was never entitled. Just the opposite, in fact. Same with Michael. You're on the inside and we're on the outside."

He picked up his pencil and twirled it between his fingers.

"Did you take the job here at MEEG because you felt you were entitled to it as his daughter?"

"That was part of it. Abraham presented it to me as my birthright and I agreed with him. Does that make you feel threatened?"

He shrugged. "I don't know. My mom feels that way—that you're taking something from us."

"She's right. What was originally to be given to one child is now being shared with three. You're getting two-thirds less than what you would have received had we never showed up. That has to make you feel something."

Isaac closed his eyes, opened them quickly. "Right now, I can't go there. I'm still dealing with the fact that my half brother has ruined a relationship that I thought would last a lifetime. I probably hate Michael as much as he hates me. Maybe more."

"He's my brother, Isaac, so I have to stand with him."

"I'm your brother, too," he said, "your half brother."

The words were a jolt to her system. He *was* her brother. "To be honest, it's not real for me. I don't even know you."

"You don't really know Abraham but you've accepted him as your father. Or, you've accepted his largesse."

Deborah tried not to be insulted by Isaac's words but she found it difficult. "To answer the question that you haven't asked, I don't love Abraham like a father but I wish I did. It's going to be a long road for both of us. There's a lot of mistrust and hurt between us, mostly on my side."

"So do you think Abraham's plan will work?"

She shrugged. "I want it to. It's in my best interests that it does. What about you?"

"Honestly?"

She nodded.

"My life would be a lot less complicated if Michael were not in it."

"Well, that leaves us at a stalemate because I'm not going anywhere and neither is Michael. If I have anything to say about it, he'll be given a position here at MEEG in the same way that you and I were given one."

Isaac nodded. "I guess we'd better get back to the stated purpose of this meeting. What do you have to tell me about Running Brook?"

Deborah handed Isaac the folder of materials she had prepared for him. She outlined the projects she wanted to keep and why, as well as the ones she wanted to discontinue. He listened intently and asked pertinent questions. When she left, she was more determined than ever to see that Michael's interests were protected. She also had a greater respect for her half brother.

Chapter Forty

Dressed in a pair of his favorite navy silk pajamas and robe that Saralyn had brought him from home, Abraham sat in the recliner in his hospital room and perused a stack of about twenty national newspapers while CNN blared from the television. He put the hometown paper, the *Atlanta Journal,* in the trash pile and reached for the *Wall Street Journal.*

Hearing a knock on his door, he looked up. "Come in," he said, pulling off his reading glasses and putting them in the breast pocket of his robe.

"Good morning," Deborah said when she entered the room, followed by her mother. "I hope we're not disturbing you."

Abraham shook his head. "Not at all. I'm glad you came by." As usual, his daughter mesmerized him. He felt his mother's spirit strongest when she was around. He got up from his chair. "Leah, you can take this chair and I'll sit on the bed," he said. He pointed to a chair in the far corner of the room. "Pull that one closer, Deborah, so we can all talk together."

"How are you feeling this morning?" Deborah asked after she'd pulled the chair over and sat in it.

"If the doctors are to be believed, I'm doing great. They're kicking me out of here later today or first thing in the morning."

"That's good," Deborah said. "I bet you're ready to get back to MEEG."

Abraham had been thinking about that, and he wasn't sure what he wanted to do. If he needed to bow out for a while to ensure that Isaac stayed at MEEG, he was willing to do it. "Is the place falling apart without me?"

Deborah shook her head. "Not at all," she said. "That's not what I meant."

Abraham chuckled. "I was teasing you," he said. "How are things with Running Brook? I'm sorry I wasn't there to help you settle in."

"That's all right. Alan stepped in and showed me the ropes. He's been a lot of help during my adjustment. So has Isaac."

Abraham smiled. "I like hearing that. How are you and Isaac getting along?"

"So far, so good," she said. "He seems fair. That's all I can ask."

"He's a good boy," he said.

Leah grunted, her first contribution to the conversation. "He's a man, Abraham, for goodness sake."

Abraham didn't know how to respond to her snappish remark. Apparently, neither did Deborah because she just stared at her mother.

"Sorry," Leah said. "It's early and I didn't have my coffee."

Deborah's widened eyes told him Leah was lying. It was unclear why.

"No problem," Abraham said, wanting to smooth over the situation. "Besides, you're right, but I still think of him as my boy. I guess I'll always think of him that way."

Leah gave him a too-sweet-to-be-real smile. "I know what you mean. That's how I think of Deborah and Michael. No matter how old they get they'll always be *my* kids."

Abraham felt her words as if they were a strong blow to his chin. In her sweetness, she had reminded him that he hadn't been there for Deborah and Michael in the way he had for Isaac. He glanced at Deborah. "I'm sorry if I put that badly."

"It's fine," she said, but her voice was tight and her smile was gone.

He was a smart man. How could he make such a dumb, insensitive comment? "How is Michael?" he asked.

Deborah leaned forward in her chair, all business. The loving daughter who'd entered his room a few minutes earlier was gone. "We wanted to talk to you about him."

"Is something wrong?"

Deborah nodded.

"Tell me," he said, concerned. "You know I'll do whatever I can to help. Michael's my son as much as Isaac is."

Deborah sat back a bit. "That's what you say," she said, "but your actions show differently."

Abraham's defenses shot up. He felt as though he was being attacked, and he didn't like it. He glanced at Leah for support, but her face was blank. He turned back to Deborah. "What do you mean?"

"I head up Running Brook Productions at MEEG, and Isaac is acting MEEG CEO and president. We both have seats on MEEG's board. What does Michael have?"

"He has a seat on the board," he reminded her. "I explained to you that Leah was holding it for him."

"I know what you said, Abraham, but it doesn't make a lot of sense and it's not fair to Michael. How do you think the setup makes him feel? Certainly not like a son."

He turned to Leah. "I thought we both agreed that Michael couldn't be trusted to make decisions at MEEG because he was too angry with me."

"We did," she said, "but Deborah has a point. You—*we*—made the decision thinking first about what was best for MEEG. We should have been thinking about what was best for Michael. As his mother, I know that's what I should have been thinking."

Abraham shook his head. "I don't know what to say. I don't know what you want me to do."

"All you have to do is honor your word. Deborah and I have decided that Michael is ready for his seat on the board. We've told Alan. Were you still incapacitated, it would be a done deal. But, as it is, we know you can override us. We're here to ask you not to do that."

Abraham stood and began to pace the room. "I don't know," he said, thinking of all the hard work and love he'd put into MEEG. He wasn't ready to open her up to someone who didn't have her best interests at heart. "I don't trust Michael. The things he's done, including fighting with Isaac at the board meeting, that's not the attitude I want at MEEG."

"You're being too hard on Michael," Deborah said. "You say you don't trust him. Have you considered that he doesn't trust you? You don't have the best track record where we're concerned."

Abraham heard the anger and pain in her voice, and his heart ached. This woman was his child, flesh of his flesh. So was Michael. "You're right, but this is business."

Deborah shook her head. "When you asked me to come to MEEG, you told me you were giving me my birthright. Well, where is Michael's birthright? He's still a little boy looking through the department store window at his father buying toys for another kid. How do you think that makes him feel?"

Abraham went back to bed and sat down. He felt tired, very tired. "You've given me a lot to think about."

"And—"

"That's enough, Deborah," Leah said, causing Abraham to shoot her a thank-you glance. She turned to Deborah. "Why don't you give me a few minutes alone with Abraham?"

"But—"

Leah shook her head. "It's fine. Go ahead."

Abraham watched the daughter he didn't really know leave his hospital room. "I didn't realize she was still so angry," he said to Leah.

"Then you're a bigger fool than I am."

He flashed angry eyes at her. It was one thing to take a verbal beating from his daughter. He was not about to take one from Leah. "Make your point," he said, kicking off his shoes and stretching out on the bed.

She came and stood over him. "I was too easy on you, Abraham. I should have made you do better by them when they were growing up, but I had my pride and I was determined to make a good life for them without you. We can both see how successful I was with that."

Abraham closed his eyes as the weight of guilt oppressed him. "What do you want from me?"

"I want you to do what Deborah asked. For once in your life, I want you to put Michael and Deborah first. For once in your life, I want you to do something to make them happy."

"What do you think I've been doing these last four months? I've been reaching out to both of them. I can't help that Michael won't give an inch."

Abraham noticed the tears in Leah's eyes and his guilt turned to hopelessness. "All these years," she said through her tears. "All these years I made excuses for you because I could always point to that little bit of money that you sent us. How do you think I felt when Saralyn told me that she was the one sending the money, not you? I can't believe you, Abraham. You had your wife write checks for your mistress and your illegitimate children? What kind of unfeeling monster are you?"

Abraham closed his eyes. He almost wished for the return of the days when he'd been in a coma. "I have no excuse, Leah," he told her. "That's the man I was then but it's not the man I am now."

She wiped at her tears and her clear eyes met his. "Show it," she said. "Show it by doing right by Michael."

Without waiting for him to respond, she turned and headed out of the room.

Chapter Forty-One

Isaac pushed back his desk chair and stared out the window. He rolled his shoulders forward to get out the kinks. He knew he should stand and stretch but he was too tired to move. His new work responsibilities coupled with his worry over his dad's health and the demise of his marriage were taking their toll. He was exhausted, physically and mentally. Now would be a great time for a cruise, a week or two away from everybody and everything.

Thoughts of the cruise brought memories of Rebecca and happier times in their marriage. Their first cruise had been her birthday gift to him. She'd packed his suitcase, put him on a plane to Miami, and only revealed their ultimate destination when the plane landed. He hadn't been that excited about the idea of a fourteen-day South American cruise but he was deeply touched by her gesture. The trip turned out to be one of the most relaxing vacations he'd taken.

Rebecca. He'd had such high hopes and so many plans for their life together. Those plans were now gone. His life had become destabilized all around. The father, whom he'd always looked up to as larger than life, had shown that he was instead merely another deeply flawed husband and father. And his new half brother and half sister were at the heart of all of it. Sometimes it was too much.

His phone rang as he opened his desk drawer and pulled out the bottle of pills his doctor had prescribed. "Yes, Val," he said to his father's secretary.

"A Mrs. Josette Thomas is here to see you."

Josette? He wondered what she wanted. "Send her in," he said, quickly popping a couple of pills and putting the bottle back in the desk drawer. Then he got up to meet Josette at the door.

"What brings you by?" he asked. "Is it Michael?"

She shook her head. "Nothing like that. I had lunch with Deborah and thought I'd drop in and thank you for letting me cry on your shoulder the other day at the hospital. I can't seem to control the tears these days."

He smiled. "That's all right. As long as I have a shoulder, you're welcome to cry on it."

"That's sweet of you to say," she said. "How's your father?"

"He's going home in a day or so."

She nodded. "That's good to hear. I guess that means he'll be coming back to MEEG soon. Are you going to stay on after he does?"

Isaac wiped his hands down his face. "I don't know," he said.

She studied him. "All this is tough on you, isn't it?" she asked.

Isaac realized that he wanted to talk about it. Josette had shared her concerns about the family drama with him, so he'd try to do the same with her. "I thought I was handling it," he said, "but every day there is something else."

"Does Abraham have other children out there?" she asked.

Isaac laughed a dry laugh. "I certainly hope not. It's just that I keep learning more about the two he has."

"Give yourself a break, Isaac," she said, patting his forearm. "It's okay to need some time to adjust to Michael and Deborah's presence in your life."

"Deborah I can handle," he said. "Michael is another matter. Have you forgotten that we got in a fistfight at the board meeting?"

"I haven't forgotten," she said. "Michael shouldn't have come. I tried to talk him out of it but he didn't listen. He's unreasonable when it comes to things about Abraham, and that includes you. He's my husband and we're about to have a child together, but you have to know that you shouldn't trust him."

Isaac appreciated her honesty. "I know," he said, thinking of Rebecca. "He takes pleasure in ruining the good things in my life. "

She looked away briefly. "I try not to think about it so much," she told him, rubbing her belly. "Focusing on the baby helps. You should focus on the good things in your life—like your relationship with Rebecca."

Isaac laughed. "If only I could."

"Are you and Rebecca having problems?" she asked.

He met her eyes. "We're getting a divorce."

"Oh, no," she said, covering her mouth. "I'm so sorry. Are you sure you two can't work it out?"

"Positive," he said.

"Look, Isaac, I know I'm the last person you want advice from, but let me offer some anyway. You and Rebecca can get past your problems, if that's what you want. Look at Michael and me. After I learned of his lies, I wanted to get as far away from him as possible." She rubbed her belly. "Now I'm determined to make our marriage work."

He looked at her stomach. "Maybe things would be different

if we had children or if Rebecca were pregnant. As it stands, it's easier to say it was a mistake and let it go."

Josette shook her head. "Don't give up so easily, Isaac. You love Rebecca, don't you?"

He eyed her. "Love doesn't seem to be in the cards for me." He paused and then asked the question that had been on his mind for some time. "What is it about Michael that draws women like you and Rebecca to him?" As soon as he asked the question, he wanted to take it back.

Josette's eyes widened and she sat up straighter. "Me and Rebecca? What are you talking about?"

Isaac began shaking his head. "Nothing," he said, truly sorry for his lapse. "Forget I said anything."

She shook her head. "You can't drop something like that and expect me to forget it. What did you mean by 'women like me and Rebecca'? How does Michael even know Rebecca?"

Isaac walked to the window. "Let it go, Josette," he said. "Just let it go."

She stood and walked over to him. She grabbed his arm and turned him toward her. "You have to tell me. Is there something going on between Michael and Rebecca?"

Isaac looked into her sad eyes, which were now damp with unshed tears. He hated himself for the pain he was about to cause her. "I don't know if anything is going on now," he said, "but they were once involved."

"I don't believe it," Josette said, backing away from him. "I don't believe it. You're lying to hurt Michael and me. You want to hurt him the way he hurt you."

Isaac reached out and pulled her into his arms.

"Tell me it's not true," she said, her face pressed tight against his shoulder. "Tell me it's not true."

Unable to hurt her more than he had, he told her what she wanted to hear and prayed she believed him.

He caught a movement out of the corner of his eye and turned his head to see Rebecca standing in the doorway. Her wide-eyed expression told him what she thought she was seeing. Saying nothing to her, he turned back to Josette and continued to murmur words of comfort to her. Though he didn't hear the door close, he could feel when Rebecca left the room.

Chapter Forty-Two

Seated on one of the marble benches in front of the MEEG Building, Saralyn checked the white gold watch Abraham had given her on their twenty-fifth anniversary. She wasn't surprised that Michael was late. In fact, she'd expected him to pull such an amateurish power play. The kid wasn't even in her league. So she'd let him think he had the upper hand. Poor boy! She pulled her Kindle out of her purse and resumed reading the latest Kimberla Lawson Roby novel.

"Well, I hope you've been waiting a long time," said Michael Thomas, his tone arrogant.

She looked up from her Kindle. "It was worth the wait."

Michael sat down on the bench next to her. He eyed her. "I'll be honest," he said. "Your call surprised me."

She clicked off her Kindle and put it back in her purse. "You had to know that sooner or later we'd have a showdown."

He grinned Abraham's grin and her stomach roiled.

"Silly me," he said, each word steeped in sarcasm. "Here I was thinking we'd be part of a happy family, sharing Sunday dinners and spending the holidays together."

"You've got a wicked sense of humor," she said. "And a vivid imagination. We'll never share a family dinner."

He pressed his hand to his chest. "Now you've hurt my feelings. I so hoped that I'd lucked out in the stepmother department. It seems I've drawn the Wicked Witch of the East instead. Too bad."

Saralyn bit back a scathing retort. She refused to give him the satisfaction of knowing his words bothered her. "You've missed your calling, Michael," she said. "You could give Steve Hardy a run for his money. Have you ever considered stand-up?"

Michael rubbed his chin as though he were considering her career suggestion. "You know, you may be onto something. I don't think I'd like stand-up but I think I'd do well with a radio show like Steve's." He framed his hands around an imaginary marquee. "I can see it now, 'The Michael Thomas Morning Show.'" He turned to her. "Think I could talk the old man into buying a radio station for me?"

"When hell freezes over," she said, before she caught herself.

Michael laughed, taking satisfaction in her slip. "I wouldn't be too sure. He bought my sister, his only daughter, a production company. As his son, I deserve something equivalent if not more."

Over my dead body. "Personally," she said, "a man like you shouldn't need anyone to give him a business. A real man would want to build his own business."

Michael raised a brow. "You mean the way your son, the most manly Isaac, built his 'own' business?"

He's such an ungrateful brat. "Enough of these insults. Why don't we get down to business?"

Michael shrugged and then leaned back, stretching out this legs, the portrait of aloofness. "You called me," he reminded her.

"It's your meeting, so handle your business. What do you want?"

She itched to wipe that smirk off his face. "I want to know what you want from me and my family."

"Simple," he said. "I want what's mine as Abraham's son."

Now she laughed. "Come again?" she said. "Abraham has one son, one heir. That won't change. I can guarantee it." Then she added, "I'm a reasonable woman. I'm willing to provide you and your sister a lump sum payment of one million dollars."

His eyes widened with interest. "Each?"

She nodded, feeling pretty confident the figure would sway the boy, since she knew it was more money than he'd ever seen. That company of his was doing well—she'd checked—but not that well. He was no Jay-Z. "Take the money," she said. "It's more than you deserve."

Still reclining, Michael folded his hands across his stomach. "How much is MEEG worth?" he asked.

Saralyn sensed he knew the answer to that question. "MEEG is of no concern to you. It belongs to me as much as it does to Abraham."

Michael laughed. "You must think I'm stupid, lady. I probably know more about MEEG's finances than you do, and I certainly know what it's worth. If I didn't, your two million dollar offer would give me a good idea. Why should I take pennies from you when I'm entitled to more from the old man?"

Saralyn crossed her legs. She'd expected this response. "The old saying, 'A bird in the hand is worth two in the bush,' applies here. I can have your check tomorrow. Take it. I promise you that I'll tie you up in court for years if Abraham tries to give you any part of my son's inheritance."

"Little Isaac has his mom fighting his battles. How manly of him."

Saralyn refused to be baited. "I'm waiting for your answer."

Michael eyed her. "Does the old man know you're here?"

"Does it matter? The check will clear either way."

She could tell he was thinking about it. She knew money would do it. Leah might have ridden in on a high horse saddled with her recently acquired morals, but not this wannabe. He was probably already spending the money. He'd probably plow through it in less than a year.

"What do you want in exchange for this payoff?" he asked.

"I want you, your sister, and your mother out of MEEG and out of our lives."

He eyed her. "My sister is not going to want to give up her production company."

"She'll have a million dollars. She can start her own company. But that's your problem, not mine. I give you the money. You and your family vanish. It's simple."

"You'd trust me?"

Now she laughed. "Please. I'm not a fool. When you get the check, you'll sign a contract releasing all rights to Abraham's estate. And you'll have to get your sister to sign as well."

"You've thought of everything."

"I'm not here playing games, Michael. My family was doing fine before all of this exploded. I want things back the way they were."

"Abraham's not going to like it."

"He'll get over it. I'll be sure to let him know about the check, and then I'll convince him that all any of you ever wanted from him was money. He'll get over you."

"You can't be sure."

"Look," Saralyn said, growing tired of the conversation. "Abraham is really no concern of yours. Do you want the check or not?"

Michael met her eyes. "Make it two million each and you've got a deal."

Chapter Forty-Three

Rebecca stepped off the elevator wiping tears from her face. She'd thought her crying would end during the drive from MEEG to the hospital, but that had not happened. She couldn't get the scene at MEEG out of her mind. Seeing Josette cuddled in her husband's arms had been painful, but the dismissive glance he gave her when he looked up and saw her at his door had been devastating. Though she still loved him, she didn't know how much she could take. She couldn't be the only one fighting for their marriage. Knowing she would get no sympathy from Saralyn, she'd decided to seek out her father-in-law's advice. Abraham was her last chance.

His door was open and he was sitting in his recliner, a newspaper in his lap, his eyes closed. He needed his rest, she knew, so she decided to sit in the other chair and wait quietly for him to awaken. As she waited, she thought it ironic that she'd come seeking help from the man at the root of her problems. If Abraham hadn't made his grand revelation, she wouldn't have had to confess to Isaac and her marriage would still be in tact.

Stop fooling yourself, a quiet voice said. *The truth was always going to come out, and when it did, it was going to do damage.* Accepting the rightness of those words, she closed her eyes and tried to stop thinking.

"When did you get here?" Abraham said.

She opened her eyes and found him, alert, looking at her. "A few minutes ago," she said. "I hope I didn't wake you."

He shook his head. "I was dozing. It seems I do a lot of that these days. I must be getting old."

Rebecca smiled. "I doubt it. It's hard to believe that only a few days ago you were in a coma. You've recovered in no time at all."

"I guess I come from good stock," he said. "And I know I have an angel watching over me."

Rebecca wished she had an angel. "Must be nice," she said.

"You sound like you could use an angel. What's wrong?"

Rebecca looked away. She felt a bit foolish. She was a grown woman. What was she doing taking her problems with her husband to her father-in-law? He'd probably take Isaac's side anyway.

"I know something's wrong," Abraham said when she didn't answer his question. "Something happen with you and Isaac?"

She turned back to him, surprised that he'd guessed. "Has Isaac said anything to you?"

He shook his head. "It was a guess. I thought you two were acting oddly when you visited the day I came out from the coma."

She couldn't help but smile. "I thought you said you were getting old."

He winked at her and grinned a grin she knew had stolen many hearts. Abraham Martin could have any woman he wanted, which is what landed him—and them—in this pickle they were in. "I'm getting older," he said, "but I'm also getting better."

She relaxed a little. Maybe Abraham would be her advocate. "You're definitely getting better."

He tossed his newspaper to the bed and folded his arms across his stomach. "Tell me," he said. "I want to help."

She looked down at her hand, twisted the three-carat diamond solitaire Isaac had placed on her finger the day he'd asked her to marry him, the happiest day of her life. She looked back up at Abraham. "It's a long story."

He pushed the recline button on the side of his chair, lifting his legs. "They're not exactly beating down my door with important meetings, so I have time."

The lightness with which he approached their conversation gave her the confidence she needed to tell him. She started with her past relationship with Michael and ended with the wedding and anniversary gifts.

Abraham lowered his feet to the floor and leaned toward her. "Is Isaac angry because you didn't tell him about the relationship with Michael or because you didn't tell him about the gifts?"

"Both." She couldn't tell him that Isaac also thought she had married him for his money. She needed his support, and that information might cause her to lose it.

"It figures," Abraham said. "I really caused a mess, didn't I?"

Rebecca felt badly for her father-in-law, but she nodded.

"What am I going to do about Michael, Rebecca?" Abraham asked her. "He's such an angry man, angry and vindictive."

She wasn't concerned about Michael right now, not when her marriage was sliding off a cliff. "All I know is that he wants what Isaac has. He wants everything you've given Isaac to be his, including MEEG."

Abraham pounded his fist on the arm on his recliner. "That—" He stopped himself, sighed deeply, and said, "I'm sorry, Rebecca."

She pressed her hand on his. "It's all right. It's an emotional time for all of us. Isaac wants a divorce."

Abraham squeezed her hand. "Give him time," he said. "He's hurt. But deep inside he knows you love him and he loves you."

"I do love him," she cried. "More than anything."

"I know you do," Abraham said, "or I wouldn't be sitting here talking to you."

She was relieved to have Abraham's support but was curious about it. "I don't want to look a gift horse in the mouth, but why do you believe me? Saralyn certainly doesn't."

Abraham gave a dry laugh. "Saralyn wouldn't. Despite her prim exterior, she is a hard woman. Everything is black and white to her. There's wrong and then there's right. That clarity makes her very reliable, but it also makes her very intolerant."

"Now you tell me."

He squeezed her hand again. "Isaac is a lot like her."

She held her breath and asked the question she wasn't sure she wanted to ask. "Do you think he'll forgive me?"

"I want him to," Abraham said. "Because I need his forgiveness, too."

His words made Rebecca feel selfish. Abraham had his own problems with Isaac. He couldn't be an advocate for her when Isaac no longer listened to him. She'd have to deal with her marital problems on her own.

Chapter Forty-Four

W hoa," Michael said to Rebecca, who had practically run him over in her attempt to get on the elevator. "You'd better watch where you're going." He pulled her to the side as the doors closed and the elevator began its descent.

"Let me go, Michael," she said, trying to pull away from him.

"What's wrong?" he asked.

She jerked her arm away. "It's all your fault," she said.

"What have I done?" he asked.

She shot him a hot glare.

"Oh," he said, as the elevators doors opened and he followed her out. "Problems in paradise, I guess."

"Don't talk to me," she said, striding toward the exit.

He followed her out and toward the parking lot. "What happened?" he asked her.

She stopped and turned to him. "Isaac asked me for a divorce. Are you satisfied?"

Without waiting for an answer, she turned and kept walking to her car. He caught up with her. "I won't lie and say it's not good to see old Isaac's marriage go up in flames but—"

She stopped. "No buts, Michael. Don't you get it? You hurt Isaac but you hurt me, too. Don't you even care about the collateral damage in your vendetta against Isaac and Abraham? What have I done to you?"

"Look," he said, "I haven't said anything to your husband so you can't blame me."

"I do blame you," she said. "You threatened me. You've been threatening me since the day you sent that wedding gift. I just didn't know it was a threat."

"You're hurting now," he said, "but one day you'll thank me for getting you away from that pansy boy. You need a real man."

Her palm connected with his jaw before he could avert it.

He rubbed his jaw. "Feel better?" he asked, smiling.

"No, I don't feel better, and I won't feel better until you hurt the way you hurt others. That day is coming, Michael. Mark my words."

He grabbed her wrist. "Is that a threat?"

She grinned a wry grin. "More like a premonition."

He dropped her wrist and laughed. "Now I'm really scared. A premonition. You can do better than that."

She studied him a long moment. "Word to the wise. Instead of trying to ruin other people's relationships, you ought to be focusing on your own."

"What do you mean by that?"

"Josette is no fool, Michael. She's not going to put up with you forever. She's an attractive woman, attractive enough to catch some man's eye."

"So you want me to worry about my pregnant wife being unfaithful. I think I can handle it."

Rebecca laughed. "She won't be pregnant forever."

"Let me worry about Josette."

"You need to do more than worry," she said.

"If you've got something to say, Rebecca, say it. I don't have time for riddles."

"What goes around comes around, Michael. You got satisfaction from knowing you slept with Isaac's wife. Maybe he'll return the favor."

Michael laughed, but uneasily. "Don't tell me you're jealous of my pregnant wife. You're pitiful, Rebecca. There is nothing between Isaac and Josette and there never will be."

Rebecca tilted her head to the side. "I wouldn't be too sure," she said. "People are drawn to each other for a lot of different reasons. Isaac's hurt because of my relationship with you. If Josette knew, she'd be hurt, too. They could end up consoling each other."

Michael ran a finger down her cheek and she stepped away. "Isaac won't touch Josette because I've slept with her. He stopped touching you after he found out about us, didn't he?"

Rebecca shook her head. "You're a foul man, Michael. You deserve whatever Isaac and Josette do to you. If I didn't love Isaac, it would be worth it to see you get your payback. Because I do love him, I advise you to keep your wife happy so she doesn't have to come crying on my husband's broad shoulders. There's not room for both of us there."

"Don't worry about my wife," he said.

"Keep her away from my husband and we won't have a problem."

Michael watched her get in her car and drive away. He'd have a long talk with Josette tonight. No way was Isaac going to poach on his turf. He turned back toward the hospital. But first he had to go mess with the old man's mind. Saralyn had given him the ammunition he needed to knock the old dude down a peg or two.

Chapter Forty-Five

Abraham stopped abruptly when he opened the bathroom door and saw his youngest son sitting in his recliner, the remote in his hand, flicking the channels of the television.

"It's a shame," Michael said, his eyes on the television. "All these stations and you still can't find anything decent to watch." He turned to Abraham. "I'd think a mogul like you would have a DVD player up in here. Don't tell me they're making Abraham Martin live like the regular folk. What is this world coming to when a man's money can't buy him some perks?"

Abraham finally closed the bathroom door. Michael's monologue had given him the time he needed to gather his wits and calm his heartbeat. How odd it was to look into his own face on this stranger, for that's what Michael was to him. A younger version of himself, yes, but still a stranger. "Even I have to play by the rules," he said, taking the chair next to the recliner.

Michael scoffed. "Right." He flicked the channels until he found CNN and then tossed the remote on the bed.

"Did you come here to watch television?" Abraham asked.

Michael turned to him. "You've never done anything else for me. You ought to be willing to let me watch your television." He stood. "But if you aren't, I can go home and watch my own television."

Abraham reached for his arm. "Don't go," he said. "But don't play games either. We both know you didn't come here to watch television. That's not your style."

Michael shook off Abraham's hand. "What do you know about my style?"

Abraham settled back in his chair. "I know you came to see me when I was in the coma."

"I should have known you were awake. What were you doing— faking it?"

Abraham shook his head. "I was out of it, but bits and pieces of conversations have come back to me. I remember that you were here and that you were angry. I remember being happy you were here."

Michael sat back down. "Then you definitely didn't hear what I said. My words were not spoken to make you happy."

"I'm awake now," Abraham said. "Tell me what you said to my face, like a man."

Michael laughed. "It's takes a man to challenge another man," he said. "You can't challenge me because I don't consider you a man."

Abraham took his son's words as a blow to his chest. "I'm a man, Michael," he said. "Not a perfect one, but a man nonetheless."

"If you say so," Michael said. "My mama raised me to believe a man handles his responsibilities, rather than runs away from them. I don't know how your mama raised you."

The words from his mama's letter came back to Abraham. "I'll agree that my life doesn't reflect what she tried to teach me. She was a good woman, Michael. I'm sorry you never met her."

Michael shot him a glance. "Who says I never met her?"

Abraham raised a brow. "She never mentioned it."

"I didn't exactly introduce myself as her grandson," he said.

"I wish you had," Abraham said, knowing his ma would have welcomed him. "She would have been a better grandmother than I was a father."

"We'll never know that for sure, now will we?"

Abraham shook his head. "I can't change the past, Michael, but if you'll give me a chance, I'll do better in the future. I can promise you that."

"And your promises are supposed to mean something to me?" He laughed. "Give me a break."

"I can't really blame you for not believing me," Abraham said. "I probably wouldn't believe me either if I were in your shoes. So, given that, how do we move forward from here?"

"I guess that's where the money comes in."

Abraham's heart fell. "Money?"'

The corners of Michael's lips turned up in a slight smile, and Abraham knew they'd come to the reason for the boy's visit. "We're both businessmen," Michael said. "Sometimes the easiest way to handle a problem is to throw money at it. I think this situation fits that category, and it seems your wife thinks so, too."

"What's Saralyn got to do with this?"

Michael's smile widened. "She made me an offer I couldn't refuse."

"What?" he asked, his eyes wide. "How much?"

Michael told him the number. Abraham couldn't believe it, couldn't believe that Saralyn had gone behind his back and done such an outrageous thing.

"Personally, I think she had the right idea," Michael was saying, "but I think her number was a bit on the low side. It should be worth more than that to get me and Deborah out of your lives for good."

"I don't want you and Deborah out of my life," Abraham said, keeping his voice in check. "I want to get to know you. Like it or not, I'm your father."

Michael's smile faded. "Look, old man," he said. "Even if you did have good intentions toward me and Deborah, you can see that this plan of yours is not going to work. You'll end up losing the son and wife you wanted, trying to get over the guilt of throwing away the son and daughter you didn't want. I'm trying to give you an easy out here. Deborah and I have lived without a father this long. I'm sure we can make it the rest of the way without you."

"What if I can't make it without you?" Abraham asked.

Michael smiled again. "You see, that's your problem. Everything is about you. In case you haven't noticed, there are a few other lives involved in this story."

"I'm sorry for the past," Abraham said, wondering how many times he'd have to say those five words before they were believed. "And I won't give up on the future."

"Even if it means losing your wife and your son? Because that's what will happen. Your wife practically told me straight out that she'd divorce you if you continued on this path."

Abraham knew he needed to have a long conversation with Saralyn and Isaac. He had to do a better job of making them understand what he was doing and why. "I'm not going to pay you to get out of my life. I'll never do that."

Michael's eyes grew hot and he stood. "You don't care about me," he said, looking down on him. "You don't even know me. And you've made it very clear that you don't trust me."

Abraham knew Michael was talking about the MEEG board. "How can I trust you, given everything you've done?" he asked.

"How can I trust you given everything *you've* done?"

Abraham had no ready response. "What do you want from me, Michael?"

"I don't want anything from you," he said. "Not your money, nothing."

"Then why did you come here today?"

"I wanted to tell you to your face what you and your wife could do with your money. I won't be bought like my sister and I won't be bought off like some lowlife blackmailer." He stalked to the door, opened it, and then turned back and added, "You're going to have to deal with me, old man, and you'd better be ready for me."

Abraham watched as the door closed after Michael. He raised his eyes heavenward. "What am I supposed to do now, Ma?"

Chapter Forty-Six

Michael didn't like being summoned to Alan's office like he was some wayward kid. "Look, Alan," he said, "I went to see the old man. I didn't commit murder."

Alan stopped his pacing. "You're too emotional, Michael. It's causing you to make stupid mistakes. Going to see Abraham in the hospital was as childish and petty as attending that board meeting. What was the point? What did either gain us?"

They may not have gained *us* anything, but I certainly felt good sticking it to them, Michael thought. Sometimes the anger inside him grew so hot that he felt he'd blow up if he didn't let some of it out. "I hear you," he said. "It won't happen again." *Unless there's an opportunity that's too good to pass up.*

Alan stared at him. "I hope you're telling me the truth. Abraham is no fool. If you keep getting in the family's face, you're going to undo everything your mother and sister are trying to do for you. Don't you see? Everything is lining up for us. All we need is for your wife to have that baby, and then we're in the driver's seat."

"Knock, knock."

The sound of Deborah's voice startled Michael, and he turned around in time to see her enter.

"I knew you were—" she said to Alan, but stopped when she saw Michael. "What are you doing here?" she asked. She looked to Alan. "Did Abraham overrule us on the board seat for Michael?"

Alan shook his head. "He hasn't said a thing to me about it."

"You worry too much, sis," Michael said. "Alan was preparing me for what to expect at the next meeting."

She folded her arms and tapped her feet. "Well, I hope he told you that fighting was out."

Alan chuckled, but Michael saw nothing funny. "That was a onetime thing."

"I hope so," she said. "I've never been more embarrassed in my life. Saralyn already thinks we're a bunch of lower life-forms who aren't good enough to be in the same room with her, and you only gave her data to support her prejudice."

Michael shook his head. "If you're thinking we're going to win over Saralyn, you'd better think again. Earlier today she offered me, and you, a boatload of cash to get out of MEEG and out of their lives. It was a good offer, too."

Deborah pressed her hand against her chest. "I can't believe she'd try to buy us off. Her opinion of us is lower than I thought."

Michael didn't like upsetting his sister, but sometimes her rose-colored glasses blinded her to the reality of their present situation. He felt it was his job to give her some clarity. He didn't want her to be hurt. "You said it yourself. She doesn't think we're good enough to breathe the air she breathes, much less be a part of their precious MEEG. If she had her way, both of us would be kicked out of here in a heartbeat."

She turned to Alan. "Is he right about Saralyn? Is she going to fight us the entire way?"

"I'm afraid so," he said. "I think there's little to no chance Saralyn will ever accept you here at MEEG or as Abraham's daughter. I don't think it's in her to do so." He softened his voice and added, "It's the past. She can't deal with it, and you being here forces her to face it."

Michael saw the sadness settle over his sister, even as he wondered about the caring he'd detected in Alan's tone. "We've lived our whole lives without her acceptance," he said to his sister, deciding to deal with Alan later. "We don't need it now."

"Things are different, though," she said. "She's in our lives and we're in hers, whether we want to be or not."

"It doesn't have to be that way," Michael said. "We can keep our interactions to a minimum."

"I suppose you're right," she said, but he could tell her disappointment ran deep. She obviously wanted more than minimal interaction with the Martins.

"I'm sorry, sis," he said. "I know you wanted something more, but I don't see it happening. There are no Thomas-Martin family dinners or holiday celebrations in our future. Not as long as Saralyn Martin has any say."

When Deborah didn't respond, Alan got up and walked to her. "Why don't you sit down," he said, guiding her to a chair near the desk, "and tell me why you came to visit me."

He sat on the edge of his desk in front of her.

"What?" she asked, blinking up at him.

"You came by the office," he explained with a slight smile. "I assume you needed something."

"Oh," she said, shaking her head as if to clear away the cobwebs. "Nothing important. I was leaving, saw you were still here, and wondered if you wanted to get a bite to eat." She turned to Michael. "Why don't you call Josette and the two of you join us?

Tonight is Mama's staff meeting at school and I didn't want to eat alone." Turning back to Alan, she added, "A relaxing dinner with good conversation and even better food would be a lovely way to end the day, wouldn't it??"

Michael cut Alan a quick glance, silently reminding the older man of his warning to stay away from his sister.

"Well," Alan said, pulling off his glasses and cleaning them with the wipes he kept in his desk drawer, "I have a bit more work to do yet."

"You need a break," Deborah said. "I bet you worked through lunch, didn't you?"

"How'd you guess?"

Deborah's answering smile took Michael off guard. Could his sister really be falling for this guy? If she was, Alan needed to put an end to such nonsense.

"Are you psychic?" Alan asked, chuckling.

Not exactly what a man does when he's trying to rebuff a woman's advances, Michael thought.

She shook her head. "Not really. I called earlier and your secretary told me your morning meeting ran through lunch and you had a one o'clock."

"So you've been checking up on me?"

She shrugged. "I was going to ask you to lunch. We haven't talked much in the last few days and I've missed our conversations."

"You've missed asking me questions about Abraham, you mean."

She shook her head. "Honestly, I have a few more questions about Alan Weems. What can I say? I enjoy your company. I thought it was mutual."

"Hey, you two," Michael interrupted. "When did I become invisible?"

Deborah chuckled. "Sorry about that, Michael," she said. "I was only teasing Alan. He's a good sport." She winked at Alan. "Aren't you?"

"You're a very charming *young* lady," he said, emphasizing the *young.*

"Oh," she said, "so that's why you've been ignoring me. You're worried about our ages." She glanced at Michael. "Do me a favor and tell Alan that he's the type of man I usually date."

Michael stood. "Look, this is getting a bit too deep for me." He kissed his sister on the forehead. "Thanks for the dinner invite, sis," he said, "but Josette and I have to pass." He turned to Alan and stuck out his hand. "Thanks for everything. I'll keep in mind what you've told me, and you do the same."

Alan shook his hand. "I look forward to seeing you at the next board meeting."

Michael nodded and then leaned over and whispered to his sister, "Behave yourself. You've got to stop with these old guys."

Deborah chuckled as she watched her brother leave the room.

"What's so funny?" Alan asked.

"You're not the only one worried about our ages."

Alan shook his head. "To be precise, I'm worried about the differences in our ages."

"I'm not," she said, serious now. "Age is a state of mind."

"Spoken like a twenty-something," he said. "You know I'm old enough to be your father?"

"So you've told me," she said. "But it doesn't matter to me. I've always dated older men."

He raised a brow. "I wonder why that is."

She laughed, knowing he was insinuating she had father issues. "That's probably part of it," she said, in response to what she assumed he was thinking. "But also, I find older men more interesting than young ones. Guys my age are still figuring out who they are and what's important to them. I like men who already have those answers."

"Do you have them for yourself?" When she nodded, he asked, "So what's important to you, Deborah Thomas?"

She glanced around his office, inclined her head toward the framed picture of a young woman on her desk. "Family. Work. No different than you. Who is she?"

He ran his hand caressingly around the frame. "My sister."

"Are you close?" she asked. "I'd love to meet her. I bet she could give me all the dirt on you, and enjoy doing it, too."

He chuckled. "Yes, she would have. She was killed in an automobile accident ten years ago. She gave me the photograph as a gift, our last Christmas together."

"I'm sorry," she said.

He rubbed his hand down the frame. "So am I. She was a wonderful girl, so full of life. You remind me of her."

"I'm honored."

He smiled. "That's what I mean. Instead of being insulted that you remind me of my sister, you're honored."

"Insulted? Never. I hope the reminder is not a painful one. Is it? Is that why you're reluctant to have dinner with me?"

He shook his head. "Just the opposite. You remind me that she was full of life and lived her life on her own terms, and to the fullest."

"Sounds like she may have given her older brother a headache or two."

He laughed. "Or three hundred. She could be infuriating, but she had a way of making me see things her way. I often found myself supporting her on things I knew were not the best for her."

"She sounds like Michael, more than she sounds like me."

He studied her. "No, she's more like you. Alisha made mistakes, but she made them for good reasons. There wasn't a malicious bone in her body."

"Ouch!" she said.

"Oh," he said, "I'm sorry. I didn't mean to speak ill of your brother."

She waved off his concern. "I can't argue with the truth. Michael has often used his charm for evil. I hate to say it, but it's true. But let's not talk about Michael or MEEG. Let's enjoy a nice dinner and forget all the Thomas-Martin-MEEG drama."

He lifted a brow. "Do you think that's possible?"

She shrugged. "It's certainly worth a try."

Chapter Forty-Seven

Leah and Melvin sat huddled in the back of the darkened theater, giggling like teenagers as they waited for the movie to start. They'd arrived early, as they usually did so they would have some time to talk. "You're eating all of the popcorn," Melvin said, taking the box from her and handing her a box of Choco-Bits. "Here, take these."

Leah took the Choco-Bits. "I'm going to get fat," she said.

He kissed her on her nose. "There'll be more of you to love."

"That's what you say now," she muttered, putting one of the Choco-Bits in her hand.

"Women," he said, taking back the box of chocolate. "Give me your hand." When she opened her palm, he turned the box and poured her a handful of Choco-Bits. "Now you have some candy."

Leah looked down at the contents of her hand and then up at him. "What's this?"

"What does it look like?" he said with a warm, loving smile.

Leah raked the Choco-Bits back in the box until she was left with a piece of gold that was certainly not chocolate. "It looks like a ring," she said, staring at the diamond still in her palm.

"It is a ring," he said, taking the ring from her palm. "I envisioned giving it to you over some romantic dinner and shouting my joy for all the other diners to hear, but doing it here seemed more appropriate. We had our first date here and some of our most important conversations have occurred here. So what better place to ask you to marry me?"

Her eyes teared up. "You can't be serious."

"I'm very serious," he said. "I love you, Leah. You have to know that."

She sat staring at the ring. She couldn't believe it. This wonderful, kind, and loving man loved her and wanted to marry her. "I don't know what to say."

"Say yes."

She thought of all the reasons why she couldn't marry him. "My children—" she began.

"I'm not asking them," he said. "I'm asking you. Besides, they're adults. Michael's already out of the house, and Deborah'll probably be glad to see you move out so she'll have some privacy."

"Move out?"

He nodded. "You'll move in with me after we're married," he said. "I've already decided."

She smiled. "And I have no say?"

He shook his head. "Not on this one. I'm old-fashioned that way. The wife moves in with the husband, not vice versa."

Leah grew warm inside. She loved this man more than she'd ever imagined loving a man after Abraham. But the timing couldn't have been worse and he had to know it.

"I'm waiting," he said.

She cupped his cheek in her palm. "I do love you, Melvin, but marriage, I don't know."

His smile vanished. "Okay, let's hear your reasons, though I'm sure I know what they are."

"Don't be this way," she said. "It's the timing. So much is going on now with my kids and Abraham. I couldn't think of a worse time to spring this news on them."

Melvin ran a finger down her cheek. "You can't keep putting your happiness on hold," he said. "You can't keep putting me on hold. Besides, I don't think there will be a right time in your eyes. We have to take the best time, this time. A lot of people never get the second chance we've been given. We should be putting our relationship out there as an example of how God can bless a couple. Instead, we're hiding it and sneaking around as though we're doing something wrong. It's not right, Leah. You have to know that."

Leah felt a shiver go up her spine. Was this her day of reckoning? "You have to understand—"

"I've been understanding for more than a year," he said. "For more than a year you've set the parameters for this relationship and I've allowed it because I've known from the first day I met you that you were the one for me. I know you've figured it out, too. Now I'm asking you to trust it, trust me, trust yourself, trust God."

"I don't know," she said. "I don't know."

"You love me, don't you?" he asked.

She nodded. "You know I do."

"Then I want you to act like it. Take a leap of faith, Leah."

"But your church—"

He pressed a finger against her lips. "That's why they call it faith. It's okay not to know exactly how everything is going to turn out. Just know that whatever happens, we'll face it together. Do you love me enough to do that?"

Chapter Forty-Eight

Josette couldn't get Isaac's words out of her mind. Had Rebecca and Michael slept together? Were they still sleeping together? Her arms folded across her stomach, she paced the bedroom she shared with her husband, wondering if she'd ever share the bed with him again. How much was she expected to take from Michael? Their whole life together was based on lies, lies that seemed to grow each day. What had she done to be such a victim?

Nothing, she told herself. All she'd done was fall in love. "What have I done to you, little one?" she said, speaking to the baby inside her. "And what should I do now? You need your daddy, but I don't know if I can live in a marriage of lies and deceit. What kind of life would that be for you?"

Josette went to the bathroom and sat on the stool in front of her vanity. Though she was sad, her eyes were clear and dry. She didn't have the tears or the energy to expend on Michael and what he might do. Her only concern now was for her baby.

The beep of the exterior door alarm sensor told her that Michael had arrived home. There was a time when she would have rushed down the stairs to meet him. Those days were long gone. He called out to her but she didn't answer. She wasn't ready to speak to him yet, as she was unsure what she would say.

Hearing his footsteps coming up the stairs, she began cleansing her face to give herself something to do.

"Didn't you hear me calling you?" he asked when he entered the bedroom. "Why didn't you answer?"

In the mirror, she watched him walk toward her, yellow roses in hand. Now that was a surprise. When he reached her, he pressed his chin on the top of her head and smiled into the mirror at her. "How's Mommy doing today?"

Josette felt her heart soften toward him. He was such a charmer! "Mommy's had a long day," she said, her voice not as flat as she would have liked.

He handed her the roses. "I thought these might cheer you up."

She took them from him and smelled them. "Thank you, Michael," she said.

He spun her around on her stool. "Nothing but the best for my lady," he said, before kissing her.

Josette's heart began to harden as he kissed her. She knew that kiss. It was meant to dominate and to control, to show her how much she needed him. She forced herself not to respond. His reaction was to deepen the kiss. It didn't work.

He lifted his lips from hers. "What's wrong?" he asked.

Instead of answering, she got up. "I need to put the flowers in water," she said, stepping around him. She headed downstairs with Michael behind her.

"Have a bad day?" Michael asked as she put water in a vase.

She placed the flowers in the vase. "I've had better."

"Didn't you have lunch with Deborah?"

She nodded.

"Did she say something to upset you?"

She turned to him. "Deborah? No. We had an enjoyable lunch. Afterward, I stopped by to see Isaac."

He leaned back against the counter. "Ahh, I think I understand."

"Understand what?"

"You see Isaac and all I get is attitude. Don't let that man come between us, Josette. You can't trust him."

Josette couldn't help herself. She laughed. "You're kidding me, right? I can't trust Isaac? It's you I can't trust."

"What's he been telling you?"

She looked up at him. "What are you so worried about, Michael? It's been a long time since you've been this interested in my moods or my comings and goings."

"Look, I don't like the idea of another man hanging around my wife."

Josette was beginning to feel like she was in the middle of a bad dream. "Isaac is not another man, Michael. He's your half brother. Why can't you accept him as such?"

"He's no brother to me."

Josette studied him. "Maybe you're right. You and Isaac Martin are as different as night and day. I've had more serious conversations with him lately than I've had with you."

Michael reached out and pulled her to him. "I won't tolerate your even thinking about starting something with Isaac."

She pushed out of his embrace. "And I won't tolerate you sleeping with Isaac's wife!"

"You're talking crazy."

When he would have turned away, she reached for his arm. "Are you sleeping with Rebecca?" she asked.

"I don't believe you're asking me this," he said. "I'm insulted."

"You haven't answered the question. Are you sleeping with her?"

"No, I'm not sleeping with her," he said. "Are you happy now?"

She studied him. "I'm not sure I believe you."

"I swear to you that I'm not sleeping with Rebecca."

"Have you ever slept with her?"

"Let's not go down that road, Josette. I never claimed to be a virgin before we married, and at the risk of being rude, neither did you."

He was right, but he still hadn't answered the question she needed answered. "Let's cut to the chase here, Michael. Have you slept with Rebecca since we've been married?"

He brushed a finger down her cheek. "I haven't cheated on you with Rebecca. I would never cheat on you."

Josette allowed Michael to pull her into his arms. Her dry eyes were now wet. She didn't believe a word he had said.

Chapter Forty-Nine

It's good to have you home, Mr. Martin," Mrs. Hall gushed when Isaac and his father entered the mansion in Forest Park. "I knew you'd come here instead of to that condo downtown. A man needs to recuperate where he can get some fresh air and enjoy nature."

Abraham chuckled. "I agree with you, Anna," he said. "This place will always be home to me." He inclined his head toward Isaac. "It's the boy here and his mother who love living downtown."

"Mr. Isaac loved it out here when he was a boy," she said, smiling at Isaac as if he were still a little boy. "He'd play hide-and-seek in that big old garden, and the nanny and Mrs. Martin would have the hardest time finding him. Do you remember that, Mr. Isaac?"

Isaac smiled. "Of course I do," he said. "But what I remember most are your meals. I thought you were the best cook in the world, and still do."

She blushed. "Well, that's kind of you to say, Mr. Isaac."

His father snorted. "What I remember is that he wouldn't eat the food they served in the cafeteria of that fancy elementary school he attended. We had to deliver him a lunch every day until he got tired of the other kids making fun of him."

Mrs. Hall laughed.

"I wasn't that bad," Isaac said.

Abraham raised a brow. "You have a selective memory. You were spoiled rotten. Blame your mother."

Mrs. Hall shook her head. "Mr. Isaac is not the only one with selective memory, Mr. Martin. I remember *two* adoring parents spoiling their only son. Along with a housekeeper and a nanny. Mr. Isaac had us all doing his bidding."

"Okay," Isaac said, "that's enough talk about me. It's almost dinnertime so I know you have something wonderful on the menu."

"I certainly do," Mrs. Hall said. "But you two have some time to freshen up before it's ready."

Isaac smiled as he watched the older woman walk toward the kitchen. "She runs this place, doesn't she?"

Abraham laughed. "Always has, but don't tell your mother. Anna has done a great job of treating Saralyn as her boss while bossing her around. I should have hired her at MEEG."

Isaac followed his father into his study. The masculine room had his father stamped all over it. Unlike his MEEG office, this study reflected the personal side of Abraham Martin. A built-in wall cabinet held the academic and sporting honors and trophies he'd been awarded in high school and college. The credenza was cluttered with family photos. Isaac's favorite was the one with his mother and father and his grandmother Iris. There were a couple of him as a youngster that he wished his father would remove from his collection. He felt closer to his father in this room than he did in any other place.

"Feel free to make yourself a drink," Abraham said as he settled on the couch and lifted his feet onto the ottoman.

"You want something?" Isaac asked. He studied his father, whose strong voice was contradicted by the tiredness in his eyes. Seeing his father weak would take some getting used to.

Abraham shook his head. "Not while I'm on medication, but you go ahead."

Isaac knew he didn't really need alcohol either since he was on medication himself. "I'll have some ginger ale. Want one?"

"Okay, you've convinced me."

Isaac went to the wet bar in the corner of the room, put ice in two glasses, and poured the ginger ale. He handed one glass to his father and took a seat beside him on the couch. "Bet you're glad to be home," he said.

Abraham closed his eyes and leaned his head back. "If only I didn't tire so easily."

"You'll be back to one hundred percent before you know it," Isaac said, repeating the doctor's prognosis. "You've come a long way in no time at all. You were in a coma two short weeks ago."

Abraham opened his eyes. "I'll stop complaining," he said. "I have a lot to be grateful for." He rested his hand on Isaac's shoulder and squeezed. "Having a son like you is one of them. I love you, son."

Isaac swallowed. "I know," he said. "I love you, too."

"But you still haven't forgiven me?"

He didn't have an answer. If only it were as simple as forgiving his dad. But it was more complicated than that. So much more. His father's lie had far-reaching consequences, and Isaac felt he was suffering much more than his share.

When he didn't respond, Abraham removed his hand from his

son's shoulder and sat up a bit straighter. "Okay," he said, "I won't press. You want to bring me up to date on things at MEEG?"

Isaac slid his father a glance. "I'm sure Alan has been giving you regular updates."

Abraham shrugged. "I'm not asking Alan," he said. "I'm asking you."

Isaac gave him a rundown of the major projects, ending with Running Brook. "There's not much to report on Running Brook. Deborah has made some initial decisions about projects she wants to continue and those she wants to terminate. That's about it."

"How are things working out with her?"

Isaac lifted a brow. "Professionally or personally?"

"Professionally first."

"Alan's working more closely with her than I am. He'd have a better read on her."

"That's good," Abraham said. "I should have known he'd step in for me. I can always count on Alan."

Though he knew his father meant no harm, Isaac took his words as a reprimand. "I can't hold her hand, Dad. I have my own job to do."

Abraham's eyes widened. "I know you have a lot on your plate and I don't expect you to hold her hand. Actually, I don't expect her to need much handholding. She's a bright woman, Isaac. Give her a chance."

All his life his father had held him to high standards. This was no different. He was still expected to be the bigger person. "She doesn't need me to give her any chances," he said. "You've given her a once-in-a-lifetime chance. She'd better make the most of it."

Abraham tilted his head to the side. "You don't like her?"

Isaac shrugged. "I don't know her."

"She's your sister," Abraham said.

Isaac shook his head. "She's your daughter. She's not my sister."

"Blood tells."

"I'm not talking biology, Dad. I don't know her and she doesn't know me. I've accepted her as a colleague. Don't ask for more right now."

Abraham nodded. "I know the situation is hard for you and your mother, but I don't know what else to do. This is new territory for me, too, so I'm learning and doing the best I can. I need your help with this, Isaac. I wouldn't ask you if I didn't know you had it in you to do it."

Isaac's palms grew damp and his face hot, imminent signs of an oncoming panic attack. "Why now?" he asked, practicing the visualization technique his therapist had suggested. Visions of his South American cruise passed through his mind. "You ignored them all these years. Why embrace them now?"

"If not now, when? I'm not getting any younger, Isaac. You have to use the time you're given wisely. You can't always count on tomorrow coming."

Isaac shook his head. "You're not dying, Dad."

"I hear what you're saying, but none of us know how long we have. I thought your grandmother would live forever, and then all of a sudden she's gone. Her death forced me to take stock of myself."

Isaac didn't want to listen to his father's case for doing what he wanted to do and would do, despite any objections. That was his dad's way. When an opponent didn't agree, he'd just beat them down until they did. "What's taking Mom so long?" he wondered aloud.

"She said she'd be late and not to hold dinner for her," Abraham said. "I'm glad because I've made a decision that I wanted to share with you first."

Isaac got up and poured more ginger ale. He was tempted to rub an ice cube down his neck. "Please, Dad," he said. "I've had enough revelations from you to last a lifetime. I don't need to hear about another set of kids."

"It's nothing like that," Abraham said, waving off the comment. "You know I made a place for Deborah in MEEG, and I'm sure you've noticed I haven't done the same for Michael."

"Seems a smart move to me. The man hates us."

"He doesn't hate you, Isaac. He hates me. He only resents you. I'm sorry about that, but have some compassion for the boy. You grew up with a mother and a father and all this." Abraham lifted his arms wide to illustrate the breadth of all his family had. "Michael grew up with a single mother who struggled to provide a good living for them, all the while knowing he had a rich father across town who couldn't be bothered to help. Neither he nor Deborah had any of the opportunities you had. No summer camps, no private schools, no tutors, no summer trips to Europe and Africa. Of course, they're bound to be a little resentful of you."

"A little resentful? What planet are you living on, Dad? Your underprivileged son has been taunting my wife with gifts since the day we were married. Did you know he and Rebecca had a relationship?"

Abraham nodded. "Rebecca told me. But that relationship was over long before Rebecca married you. I don't see how you can hold it against her or him."

"I'd agree with you if Michael had left it at that, but he went too far when he started taunting me and Rebecca with gifts. Before I even knew he was my brother, he was rubbing it in my face that he'd slept with my wife. I think that goes a bit beyond being a little resentful." Isaac rubbed his hand across his head. "You know what, Dad? I don't even know why we're having this argument. MEEG is your company and you can do what you want with it. I came back after your accident, knowing Deborah was there, and promised to stay until your return. But I can't keep that promise if you bring Michael in. You can let him run the company for you or with you, but I won't work with him."

"That's not you talking, Isaac," Abraham said. "Those are your mother's words. You're more generous than your words suggest."

"Don't fool yourself, Dad. These are my words. I'm generous but I'm not a masochist, which I'd have to be to work with Michael."

Abraham studied his son. "I know Michael has hurt you," he said. "But that was when he was your enemy. You don't have to be enemies anymore. You can be brothers. That's one of the reasons that I want to bring him into MEEG, so he won't have a reason to hate you."

"Wake up, Dad," Isaac said. "You can't snap your fingers and turn us into the Brady Bunch. There is a lot of bad blood between the two families. Neither wishful thinking nor gifting MEEG board seats is going to change that. This is one time the great Abraham Martin is not going to get his way. You're not going to have your offspring working side by side with you carrying out your legacy at MEEG. It ain't gonna happen."

"It could, if you would give it chance. You're my son, Isaac, my oldest son. You have the inner strength to make it happen."

Isaac put down his glass and stared at his father. "You don't get it, do you? I left MEEG because of you. I don't want to work with you. It took my leaving for me to realize that. I could breathe in my new position, Dad. I couldn't breathe when I was working with you at MEEG. You sucked all the air out of the room with your plans and expectations. It was too much. I can't live like that again. I won't."

Isaac watched as his dad sank back on the couch. "I had no idea you disliked working at MEEG."

Isaac shook his head. "You're not listening to me," he said. "I can tolerate working at MEEG, but I can't tolerate working with you. And I won't tolerate working with Michael."

"You're not leaving me too many options. Either you have MEEG to yourself or you're out—is that what you're telling me?"

Isaac shook his head. "I'm telling you that it's fine with me if you, Deborah, and Michael run MEEG together. I won't stand in your way and I'll try to rein in Mom when she tries to interfere, though I'm not sure how successful I'll be."

"You don't mean that, Isaac. MEEG is your heritage. I built it for you."

"No, you didn't," Isaac said, walking over to sit on the ottoman in front of his dad. "You built it for you and it's yours. I'm proud of what you've accomplished but I can't and won't stand in your shadow any longer. It's not a healthy place for me to be."

Chapter Fifty

Saralyn arrived home later than planned. It had taken longer than expected for her to identify the things from the penthouse that she wanted moved to the mansion. She'd miss living downtown but her place was with Abraham. If he wanted to recuperate here, she'd be right by his side, as she'd been for all of their marriage, the good and the bad.

She admitted to herself, though, that these times were as bad as they'd ever been. Her husband was making decisions about her and Isaac's future without even consulting her. Now that she had him out here to herself, she was sure she'd be able to talk some sense into him.

Mrs. Hall met her when she opened the front door. "Welcome home, ma'am," the older lady said.

"I'm sorry I missed dinner, Anna," Saralyn told her, knowing and appreciating how much effort she put into her meals.

"Don't worry about it," Mrs. Hall said. "Are you hungry? I can fix you a plate."

Saralyn shook her head. "I had a sandwich and salad when I was downtown. Where are my husband and son?"

"Mr. Isaac left a while ago," Mrs. Hall said. "Mr. Martin is in his study."

"Thanks," Saralyn said, then turned toward Abraham's study. She was disappointed she'd missed Isaac because she looked forward to spending time with both her men tonight. Family time had been short in the last few months, since Isaac left MEEG and the relationship between him and his father had grown increasingly strained. She smiled when she walked through the study doors. Abraham sat slouched back on the couch, his feet propped on the ottoman in front of him, head back, eyes closed. Love for him flowed afresh within her.

Despite the doctor's orders for him to take a break from work while he recuperated, there was a stack of documents on his lap. A closer inspection showed that some of them had fallen to the floor. Shaking her head, she bent and picked up the documents and then collected those on his lap. She scanned them as she headed for his desk to put them away. She stopped when she spotted the name Michael Thomas.

She read the contents of the document then turned toward her still sleeping husband. "Abraham Martin!" she yelled. "Are you out of your mind?" She marched toward her husband as he sluggishly awakened from his sleep.

"Saralyn. What's going on?"

She dropped down on the ottoman and shoved the document in his chest. "What's going on with me?" she parroted. "What I want to know is what's going on with you? You can't seriously be thinking about making Michael Thomas an officer in MEEG. Tell me I read that document wrong."

Abraham wiped the sleep from his eyes. "Calm down," he told her. "We're not alone in this house."

Saralyn jumped up from the ottoman, stomped to the study door, and slammed it closed. "Now tell me I read that document wrong, Abraham."

Abraham sighed. "You didn't read it wrong."

She stalked back over to him. "Why are you doing this to me? Why are you doing it to Isaac? Don't you know what Michael has done to him? Are you trying to push Isaac away?"

"Of course I'm not trying to push him away," he told her. "Stop talking crazy."

She folded her arms and tapped her feet. "You're the one who's crazy if you think I'm going to put up with this."

"I can't talk to you when you're like this," he said, but she recognized the dismissive tactic for what it was.

"Oh, no," she said. "You're not going to brush me off so easily. You can't keep making all these unilateral decisions. You should have consulted me before you offered that Deborah a job, before you put her and that mother of hers on the board, and definitely before you did anything for that miscreant Michael."

"He's my son, Saralyn."

"Isaac is your son, too, but it seems you've forgotten that in your quest to appease your other children."

"That's not true," he said. "The problem is that you've fought me all the way. You haven't tried to understand what I'm going through."

She wanted to throw something at him. "What you're going through? What about me? What about Isaac?"

He sighed. "Why do you have to fight me every step of the way, Saralyn? Why can't you work with me on this? Throughout our marriage, you've always supported me, been there with me. Why does this have to be different?"

"Are you crazy? This isn't a simple business deal, Abraham.

We're talking about your mistress and her children. This *is* different."

He got up and came to her. "It doesn't have to be," he said, rubbing his hand down her arm.

She snatched her arm away from him. "Your sweet talk is not going to work this time. You've got to choose: them or us. It's that simple."

"Don't threaten me, Saralyn."

"It's not a threat. If you don't stand up for me and Isaac, I'll have to do it."

He eyed her. "What are you talking about?"

She might have been angry, but she was not stupid enough to tell Abraham of her trump card. Her husband was a smart man, and if he knew what she planned to do, he might be able to find a way to thwart her. "You heard me. I've always stood by you, Abraham. I even forgave you when I first found out about Leah and those kids. Do you know what it took for me to do that, knowing that you'd been lying to me for years? It took a lot."

Abraham reached for her. "I know, Saralyn. I know."

She shook her head. "If you did, things wouldn't be the way they are today."

He looked away. "They're my children, too, Saralyn," he said. "I can't walk away from them again. What kind of man would I be if I did that?"

"I know you don't want to hear this, Abe, but it's too late for you to be a father to them. You can't make up those years. Bringing them into MEEG is not going to make them see you as their father. You're a stranger to them, a rich stranger. Why not make this simple? Give them some money—a lot of money if you want, I won't fight you. Give them the money and let them leave. That's all they want anyway."

Abraham shook his head. "You're wrong," he said. "Michael told me about your offer. He's not taking it."

"What do you mean he's not taking it? Of course he's taking it. The boy's a lot of things but stupid isn't one of them. He's taking the money, all right."

Abraham hated hearing his wife speak that way. "He's not taking it, Saralyn. I don't care what he told you. He told me that he's not taking it. He only said he would so he could throw your offer back in my face. How could you, Saralyn? How could you try to buy them off?"

"I'm not ashamed of what I did. I did it and I would do it again. You aren't the only fighter in this family, Abraham. I'll do whatever I have to do to protect my family, my son. You can be my ally in this or you can be my enemy. It's up to you."

He reached for her again. "Saralyn—"

"You have a decision to make," she said, sidestepping him and heading toward the door. She opened it and then turned back to him. "I know this is hard for you, Abraham, but I'm not sorry. You've accomplished everything you wanted in life with your charm, your good looks, and your brain. This time it's going to be your heart that either gets you out of trouble or buries you deeper in it."

She left the room and closed the door behind her. As she made her way to the stairs, she knew that regardless of what Abraham did, she'd have her attorney file the separation papers tomorrow. If she couldn't count on Abraham's love for her and Isaac to stop the nonsense, she'd have to rely on the law.

Chapter Fifty-One

Josette drove around the block where Isaac and Rebecca lived several times before she got up the nerve to pull into one of the visitor spaces in front of the high-rise luxury condo building. She was familiar with the building, as one of Michael's goals when he "hit it big" was to buy a condo here. At least now she understood the appeal the building had for him. She wondered if he had any goals that didn't stem out of his disdain for Abraham Martin. Despite everything she'd learned about Michael recently, she still couldn't shake the notion that she'd made the right decision when she married him. And that was totally crazy. How could it be the right decision when her husband was a habitual liar and, she suspected, a serial adulterer?

Shaking off those thoughts, she headed for the lobby. The doorman greeted her, and she told him she was there to see Mrs. Martin. "Which one?" he asked, with a grin that told her he'd asked the question often.

She smiled at him. "Rebecca Martin, Mrs. Isaac Martin."

"I'll ring her," he said, picking up the phone. "Name, please."

She told him and prayed Rebecca would see her.

He hung up the phone. "Follow me, please," he said, leading her to the bank of elevators. He punched the Up button, waited for the doors to open and her to enter, then pushed the button for the tenth floor. "It's 1002," he said. "Take a left after the doors open. You can't miss it."

"Thanks," Josette said as the doors closed; 1002, she repeated silently.

When the elevator doors opened, she stepped off and followed the doorman's directions. She took a deep breath before she rang the bell. The door opened before the first full ring.

"Come on in," Rebecca said, as if Josette were a friend dropping by for a bout of gossip.

Josette grew uneasy as she began to consider the wisdom of her visit. What did she hope to gain by coming here?

Rebecca pointed to a leather couch. "Have a seat," she said. "Can I get you something to drink?"

Josette shook her head. Was this the Twilight Zone? It certainly felt like it. She had to get things back on keel. "I didn't come here for tea," she said, taking the offered seat.

Rebecca sighed and then sat in the leather chair next to the couch. She folded her legs under her, as calm as she could be. "So why did you come?"

Josette studied this woman she suspected was sleeping with her husband. She couldn't shake the comparison. They were married to two brothers, and this woman had slept with both of them. Maybe those people on *Jerry Springer* were real, after all. "You have no idea?"

Rebecca laughed, but it wasn't a real laugh, more a nervous reaction. "You either came about Michael or about Isaac. They're all we have in common. So which one is it?"

Josette studied her. She could see why men were attracted to
Rebecca. She was one of those women who exuded sexuality
and self-confidence without even trying. What Josette couldn't
figure out was how the same man could also be attracted to her
when she was so different from Rebecca. Of course, she didn't
exude sexuality now that she was pregnant, but she hadn't
exuded it before. She was more the girl-next-door, while Re-
becca was the siren down the street. "I'm here about Michael,"
she finally said.

"Interesting," Rebecca said. "You spend so much time with my
husband these days, I thought you might want to talk about him."

"What are you talking about?"

Rebecca unfolded her legs and leaned toward Josette. "First,
you're crying on Isaac's shoulder at the hospital, and then you're
crying on his shoulder in his office. It seems to me you should be
crying on your own husband's broad shoulders, not mine."

"You're joking, right?"

"Do I look like I'm joking?" Rebecca said. Her harsh tone sig-
naled there would be no bout of gossip. "I take women coming
on to my husband very seriously. I've been meaning to talk to you
about it."

"You can't be serious," Josette sputtered. "What are you accus-
ing me of?"

Rebecca shrugged. "I'm not accusing you of anything . . . yet.
Isaac wouldn't cheat on me. But I'm sure he's told you that we're
having problems, and you wouldn't be the first woman to take
advantage of a man when his marriage was on the rocks."

"Maybe you're reflecting your lack of morals onto me," Josette
said, unable to believe how quickly the conversation had turned
against her. "I am not making a move on Isaac."

"Actions speak louder than words," Rebecca said. "Try staying
away from him."

Josette stood. "I came here to ask you one question, but I don't even have to ask it now. You're sleeping with Michael, aren't you? That's why you see evil wherever you look."

"I am not sleeping with Michael," Rebecca said.

Josette studied her. "Why should I believe you?"

"Because I'm telling you the truth. I'm not sleeping with Michael, but I did in the past, long before I met Isaac."

The truth sent Josette back to the couch with a thud. The truth hurt. But she'd come for answers and she wouldn't leave until she got them. "How long were you and Michael an item?"

Rebecca leaned close again. "I'm going to be honest with you because I've already been honest with Isaac. I started sleeping with Michael before the two of you got married, and I continued sleeping with him for a few months after you were married."

Josette blinked rapidly. Rebecca's words pierced her heart. It was one thing to think your husband was a liar and a cheat. It was quite another to know it for a fact. She rubbed her hand across her belly. Thank God for her baby. This child was the only thing keeping her from screaming and tearing into Rebecca.

"I'm sorry," she heard Rebecca say. "I know it's not much, but I really am sorry."

"Sorry Isaac found out," Josette spat out.

Rebecca looked away. "That, too." She turned back to Josette. "I told him the truth before he found out. I had to tell him."

Josette nodded. She understood. "Before Michael told him."

"You know your husband, don't you?"

She smiled a little. "It seems we both do."

"Look," Rebecca said. "Let's talk woman-to-woman for a minute. Isaac's feeling lonely and betrayed right now and he's wondering if he made a mistake by marrying me. And you're probably feeling the same way. Michael lied to you about a lot of stuff, I know, and you're wondering if you made the right choice when you chose him."

Josette looked way, blinking back tears. Rebecca had read her very well.

"We have two very different marriages here," Rebecca said. "I'm not interested in swapping partners and I don't think you are either, not really. You're angry with Michael just like Isaac is angry with me. I only ask that you don't let the anger make you do something you'll regret. You and Isaac don't have a future together, any more than Michael and I do."

Josette looked down at her fingers. "Did you love Michael?"

Rebecca shook her head. "No. Michael and I had more of a business relationship, though there was a time when I had hoped there would be more. Michael didn't want more, at least not with me. The sex was something that just happened. It didn't mean anything beyond physical release to either of us."

That there was no love between Rebecca and Michael didn't ease Josette's pain. Michael had still betrayed their marriage vows.

"Because I love Isaac, you're in a position to hurt me, to do to me what I did to you by sleeping with Michael after he married you. I can't hurt you the same way because Michael doesn't care about me and I don't care about him. So you have the upper hand. I want my marriage to work, Josette. I love Isaac, but he's never going to believe that if you're always hanging around him."

"I'm not trying to take Isaac from you."

"You don't have to try. I'm sure you've noticed that Isaac is a caretaker. He knows you're hurting and he wants to stop it. That can easily lead to something else, especially when you're always in his face reminding him of what monsters Michael and I are."

It was Josette's turn to give a nervous laugh. "This conversation is certainly not what I expected when I walked through your door."

Rebecca laughed, this time genuinely. "You were going to scratch my eyes out?"

Now Josette gave a real laugh. "After I cussed you out and told you to stay away from my husband."

"I really am sorry for what I did, Josette. I can only imagine how hearing about it makes you feel. I get sick to my stomach every time I think of something happening between you and Isaac. We women have to be better to each other than we are. I was wrong."

Josette thought of her baby and this woman who would be her baby's aunt. "I forgive you," she told Rebecca, surprising herself. "Life's too short, and I'm having a baby who's going to be your niece, if you can believe that."

Rebecca laughed. "Think we can get on an episode of *The Maury Show*?"

Josette chuckled, having thought something similar. "Saralyn would shoot us both before she'd let that happen."

Both women were silent for a few moments. Rebecca spoke first. "What are we going to do about our husbands, Josette?"

Josette rubbed her belly. "I have no idea, but we have to do something. More than anything, I want peace in this family."

Chapter Fifty-Two

Leah sat at the desk in her cramped office at the community college and tried unsuccessfully to concentrate on the student paper she was grading. Her mind kept wandering to Abraham's impending visit. She had turned down his initial request to meet him at the mansion, insulted that he thought for even a moment that she'd come to his home. Abraham was a selfish man who always thought of himself first.

She picked up the pages of the student paper and turned her chair toward the window, hoping a new direction would help her concentration. She began reading again, but was back to thinking about Abraham before she finished the page. She'd always known he was selfish, had accepted it as a character trait rather than a character flaw. And that was her character flaw: making excuses for him and putting up with his unacceptable behavior. Why? Love, of course. Or rather, what she'd thought was love.

Now that she knew a different kind of love, the kind that held her in esteem, that put her first, she knew that what she'd had with Abraham wasn't love. She'd loved what they could have been together, and he'd loved that she loved him. She couldn't blame him. Not many men would pass up the adulation she had heaped on Abraham.

"Sorry I'm late."

She turned, tossing aside her thoughts, and saw him standing in her doorway. His eyes seemed tired and for a moment she felt guilty for having him make the trek over instead of going to his home. Brushing her guilt aside, she pointed to the straight-back chair near her desk. "Have a seat," she said. "What was so important that we couldn't discuss it over the phone? You look like you should be resting."

He sat, crossing one leg over the other. "I feel better than I look," he said, with a smile meant to disarm.

As she observed him now, she realized nothing had changed. He had more money, but the arrogance and self-assurance had always been there. It was just a bit more polished. "I assume this visit is about Michael or Deborah."

He nodded. "It's odd, isn't it? After all these years, we're being parents to our children."

"Correction," Leah said, her voice tight. "I've *always* been a parent to our children. You're the one who's new to the game."

He uncrossed his legs and leaned forward. "I worded it wrong," he said, "but you know what I mean."

She shook her head. "Not really. The children you refer to are adults. It's not like we're discussing finding a place in the family budget for fees for Michael to join the basketball team or getting help for Deborah's struggles with math. They needed parenting then, Abraham. I'm not sure they need it now."

He sat back in his chair. "Well, it seems I can't do anything right these days."

Leah didn't say anything. It wasn't her job to make Abraham

Martin feel better. She'd covered for him too long, only to find out that he had given her and her children little to no thought over the years. Saralyn had opened her eyes to how things really were. She didn't think she'd ever see Abraham the same way again.

He sighed. "I wanted to talk to you about Michael and MEEG . . ." He paused. "I know we talked about giving him a seat on the board immediately, but that move is going to take a bit more finesse than I had expected."

"What does that mean? Isn't MEEG your company?"

"It's more complicated than that."

Leah nodded. "I see," she said, and she did. Apparently, Abraham was getting push-back from Saralyn. Leah had to give it to her. Saralyn took care of business.

"I don't think you do understand," Abraham said. "It's going to happen, but it'll take a bit more time."

Leah sneered at him. "What's more time when Michael has waited thirty years?" She inclined her head toward the door. "If that's it . . . "

"You have to understand, Leah," he said. "I'm going to do right by him, but I need more time."

Leah slammed the sheets of paper in her hand on the desk. "I understand, all right," she said. "I understand that my children stand with you where they've always stood—nowhere. We would have been better off if you'd continued to ignore us. All I asked was for you not to hurt them. Why didn't you get your house in order before you reached out to them? Why did you make promises that you can't keep?"

"I'm keeping my promises to them, Leah," he said. "I had reservations about Michael from the start, if you'll remember."

"I remember, all right," she said. "I remember how I went along with that initial plan because it was easiest for you and I was so happy you'd finally decided to embrace your kids. After thirty years I was still putting you and your concerns ahead of my kids.

I should have sued you for child support from day one. If I had, we wouldn't be in this situation now."

Abraham sat looking at her, his eyes wide with surprise. He obviously hadn't expected her outburst. "Look," he pleaded, "I'm sorry about the past, but I can't do anything about it."

Leah laughed at him, laughed to keep from crying. "You still don't get it, do you? This is not about you. This is about me not doing what was right by my kids. This is about me not putting my kids first." She took a deep breath. "I let guilt keep me from doing the right thing."

"What are you talking about?" Abraham asked. "What guilt?"

"Guilt about a miscarriage. I got out of your life and kept my children hidden and deprived because of the guilt I felt about Saralyn's miscarriage."

"We shared that guilt, Leah."

She took a deep breath, not wanting his words to sway her. "I'll talk to Deborah and Michael about your change in plans," she said.

"I'd like for us to talk to them together," he offered.

She shook her head. "This is between me and my kids. We can talk to them together after I talk to them alone, if they're interested."

"But it'll be better if we do it together."

She lifted a brow. "Better for whom? You? Certainly not them."

"They're my children, too."

"I'm glad that finally means something to you, but it doesn't mean to you what it does to me. You know, I'm learning a lot from you and Saralyn. You've always known what I'm only now learning—take care of yourself and your children first. Do you know that Saralyn offered me money to get us out of your lives? Did you put her up to it?"

"Of course I didn't put her up to it. I didn't even know about it. I can't control her. She even offered Michael money. I was appalled."

That witch. "Look, I think we've said all we need to say. I know where you and your family stand, and you know that I stand—*fully with my kids*. Now if you don't mind, I've got papers to grade."

He looked at her a long minute, and Leah thought he was going to say something more. Instead he got up. "You'll call me after you talk to them? I really want them to hear my side."

Without looking up, she said, "If they want to talk to you, you'll be the first to know."

Chapter Fifty-Three

Since Michael's secretary wasn't at her desk, Deborah went directly to his office and made herself comfortable by stretching out on the sofa in the corner. This office was more familiar to her than her own, and she felt much more comfortable here at Thomas Management Group than she did at MEEG. Here, the furniture was serviceable—more IKEA than the custom Fulbright designs found at MEEG—and as a result more casual. Though she appreciated what Abraham was trying to do for her, and for Michael, sometimes she felt so out of place at MEEG she had to leave the building. Today was one of those days. She had considered going to visit her mother out at the community college, but her brother's office was much closer.

"What's this? Sleeping Beauty come to visit?"

Deborah's eyes snapped open and she sat up on the couch. "You scared me," she said, her hand to her chest. "You need to give a person warning before you startle them out of a deep sleep."

Michael raised a brow. "You're joking, right?"

"No, I'm not joking," she said as he came toward her.

He took a seat next to her and put his feet up on the coffee table in front of the couch. "It must be nice," he said, "to be able to sneak away from the job and grab a few z's. Is that one of the perks of being the boss's daughter?"

She punched him on the arm. "Please. I'm not at the perks stage yet. I love the work but there's something about the MEEG Building that intimidates the heck out of me. Do you think I'll ever get used to all that . . . that richness?"

Michael chuckled. "Sure. I know I would. And it wouldn't take me long, either. I can't believe you aren't soaking it up. Your digs over there are a hundred times better than at your old job."

"Make that a million times better. I'm thinking it's too rich for me. I can't quite get comfortable."

"Hang in there, sis. You'll get used to it."

"I'd get used to it quicker if you were there with me. Any formal news yet about the board position?"

He shook his head. "I'm not holding my breath."

"You should give Abraham more credit. He's trying, Michael."

He tapped her on her nose. "A family can only have one flaming optimist, and that's you."

"That doesn't mean you have to be a flaming pessimist."

He laughed. "Yes, it does."

She punched him again. "What am I going to do with you?"

He lowered his feet to the floor. "I'm hungry. Now that you're the head of a big-time production company, you can treat me."

"I'm game," she said. "How about Sylvia's?"

"Sylvia's? With a fat check like yours, you ought to be taking me to The Sundial at the top of the Peachtree. You've got to start thinking big, sis, as fits your new station in life."

Now she laughed. "You're so full of it, Michael."

He tried to charm her with his trademark grin. "But you love me anyway."

She frowned. "Only because you're my brother. You'd better be glad of that."

"I am," he said. "You can work a brother's nerve sometimes, but you're an all right sister."

"I'll try not to let all that praise go to my head." She got up. "Where do you want to go for lunch? And be serious this time."

He looked at his watch. "You can pick the place. I just need a few minutes to make a phone call."

"No problem," she said. "I need to make a stop at the ladies' room before we go anyway."

"I'll be ready when you get back."

Nodding, she headed for the door. She stopped abruptly when she met Alan as he entered the outer office. "What are you doing here?" she asked.

He smiled at her. "The same reason you're here, I'd guess. To see your brother."

"About what?" she asked. "Does this have anything to do with Michael's position on the board?"

He took her elbow and turned her back toward Michael's office. "I wanted to tell him first," Alan told her, "but I guess I'll have to tell you together."

Deborah knew it was bad news.

Michael put the phone down when they entered his office. "Alan," he said. "What brings you by?"

"MEEG business," the attorney said. "Why don't we all sit?"

Michael sat in his desk chair, while Alan and Deborah sat in the visitor's chairs in front of the desk.

"I think I know what's coming," Michael said.

Alan glanced at Deborah before turning back to Michael. "Abraham has asked me to withdraw your board seat."

"He can't do that," Deborah said. "He said he would go along with what Mama and I decided."

Alan turned to her. "The seat is not withdrawn for good," he told her. "Just for the time being."

"Why would he do this?" she asked. "And why wouldn't he tell us himself?"

"I'm not here in an official capacity, Deborah. I came to give Michael a heads-up. I'm sure Abraham plans to tell both of you. I probably shouldn't have put myself in the middle of it, but I felt Michael needed to know sooner rather than later."

Deborah appreciated his thoughtfulness. That was the kind of man Alan was, she thought.

"Thanks, man," Michael said. His face was shuttered to hide his emotions from Alan, but he couldn't hide them from her. He was angry and hurt. The anger she expected and could deal with. The hurt was new. She wanted to hug her brother but knew he wouldn't appreciate it with Alan present.

"Deborah was about to take me to lunch," Michael said to Alan. "You're welcome to join us."

"I'll have to take a rain check," he said, standing up. "I have a lot of unfinished business on my desk." He shook hands with Michael and smiled at her. Then he left the office.

"I'm sorry, Michael," she said. "I'm definitely going to have a few words with Abraham about this."

He shook his head. "No you're not. MEEG is Abraham's company and he can do what he wants with it."

She slid to the edge of her chair. "But—"

He cut her off with a raised palm. "If Abraham comes to you, fine, but don't you go to him, not on my behalf."

She slumped back in her chair. "How can I continue to work there after this?" she asked.

He came around and sat on the edge of the desk facing her. "You stay because you enjoy the work. In the process, you build your résumé and keep active in your network. That way, if

Abraham changes his mind about you, you will already have the experience and the exposure to move on to something better. It's a great opportunity, sis. You have to make the best of it."

"How can I? I'm not even sure I trust Abraham. He could come in tomorrow and give me my walking papers."

"He could, but I don't think he will. He's already given you a job and a seat on the board. Alan didn't say anything about him withdrawing yours, just mine. Face it, sis, I'm not exactly on the man's fan list. He has to have reservations about me. He'd be a fool not to. And Abraham Martin is a lot of things, but fool is not one of them."

She eyed him skeptically, wondering if the hurt she'd read in his expression had been something else altogether. "You sure are taking this well," she said. "Where is the Michael Thomas who had a knockdown, drag-out fight with Isaac Martin in the MEEG boardroom?"

He grinned at her. "He's remembering his mother's home training." He stood. "I have my own ways of dealing with Abraham Martin. For now, let's forget him and enjoy lunch. He'll get his when the time is right."

"What do you mean by that?" she asked, alarm bells sounding.

Michael shrugged. "Nothing in particular. Just remember those Sunday school lessons about reaping and sowing."

The alarm bells sounded louder in Deborah's ears as her brother led her out of the office and to the elevator. She had no idea what they meant or what to do about them.

Chapter Fifty-Four

I saac rubbed the back of his neck as he entered his condo later that evening. He'd worked nothing but long hours since coming back to MEEG, and he knew that was what his future held for him as long as he worked with or for his father. Those were Abraham's rules. Owners worked longer, harder, and smarter than everybody else combined. There was a time when he had lived by that motto in his need to gain his father's approval. Those times ended when he found out about his father's other children. Approval from a liar and adulterer didn't seem to mean much. He tossed his briefcase on the kitchen counter, loosened his tie, and opened the refrigerator.

"This is stupid, Isaac," Rebecca said.

He looked up over the refrigerator door and saw her leaning against the frame of the entranceway to the kitchen. "What's stupid?" he asked, pulling out one of the covered baking dishes.

"This," she said, moving away from the wall and toward the

island where he'd placed the baking dish and a can of diet soda. "You come in late each night after I've gone to bed, sleep in the guest room to ignore me, yet you eat the leftovers I leave for you. Now that's stupid."

He pulled down a plate and forked some of the casserole onto it. He then covered the plate with a paper towel and put it in the microwave. "Not stupid," he said, after he punched in the cooking time. "Practical. No need to let the food go to waste."

She sat on a stool at the island. "Neither is there a reason to let our marriage go to waste."

He popped the tab on the soda and took a long swallow. "Let's not get into this tonight, Rebecca," he said, feeling a headache coming on. He reached into his pocket for his pill bottle and remembered he'd tossed it after he'd taken the last pill at work earlier today. He needed to call in a prescription.

"If not tonight, when?" she asked. "You ignore me, don't talk to me. When are we supposed to talk?"

The microwave sounded, and he walked over to it and took out his food. He grabbed a fork, came back to the island and sat. "This is good," he said after one bite. "You're a very good cook."

"What? A compliment from you? I can't believe it."

He eyed her. "Cut the sarcasm, Rebecca," he said. "I'm trying to be cordial."

"I don't want cordial," she said. "I want a long and loud fight where we air all our grievances, and I want to follow it up with a lifetime of never hurting each other again."

"You don't want much, do you?"

She met his eyes with hers, held them. "I love you, Isaac. I want it all."

He didn't say anything. What was there to say? He was tired of words. Words brought expectations and he was tired of trying to meet the expectations of others. His father expected him to lead MEEG with his arms open to a brother and sister he hadn't known existed until a few months ago. His mother expected him to bunker down in war formation and hold the fort against the infidels. His wife expected him to forgive the unforgivable. He'd lived all his life meeting the high expectations set for him, and now he was tired. All he wanted was rest. He didn't have the energy or the will to even try to be what his father, his mother, or his wife wanted. He finished his meal, rinsed out his plate and glass, and put them in the dishwasher.

"Don't walk away, Isaac," Rebecca said, when he would have left her sitting at the island.

He turned back to her. Though she had hurt him terribly, he didn't take any pleasure in hurting her. "I don't have anything inside me to give you, Rebecca. I can't fight for our marriage because there is no fight in me. I'm so tired of all of this. All I want is peace."

"I want that, too," she said. "Peace between us."

He shook his head. "Have you seen a lawyer?"

"I don't want a divorce so I don't need a lawyer."

He rubbed the back of his neck. "There's no value in drawing this out. If your lawyer doesn't contact me in a week, I'll have mine contact you. Let's get this over as painlessly as possible."

"That's impossible," Rebecca said. "I still love you."

"Words again," Isaac said, as the voices of his mother, his father, and Rebecca battled each other in his head. He raised his hands and covered his ears. Instead of blocking out the sounds, the action seemed to confine and intensify them in his head.

"Isaac," Rebecca called. "Are you all right?"

He opened his mouth to tell her that he wasn't sure, but slumped to the floor as darkness overtook him.

Chapter Fifty-Five

Abraham had been holed up in his study since he returned from his visit with Leah. To say that visit hadn't gone well was an understatement. He was getting it from all sides. He seemed unable to please anybody, including himself. He lifted his eyes heavenward. "Ma," he called. "I've accomplished everything in my life I set out to accomplish. Why can't I pull this off?"

Before he could get an answer, a knock sounded at the study door. "Mr. Martin," Mrs. Hall called. "You have a delivery."

Annoyed by the unnecessary disturbance, he called back, "Sign for it, then, the way you usually do."

"You have to sign," she said through the door that he knew she wouldn't open unless he gave her permission.

"Okay," he said, wondering what the package could be. When he pulled open the study door, Mrs. Hall was standing near the front door. She opened it when he reached her.

The deliveryman said, "Abraham Martin?"

He nodded. "Yes."

The man gave a wry smile and handed him a manila envelope. "You've been served," he said. Then he turned and jogged down the steps.

Mrs. Hall closed the door as Abraham opened the envelope. The heading on the first page sent him rocking on his heels: PETITION FOR FORMAL SEPARATION. He looked at the paper and then up at Mrs. Hall. He saw the question on her face but didn't answer it. "Where's Mrs. Martin?" he asked.

"Upstairs in her bath," she said.

He nodded. "That'll be all," he said. "Why don't you call it a night? I'm going up myself."

She nodded. "Good night, Mr. Martin."

He muttered a good-night and headed up the stairs. *Petition for Formal Separation!* He couldn't believe Saralyn had gone this far. The woman had definitely crossed the line. "Saralyn," he called to her when he entered the master suite. He closed the door behind him and followed the strands of music to her bath, a huge sunken tub flanked by a stereo system and plasma television. It was all a bit much, in his opinion, but it was what she wanted so she had it.

He found her as he expected, as relaxed as ever, eyes closed, head resting on the back of the tub. "Saralyn," he called again.

"I heard you the first time," she said, no change in her position. "You know I don't like to be disturbed when I'm in my bath."

Abraham sat on the side of the tub. "And I don't like being served separation papers by some young buck thinking it's some big joke." When her eyes fluttered open, he waved the papers in her face. "What is this supposed to mean?"

She closed her eyes again. "You can read," she said. "You know what it means."

He wanted to snatch her out of the tub and shake some sense into her. Instead he got up and paced around the tub. "I don't believe this," he said. "You actually had me served with separation papers. I didn't even know you wanted out of this marriage."

She opened her eyes and looked at him. "I don't want out of our marriage. What I want is your attention."

"Well, lady," he said, "you've got it. Now what are you going to do with it?"

"Wrong question," she said, her eyes closed again.

The more she maintained her calm, the more agitated he became. "Wrong question? What are you talking about?"

"The question is not what am I going to do. The question is what are you going to do about Deborah and Michael and MEEG."

Abraham dropped down on the side of the tub again. "Is that what this is about? You're threatening a separation if I don't do what you want?"

"I'm not threatening anything. Those papers give you time to choose."

"Open your eyes, look at me, and tell me what you're talking about."

She did as he asked, albeit reluctantly. "You're being dense, Abraham. It's perfectly clear what I'm doing."

"Forgive me, wife," he said. "I've never received separation papers before so I don't understand the protocol."

"I've got a tip for you. Sarcasm is not the appropriate response."

Abraham sighed. They were going around in circles, getting nowhere fast. "I'm listening," he said.

"Those are separation papers," she said.

He bit down on his lip to keep from telling her to hurry up and tell him something he didn't know.

"Those papers stop any major transactions at MEEG that might reduce the value of my share of the marital property. They're an injunction preventing you from making any hasty decisions about MEEG in regard to those kids of yours."

Abraham could only stare at his wife. When he found the

words, he said, "You went to this length to stop me from sharing MEEG with Michael and Deborah."

She nodded. "Exactly. You've been acting like the sheriff in a two-person town, making decisions without consulting me. Well, those separation papers end your reign of autonomy. Either we reach some agreement on MEEG, or we sell it and split the proceeds. Or I could buy you out."

He didn't bother to respond to that nonsense. Instead, he asked, "Do you really think separation papers were necessary?"

"I filed them, didn't I? I had to do something to save this family."

"Save the family? You're destroying it. People don't separate when they're fighting for their family."

"The only thing those papers change is how you operate MEEG. I'm not moving and you don't have to. I'm bringing in a third-party mediator to help us make decisions."

Abraham stood. "You're crazy. No way is some paper-pushing mediator going to tell me how to run my business."

"*Our* business, Abraham," she said. "The first thing you need to do is stop thinking of it as your business. It's mine and Isaac's as much as it is yours."

Abraham didn't know what to say so he said nothing. When the phone rang, he was happy to answer it. "Hello," he said.

"It's me, Rebecca. You need to get down to DeKalb General immediately. Isaac was rushed here about thirty minutes ago."

"What? Isaac? What's going on, Rebecca?"

Saralyn grabbed a towel and jumped out of the tub. "What's going on?" she asked, tugging on his arm.

Abraham shushed her. Rebecca babbled on, clearly distraught and in tears. "We're on our way," he told her. "We're on our way."

After he hung up, he turned to Saralyn and said, "Isaac passed out. He's in the Emergency Room at DeKalb General."

"Oh, no," Saralyn said, "not my baby." She weaved on her feet as though she were going to pass out herself. Abraham reached out and gave her a quick hug.

"The boy's strong, Saralyn," he told her. "He's going to be fine. Now get dressed so we can get down there."

As Saralyn did as she was told, Abraham prayed for his son's life.

Chapter Fifty-Six

Abraham spotted Rebecca as soon as he and Saralyn stepped into the Emergency Room waiting area. "I'm so glad you're here," she said, rushing into their arms. "I was so scared. He fell to the floor right in front of me. I thought he was dead."

"Don't say that," Saralyn chided, stepping out of the group hug. "My son is not going to die."

Abraham shot a hot glare at Saralyn while he tried to calm his daughter-in-law. He led her to a quiet corner of the waiting area. "Tell me everything," he said, settling her into a chair and sitting next to her while Saralyn went to the desk and talked to the nurse.

"We were arguing," Rebecca choked out. "We were arguing, and then he grabbed his head and couldn't talk. He just sank to the floor." She buried her face in Abraham's shoulder. "He has to be all right," she said. "He has to be."

Abraham rubbed her shoulders, calming her and calming

himself at the same time. "Have they let you see him since they brought him in?"

"For a brief moment," she said, "but his eyes were closed and he didn't say anything." She lifted her head and her fear-filled eyes met his. "What if he's in a coma the way you were?"

"Let's not ask for trouble," he said. "We'll wait and see what the doctors say."

Rebecca seemed to get ahold of herself. "Thanks for coming so quickly," she said.

"Of course, we'd come," he said. "He's our son. Where else would we be?"

"I don't know what I'm saying," she admitted. "I was so scared when I was here alone."

"Well, we're here now," he said. He looked up to see Saralyn coming toward them. "What did you find out?" he asked her when she reached them.

"Nothing really," she said. "All the nurse would say is that they're running tests and the doctor will speak with us shortly." She looked at Rebecca. "What happened?"

Rebecca sighed and Abraham knew she didn't want to go over it again. "We were arguing," she explained.

"Arguing about what?" Saralyn accused. "Please tell me it wasn't about you and Michael Thomas."

"Saralyn!" Abraham chided.

"Don't Saralyn me," she said. "We both know Isaac and Rebecca are having problems in their marriage because of her relationship with your other son."

Abraham felt the condemnation he heard in her voice.

"The argument wasn't about Michael and me."

"What was it about then?" Saralyn probed, unwilling to let the subject drop.

"Isaac wants a divorce and I don't."

"I knew this was about Michael Thomas."

Rebecca shook her head. "We were arguing and then Isaac was grabbing his head, mumbling something about high expectations and how tired he was and how he wanted to rest."

"I should have known," Saralyn said to Abraham. "All this stuff with those Thomas kids got to him. I told you to get those people out of our lives," she spat at him. "Look what you've done to our son. Is this what you wanted?"

Abraham refused to be baited by Saralyn. He knew she was scared and itching for a fight as a way to deal with her fear. He wanted to hold her, give her comfort, and take comfort from her, but he knew reaching for her would not be a wise move.

"Mrs. Martin."

The three of them looked up to see a young doctor standing before them.

"I'm Mrs. Martin," both Saralyn and Rebecca said.

"Mrs. Isaac Martin."

Rebecca stood, and he and Saralyn stood with her. "I'm Mrs. Isaac Martin," Rebecca said. "And these are his parents, Abraham and Saralyn Martin. How is my husband?"

The doctor acknowledged Abraham and Saralyn with a slight nod. Then he said to Rebecca, "Your husband's condition is serious. We're running tests to find out how serious."

Rebecca and Saralyn both slumped back against Abraham at the doctor's words. It seemed they would have sunk to the floor in despair had he not held them up. He probably would have sunk right along with them if he hadn't needed to be strong for them.

"Is he going to die?" Saralyn asked, voicing the fear she'd earlier chided Rebecca for expressing.

"Not if I can help it," the doctor said. Abraham liked the arrogance he heard. The doctor's stature increased in his eyes. "The initial tests suggest your son has signs of liver disease. We have to run some additional tests to figure out how severe it is."

"Can it be cured?" Rebecca asked.

"Once we know the severity, we'll know the treatment options. The best case is if we can treat it with oral medication. The worse case is a liver transplant."

"Transplant?" all them of them echoed.

"That's the worse case scenario. We should know within the next couple of hours where we stand. I'll come out and give you an update as soon as I know more."

"Thank you, Doctor," Rebecca said.

"Take care of my son," Saralyn added.

Abraham nodded, man-to-man. The doctor's answering nod told him his plea had been understood.

Chapter Fifty-Seven

Deborah and Alan sat at the small conference table in her office eating the Chinese food they'd had delivered. Deborah dunked a fried wonton in a small plastic cup of soy sauce and then popped it in her mouth. "This is one part of the job that I could do without," she said.

"Welcome to the big leagues," Alan said. "Power always comes with a price tag."

"So I'm learning," she said, looking at the three short stacks of contracts before her. They represented contracts she was going to continue, contracts she was going to terminate, and contracts that were on the borderline. The borderline stack held the most contracts. "I'd like to go ahead and let the writers in the first two stacks know their status."

Alan nodded. "The legal department will get the letters out within the next week."

She looked at the second stack, the contracts for termination.

"Those writers are going to be crushed," she said. "Making dreams come true is certainly a lot better than killing them."

Alan chuckled. "I think you're exaggerating our power. You aren't killing dreams. You're giving those writers a chance to resell their work. Remember that those termination letters will each go out with a check for the remaining balance of the advance specified in the original contract. Some of the writers will probably be glad to be able to explore other opportunities for their work."

"I can tell you've never rejected a screenplay or a treatment."

He swallowed the last of his kung-pai chicken and then brushed his lips with a napkin. "But I've been around enough to know how things operate. Now that you're the head of production, the buck stops with you. Like I said, the price of power."

She folded her hands under her chin. "Is it about power for you?" she asked. "Is that why you're in this business?"

He shrugged. "It didn't start out that way, but power can be seductive and all-consuming. Once you have it, you don't want to give it up."

"That sounds more like Abraham than you," she said. "You don't seem caught up in all of this."

He smiled. "You're being generous and forgetful. I've spent a lot of my life in this building. Sometimes I wonder if the trade-offs were worth it. One thing power doesn't do is keep you warm at night."

"Why haven't you married?" she asked. "Abraham managed to get married, have a family, and have kids on the outside. What makes you so different from him?"

"Don't get me wrong," Alan said. "I've had my share of relationships, but nothing really serious. I was devoted to my sister and my work, in that order. I didn't have the emotional capacity to support another demanding relationship. A lot of men don't have it but they get married anyway and their families suffer."

"Like Abraham?"

"I didn't say that," he said. "Saralyn was fully committed to Abraham and she knew the sacrifices she'd have to make in order for them to achieve their dreams. That's what she bought into when she married him."

"I'll bet she didn't buy into him cheating on her with my mother."

"I'm sure she didn't, but I think women married to powerful men like your father live by a different set of rules and hold their husbands to a different set of standards. What might kill an ordinary marriage becomes a minor bump in the road in Saralyn-Abraham type marriages." He shrugged. "I know that sounds pessimistic but I think it's true."

"You may be right," she said. "I think that's one of the reasons I'm attracted to older, more established men who've gotten past the 'making a name for themselves' stage. They're at the point where they want to spend more of their time enjoying what they've accomplished."

"You're a bit too wise to be so young," he said, brushing a crumb from her cheek. "You must have an old soul."

"Thanks, I think," she said with a smile. "No matter what you say, I still can't believe you've never been in love, never wanted to get married."

He smiled, but there was sadness behind the smile. "Now you're sounding your age."

She punched him in the shoulder.

His sadness faded and he chuckled. "Okay, I've never been in love, but I have to admit, though, that I was tempted to get married after my parents died and Alisha became my responsibility. I began looking at each woman I dated as a potential mother for her. Fortunately, or unfortunately, there didn't seem to be much overlap in the women I wanted to date and the women who make good mothers."

"I know you made a good life for you and your sister."

He nodded. "Life was good. Alisha was happy. Women were plentiful, but not too demanding, the way I liked them. I always figured Alisha'd get married, have a passel of kids, and I'd be the doting uncle-slash-grandfather. So much for those plans."

Deborah reached for his hand. "I'm sorry, Alan. Your sister was lucky to have such a loving and caring brother."

"I was the lucky one," he said, shaking his head. The sweet smile on his face told her that he was recalling a special memory with his sister. She didn't ask what it was because she didn't want to intrude.

"Your sister would want you to be happy, Alan. It's not too late for a family of your own. I'm sure a lot of women would consider themselves blessed to land a distinguished man like you."

He grinned at her. "Volunteering for the job?"

She grinned back. "I'd need a detailed job description first."

He laughed. "You see, that's something Alisha would have said. She always had a ready response."

"She probably owed her quick wit to you. I know Michael forced me to develop one. He could be merciless, so I learned early to give as good as I got. Something tells me the relationship you shared with Alisha was a lot like the one I share with Michael."

He raised a brow.

"I'm not saying you're like Michael in all ways, but you and your sister were close because all you had was each other. That's the way it was with me and Michael, and to some extent our mother."

"Some extent?"

"It's hard to explain," she said. "Michael and I have always been more than a little protective of her. So instead of taking our complaints and disappointments to her all the time, we learned to take them to each other so we wouldn't add to her burden."

"What was it like for you, growing up, I mean?"

Deborah thought before answering. "How do I describe it? We were happy, you know, but there was always the shadow of Abraham looming above us. Sometimes I wonder if it wouldn't have been better all around, kinder even, if Mama had told us our father was dead or that she didn't know who he was. It was hard to know that he was around but didn't care enough to be involved in our lives."

"You amaze me," he said. "After all you've suffered at Abraham's hand, you accepted him when he reached out to you. How did you do it? *Why* did you do it?"

"I've asked myself that question many times and the only answer I can come up with is that he's my father. I'm a part of him and he's a part of me. Biology isn't everything, but it's strong."

"For you," he said, "but not for Michael."

She shrugged. "I don't know. I think it's easier for me to accept that I still need a father because I'm a woman. I'm expected to be soft and forgiving. Michael's entire identity is that he was forced to become a man without Abraham's help so he doesn't really need him now. That's why I think Abraham should cut him some slack. Michael has had to be the man of the family since he was a boy. Abraham needs to be the man now. He needs to do right by Michael without expecting Michael to fall at his feet. That's not going to happen. Not in this life."

"For what it's worth, I do believe Abraham plans to do right by him. He needs more time to work things out."

"You know, that explanation really doesn't work for me. Abraham has had thirty years already. How much more time does he need? What he needs is to be a man and do what's right. Michael is as much his son as Isaac is. He should treat him as such."

Alan chuckled. "I'm not sure that's what you want," he said. "You know the old saying, the grass is always greener on the other side of the fence. Well, life between Abraham and Isaac hasn't always been smooth. Power can mess up a man's thinking. The only softness Isaac has seen since he got out of elementary school has been from his mother. Abraham has been all about making him a man and getting him ready to run MEEG one day."

Deborah wasn't ready to hear a list of Saralyn's better qualities, especially when the woman held them all in such low esteem. "As someone who grew up without a father," she said, "I'm pretty convinced that having a father who expected too much from you is a thousand times better than having one who didn't care at all."

Alan was about to respond when his cell phone rang. He checked the number and then said, "I need to take this."

He stood and walked to the windows for some privacy. She cleared the table of their leftovers. When he came back to the table, he said, "Isaac's been taken the hospital. Something about his liver. "

She jumped to her feet. "Liver? Isaac? I can't believe it."

"Neither can I," he said. "I was talking to him earlier today and he was fine." He shook his head. "I need to get back to my office, make some phone calls, find some liver specialists. Abraham and Saralyn want only the best working on Isaac's case."

"Who can you call at his hour?"

He gave her an indulgent smile. "Another perk of power. I can't think of anybody in Atlanta who'd refuse a late night call from Abraham Martin's attorney."

Deborah swallowed. Hard. The perks of power, all right. "Is there anything I can do to help?" she asked, knowing Abraham must be beside himself with worry, despite all his power.

"You can hop on the Internet and find out what you can about liver disease and liver transplants. The more information we have, the better we'll be able to help."

"I'm on it," she said. She went back to her desk and fired up her computer.

"Thanks," he said. "I'll drop back by after I finish my phone calls, and we can ride to the hospital together."

"I'm not sure that's a good idea," she said, remembering the last time she was in an Emergency Room with Saralyn Martin.

"It's up to you," he said, "but I think it would mean a lot to Abraham to know you were there."

She thought about the conflict she'd face with Saralyn at the hospital, and about Abraham's recent about-face with regard to Michael and the board seat and how that made her and Michael feel. It didn't really matter now, did it? Abraham was her father and Isaac was her half brother. "I'll go with you," she told him.

He smiled at her choice and left to make his calls. She typed *liver disease* into Google and began her Internet search.

Chapter Fifty-Eight

Leah paced in front of the couch where Melvin sat in his living room. "Can you believe that man?" she asked, winding down from a twenty minute monologue of Abraham's visit to her office. "I was a fool to think he'd changed."

Melvin patted the seat next him. "Come, sit down. "

Leah didn't want to sit. She was too wound up.

"Come on," he said.

Reluctantly, she sat next to him. When he pulled her into his arms, she relaxed against him. "No man has ever loved and cared for me the way you do," she told him. "I'm so blessed to have you in my life."

He kissed her forehead. "I feel the same," he said, taking her left hand in his. He circled a finger around her bare ring finger.

Leah didn't have to guess what he was thinking. She peered up at him. "You know I love you, don't you?"

He dropped her hand. "I love you, too," he said. "And I've

asked you to marry me. Have you thought any more about my proposal?"

She eased up and away from him. "There's been so much going on—"

He lifted his palm to stop her. "I've heard it all before," he said. "It won't make any more sense to me tonight than it's made before. Maybe something else is holding you back."

She had no idea what he was talking about. "There is nothing else."

He met her eyes. "Maybe I should have said 'somebody' else."

His accusation hurt. "Melvin, you can't believe that. You're the only man in my life. You have been the only man since we started seeing each other over a year ago."

He shook his head. "I'm not sure that's true."

"Well, you're going to have to school me. Who is this mystery man?"

He reached out and touched her cheek. "Abraham."

"Abraham?" That answer truly shocked her.

"Think about it. The man practically consumes your life."

"That's not true," she said.

He nodded. "Yes, it is. What was your first reservation about dating me? It was that Abraham and Saralyn were members of my church."

"That doesn't prove anything," she said. "I was trying to protect you from Saralyn."

"That may be true," he said. "But you have to admit that your past with Abraham has been very much a part of our relationship."

"I thought you deserved to hear about my past from me," she said. "I was only trying to be honest. I had no idea you'd use that against me."

"I'm not using anything against you. I'm not even angry with you. I want you to be honest with yourself so that you can be honest with me."

"I have been honest with you."

"But have you been honest with yourself? Abraham was your first love. You have two children together. Even though it's been nearly thirty years since you've been together, I think you always held out hope that he would someday love the children you had together. I don't blame you for that. It's what any mother would want for her children."

"Then why are you asking if I love Abraham?"

"Because you didn't end the relationship with him because you stopped loving him. You ended it despite your love for him."

Leah wanted to tell Melvin he was wrong, but she couldn't. In some ways, loving her children forced her to hold some warmth in her heart for Abraham. How could she see him in her son's face every day, or see his mother's face in Deborah's, and not feel something for him? But it was more complicated than that. A part of her hated Abraham for the way he'd treated them. To keep that hate from consuming her, she'd made excuses for him. Excuses that began to blow up in her face when Saralyn schooled her on the way things really were. Now the hate was coming back. It wasn't love for Abraham that was holding her back; it was hatred. That realization shocked her.

"What are you thinking?" he asked.

"I'm thinking that I don't deserve you," she told him. "I'm not in love with Abraham, Melvin, not the way you think. But you're right that he does consume me. I've spent all my life either loving him, hating him, or making excuses for him, sometimes all three at the same time. He's my baggage."

"Baggage we can deal with," he said, with a warm smile. "All you have to do is let it go."

Her eyes grew damp and she began to blink fast. "How can I? He's back in my life now more than ever."

"You have to draw lines, Leah, establish some boundaries. Your children aren't babies anymore. They don't need you running interference for them with Abraham. Their relationship with him doesn't have to go through you."

"But I don't want them to be hurt."

"You can't control that, and you shouldn't. When you love somebody, you risk getting hurt. Sure, Abraham is going to let your kids down just like he let you down. It's inevitable. But they're strong; they're going to survive. And in the process, they'll forge their own relationship with him, not the relationship that you've always wanted for them, always prayed for them."

She began to weep softly. "I've spent my whole life protecting them from him and his disinterest. I don't know if I can stop."

"I know you can."

She smiled through her tears. "You're biased."

"Maybe," he said. "But I'm also right. It'll be hard but you'll do it. You have to let them go."

"But what if they think less of me as they get to know him better?" she asked, surprising herself with the question. She hadn't known she had this fear, but voicing it seemed to lift some unseen burden.

Melvin pulled her into his arms, and she wept harder. "Oh, sweetheart," he said, "that's impossible. Deborah and Michael have enough love in them for both you and Abraham. You have to trust them."

Melvin held her close as she cried herself out. "I do love you," she said.

"Prove it," he challenged. "Tell your children you want to marry me. Trust them to want your happiness as much as you want theirs."

"Now?"

He nodded. "This is the best way. Telling them will signal that your have your own life and that your relationship with them is separate from their relationship with Abraham."

"You make it sound so simple," she said.

He tapped her nose with his finger. "It is simple, but I didn't •
say it would be easy. The good news is that we'll face it together.
That's what marriage is all about, Leah: being there for each other,
holding each other up in the tough times."

Leah let his words shower over her. Did she have the courage to
do as he asked? Before she could answer, his phone rang.

He lifted an arm from around her and reached for it. When he
saw the caller ID, he pressed a soft kiss on her forehead and said,
"I've got to take this. Church business. I'll be right back." Then he
got up and went into the kitchen to take the call.

His absence gave her more time to think about the things he'd
said to her. The more she thought about them, the more she knew
he was right. She needed to move on with a life that was not cen-
tered on her children and their father, and her kids needed to see
her do it. They needed to be free to establish a relationship with
Abraham, knowing she was happy with the life she had.

She got up when she heard Melvin reenter the room. His dour
expression killed the insight she had been about to share with
him. "What's wrong?" she asked.

"It's Isaac Martin. He was rushed to the hospital, something
about his liver. I need to get over there and be with his wife and
his parents." He extended his hand to her, palm up. "Will you go
with me?"

Instinctively, Leah knew he was asking her to go public with
their relationship. The only reason she had for not doing it was
the havoc Saralyn might cause in his congregation. Could she
put an end to her patterns of the past and move forward with a
renewed life? The outstretched hand before her told her she could.
All she had to do was take the help he offered.

Chapter Fifty-Nine

Abraham sat in his son's hospital room with Saralyn and Rebecca. Isaac was asleep, but neither of them wanted to leave his side. The doctors had told them that his son was in for a tough trek so the rest was good for him. Abraham was content to let him sleep. Rebecca seemed to need to touch him. She'd been holding his hand and murmuring words of love and hope since they entered the room. Saralyn had staked out the role of nurturer, her focus on her son's comfort. Did he need another pillow? Should they freshen the pitcher of water beside the bed? Now she was arranging a huge bouquet of flowers to give his room some "life."

Abraham knew the women were doing what they needed to do to deal with the uncertainty before them, so he let them be. Earlier, he'd suggested that they step out and get some fresh air, but that suggestion was met with icy glares. He gave up, even though he knew they needed to leave the room and take some time for themselves. He needed that, too, but couldn't make himself leave either. He sat staring at his son lying in the bed, and wished he could trade places with him. He didn't see a hale, thirty-year-old man before him; rather, he saw a small, frail, little boy who needed his father's strength to pull an overloaded wagon across the patio.

He wiped at his eyes. Why? Why Isaac and why now?

Before he could ponder the questions, the door to the hospital room opened and in walked the doctor. Standing, Abraham could hear his heart pound as he prayed that Isaac's condition could be treated with medication. He looked from his wife, standing less than a foot away from him, to Rebecca, seated next to the bed holding Isaac's hand. All three of them seemed to be frozen in place by fear and anxiety.

From her position seated next to Isaac, and still holding his hand, Rebecca asked, "Is it good news, Doctor?"

Taking a step closer to Saralyn and reaching for her hand, Abraham prayed harder. Isaac was strong, he told himself. Everything would be fine. He squeezed Saralyn's hand to transmit the same message to her. He wanted to look at her and give her the same reassurance with his eyes, but he was afraid she'd see his fear instead.

The doctor made eye contact with him and Saralyn before answering Rebecca's question, "I'm sorry," he said, "but Isaac is going to need the liver transplant."

Saralyn's hand went limp in his, and he braced her with an arm around her waist. She turned her face into his side and began to cry. Rebecca's eyes filled with tears but no sound came from her. She lowered her head to Isaac's hand and wept silently. Abraham felt her pain as if she'd screamed from the bottom of her heart. Isaac had to get better, if only to learn how much this woman loved him, regardless of what had gone on in the past.

Abraham rubbed Saralyn's back and encouraged her to sit.

When she did, he poured her a glass of water. "Drink this," he said. "You'll feel better."

Her eyes told him she didn't believe him, but she drank anyway.

Glancing over at Rebecca and seeing her head still resting on her and Isaac's clasped hands, he went to her. The soft weeping that greeted him almost sent him over the edge. He bent down and kissed her head, whispered whatever words of comfort came to his mind.

The doctor, who'd undoubtedly given this message time and time again, merely waited for them to adjust to the disappointment before plodding ahead with options and alternatives.

Fighting back his own grief and disappointment, Abraham stood and asked the doctor, "What's next?"

The doctor walked closer to the bed and placed his clipboard on Isaac's bed tray. "There are two types of liver donors," the doctor began, "cadaver donors and living donors."

Saralyn moaned at his words and Rebecca finally raised her head. Abraham could only bite down on his lower lip.

"As the names suggest, with a cadaver donor, the liver is taken from a deceased person who was an organ donor. There is a very long waiting list for one of those livers. If Isaac had a cadaver donor, we'd simply remove his diseased liver and replace it with the donor liver.

"The second type, living donors, is gaining in popularity and occurrence because the liver in a healthy donor will regenerate itself. A living donor is typically a living relative who is in excellent health and has a compatible blood type. Possible donors will have to be tested. After we identify a match—or if there are multiple matches, the best match—we'll schedule surgeries for the donor and for Isaac. During the surgeries, Isaac's liver will be removed and about half of the donor's liver will be removed and transplanted into Isaac."

The doctor paused as if to let his words sink in. After a short moment he continued, "In Isaac's case, the best option is the living donor route. In addition to being quicker than the cadaver donor route, the success rate is higher. There is minimal risk to both Isaac and the donor, though as with any medical procedure, there can be complications."

"I'll get tested," Abraham said.

"So will I," Saralyn said.

"Me, too," Rebecca added.

The doctor looked across the three of them. "Of course, I want all three of you to be tested, but I have to tell you that none of you are good candidates." Turning to Rebecca, he said, "You're not a blood relative so you wouldn't be my first choice." Then he turned back to Abraham. "Mr. Martin, you recently had your own health problems. You wouldn't be a good risk for this procedure."

"What about me?" Saralyn asked.

"Of the three of you here, you may be the best option. The only problem is your size. Your son is much bigger than you, suggesting that his organs are as well. The size of your liver may eliminate you as a viable candidate. Do you have any other children?" the doctor asked. "Siblings are typically the best candidates." He flipped a couple of pages on Isaac's chart. "I see that Isaac has none. How about half siblings? The match may not be perfect but if there is a half brother about Isaac's size, he should definitely be tested."

Abraham refused to look at Saralyn. All he could think about were the awful things she'd said to and about Michael, and the recent decision he'd made to withhold the boy's seat on the MEEG board. Now they needed him to save Isaac. Would the boy do it? He didn't know.

"He has a half brother and a half sister," Rebecca finally said, turning Abraham's attention to her. "The brother, Michael, is about Isaac's size."

The doctor picked up his clipboard. "Let's get him in here and tested, then," he said. "We need to move quickly."

Saralyn stood. "Wait a minute, Doctor," she said. "Can't there be other living donors out there?"

"Anything is possible, Mrs. Martin," he said. "You're welcome to have as many people tested as are willing to be tested, but the statistics suggest that the half brother is the best candidate."

"Thank you," she said. When the doctor left the room, she turned to Abraham. "You have to convince him to be tested, Abraham," she pleaded. "Give him whatever he wants, just don't let my baby die."

Chapter Sixty

Josette sat at the foot of her bed and stared at the two suitcases and the vanity case she'd packed. She was really going to do it; she was going to leave Michael. She didn't see that she had any other choice. She couldn't let him keep lying to her with no consequences. She needed to take a stand, and this was the only way. Hearing the truth directly from Rebecca's lips had knocked the rose-colored glasses off her face. Now she clearly saw her husband for the man he was, and she didn't like what she saw. He was her child's father, so they'd always have a bond, but she no longer saw herself as his devoted and loving wife.

For the first time in a very long time, she didn't look at the clock when she heard him enter the house. She sat calmly and waited for him to come upstairs. She didn't have to wait long.

He knew something was wrong as soon as he crossed the threshold to the bedroom. She could see it in his wide-eyed expression when he saw the packed bags in the middle of the floor.

"What's this?" he asked, looking from her two packed bags to her.

"What does it look like?"

"It looks like somebody's going on a trip."

"Since I'm somebody, it seems you're correct."

He stared at her. "Where are you going?"

"Away from you," she said, her voice tighter than she wanted it to be. She told herself to breathe, remain calm.

He stepped around the bags and leaned against the dresser, facing her. "You can't keep running to my mother's every time you get upset with me," he said. "It's childish."

His words made her flinch. Going to his mother did make her seem childish, not to mention stupid. Leah and Deborah would always take Michael's side. They had deceived her from the beginning. She couldn't trust them. Oddly, the only person she felt she could trust to tell her the truth was Rebecca. "I'm not going to your mother's," she said.

"Then where are you going?"

She met his eyes. "I told you," she said, unwilling to get more specific. She'd rather keep him guessing than tell him she would be staying in the guesthouse of one of Rebecca's friends a few mere miles from their home. "Away from you."

"What's that supposed to mean?" he asked. "Stop talking in riddles. You wanted my attention. Well, you've got it."

He was too smug for his own good. She wanted to wipe that smugness off his face. She rubbed her belly. "Your daughter and I are taking a vacation, a long one."

He glanced down at her belly. "Not too long, I'd guess."

She hated his dismissive attitude. He should be asking why she was leaving and begging her to stay, like a normal husband would. Then she remembered that she was dealing with Michael

Thomas, definitely an atypical husband. "I went to visit Rebecca today," she said, giving the conversation a stiff shove in the direction she wanted it to go.

He jerked his head up. "Rebecca? Rebecca Martin, Isaac's wife?"

She didn't bother to answer, only stared at him. How many other Rebeccas did they know?

"Why'd you go see her?" he asked. "I told you there was nothing going on between us."

"That's not what she said."

"Then she's a liar," he said.

"Somebody's a liar. I'm not sure it's Rebecca, though."

He moved away from the dresser and began pacing in front of the packed bags. "So now I'm a liar?"

"If the shoe fits . . . "

He stopped pacing and pinned her with a stare. "You can't believe anything that woman says. She's always had a thing for me. She and Isaac are having problems and she can't stand that we're happy. Don't let her play you."

Somebody was playing her, all right, but it wasn't Rebecca. "Stop lying, Michael," she said, losing patience with him. "For once, be honest with me. I already know you slept with Rebecca after we were married. Why won't you admit it? She did."

He studied her, as if weighing the pros and cons of telling the truth. Finally, he said, "It was only a few times, and it didn't mean anything."

She blinked fast to keep the tears that had quickly filled her eyes at bay. "It meant something to me. I took my vows seriously and I thought you did, too."

He didn't say anything. Just looked at her with those pseudo sad eyes, hoping his charm would sway her. Same old Michael.

"Why did you marry me, Michael? What do you want from this marriage?"

He sat down next to her. "Why are you asking me all these

crazy questions? I want what everybody wants—a wife, a family, a home where I can love and be loved."

Now this was the Michael she'd fallen in love with. She'd thought he was lost to her. "You can't build that kind of life on lies, Michael. It doesn't work that way. It doesn't work that way for me. I need honesty. I need to know I'm loved."

"I do love you," he said. "You know I do."

She shook her head. "I used to know it. Now I'm not so sure. You married me without telling me of your relationship to Abraham and Isaac. You cheated on me with Rebecca. And you lied to me about both for a very long time."

"I didn't lie to you," he said.

"Of course you did. You lied by omission." She caressed her stomach. "This baby is our future, Michael. What kind of father will you be to her? Will you be another Abraham?"

"Never," he said. "I'd never abandon my children."

"You already have," she said softly. "You're here physically, at least some of the time, but emotionally you're somewhere else."

"That's not true."

"Yes, it is. You don't have any energy left for the baby and me because you expend it all on your hatred for Abraham and all that he has. He consumes you, Michael. What good will it do to exact revenge on Abraham if you lose your family and everyone who loves you in the process?"

"I'm not going to lose my family."

She shook her head slowly. "Leah and Deborah will always stick with you, that's true. You three are as tight as the Three Musketeers. I envy your closeness and wish that we had a sliver of it in our marriage, but we don't. Do you know why that is?"

"You have all the answers, so you tell me," Michael said, moving from charm to peevishness.

"I don't have the answer to that one, and that's why I need to get away for a while. I need to figure out what I'm going to do after the baby is born. Right now, I don't think I'll be coming back to this house, to you."

"Those are your hormones talking," Michael said. "Of course you're coming back here."

"You're not listening to me, Michael. Our marriage is in trouble and it's going to take some serious work to fix it. I don't know if you're up to it."

"You're talking crazy."

She refused to let him turn the conversation. "I'm deadly serious. You're going to have to fight for me and the baby, if you want us, Michael, and it's a kind of fighting you're not used to."

Her cell phone rang and she answered thinking it was the car service she had scheduled to pick her up. But the caller ID told her it was Deborah. She handed the phone to Michael. "It's your sister," she told him.

With a scowl, he took the phone. "Yeah, Deborah," he said. "What can I do for you? Josette and I were in the middle of something."

He handed the phone to Josette. "She wants to talk to you."

"It's Josette, Deborah."

"Good," Deborah said. "I didn't want to tell Michael this over the phone, but Isaac Martin is in the hospital."

She pressed her free hand to her chest. "Is it serious?"

"Very. He needs a liver transplant."

"What?" Josette said, thinking about the kindness Isaac had shown to her the day she'd visited his office. He was a good man. She didn't want him to be sick.

"I know it's a shocker. It was to me, too. They are asking for blood relatives to test as possible donors. That includes me and Michael."

Josette glanced at Michael. It would be a miracle if he agreed to the test. Just like it would take a miracle to restore their marriage. Did she believe in miracles?

"Look, Josette," Deborah said, "they wanted to start testing to-morrow but Alan convinced the hospital to start tonight. I need you to get Michael to the hospital so we can convince him to get tested. If you tell him why, he won't come."

More deception, Josette thought. This family was full of it. "I'll do what I can," she said. "And regardless of what Michael decides, I'll be there." She hung up the phone.

"What is it?" Michael asked.

"Isaac's in the hospital," she said. "He needs a liver transplant. They're asking all blood relatives to be tested. I'm going and I want you to go with me and be tested."

Michael shook his head. "No way. No how. Why should I do anything for them? What have any of them done for us?"

"When I said you were going to have to fight for me and the baby, this is what I meant. You're going to have to fight your baser instincts and do what's right. You can't let the need for vengeance destroy your capacity to love. If there is to be any chance for me and this baby to come back to this house, you have to come with me to the hospital."

He folded his arms across his chest. "So I have to give up my liver or you're going to take my kid away?"

She shook her head. "I'm not asking you to give up a liver. All I'm asking you to do is to be tested. You may not be a match."

He lifted a brow. "And if I am?"

"We'll cross that bridge when we come to it."

Chapter Sixty-One

Did you see this coming, Ma? Abraham thought as he sat alone in the hospital waiting room. Did you know that Isaac would need one of his half siblings to survive? A solid affirmative settled in Abraham's stomach. His mother had known this tragedy was coming, and tried to prepare the family for it. If only he hadn't deserted Leah and those kids. If only he'd brought Isaac, Deborah, and Michael up as siblings instead of keeping Deborah and Michael outside the family circle. Why had he and Saralyn chosen to make their world, their family, smaller instead of larger?

Isaac had always wanted a brother or sister. And all this time, he'd had both: two adults who now meant nothing to him, just as Isaac meant nothing to them. A sibling bond was more than biology. It grew out of a shared history. Abraham had no doubt Michael would donate a liver, whatever was needed, to save Deborah. But he was unsure if Michael would even lift a finger to save Isaac.

He wondered what he would do in the boy's situation. If he were as young and ambitious and calculating as Michael, he thought, he'd use the situation to his advantage. Unfortunately, he had no clue what Michael wanted from him. He'd already extended his hand to the boy once, and Saralyn had offered him money. Michael hadn't been interested in either.

According to Leah and Deborah, what Michael needed was unconditional acceptance, and recognition that he was an heir in MEEG—the one thing Abraham had thought he shouldn't give him. Now, he didn't know if Michael would even take it.

"Abraham," a familiar voice called. "I got here as soon as I could."

He looked up to see Reverend Reeves and Leah coming his way. What was she doing with his pastor? Standing, he said, "Leah, what are you doing here? How did you find out?"

"I was with Melvin when he got the news. I'm so sorry, Abraham. If there's anything I can do, please let me know."

Guilt welled up in Abraham as he recalled their recent conversation about Michael. The boy couldn't be trusted with a position at MEEG, but he could be trusted to donate an organ to Isaac. He couldn't help but feel like a hypocrite. Yet that was a minor price to pay for his son's life.

Deciding he'd rather have his conversation with Leah in private, Abraham reached out his hand to Reverend Reeves. "It's good to see you, Reverend," he said. "Your coming means a lot to me, and I know it'll mean a lot to Saralyn and Rebecca."

"I had to come," Melvin said. Pointing to a row of empty seats along the back wall, he added, "Now sit down before you fall down." Abraham did as he was told. When they were seated, Melvin directly next to him and Leah next to Melvin, the reverend asked, "How is Isaac? And how are Saralyn and Rebecca holding up?"

Abraham wiped his hand down his face. "Saralyn and Rebecca

are doing about as well as can be expected, given the news we just received. Isaac needs the transplant. According to his doctor, his problem is too severe to be treated with oral medications. I'll have some specialists here tomorrow for a second opinion but for now we're operating under the assumption that a liver transplant will be needed."

Melvin rested a hand on Abraham's shoulder. "I know this was hard news to hear, Abraham, but don't be disheartened. Isaac will find a donor. I'll get tested and I'll have an announcement made in church so that others will know to be tested."

"You should look into having a test site at the church to give people easier access," Leah suggested. "Maybe one Wednesday night around Bible study time and then another one on Sunday."

Reverend Reeves kissed Leah's cheek. "That's a great idea and that's exactly what we'll do."

Abraham tried to look past the reverend to Leah, but he couldn't see her face, couldn't read her expression.

"I want to say a few words to Saralyn and Rebecca and then I would like to pray with all of you," Melvin said. "After we do that, Leah and I will get to work organizing the church testing site."

Abraham nodded. "Go on in, Pastor," he said. "I'll be there shortly. I need to discuss something with Leah."

Melvin glanced at Leah, who gave a slight nod, and then he left them alone.

Abraham cleared his throat. "I hate to ask you this, Leah," he said, "especially after our conversation the other day."

She met his eyes directly. "I hate that you have to ask me," she said. "But I would do the same thing if it were my son."

"The doctor wants to do a living donor transplant," he said. "The donors are usually blood relatives. Unfortunately, neither Saralyn nor I are good matches."

Leah finished for him, "You want Deborah and Michael to be tested. Is that what you're asking?"

"They're his half siblings and the doctors think they could be a match, Michael more so than Deborah because he and Isaac are similar in stature."

Leah didn't answer immediately, and Abraham wondered what she was thinking. Her straight face gave away nothing. When she finally spoke, she said, "It's a lot to ask, Abraham."

"I know it is," he said. "I wouldn't ask if there were any other options. There aren't. Do you think they'll do it?"

"Deborah has a soft heart. She'd do it for a stranger so I'm sure she'll do it for Isaac. Michael is another story. I'm not sure about him."

Abraham closed his eyes and leaned back in his chair. "Sins of the father," he murmured. "What have I done to my children?" When he opened his eyes, he looked directly at Leah. "I still have to ask him," he told her. "You understand, don't you?"

She nodded. "Like I said, in your shoes I'd do the same."

"Will you try to convince Michael?" he asked. "Isaac could die without the transplant."

Leah shook her head. "I can't, Abraham," she said. "It's not my place. They're adults. I can give them my opinion but I can't tell them what to do."

"Could Michael live with himself if Isaac died?"

She smiled sadly. "You lived with yourself and prospered for thirty years, never even thinking of Michael as your son. I don't advise playing the guilt card with him. It won't work."

Her words shamed him. Abraham knew she was right but he was out of ideas. "How should I approach him, then?"

"Approach him like you'd approach a business associate you'd once done wrong and with whom you'd now like to play ball," she said. "Tell him why you're asking and how it makes you feel to ask. Be honest and forthright. And, most of all, listen to the answers he gives."

Abraham nodded. "Thanks," he said. Then he got up. "I'd better get back to Isaac's room. The pastor said he wanted to pray." He hesitated, then asked, "Do you want to join us? We can use all the prayer we can get."

She shook her head. "I don't belong with you and your family now," she said. "I came to support Melvin and to offer my best wishes for Isaac. I've done that."

"What's with you and Melvin?" he asked, his head tilted. The kiss that Melvin had given her on her cheek had not gone unnoticed.

She met his eyes. "He's asked me to marry him," she said. "We've been seeing each other for about a year or so."

"A year? I didn't know."

"We kept it a secret."

"Well, I'm glad for you. He's a good man, Leah. He'll treat you right."

She smiled at him. "He already does."

He tried to smile back but his lips didn't turn up far enough. Then he turned and headed toward his son's room.

Chapter Sixty-Two

Deborah walked hand in hand with Alan through the hospital waiting room. She wasn't sure what holding her hand meant to him, but she took it as a sign that he was becoming more comfortable with the idea of a relationship with her. She stopped walking when she spotted her mother dialing on her cell phone. "Mama?" Leah turned around. "What are you doing here?"

Leah closed her phone. "Deborah, you're here. I was about to call you about Isaac." She hugged her daughter. "How did you find out?"

Deborah pointed to Alan. "I was with Alan when he got the call." Alan and Leah exchanged greetings. "How did you find out?"

"It's a long story," Leah said. "I was with Abraham's pastor when he got the call."

"Abraham's pastor? How do you know Abraham's pastor?"

"Like I said, it's a long story."

Alan put a hand on Deborah's shoulder. "I'm going to go check on Isaac. Will you be all right?"

Deborah nodded. "Go on ahead. Mama will catch me up." After he left, she turned to her mother. "Now tell me the long story."

"I don't want to get into it here," Leah said. "This time should be about Isaac."

"Look," Deborah said, "I've done what I could do for Isaac by getting tested. Now tell me the long story."

Leah sighed. "I didn't want to tell you here, but since you're so insistent, I'm dating Melvin Reeves, Abraham and Saralyn's pastor."

"What?" Leah asked. "You're dating? Since when did you start dating?"

"Don't sound so surprised. I'm not dead yet."

"That's not what I meant," she said. "It's just that I haven't known you to date. Sure, you went out a few times over the years, but nothing more. I'm happy for you. It's about time. But a pastor?"

Leah chuckled. "That's why we kept it a secret."

Deborah's ears perked up. "A secret? How long have you been seeing this pastor?"

"A little over a year," Leah said. "We kept it a secret because I feared Saralyn would cause problems for him with his congregation if she knew I was the woman in his life. I didn't want him to have problems in his church because of me."

Deborah heard her mother's words, but that she hadn't shared something so important concerned her. "I can see you keeping it a secret from outsiders, but I can't believe you kept it a secret from me and Michael for a year. How could you, Mama?"

"Don't blow this out of proportion," Leah said. "I explained why we kept it a secret."

"Your explanation doesn't make sense," she said, hurt at her mother's deception. "Michael and I aren't people off the street out to do you harm; we're your children. How could you not tell us?"

"I thought it was best, Deborah," she said. "It was my decision to make and I made it."

She eyed her mother skeptically. "I don't remember you going on any dates with this pastor. When did you see each other?"

"Mostly after my evening classes."

Deborah's eyes widened. "When you told me you were at faculty meetings or meeting with students?"

Leah nodded.

"Mama," Deborah cried, wondering where this side of her mother had come from, "you lied to me. You flat-out lied to me. You should at least feel bad about it."

Leah sighed. "I didn't know where the relationship was going at first. It seemed to gain legs as we got to know each other better, and I was afraid I'd jinx it by going public. It was easier to keep on as we were."

"To keep lying to us. To me."

"You're not listening to me, Deborah. This wasn't about you. It was about me. It was something I wanted for myself. I didn't want you to know at first because of the Abraham-Saralyn connection through Melvin's church. This relationship began before Abraham decided to reinsert himself into your lives."

"Well, Abraham's been back for more than five months now. You had plenty of time to tell us, Mama."

"It's complicated, Deborah. By then I had grown to like Melvin—a lot. All I could think was that Saralyn would somehow use our relationship to cause problems between him and his congregation. I didn't want that."

Deborah still didn't understand. She and Michael would have kept the secret. There had to be more to this than her mother was telling. "I hear what you're saying, but it still doesn't make sense to me."

"I know it doesn't," Leah said. "Let's talk about it later, after you've met Melvin. He's a wonderful man. He's been wanting to meet you and Michael for a long time. I've been the hold-up."

Deborah smiled, relieved that at least one half of this secret couple had some sense. "Now this sounds like a man I can like."

Leah reached for her daughter's hand and squeezed. "You'll love him," she said. "I know you will." She pulled out her cell phone. "Now I've got to call Michael."

Deborah shook her head. "I already called him. I don't know if he's coming, but Josette said she'd try to get him here. I told her about the transplant and being tested."

"Do you think he'll do it?"

Deborah shrugged. "I honestly don't know. I told Josette to get him here without telling him the details of Isaac's condition. You and I will convince him to be tested once he gets here. I think we can do it, don't you?"

Leah shook her head. "No, we won't," she said. "It's not your place to tell Michael what to do in this situation, and neither is it mine. I'll give him my opinion, but I'm not going to try to convince him of anything. I only wish he had made peace with Abraham before now."

"No kidding," Deborah said. "Alan told us the other day that Abraham was pulling back on giving Michael a seat on the board. Michael seemed to take it okay, but Abraham's decision did nothing to improve Michael's opinion of him."

"Well, this is between Michael and Abraham and Isaac."

"But what if Michael doesn't get tested and Isaac dies? How will he feel then? Do you want him to live with that regret? I don't think I could live with myself if I didn't at least try."

Leah noticed her daughter used the same logic as Abraham. "Well, that's you," she told her daughter. "You can't expect Michael to make the same decision. And you have to make your decision for the right reason. You have to do it for Isaac, not to win points with Abraham or Saralyn, or to try to make Abraham proud of you. You can't go into this expecting some change in their attitudes toward you, and neither can Michael. If you did, you'd be deceiving yourselves."

"Isaac is my half brother, Mama. I can't do nothing."

"I'm not saying you shouldn't help him. In fact, I'm glad you've come to that decision. All I'm saying is that you have to give Michael the freedom to do the same. If something goes wrong during the surgery and Michael is harmed in some way, I don't want you to feel guilty. Could you go to work each day with Isaac and know that Michael died saving his life?"

Deborah shook her head back and forth. "I hadn't thought of it that way."

Leah grasped her daughter's hand. "This is Michael's moment, Deborah. We have to let him make his way through it. All I can tell him is not to use his decision as a way to gain revenge on Abraham. Other than that, it really is his choice."

Deborah wasn't sure she fully agreed with her mother, but there was little else she could say. Their family matters were much too complicated. And now with the introduction of her mother's new man, their family matters had gotten even more complex. She hadn't even thought that was possible.

Chapter Sixty-Three

Don't ask Michael, Dad," Isaac told his father. He sat up in his hospital bed, Rebecca on one side, his mother on the other. His father stood at the foot of the bed. "It's too much."

"Of course we're going to ask him," his mother said before his father could answer. "And he's going to do it."

Isaac turned to his mother. "Why would he, Mom? Why would he allow himself to be cut open and a part of his body removed for me? Tell me why he would do that."

"He's your brother," Rebecca said softly. "That will matter."

Isaac reached for Rebecca's hand, brought it to his lips and kissed it. Then he looked deeply into her eyes. "You know him better than we do," he told her. "So be honest. Would the Michael you know, the Michael who has tried to make my life miserable, do you really think he'd give me part of his liver?"

He watched tears well up in his wife's eyes and had his answer.

He looked to his father, who still hadn't said anything. "It's not your fault, Dad," he said. "You don't control Michael."

Abraham cleared his throat. "I know that, but I also know that I haven't handled things right with him from the beginning. If I had, you two might be as close as brothers should be and this decision wouldn't be an issue for either of you."

"You can't play the woulda-coulda-shoulda game, Dad. It's a no-winner."

"We can offer him money, a seat on the MEEG board, whatever he wants," his mother said. "If he won't do the right thing out of the goodness of his heart, then he'll do it out of his own self-interest."

Isaac shook his head as he smiled sadly in his mother's direction. "I love you, Mom," he told her. "You know that, don't you?"

"Of course I do. What a silly question."

"Well, I'm going to say something that may hurt. If the tables were turned and it was Michael Thomas needing the transplant, would you be encouraging me to be tested to be a living donor? If I were a match, would you want me to go through with the transplant?"

His mother didn't answer, instead looked away. While her answer disappointed him, he appreciated her honesty.

"Somewhere along the line," he said, "we made Michael and Deborah the enemy. Truth be told, there's very little difference between them and me. None of us controlled the conditions of our births, yet we're living under the shadows of those conditions. It's amazing that I can see that so clearly now but I couldn't see it before."

"I'm sorry, Isaac," his father said again. "So sorry."

Isaac smiled. "One thing that being sick and feeling your mortality does is give you a bit of clarity. I forgive you, Dad," he said. "You made a whopper of a mistake thirty years ago but at least you tried to make it right, albeit it took a long time."

His father wiped his eyes with his hand. "Thank you, son," he said.

"Don't thank me," he said. "I guess it's the Martin way. It takes us a while to see the error of our ways, but when we do, we make every effort to rectify it."

"Michael's a Martin, too," Rebecca said. "That should give us hope."

Isaac kissed his wife's hand again. "I need you to forgive me, Rebecca," he told her.

Her eyes widened. "For what?"

"For being a self-righteous you-know-what. I do love you and I want to make our marriage work." Tears flowed down her cheeks. "It's going to take some time to rebuild the trust between us but I'm willing to work at it if you are."

"Of course I am," she said. "Thank you, Isaac."

"You're not dying, Isaac," his mother snapped. "So stop talking like it."

Isaac laughed. "I know I'm not dying," he said. "But you have to admit I've never been this close to death before."

"Still," his mother said, "stop with all the forgiveness. You'll have plenty of time for that later. Let's talk about the good times we'll have when you get out of here. The first thing I think the four of us should do is take a long, a very long, vacation. We're blessed people and we have a lot to be thankful for."

"A vacation sounds nice," Rebecca said. She looked at Isaac. "A getaway would give us some time together."

"I'm all for going on vacation," Isaac said, "but what I look forward to once I get out of here is making peace with the Thomases."

"Please, Isaac," his mother said. "The boy may not even give you his liver."

"That's his right, Mom, but it doesn't stop him from being my brother, nor Deborah from being my sister."

"Half brother and half sister," his mother muttered.

"I want you to promise me something, Mom," he said.

She eyed him skeptically. "What?"

"I want you to promise to try to get along with them. I know it's a lot to ask, but we can't keep going on the way we are. I can't live in a family at war, and whether you like it or not, Michael and Deborah are my family, too."

"After what Michael has done to you—"

"If I'm willing to put it in the past, then so can you."

"I don't know," his mother said.

"I do," he said. "There's nothing Saralyn Martin can't do once she sets her mind to it. Set your mind to this, Mom. Do it for me. There's been too much stress and drama lately. All I want is peace."

"Amen to that," Abraham said.

"You all make it sound so simple," his mother said, "but peace has a price."

Chapter Sixty-Four

Abraham stepped out of Isaac's hospital room for a few moments. He needed some space to clear his mind, his heart. While he was proud of the sentiments his son had expressed, he was concerned that Isaac was giving up. Like Saralyn, he also thought the boy sounded like he was giving his last words, and he was not about to give up that easily.

Just then he spotted the group he was looking for and strode directly toward them. Alan saw him first. Then Melvin, Leah, and his dear daughter, Deborah, turned in his direction. "I'm glad you all are here," he said, meaning it. He stepped closer to Deborah and pulled her into a long, warm embrace. He whispered, "Especially you," in her ear and felt her smile in return. When he ended the embrace, he kept her close. "Isaac is awake and talking," he said. "You're all welcome to go in and say hi."

Melvin spoke first. "I'll say a quick good-bye, then Leah and I are going to head out. It's late but we've got to get started on getting those test sites set up at the church."

Abraham nodded and shook the pastor's hand. "Thanks for coming. It meant a lot."

As Melvin walked back toward Isaac's room, Abraham said to Leah, "It's okay if you go in as well."

She shook her head. "Maybe later."

He nodded his understanding. Perhaps one day things would be better between her and Saralyn, but today was not that day. "How about you?" he asked Deborah.

"I want to see Michael first."

"He's coming here?" Abraham asked.

"It seems like it. Josette called a few minutes ago and said they were on their way."

Abraham squeezed her shoulders. Maybe things would work out after all.

"Don't get your hopes up too high yet," Deborah said. "Michael doesn't know about being tested for the transplant."

Abraham's hopes sank at the news. Deborah knew her brother better than anyone, and she was clearly skeptical about his response to being a donor for Isaac. "It'll work out," he told her, not wanting her to bear the burden of her brother's decision. "If not Michael, we'll find another donor." He kissed her forehead. "I need to steal Alan away for a few minutes, if it's all right with you ladies."

After both women nodded, he said to Alan, "How about joining me for a cup of coffee?"

Alan looked at Deborah.

"Go ahead. I'll be fine."

With that, Abraham and Alan headed for the elevators to the hospital cafeteria.

"How are you holding up?" Alan asked when they were in the elevator.

"Still standing," he said. "But not much more. I've fought my share of battles, but nothing like this. I'd easily and readily change places with Isaac. In a heartbeat."

"I know what you mean," Alan said.

Abraham turned to him. "You do, don't you?" he said, remembering Alisha's death. "How did you make it through it, Alan?"

"What other choice did I have? I couldn't bring her back and I couldn't go with her. I was left to go on without her."

"She was a wonderful girl, Alisha," Abraham said.

"I know."

"I was wrong to start seeing her," Abraham said.

"Let's not do this now," Alan said as the elevator doors opened and the two men stepped off and headed in the direction of the hospital cafeteria.

Abraham maintained his silence until they'd gotten their coffee and taken a seat at one of the tables in the hospital cafeteria. "I'm sorry I betrayed you, Alan," he said. "I know you didn't like my seeing her, given my marital status and her age. I'm sorry I refused to see the harm our relationship would bring."

"It's the past," Alan said, sipping his coffee.

"Is it?" Abraham challenged. "Our relationship changed when you found out I was seeing her, and grew even more distant after her death." When Alan's eyes grew wide with surprise, Abraham added, "I may be a self-centered man, Alan, but I'm not blind."

"You never said anything."

"What could I say?" Abraham said. "I'm sorry I seduced your little sister? I'm sorry I broke her heart? I was too coldhearted to even think those thoughts. I kept waiting every day for you to leave MEEG or to beat me up or something, but you never did. Why?"

"Because she loved you," he said simply. "As she lay dying, she asked me not to blame you. I'd never denied her anything, and I couldn't very well start then."

"I never knew."

"There was no reason for me to tell you," he said. "It was between me and Alisha."

"You're a better man than I am, Alan," Abraham told him. "You always have been. At times I've resented you for it."

"And there've been times when I've resented the way you take what you want without regard for the consequences. You did it with Alisha. And before her, you did it with Leah and those kids."

"Well, it seems the consequences have caught up with me. The son I raised and loved needs a transplant, and his best donor may be the son I denied and ignored. What am I going to do, Alan?"

"You're going to do what you set out to do," he said. "You're going to do right by *all* of your children."

Abraham sighed. "Isaac doesn't want me to ask Michael about being tested."

"You have to," Alan said.

"But won't that make things worse between me and Michael?"

"It's a risk you have to take."

"And if he says no?"

Alan put down his coffee cup and met Abraham's eyes. "That's the price you have to pay."

Chapter Sixty-Five

Michael's mood had certainly improved by the time they reached the hospital, so much so that it made Josette uneasy. Her husband had gone from being totally uninterested in helping Isaac to giddy at the prospect of being a donor match. He was up to something. She was sure of it.

She saw Deborah when she entered the waiting room. "Where's Michael?" her sister-in-law asked, worry in her voice. "I thought you said he was coming."

"Calm down," Josette said. "He's here. He went immediately to be tested. He'll come here after he's finished."

"You told him about Isaac's condition?"

She nodded. "Michael and I have a new pact. No more secrets, no more lies. I told him as soon as I hung up with you."

"Well, you certainly took a big risk," Deborah said. "What if he had chosen not to come?"

"Then he wouldn't have come." With the Thomases, she

thought, the end seemed to justify the means. "I told you, no more secrets, no more lies. Michael's a grown man and I'm going to deal with him like he's one. All this subterfuge has got to stop."

"What are you talking about?"

"I'm talking about the lies and half-truths," Josette said. "They may get you through the moment, but they don't endure for the long run. Trust me, I know."

"Well, I don't even know what you're talking about. I was only trying to get Michael to come in to be tested. Knowing how he feels about Isaac, I didn't think he would come. That's the only reason I asked you not to tell him."

"Well, I told him and he's being tested."

"Willingly?"

"I nudged him a bit," Josette said, not wanting to get into details. "You know your brother."

"I'm not sure I do. I hate to say this but I'm surprised he went for the testing."

"This silly feud that Michael has with his father has got to stop," Josette said, running her hands around her extended belly. "This is not the environment I want for my child."

"I'm sorry, Josette," Deborah said. "Things will get better. Maybe Isaac's condition will draw us all closer."

"I hope so," she said, but she didn't count on it. "I can't live this way."

"What's up with you, Josette? You're talking in code. Something's bothering you. You may as well tell me what it is."

Josette looked up at her sister-in-law. "Michael and I are taking a break from each other," she said. "Until the baby is born."

"Will you be staying with Mama and me?"

Josette had to chuckle. Given that her past efforts at leaving Michael had consisted of nothing more than a short visit to Deborah and Leah's, she couldn't fault her sister-in-law for thinking this time would be no different. "Not this time," she said. "I really need to be alone so I can think clearly about the future for me and the baby."

"You can't be thinking about divorce," Deborah said. "Not now."

"Of course I'm thinking about divorce. I've been thinking about one since I found out Abraham was Michael's father. Michael should have told me before he married me."

"I know," Deborah said. "Mama and I both told him to tell you."

Josette shook her head. "That's not good enough, Deborah. When Michael didn't tell me, you and Leah should have. How could you let me marry him not knowing the truth? How could you?"

"It wasn't our place," Deborah said. "It was between you and Michael."

"If you really believe that, I feel sorry for you, Leah, and Michael."

"You feel sorry for us? Why?"

"Because you're stunted as a family. It's been the three of you against the world for so long that you don't know how to make room for anyone else. Leah's still alone after all these years, you flit from one old man to the next, and Michael married a woman he didn't trust enough to tell the name of his biological father. If that's not dysfunction, I don't know what is."

Deborah took a step back. "Well, you certainly have a low opinion of this family."

"It didn't start that way. I've loved you all from the beginning, when I thought I had been brought inside your circle. But I was wrong. Your silence about Abraham was proof that I was an outsider. Things haven't been the same for me since I found out. Something inside me is broken, Deborah, and I don't know how to fix it."

"Leaving is not going to fix it," Deborah said. "Running away never works."

"I know it's not the ideal answer, but it's the only one I have now. I can't live with a man I don't trust and who doesn't trust me, a man who cares more for vengeance than he does for his unborn child."

"Michael's not that bad, Josette," Deborah said.

"He's worse than you know. Michael has cheated on me, Josette." Deborah rolled her eyes. "With whom?"

"It doesn't matter," she said, deciding to keep Rebecca's name out of it. She wanted peace, not to add to the family drama.

"Do you have any proof of this cheating?" Deborah said, pushing the issue. "You've been accusing Michael of another woman for months, and he's said it's not true."

Josette gave up with a wave of her hand. "Look, I can't talk about this anymore. I'm going to go in and see Isaac."

"You can't leave the conversation hanging like this," Deborah said.

Josette nodded. "I don't have anything else to say. I'm empty, Deborah. That's what I've been trying to tell you. The only energy I have these days is for the baby." She rubbed her tummy again. "She's my focus."

"And she needs her father."

Josette shook her head. "She needs a father who will put her first, not a father who will sacrifice her on the altar of vengeance."

"If you take her away from her father, she's going to resent you when she grows up."

Josette smiled. "Don't worry," she said. "My daughter will know who her father is. I just pray history doesn't repeat itself and he doesn't ignore her until she's an adult. I hope my leaving will give Michael a chance to think about me and the baby, and how important—or unimportant—we are to him. He's got to show me that he's man enough to be a husband and a father. Right now all I see is a petulant little boy. I didn't sign up for babying a husband and a newborn. I won't do it."

She leaned over and kissed Deborah's cheek. "I'd never cut you all out of my baby's life. I want her to know her grandmother and grandfather, her aunt and her half uncle. I want her to have a supportive and loving family."

"No family is perfect, Josette."

"I'm not asking for perfection, Deborah. I just want the basics of love and honesty, someone who treats me with compassion and respect, someone who knows how to forgive, someone who values family above vengeance. Without those, what do you really have?"

Chapter Sixty-Six

I'm gonna be a match, Michael thought as he walked out of the Cancer Center, where the donor match tests were administered. *I just know it.*

"Michael?"

He turned and saw Alan heading toward the center from the opposite direction. *This has to be an omen.* "What are you doing here, man?" he asked.

"I could ask you the same," Alan said. "I'm surprised you agreed to be tested."

"Be tested? I'm praying I'm a match."

Alan eyed him skeptically. "You're praying to be a match? Now that's a bit much."

"Don't you see how perfect it would be if I were a match? We couldn't have asked for a better scenario. Forget waiting for Josette to deliver the baby and trying to invoke some obscure clause in the MEEG bylaws. If I'm a match, I'll have Abraham and Saralyn exactly where I want them, groveling at my feet to save the life of their precious son. Who said there was no God?"

"What are you planning?" Alan asked.

"It's all contingent on the results of that test. If the results indicate that I'm a match—which I'm confident they will—I'm going to have Abraham and Saralyn make me an offer I can't refuse." He chuckled. "Or I could make them an offer they can't refuse. Don't you love it?"

Alan shook his head. "I knew you hated them," he said, "but—"

"But nothing," Michael said, pointing a finger in Alan's chest. "A few months ago you came to me with a plan to take down Abraham Martin, remember? I didn't come to you. I signed on to hit him where it hurts, to give him a dose of his own medicine." He dropped his hand from Alan's chest and rubbed his chin. "How'd you put it? Yeah, show the big man that he can't get away with hurting people. Well, we've had the perfect way of doing that placed in our laps. Don't you see?"

"I can't do it," Alan said. "I can't use Isaac's illness to bring Abraham down. He's already down. I want a fair fight."

"You haven't been paying attention to how the old man works, have you? There's no such thing as a fair fight. You fight to win, by any means necessary, or you lose. It's that simple."

Alan looked at him as if he had two heads. "You know what, Michael? You may not have been raised in Abraham's home but you're definitely his son. You're more like him than Isaac is. In fact, you're exactly like him. Look at yourself. Standing in a hospital, hoping to hold the keys to a man's life in your hands so you can use them to take vengeance on your absentee father and his wicked wife."

Michael's lips tightened. "He's going to pay for what he did to me and my family. I thought you wanted him to pay for what he did to your sister."

"I did. But the funny thing is, I think he's paying for it now. We can't bring him down any lower than he is now, Michael. He knows there's a good chance that Isaac's life lies in your hands. His past has finally caught up with him. He needs the son he deserted to save the son he cherished. But he knows that even asking the deserted son for help will only widen the gap between them that he's been trying to bridge. He's at his lowest point, Michael. The game is over and everybody lost. It's time to call it in."

Michael folded his arms across his chest and gave Alan a look of disdain. "I always knew you were a weak man. Otherwise, it wouldn't have taken you so long to avenge your sister's death. Instead of taking Abraham down, you remained his flunky. Your sister is probably rolling in her grave."

Alan smiled, seemingly unmoved by Michael's taunt. "My sister is resting peacefully. That's something we have in common, Michael. Sisters who sleep easy because they always look for the best in others. Sisters who love us unconditionally. The sledgehammer that these weaker women hold over our heads is that their love comes with expectations. They expect us to be bigger than we are because that's how they see us. It would have hurt my sister had I brought Abraham down, but it would devastate her to know that I used Isaac's illness to do it. I never wanted to see that kind of disappointment in her eyes. I don't want to imagine it now that she's dead. You don't want to see it in Deborah's."

"Who are you to tell me anything about my sister? You know nothing about her."

"I know more than you think. I know she has a soft heart, and despite all you've done against Abraham and Isaac, she still thinks you're one of the good guys. If you do what you're planning to do, you'll break her heart. She'll never look at you the same again."

"Let me worry about my sister," Michael said. He tapped Alan in the chest again. "You stay away from her. I wonder what she'll think of you when she finds out our initial plans for Abraham. My guess is that she'll drop you so fast you won't know what hit you."

"Your threats don't work with me, Michael. I'm going to come clean with Deborah because I care about her."

A trickle of fear rolled up Michael's spine. "I don't believe you."

"I don't care what you believe. I'm going to tell her and she's going to tell your mother. Our plan is over."

"Good," Michael said, though he wished he could have kept Alan on his side until they lowered the boom on Abraham. "I don't need you anyway. I've been given another path to get what I want."

"You're so much like Abraham that it's no wonder you two don't get along. The funny thing is, you probably wouldn't have gotten along any better if he'd been there for you from day one. You're too much alike."

"I don't have to listen to this," Michael said, hating the comparisons of him and Abraham. He was nothing like the man. "You take care of your business and I'll take care of mine. And when the doctors confirm that I'm a match, I want a meeting with Abraham and Saralyn in the MEEG boardroom. I want to take them down on their turf." Then he turned and stalked away.

Chapter Sixty-Seven

Deborah hadn't known what to expect when Alan offered to drive her home from the hospital, but she'd never expected this news. "I don't believe you," she said.

Sitting next to her on her mother's living room couch, Alan tugged her hand into his. "Yes, you do," he said. "I have no reason to lie."

She pulled her hand away. "You've been lying since we met," she said. "Lies of omission. Was your interest in me part of your and Michael's plan?"

He shook his head, but she didn't believe him. How could she? "Your brother is very protective of you. He warned me not to start anything with you. He didn't want you to get hurt when you found out our plans. I tried to abide by his wishes, but I was drawn to you despite myself."

Under other conditions, Alan's words would have melted her

heart. Under the present conditions, they only made her sad for what could have been between them. "That makes no sense," she said, focusing on his comment about Michael and ignoring his words about their relationship. "If he knew the plan would hurt me, why would he follow through with it?"

"You know the answer to that, Deborah. Michael's need to hurt Abraham is much greater than his need to protect your heart. To be fair, he did say you'd forgive him in time. He trusts the love he has with you and your mother that much."

Deborah's heart ached. How could her beloved brother plan to use her this way? And dear sweet Alan, she never would have expected him of such deceit. She wouldn't have thought it was in his character. "So why are you telling me now?" she wanted to know.

"Because if there is to be any hope of a future between us, you had to hear it from me. And I do want a future with you, Deborah. I haven't thought much about the future since Alisha died, but I think it's time. It's been a long while since I've been in a serious relationship, and as we both know, I'm old enough to be your father, but if you're willing to take a chance on me, I promise to give you and this relationship all I have."

Deborah wanted to believe him, thought maybe there could be something between them, but she couldn't be sure. "I don't know," she said.

He stood and looked down at her, his eyes full of sadness and regret. "I understand," he said. "It's my loss, really."

She wanted to tell him that it wasn't a loss yet, but she couldn't force the words through her lips. She stood, her manners forcing her to escort him out, and as she did, the front door opened and a harried Michael entered the house.

He saw her first. "Is Josette here?" he asked. "Did you give her a ride from the hospital?" When Alan stepped around her and made himself visible, he added, "What are you doing here?"

Alan didn't bother to respond. He looked down at Deborah. "I really am sorry," he said. "More than you know." Then he headed out of the room, past Michael, and out of the house.

When he was gone, Michael asked again, "Is Josette here?"

Deborah stared at her brother as if he were a stranger. "No, she's not," she said. "The last time I saw her, she was going into Isaac's room at the hospital."

Michael marched past her to the living room and sat on the couch. "Where could she be?" he asked himself.

Deborah leaned against the doorjamb, remembering her conversation with Josette. "She did it, didn't she? She left you."

Michael looked up at her. "You're talking crazy. You know Josette, she'll be back."

Despite everything she'd just learned about Michael from Alan, Deborah's heart ached for him and his loss. He'd lost his father through no fault of his own, but the loss of his wife lay squarely at his feet. "This time is different, Michael. She's not coming back."

He eyed her skeptically. "How do you know so much? Did she tell you where she was going?"

As she looked at her big brother, her protector, her longtime best friend, she could only shake her head at what his life had become. "She just told me she wouldn't live with a man she didn't trust and who didn't trust her. I didn't understand fully at first, but I do now. You really should have told her that Abraham was our father before you married her. It shook her foundation and the foundation of your marriage when she found out. She feels as though you never trusted her and as a result she has nothing to stand on in the marriage. Without trust, what is there?"

Michael jumped up out of his seat. "Not you, too," he said. "I didn't tell her because it wasn't important."

She thought about the news Alan had just given her and how it made her feel. "Yes, it was important," she said. "You romanced her and convinced her to build a life with you without really sharing yourself with her. Then you stood before God and shared vows with her, all the while knowing that you were hiding a big piece of who you were from her."

"That's a load of bull," he said, running his hand across his head.

She sat down on the arm of the couch and watched her brother try to pace his troubles away. "Alan was telling the truth, wasn't he? You planned to use me, Mama, and Josette in some crazy plan to usurp Abraham's position at MEEG, didn't you?"

He met her eyes with his own clear ones. "That was Alan's plan. I went along for the ride."

His callousness made her heart ache. "How could you, Michael?" she cried. "Even after Mama and I went to Abraham and made the case for you, you were going to use us to undermine him. He would have thought we were in on it."

"Who cares what he would have thought?" he shot back. "We'd have what was rightfully ours as his heirs."

She patted her chest. "I would have cared," she said, tears rolling down her cheeks. "I want a relationship with him, Michael. I thought you knew that."

His eyes flared with contempt. "You make me ashamed to be your brother when you spout that crap. That old man that you care so much about went back on the deal he made with you and Mama. He can't be trusted. That old man ignored us until—"

"I don't care how long it took," she said. "Don't you get it? He's my father and I want him in my life. He can't change the past, Michael, but he's trying to do better now. You just won't give him a chance."

"He doesn't deserve a chance," he declared.

She wiped her wet cheeks with the back of her hand. "And what do you deserve, Michael? What do you deserve for undermining your marriage to Josette with lies and half-truths? What do you deserve for sacrificing me and Mama on the altar of your vendetta? What do you deserve for exploiting your half brother's illness for material gain and personal gratification? What do you deserve for seeking to destroy your unborn child's grandfather? You'd better be careful about not giving second chances. It seems to me you're going to be needing more than your share of them in the not so distant future."

"I didn't come here for this," he said, turning on her. "I came looking for my wife."

"Maybe if you had spent half as much time and energy on keeping her happy as you did plotting against Abraham, you'd know where she and her unborn child were. She's gone, Michael, and I'm glad she is. You're not ready to be a father. How can you be? You're still a child angry with an absent parent. But you're not a child, you're a grown man, and the actions you take will have long-lasting ramifications. Please think before you do something more stupid and destructive than what you've already done."

"If I wanted a sermon," he said, "I'd go to church." He headed for the door. When he reached it, he turned and said, "If Josette contacts you, tell her that I want her to come home."

"I'll think about it," she said. Then she added, "I'm not going to tell Mama about all of this, Michael, because it will break her spirit. I'm praying that you have a change of heart while there's still time. If you go through with this, I don't know if you'll ever get back what you lose in the process."

Without another word, he turned and left the house the same way he'd entered. Deborah slumped down on the couch, trying to get her mind around all that had transpired that day. Several of her illusions had been shattered. The good news was that one illusion had been restored. She was no longer angry with her mother for keeping her relationship with Reverend Reeves a secret. There

was no telling how Michael would have tried to exploit that con-
nection to Abraham, and perhaps, in the process, ruined their
mother's chance for happiness. She loved her brother, but right
now she saw him as a rabid animal, destroying everything in his
path. She feared he'd destroy himself in the process.

Chapter Sixty-Eight

A couple of days later the hospital called Michael with the news that he was a match. About an hour after that Alan called to tell him that Saralyn and Abraham wanted to meet with him. As he strode down the hallway at MEEG on his way to the boardroom for the meeting, he felt empowered and vindicated. He was about to get everything he deserved, everything he'd been denied by the old man's disinterest. But more important, the old man and the wicked stepmother were about to get a taste of what they deserved. Today was payback day all around.

Yes, he had the Martins exactly where he wanted them this morning. It was the Thomases who were giving him headaches. Deborah wasn't speaking to him, and when she did, he wasn't interested in hearing what she had to say. Josette had called last night and confirmed that she had left him, just as she'd said she would. She hadn't told him where she was, but she did promise to update him regularly on her condition and the baby's. He took that as a sign she would be back at his side very soon.

Michael glanced to his left at his previous partner in crime. Alan didn't have much to say to him this morning. Since he no longer needed Alan, he didn't really care whether they engaged in conversation or not. The man had never been anything more to him than a means to an end.

His heartbeat raced as they approached the doors to the boardroom. Alan opened the door for him and he entered, head held high. "Good morning," he said, nodding first to Saralyn and then to Abraham. The two were seated on the far side of the conference table next to each other, the picture of solidarity. Saralyn wore a haughty expression that clearly showed what she thought of him. Abraham's was more guarded, so he couldn't read him.

Abraham gave a hearty "Good morning" in return, while Saralyn said nothing. She was there, but it was clear she didn't want to be. It was also clear to him she wasn't going to pretend that her attitude toward him had changed. He really didn't care. He'd put her in her place before the meeting was over.

He took a seat across from them while Alan went around the table and sat next to Abraham. Michael had considered bringing his lawyer with him, but he didn't think he needed him since he held all the cards in this poker game. It was merely a matter of watching his opponents fold.

Alan cleared his throat. "Since we all know why we're here this morning, I suggest we forgo the formalities and get right to the matter at hand." His eyes met Michael's. "The floor is yours, Mr. Thomas."

Michael knew Alan's introductory statement was meant to shame him, but he felt no shame. He unbuttoned the buttons of his suit jacket and opened the portfolio he'd brought with him. "First, I'd like to thank you two for meeting with me this morning. I know you both have a pressing personal matter on your mind. Let me say up front, I don't intend for us to be here very long."

"Oh, please," Saralyn muttered. She glanced at Abraham. "Do we really have to sit through this?"

"Yes, you do," Michael said, his voice tight, before Abraham could answer. He hated Saralyn Martin about as much as she hated him. "Second, I want to be clear that the parameters of the deal I'm about to put forth are not up for negotiation. As we speak, my attorneys are drawing up the necessary contracts. They'll be ready for Alan's review and yours by the time we end this meeting."

Though he wasn't thirsty, Michael poured himself a glass of water from the pitcher near him and drank a swallow. He wanted to prolong the anxiety he knew Abraham and Saralyn were feeling. "I have only five requests," he began, looking down unnecessarily at his portfolio. "First, I want a permanent seat on the MEEG board of directors with full and equal voting rights. Do you agree to this request?"

"We agree," Alan said, speaking for his clients.

Michael shook his head. "I want to hear it from them. Individually."

Saralyn's lips turned into a snarl. "You are a petty little man, Michael Thomas. You will never be the man my son is."

Michael grinned at her because he knew it would anger her. Then he turned cruel. "You may never know the man your son can be if you don't answer the question."

"There's no need for that," Abraham said. "We wouldn't be here if we weren't ready to accept you terms. Let's get on with it. I agree."

Michael looked at Saralyn. "I agree," she muttered.

"Good. Now on to number two. I want you to honor the current stipulation in the MEEG bylaws that awards a board seat to the spouse of a Martin heir upon the birth of the first child to their union."

"I agree," they both said.

With that agreement, Michael had just guaranteed Josette a seat as soon as she gave birth to their child. "Good. Now on to number three. I want MEEG to purchase Thomas Management as a fully owned subsidiary, with me, Michael Thomas, as permanent CEO. I will have full control of the subsidiary along with full access to the resources of all the other MEEG holdings. The purchase price will be two times the offer Mrs. Martin made for me and my sister to get out of your lives, half in cash, half in MEEG stock. Do you agree to this request?"

Alan leaned over and whispered something in Abraham's ear. Though Abraham listened intently, he never took his eyes off Michael, who remained erect in his chair. Finally, the old man was seeing that Michael was as much the businessman as he himself was.

When Alan was finished, Abraham turned and whispered something to Saralyn. "I agree," they both said.

Michael grinned again. "Good," he said. "See, I told you this wasn't going to take long. Let's move on to number four. I want a stipulation in the corporate bylaws that requires equal distribution and assignment of MEEG shares among Abraham's three children, meaning first that shares cannot be given to one sibling without being given to the others, and second, shares cannot be sold to one sibling unless the same offer is made to the other siblings. Do you agree with this request?"

Abraham looked at Alan, who nodded. "I agree," Abraham said. Saralyn repeated the phrase.

Michael thought the meeting was going pretty well. He had just ensured that Isaac would never own more shares of MEEG than he would. In fact, he would own more since he would have the shares from the sale of Thomas Management. This meeting was going very well. "Now for my fifth and final request. Since you've been so gracious with my previous requests, I'm going to be gracious with this one and give you an option. I want Saralyn Martin removed from the MEEG board of directors—"

Saralyn jumped up from her chair. "You little miscreant. Who are you—"

Abraham tugged on her arm and pulled her back down. He leaned over to her, rubbed her shoulders and whispered in her ear. Then he looked back at Michael, his eyes full of fire. Michael was glad to know he'd finally gotten a rise out of the man. "Go on," Abraham said. "Let's finish this."

Michael nodded. "As I was saying, I want Saralyn Martin removed from the board or Leah Thomas added to the board. The choice is yours."

Without consulting with Saralyn, Abraham said, "We'll add Leah."

Michael closed his portfolio. "That concludes my business this morning. Does anyone have anything else?"

Saralyn stood. "I can't take any more of this," she said. "I'm going to see my son." With those words, she left the boardroom, slamming the door behind her.

Abraham turned to Alan. "You've got all that, right?"

Alan nodded.

"Then give me a few minutes alone with my son."

After Alan left the room and they were alone, Abraham said with a smile, "You're full of surprises, Michael."

Having gotten what he wanted, it didn't matter to him what Abraham thought. He was a bit disappointed, though, that the old man didn't look like he'd lost. He wanted to wipe that smile off his face. "What's life without surprises?"

"Except for that shot you took at Saralyn with the board nonsense, your requests were pretty reasonable. I half expected you to want all of MEEG, not just a part of it."

Michael had tempered his requests in deference to his wife, mother, and sister. It would take them some time to forgive him for his revised requests, he knew. Had he gone with the original ones, no doubt it would have taken them longer. He didn't want or need all the drama, since the baby was coming soon. "I'm a reasonable man and a pretty astute businessman," he said to Abraham. "The only thing worse than a bad hand is the overplaying of a great one."

"There's something I don't understand, though," Abraham said, curiosity shining in his eyes. "Most of what you asked for—the board seat, the MEEG equity—I already wanted to give you. I had even thought about how Thomas Management Group would fit in with my other MEEG holdings. I wanted us to work through these ideas together and in the process forge some kind of relationship. If you had accepted my hand when I offered it to you, we could have reached this point in a much more amicable way. Why didn't you?"

Michael lifted his shoulders in a slight shrug. "I didn't trust you, still don't. And given how things worked with that board seat, I was right not to. You sang a good song about wanting to bring Deborah and me into the fold, but your execution was shoddy. I took this opportunity to set things right. You ought to thank me for it."

Abraham smiled that smile again. "Give me a few days to think on it. This new magnanimous Michael is a bit much for me to deal with."

The old man was good at masking his emotions, Michael thought, for there was no way he could be happy about what had gone on in the meeting. The smile and his calm expression had to be a facade. "Don't get me wrong," he said. "I'm not going to lie and say I didn't want your head on a platter, but I couldn't find a way to do it without suffering personal losses that were just too high. At least, too high for right now. But it's not over yet. There's still time for me to take you out."

Abraham laughed, a hearty laugh that Michael knew was real. "I'll watch my back."

Abraham's laughter threw him off-kilter. He'd expected the man to be angry, defiant, but he wasn't. It had to be a trick, he thought. The old man was trying to get inside his head. Well, he would let him think he had. That way, when the opportunity presented itself and he was finally able to lower the boom on Abraham Martin, the unexpectedness of it would make it that much sweeter. Abraham was nowhere close to having paid the debt he owed. Michael stood and picked up his portfolio, ready to leave.

"One more thing," Abraham said. Michael turned back to him. "We found another donor, so we don't need you for the transplant after all."

Michael swallowed hard, tried to maintain his composure, but his knees felt like they were about to give out on him. He sat back down to keep from falling down. "What did you say?"

"I said that Isaac has another donor so he won't need your liver. It turns out someone from our church was also a match."

Michael opened his mouth but couldn't decide what to say, so he closed it, saying nothing. He merely stared at Abraham, who stared right back at him.

"You know," Abraham began, "a sit-down similar to this one is all I've wanted from you. A chance to talk, to hear about your business, to find out what makes you tick. You've done a great job with Thomas Management, by the way. I've always thought it was more than coincidence that you and Deborah chose careers in the entertainment field. It was one sign that Martin blood flowed through your veins."

Michael's head felt like it was filled with cobwebs that were clouding his thinking. He wanted to give his head a couple of swift shakes to rid himself of them, but he didn't want Abraham to know he was rattled. "What was this meeting all about, then?" he asked when he was finally able to put together a question.

Abraham leaned back in his chair, folded his arms across his stomach. He appeared completely and fully relaxed. "You're a businessman. You tell me what it was about."

Michael didn't want to voice his thoughts. It would be too humiliating. He'd come here to put Abraham in his place, and Abraham had turned the tables on him. How quickly he'd gone from victory to defeat! "You may have won this round, old man, but this war of ours is far from over. I'm going to beat you at your own game. Maybe not today, but someday."

Abraham leaned forward. "You still don't get it, do you?" Without waiting for a response, he continued, "The war ended today, Michael, and we both won. You got what you wanted and I got what I wanted."

Michael finally had to shake those cobwebs away. "You've totally lost me," he said. "I have no idea what you're talking about."

"I've accepted all your terms, so you've won," Abraham explained. "They were all things I would have freely given you anyway, so I've won as well. Win-win."

Michael wasn't sure he'd heard correctly, so he asked, "You're going to honor this deal even though I won't be giving Isaac part of my liver?"

Abraham's smile faded and the look of defeat that Michael had wanted to see earlier finally appeared on his face. "I thank God Isaac doesn't need your liver. First of all, he wasn't going to take it."

"He wasn't going to take it?" Michael said, interrupting him.

"He was adamant about not taking it, has been since he learned he needed a transplant. He wants a brother, Michael, not a donor.

It was clear to him that he'd never have you as a brother if he used you as a donor."

Michael didn't know what to say. He wasn't sure he believed Abraham. "It's easy for Isaac to say that, knowing he has another donor lined up. He'd be singing a different tuned if he didn't."

Abraham shrugged. "Maybe, maybe not. Isaac didn't even want you to be tested."

Michael snorted. "Well, he had you and Saralyn out there fighting for him on that one. Don't tell me you didn't want me to be tested. Don't tell me you hadn't already lined me up to be a donor. You and Saralyn were willing to go a long way to get your precious son a liver."

Abraham blinked his eyes, shuttering his emotions. "You'll be a father soon and understand how far a father will go for his child. In case you're wondering, if the situation had been reversed and you had needed a liver, I would have asked Isaac to be tested."

Michael felt his temper rise with those words. Just who did this old man think he was talking to? "Why didn't you have those feelings for me when I was born?" he asked in a calm voice, even as he fought the urge to shout. "Why was it so easy for you to walk away from me and Deborah?"

Abraham lifted his arms as if in supplication. "I don't have any answer that will make what I did right or acceptable. I only hope that one day you find it in your heart to forgive me. I know it's a lot to hope for, but I'm feeling hopeful these days. I've given you everything you've asked for, Michael. I don't know what else to do to show you that I want to right the wrongs I did all those years ago. What more do you want from me?"

I want you to have been there when I needed you. I wanted you at my basketball games. I wanted you at my college graduation. I wanted your advice when I started my business. I wanted you to be my father so I could learn to be a man.

Michael thought all these things but couldn't voice any of them.

"I know what I want from you," Abraham said, when Michael didn't answer his question. "I want to get to know you."

"It's too late," Michael said, but the words rang hollow to his ears.

Abraham shook his head. "As long as we both have breath in our bodies, it's not too late. All you have to do is give me a chance."

Chapter Sixty-Nine

Michael was surprised when he received the signed contracts from Alan a couple of days later. Even though the old man had assured him their deal was solid despite the fact that Isaac had another donor, he hadn't quite believed him. Old habits were hard to break. He'd read every word of the document to make sure that Abraham hadn't tried to sneak in any changes and found none. The old man had given him everything he'd asked for, and gotten nothing in return. It didn't make sense.

Regardless, he'd felt the need to celebrate, only to discover that he didn't have anyone to celebrate with. He hadn't heard from Josette beyond that first call, and he was pretty sure his mother and Deborah wouldn't be in a celebrating mood. Nevertheless, he found himself seated on their porch waiting for them to get home so he could share his good fortune with them. They arrived about an hour after he did.

"If it isn't the prodigal brother," Deborah said when she got out of the passenger front seat. She waved him over. "Get over here. We need help with these groceries."

"Why didn't you let yourself in?" his mother asked when she got out of the driver side door. "Did you lose your key?"

Michael ambled over to the car and followed his mother and sister to the trunk. "I didn't lose my key," he said. "I was just taking advantage of a beautiful spring day. Nothing wrong with that."

Deborah picked up four plastic grocery bags. "You're right about that," she said, heading for the house.

Before picking up her bags, his mother leaned over and kissed him on his forehead. "You've been avoiding me," she said. "And I don't like it." She picked up three grocery bags. "Bring the rest of these in for me, please."

Michael nodded. He removed the remaining four bags from the trunk, lowered it closed, then followed his mother and sister into the kitchen. They'd already started putting food in the refrigerator and pantry. He placed his bags on the table and began removing their contents.

"Guess what I got via express mail yesterday?" his mother asked, putting a gallon of milk in the refrigerator.

"I have no idea," he said. "So you may as well tell me."

"A contract from MEEG giving me a seat on the board."

Michael met his mother's eyes. "You deserve it, Mama. I'm glad Abraham finally realized it."

"Did you get a contract, too?" she asked him.

"Sure did," he said, not bothering to explain that his contract specified more than a MEEG board seat. He let his mother assume his was the same as hers.

"Guess what she did with it?" Deborah said.

"I hope she signed it and sent it back."

Deborah rolled her eyes. "She sent it back, all right, but she didn't sign it."

Michael turned to his mother. "Why didn't you sign it?"

After putting a five-pound bag of sugar in the pantry, Leah said, "I didn't sign it because I don't want the seat."

"But you deserve it, Mama," he said.

"Don't waste your breath," Deborah said. "She's not going to change her mind."

Leah slapped Deborah lightly on the shoulder. "Stop trying to stir up trouble. I told you why I didn't want the seat."

"Well, tell me," Michael said, thinking of all he'd gone through to get it for her.

Leah raised a brow. "If you'd answered your phone or returned your messages, you'd know already."

Duly chastised, Michael said, "I'm sorry about that."

"As you should be," Leah said. "I turned down the seat because I don't belong at MEEG."

"Yes—"

She cut him off with a raised palm. "You and Deborah belong there with your father, but I have my own life. If you'd returned my calls or answered your phone, you'd also know that I'm getting married."

Michael stopped removing items from the bag he was working on. "What are you talking about? How are you getting married?"

Deborah laughed.

After giving her daughter her version of the evil eye, Leah said, "I'm marrying Reverend Melvin Reeves."

Michael sat down in a chair to keep from falling down. His world seemed to be spinning off its axis. "You're marrying a preacher? I didn't even know you were dating."

"I've been down this road," Deborah said, "so I'm going to let you two travel it again without me." She took an apple from one of the bags and left the kitchen.

Leah took at seat at the table next to him. "I know this comes as a surprise to you, Michael. I should have told you both about

Melvin sooner." She went on to tell him how she and Melvin had met and how long they had been seeing each other.

"I can't believe you kept it a secret from us," he said.

"Melvin is the pastor of Saralyn and Abraham's church," she explained. "That made things complicated."

Michael understood. A grin spread across his face when he thought of Saralyn's reaction to the news. "Do they know?"

She shook her head. "We're announcing our engagement at his church on Sunday. I want both you and Deborah to be there."

Michael nodded. "Of course I'll be there. I only wish Josette could be there with me."

Leah squeezed his shoulder as she got up and resumed putting away the food. "Don't give up hope. She called yesterday and I asked her to join us."

Michael tried not to be hurt that Josette hadn't called him yesterday. "How is she?" he asked.

"She sounds good, said she and the baby were fine."

Michael appreciated his mother not asking questions about the separation or berating him for causing it. "Josette'll be home soon," he said. His mother gave him a look of pity. He turned away from it and focused on one of the grocery bags.

"I hope you're right, son. And I hope you're doing the things you need to do to make her want to come home."

Deborah's reentry into the room saved him from having to respond. She surprised him when she pressed a kiss against his forehead.

"What was that for?" he asked.

"Can't a sister show a brother some love?"

"Yeah, but there's usually catch with it."

Deborah looked at Leah. "Can you believe it, Mama? He's rejecting my love."

"Don't put me in the middle," Leah said. "My days of refereeing your fights are over. You're on your own."

Deborah looked at Michael, while tilting her head in her mother's direction. "She's gotten sassy since she's gotten engaged."

Leah didn't even bother to respond. She picked up the phone when it rang and then stepped out of the kitchen with the handset to talk.

"I'm glad you didn't have to go through with the liver transplant," Deborah said when her mother was out of earshot. "I think you dodged a bullet there, Michael. I'm fairly certain that plan of yours to outwit Abraham would have backfired on you and caused trouble all around."

Michael saw the relieved joy in his sister's eyes. He wondered if telling her what had happened would change her expression. "I went through with it, after all," he said, deciding to go all in.

Her eyes dimmed a bit and she sat next to him. "Why? What happened?"

Michael explained what had happened. "Can you believe it?"

"To be honest, I can. Abraham was right when he said he was only agreeing to what he would have given you before, other than the board seat for Mama. He probably knew she wouldn't take it anyway." Deborah chuckled. "He beat you fair and square."

"The war's not over," Michael said, even as he remembered Abraham's win-win words.

Deborah got up and patted him on his shoulder. "It's over, Michael. You just refuse to concede defeat. If you want to be a family with Josette and that baby, I strongly recommend that you start looking forward and stop looking back. Everything you want is within your grasp. Don't lose it all fighting some war that exists only in your mind."

Chapter Seventy

Michael's day was off to a good start. It had begun with a call from Josette. She'd been a bit distant and hesitant at the start of the call, but warmed up as she began talking about the baby. He'd surprised himself and told her about his ill-fated showdown with Abraham. She'd been disappointed in his actions but quite pleased that he told her about it. Women! Go figure.

She'd only asked one thing of him in the call, and he promised to do it only because she said she'd call back later that night to hear how it went. His wife was definitely honing her manipulation skills. He wanted her and the baby back with him and she knew it, so she was using that knowledge to her advantage.

So here he stood outside Isaac Martin's hospital room, having no choice but to go in. He'd considered not coming and telling Josette that he had. He decided against that course of action after calculating the price of being found lying and realizing it was a higher price than he wanted to pay. He took a deep breath and pushed open the door.

Isaac and Rebecca both turned toward him. He was relieved that Saralyn and Abraham were not there. He hoped he wouldn't have to see them again until the next MEEG board meeting. "I bet you're surprised to see me," he said, after discarding the idea of giving a traditional greeting.

To his surprise, both of them smiled. "Surprised is a good word," Isaac said.

"I'm not surprised," Rebecca said, "Josette told me she'd get you down here somehow."

It was Michael's turn to be surprised. His Josette was in communication with Rebecca? "She's a miracle worker," he said, coming to stand closer to the foot of the bed. "How are you doing?" he asked Isaac.

"Glad to be alive," he said, his face serious.

Michael couldn't think of anything else to say. Josette had asked him to come see how Isaac was doing and he'd done that. What else was there left to do?

Isaac turned to Rebecca. "Give us a minute, sweetheart."

She nodded. "Thanks for coming by, Michael," she said. "I'll make sure to thank Josette for getting you here." She smiled and then she left him and Isaac alone.

"Dad told me about the settlement," Isaac said.

Michael stiffened his spine. "I only asked for what I thought was fair."

"I'm not judging you, Michael," Isaac said. "In your shoes, I may have done the same thing. Anyway, I'm glad you came by today. I know our history is not that good, but I'd like for us to have a new start to go along with my new liver."

"I just came here to see how you were doing because Josette asked me to," Michael explained. "I wasn't looking for more than that."

"Is that a no?" Isaac asked. "Because if it is, I'll have to tell Josette that you rejected my olive branch. I don't think she's going to like that."

"You're blackmailing me?"

Isaac chuckled. "I know it sounds that way, but I'm just trying to create an amicable environment in this family. Your daughter—my niece—will be born soon and she'll draw the bonds between us even tighter. Josette is determined that we get along for the baby's sake. I don't want to let her down and I know you don't either. That leaves us with no choice other than to take a first step toward some kind of reconciliation or cease-fire. We don't have to be best friends, Michael, but we do have to be able to be in the same room without having the tension choke us all to death."

Michael agreed with everything Isaac had said. "I think I can do that," he told him, "for Josette and the baby."

Isaac extended his hand. Michael looked at it for long moments before moving to the side of the bed and shaking it. When he would have ended the shake, Isaac held onto his hand. "One more thing," he said. "And this is for Rebecca, not for me."

"What?"

"I need you to apologize to her for the gifts and for the things you said in the boardroom. Everything else that's happened between us was fair game, but it wasn't fair to bring her into it. Will you do that? Will you apologize to her?"

Michael looked into his brother's face, a face so like his own, and nodded.

Epilogue

Four months later

T hat was a wonderful meal, Rebecca," Alan said, patting his
stomach as he and Deborah walked from the kitchen to the
living room of Isaac and Rebecca's condo. "It's nice to know
modern women haven't given up on domestic skills altogether."

Deborah punched him on the shoulder. "Stop dropping hints,"
she said. "I told you I would take a cooking class."

Abraham chuckled. "This relationship must be getting serious.
It says a lot when a woman starts working on her cooking skills
for a man."

"You know what they say, Dad," Isaac chimed in. He took a
seat on the love seat next to Rebecca, after Deborah and Alan had
positioned themselves on the couch and Abraham had taken the
club chair. "The way to a man's heart is through his stomach."

"And what's the way to a woman's heart?" Rebecca asked her
husband.

Isaac planted a soft kiss on her lips.

"You've got that right, Isaac. You men take the food. We'll take romance any day."

Abraham sat back and watched, with joy, the interplay of people he loved. His heart grew warm with every smile exchanged between Isaac and Deborah. The sibling bond that he wanted for them seemed to be taking root. He thanked God for it.

He was thankful, too, that Isaac and Rebecca had found each other again. They'd gone on a late anniversary cruise as soon as the doctors gave Isaac the go ahead. They'd returned renewed and more in love than ever before.

He glanced over at Deborah as she laughed at something Alan said. He wasn't sure how he felt about that relationship, but she didn't have any substantive grounds on which to challenge it. Alan was much too old for Deborah, in his opinion, but he doted on her and she blossomed under it. A part of him knew that some of his resistance to the relationship had to do with Alan filling a role he wanted to fill. He wanted to be the indulgent father, but Deborah didn't need him to be that when she had an indulgent boyfriend. Running Brook was where he and Deborah melded. Their mentor-mentee relationship was probably the closest they'd get to father-daughter. He gratefully accepted it.

As much as Abraham appreciated the family that was with him today, he missed those who were not. Saralyn and Michael been invited, but both had declined. Saralyn had yet to get over the ultimatums Michael made when he thought they needed him to be a liver donor for Isaac. And he knew that she was still angry with him for giving in to those demands when they hadn't needed to. The bottom line was that she still wasn't ready to accept Michael or Deborah. He counted on Isaac to wear her down, though. He was her only soft spot.

Michael, on the other hand, was just not ready to give up thirty years of anger. Abraham hoped that the birth of his first child would change him. If it didn't, he didn't like to think where Michael's life would take him. Josette would accept nothing less than full surrender from him.

Thoughts of Josette, who was still separated from Michael, brought thoughts of his grandchild, which brought a giant grin to his face. Josette was due to deliver any day now. He couldn't wait to hold his first grandchild. How he wished his mother could be there for the birth of her first great-grandchild! He comforted himself with the knowledge that she was looking down from heaven with a smile. He'd taken her letter to heart and tried to become the better man she'd wanted him to be. It hadn't been an easy road to travel so far, and he didn't expect it to become easier as time went on, but he knew the struggle was worth the reward.

"What are you grinning about, Dad?" Rebecca asked. "Let us in on it."

He smiled. "Josette and the baby."

"That ought to make you smile, Grandpa," Alan said.

The phone rang and Rebecca got up to answer it. "Really," she said into the handset. "We're on our way.

"You must be psychic, Dad," she said when she hung up. "That was Leah and Melvin. Josette just called them. She's on her way to the hospital."

Deborah got up from her seat, clapping her hands. "Come on, folks," she said. "We've got to get moving. I'm about to be an aunt."

"And I'm about to be an uncle," Isaac chimed in.

Abraham looked heavenward. "And I'm about to be a grandfather." Life was good. He was living proof that a man's past sins didn't have to destroy his future. "Who's driving?" he asked. "Grandpa is much too nervous to do it."

Acknowledgments

Sins of the Father made its way into print due to the hard work of a lot of people. Though it is impossible for me to name every person who contributed, I'd like to single out a few.

My first thanks goes to Carolyn Marino, my previous Harper editor, for leaving me in the wonderfully capable hands of her assistant Wendy Lee. Thanks also, Carolyn, for being there to help us develop a great tagline.

I don't really know how to express my gratitude to my editor, Wendy Lee. Wendy, you were all the things an editor needed to be to get this book out of me. You were understanding when I needed to be understood, flexible when I needed flexibility, and stern when I needed discipline. I appreciate you for all the things you were to me and to Sins of the Father. Because of you, it is a much stronger book and I am a much more enlightened author.

As always, thanks to Natasha Kern, my agent, and Carol Craig, my personal writing GPS, for their unwavering belief in me and the vision I have for my work. Ladies, I am fortunate to have you in my life.

I offer a special thanks to the other members of the Avon/HarperCollins team who worked to get *Sins of the Father* into print and into bookstores. Once again you have blessed me with a wonderful cover and enticing back cover copy. To Michael Morris in Sales and Emma Beavers in Publicity, I know the magic you worked for *Up Pops the Devil*, and look forward to see that magic in action again with *Sins of the Father*.

Finally, a special thank you to all the readers who have picked up *Sins of the Father*. Many of you have been with me since my first book, *Bands of Gold*, was published in 1994. Others of you have found me more recently and after reading my newest works, bless your heart, now you're trying to find *Bands of Gold*. Please know that I don't take you or your hard-earned money for granted. My goal with each book is deliver an entertaining and uplifting story that will keep you turning the pages until the very end and leave you wanting more. Thank you for being my inspiration.

A+
AUTHOR
INSIGHTS,
EXTRAS, &
MORE...

FROM
**ANGELA
BENSON**
AND
AVON A

Reading Group Guide Questions

1. Abraham tries to become closer to his children by offering them access to his business and vast wealth. Do you think this is enough to make up for his absence during their childhood? Do you believe that it is possible to atone for something like abandoning your children? Why or why not?

2. Michael refuses to meet with Abraham, while Deborah is quite willing to reconcile with him. Do you think Michael is correct to act in that fashion, or do you think Deborah's way is better? If you were in their situation, what would you do?

3. Why do you think Deborah likes to date older men? Is it just because she is looking for a father figure? Do you think that she and Alan will make a good couple? Why or why not?

4. Isaac doubts Rebecca's love after he learns she's kept a secret from him. Do you think his doubts are justified? What do you think Rebecca should have done to convince him of her devotion?"

5. Saralyn and Leah both say that they were Abraham's true girlfriend, while the other was just someone Abraham cheated with. What do you think is the true story behind these relationships? How would Abraham's life be different if he had chosen Leah instead of Saralyn?

6. Leah tells Melvin that although she is not in love with Abraham anymore, much of her life has been consumed by him. Can you think of a similar situation in your life? Have you ever been unable to let go of a relationship with someone, romantic or not, despite knowing it was for the best that you do so?

7. Why do you think Michael didn't tell Josette that Abraham was his father? Do you think she should be upset with him about it? If your spouse or significant other withheld that kind of information from you, would you not trust them as much? Why or why not?

8. Do you think Josette's decision regarding Michael and the baby is a good one? How does the situation between Josette and Michael mirror the situation between Leah and Abraham? Do you think children are destined to repeat the mistakes of their parents? Why or why not?

9. How do both Isaac and Michael exhibit traits of their father? Who do you think is more "Abraham's son," Isaac or Michael, and why?

10. Do you think that Michael will ever become close to his father and half brother? Will it ever be possible for the Martins and the Johnsons to become one big family, or is their shared past too much to overcome? Why or why not?

In Praise of Siblings
An Essay by Angela Benson

I've been thinking (and writing) a lot about siblings these days. I only have one—a brother—though there were many times growing up when I thought there were six of him. The boy was a holy terror, sometimes without the holy.

I have the funniest memories of him growing up. Though he's three years younger than I am, when he was around five or six he used to beat me up. He did it because I'd never hit him back. Well, I woke up to that pretty quickly when I accidentally socked him one day. Guess what? My brother's love of hitting his big sister suddenly faded.

My brother used to torture me with dessert. Like a normal person, I would eat my dessert immediately after the meal. Not my brother. He'd save his for later that night when I had none. Then he'd sit in front of me eating his, waiting for me to ask for a bite so he could deny me. I wish I could say I never asked, but I always did.

As we grew older, I seemed to get the upper hand on my little brother. My mom worked two jobs when we were kids, so when I was old enough, she gave me cooking chores. My first dish was fried chicken. How hard could it be? I'd seen my mother cook it often. So I fried this chicken. It looked golden brown on the outside but I wondered about the inside. I didn't know, but I knew how to find out. I served my good-looking chicken to my brother. As I watched him take his first bite and saw the streams of blood flowing out, I concluded the chicken wasn't quite done yet. Guess what? I never had to cook again. Why? Because my brother re-fused to eat anything else I cooked. That bloody chicken ended it for him.

To be honest, I didn't lose any sleep about not cooking. What kid wants to cook? What kid wants to do any chores around the house? Not me. I soon figured out how to evade all chores: pre-tend I was reading or doing homework. You see, my mom was a strong proponent of getting a good education. Unfortunately for my brother, he never figured this out so he did a LOT of chores. Sometimes I felt sorry for him and wanted to clue him in on my chore evasion strategy, but I couldn't trust him not to tell Mom. So I watched him cook (yes, he cooks), clean, and iron, while I pretended to study.

As we grew older, things got a bit more serious. I remember an incident that occurred when I was off at college and my brother was still home. He called me to share a secret about a problem he was facing. He made me promise not to tell our mother. Of course, I promised. Unfortunately, as soon as we hung up the phone, I dialed my mom and told her the secret. Now, I love my brother, but there was no way I could keep that secret. To this day I don't remember what the secret was, I just remember feeling that it was too big for me too handle. It took my brother a while to get over this one and share another secret with me, but he did.

One of the dearest memories I have of my brother is the day I realized he'd become an adult with insights to help me with my problems. I remember pulling the phone away from my ear and looking it, while thinking, When did my little brother become a man? A very precious moment indeed.

I cherish my relationship with my brother, as you can prob-ably tell from these stories. Because we live thirteen hours apart, we don't see each other often, but we talk several times a week. There's a richness to our relationship because of its ups and downs, and because it seems to grow stronger and deeper through those ups and downs.

I like to read about relationships that remind me of me and my brother. I love to read about people caring for each other, through the good times and the bad. The bumps on the relationship road only make the relationship more cherished. It's not surprising, then, that my stories have strong sibling relationships. I'm waiting for the day my brother recognizes our relationship in one of my stories. When he does, I'm sure he'll want a commission.

Siblings. Mine's a keeper. I hope you know yours are, too.

Q&A with Angela Benson

You have an unusual background for a writer in that you have degrees in mathematics and industrial engineering, and you teach educational technology at the University of Alabama. Does that background influence what you write?

Not as much as you would think. I have never set a story in the engineering world or in the academic world. I guess I go to my personal life when I write rather than to my professional life. I have often thought of writing a thriller set in the engineering world, where the heroine has to save the world from "technology gone amuck," but I've never come up with a solid idea. I tried the college campus with my last book but found the setting restrictive. I'm not sure why since other authors have written engaging stories set on college campuses.

Your first novel was published in 1994, and *Sins of the Father* will be your twelfth book. Where do you get the ideas for your stories and characters?

Ideas come from everywhere, even my own life. My family is convinced my first book, *Bands of Gold,* was autobiographical. I even had a cousin call me up and ask if the book was about me. It's not; trust me. My life is not exciting enough for a novel. That said, I do use bits and pieces of my life in my stories, but I have to spice them up a lot to make them novelworthy. I had a cousin who struggled after being released from prison, so he inspired my last book, *Up Pops the Devil*.

My stories are not really about the people or events that spark the idea, though. Rather, they are about the questions those ideas raise for me. In writing my novels, I explore those questions. I grew up without a father, so *Sins of the Father* allowed me to explore what it would be like for an absentee father to return.

Faith seems to be a very important component of your books. Can you talk a little bit about the role of faith in your work?

My writing has always been about hope. My career started with writing romance novels because that "happily ever after" ending was a sign of hope. Faith is the other side of the hope. I started writing Christian fiction in 2000 because I wanted to make that faith explicit on the pages of the story. Faith, church, and religion have long played a pivotal role in the American family and in the African-American community. *Sins of the Father* is another faith story, but I consider it more inspirational fiction than Christian fiction because I focus more on the faith and less on church and religion.

How did you decide to become a writer? What practical advice would you give to a writer who's just starting out?

My earliest memory of writing fiction is from Ms. Milazo's fifth grade English class. We wrote short stories each week and read them aloud to the class. My classmates loved my stories and always clapped after I finished reading them, which made me feel really good about myself and what I'd written. The story that made me the all-time class favorite was "My Interview with the Jackson Five." This was a pretty special story for me, since I had a very strong crush on Jermaine Jackson at the time. Okay, now I've dated myself. That was more than thirty years ago.

I decided that becoming a published author was a realistic goal in 1992 at a Romantic Times Magazine Readers and Writers Convention. I remember sitting in a workshop led by three published romance writers. As I listened to them talk about how they wrote their stories, the thought that filled my mind was, They don't look any smarter than I am. If they can write a book, so can I.

Of course, the actual experience of writing a book turned out to be more difficult than I thought it would be, but I persevered. After that convention, I went back home, joined the local chapter of Romance Writers of America (RWA), and began my first novel. That novel, which I started in early 1992, was completed in early 1993, sold to Arabesque in late 1993, and arrived in bookstores in late 1994.

My advice to new writers is to keep writing. I accumulated a stack of rejection letters from publishing houses and agents. Every time I'd get a rejection, I'd send out another proposal or query letter. Remember, "The race doesn't go to the swiftest, but to him who endures to the end."

What are some of your favorite books and writers? What titles would you recommend to a reader?

Two books that touched me most deeply are Sharon Ewell Foster's *Passing by Samaria* and Julie Garwood's *For the Roses*. The stories, though very different, showed me how powerful fiction can be in helping us see ourselves, our hypocrisies, and our goodness. *Passing by Samaria,* which has racism as one of its themes, brought home for me how difficult forgiveness can be. *For the Roses,* a simple western romance, had me crying like a baby. I wasn't crying because of the romance, though. I was crying because of the relationship between five orphans, one black, who made themselves into a family.

Photo by Olan Mills, Inc.

ANGELA BENSON is a graduate of Spelman College and the author of twelve novels, including the Christy Award-nominated *Awakening Mercy,* the *Essence* bestseller *The Amen Sisters,* and *Up Pops the Devil.* She is currently an associate professor at the University of Alabama and lives in Tuscaloosa.

www.angelabenson.com

Angela Benson